A Certain Darkness

A Verity Kent Mystery

Anna Lee Huber

W F HOWES LTD

This large print edition published in 2022 by
W F Howes Ltd
Unit 5, St George's House, Rearsby Business Park,
Gaddesby Lane, Rearsby, Leicester LE7 4YH

1 3 5 7 9 10 8 6 4 2

First published in 2022
by KENSINGTON BOOKS

A CIP catalogue record for this book is available
from the British Library

ISBN 978 1 00409 915 3

Typeset by Palimpsest Book Production Limited,
Falkirk, Stirlingshire

A Certain Darkness

ALSO BY ANNA LEE HUBER
FROM CLIPPER LARGE PRINT

This Side of Murder
Treacherous is the Night
Penny for Your Secrets
Pretty Deceit
Murder Most Fair

For my grandfathers – Harold Huber and Herbert Heim – both of whom served in the military in slightly different eras. When I write about soldiers, I can't help but think of them.

I remember Grandpa Harold for his gentle ways, his farmer hands, and his ability to fall asleep in a room filled with even the most boisterous of children.

I remember Grandpa Herbert for his booming laugh; his lively storytelling of *The Three Billy Goats Gruff*; and his playful imagination, taking us to search for Winnie the Pooh in the woods behind his home.

A certain darkness is needed to see the stars.

—Osho

. . . Only when it is dark enough can you see the stars.

—Martin Luther King Jr

CHAPTER ONE

March 1920
London, England

The club was hopping. Peering through the curtains at the edge of the stage, I had a clear view of the bodies packed together on the dance floor, swaying and jazzing to the driving rhythm of the band playing twenty feet from my place of concealment. The beat of the drums and the piano pounded in my chest, and the throbbing wail of the trumpet and trombone sang in my ears, tempting my toes to tap and my hips to swing. Normally I would have been part of the undulating mass of bodies, steeped in the haze of sweat and perfume, spellbound by the sweet, syncopated sounds. But not tonight.

Tonight, I had greater concerns. Tonight, I had other fish to fry. Namely, fileting a traitor.

I heard my husband's soft foot tread moments before I felt his hand brush over the silk of my dark gown at my waist. 'Goldy says Ryde's chap is finally in place.' Sidney added a soft grunt. 'Albeit a bit windy.'

1

I fingered the filigree gold pendant dangling from my neck and nodded. I'd expected as much. Our friend Max Westfield, the Earl of Ryde, had said the man he'd convinced to speak with us from the War Office was already uneasy, and our clandestine arrangements to meet him would only have heightened his nerves. Add to that the frenetic mood of the Grafton Galleries nightclub and the crush of patrons in their glad rags either dancing or indulging in a cocktail, and the man must be close to turning tail and running. Fortunately for us, that was all but impossible.

I allowed my gaze to sweep over the assemblage once more, verifying that Crispin and his friend were still holding their positions. Tonight's crowd had seemed a boon, providing an effective cover for any who might be surveilling either Max or the man from the War Office, but it was now in danger of foiling our entire ploy. It had taken the man much too long to make his way through the throng to the far stage door. There wasn't a moment to lose.

I nodded to the clarinetist on stage who stamped his foot and tipped his head back and arched his spine to lift his instrument into the air as a warbling trill of notes blared forth. Even with his hearing damaged from his time at the front as an artillery officer, Crispin couldn't miss that cue. He stumbled backward as if losing his footing, and flailed his arms, spilling several bystanders' drinks before elbowing his friend in the nose. My eyebrows arched skyward as the friend bent forward, cupping his hands around his face. The men were supposed to be playacting, but from this distance that had certainly looked real. Either their acting abilities were greater than I'd anticipated, or Crispin had gotten carried away.

'Ham,' Sidney scoffed good-naturedly from over my shoulder, making me suspect it was the former, for he knew both men far better than I did.

Crispin's friend launched out at him with a fist, making Crispin stagger back into several onlookers, before he came back at him. News of the brawl quickly swept through the crowd, drawing eyes and interest. Trusting the distraction would be enough, and Goldy would know the right time to take advantage of it to usher the man from the War Office through the stage door, Sidney and I turned to hurry back through the wing of the stage to Etta's dressing room.

Etta Lorraine was the most talented jazz singer this side of the Atlantic, as well as a good friend and eager coconspirator. She'd served as a mediator and courier for my ongoing clandestine work for C, the chief of the British Secret Service, more than once.

I rapped on the door before opening it to be engulfed by the scent of flowers from Etta's admirers filling at least half a dozen vases, and the musk of powder and kohl decorating the vanity's surface along with a smattering of brushes. It was certainly an improvement over the dank, musty corridor.

She glanced at me in the reflection of the mirror as we entered before continuing to apply her crimson lip salve. 'Spring your trap?'

'Yes.' I shared a look with Sidney. 'Now, let's hope it proves worth the effort.'

Etta rubbed her lips together and then turned her head to the left and then the right, before nodding, apparently satisfied with her appearance. As she should be, for she looked stunning, as always. She tended to favor metallic-colored gowns, and tonight was no exception. The warm copper sequins and fringe seemed to ooze over her frame like melted caramel. Her cinnamon-brown eyes snapped with a fire reflected in the topaz-accented teardrop earrings brushing the tips of her mocha shoulders.

We kissed the air next to each other's cheeks as she turned to greet me, her *Tabac Blond* perfume wafting up from her neck. Then she offered her cheek to Sidney, who bussed it lightly. Her eyes dipped to my midnight blue bodice as she leaned her hip against the vanity table. 'You don't normally wear such dark colors, Verity, but I must say, they suit you.' She reached up to tug one of my castle-bobbed curls. 'It's your hair. Makes the red gleam.'

I draped a hand somewhat self-consciously across my chest. 'Yes, well, they do come in handy when you need to skulk through dark corridors.' She hadn't mentioned the unfashionable cut of my neckline, but I felt conscious of it nonetheless, and slightly annoyed by that fact. Most of the current evening and dancing gowns tended to favor a square neckline with thin straps, but the bullet I'd taken in my shoulder some three months past, and the resulting scar, had put paid to any such wardrobe options. I'd been forced to turn to my modiste for help in designing a new evening wardrobe to accommodate my injury and was personally quite pleased with the wider straps and plunging vee neckline. In truth, it was far more flattering to my shapely figure. But that didn't mean I wasn't still a trifle uncertain. A position I was unaccustomed to, normally feeling confident about being the most stylish woman in the room.

As if sensing my insecurity, Sidney pressed a hand to the small of my back. Its warmth penetrated through the silk and infused into my backbone, offering me a reassurance I chided myself for craving.

Etta nodded. 'You've the use of my dressing room as long as you need it.' She looked toward the door. 'Is Ryde joining you?'

'No, we thought it best to send him elsewhere,' I replied. 'To try to throw some of the hounds off the scent.'

'Do you think it worked?'

I heaved a weary sigh. 'At this point, we can only hope.'

Our gazes met and held in commiseration.

There was light knock on the door, and she

straightened. 'That'll be your man. And I believe I need a drink before my next set,' she added over her shoulder as she sashayed toward the door. 'So, I'll leave you to it.'

'Thank you.'

She lifted her hand in acknowledgment and then opened the door. A man whose dark blond hair was coated with copious amounts of Brilliantine nearly tumbled inside, coming to an abrupt stop at the sight of Etta. His eyes widened in uncertainty, but also a bit of awe, while she all but ignored him, pressing her hand to her beau Goldy's chest as she skirted past him and out into the dark corridor. Goldy nodded at us, letting us know he would be nearby, and then shut the door, all but forcing the other man to take his last stumbling step inside to join us.

I waited to speak, pausing a moment to study the man before me. He was no more than average in build, with pale gray eyes and a weak chin. From the manner in which he tugged at his evening coat and straightened to his full height, it was obvious he was a military man, but judging by the shiftiness of his eyes and the apprehension shimmering in their depths I pegged him for a subordinate staff officer – likely a second lieutenant – or a clerk.

'Lord Ryde said you like birds,' I remarked, beginning the coded exchange Max and I had worked out prior to this meeting in order to verify the informant's identity.

6

'Aye,' he replied, before pausing to clear his throat. 'Especially pipits.'

His Scottish brogue had surprised me, for I would have expected it to be something Max would have priorly remarked upon. So, in spite of his correct retort, I examined him more carefully as I uttered the second part of the code. 'And reptiles.'

'There's nothin' like a good cup o' tea in the mornin' to set ye right,' he stated, displaying no hesitance at the incongruous nature of the last call and response. It was evident he'd been prepped, which eased my concerns.

I crossed my arms over my chest. 'Ryde says you have information for us about the investigation into the explosion that killed Brigadier General Bishop and nine other men.'

An explosion I was intimately familiar with as I'd been injured in it. In the spring of 1918, as the Germans had made their last big push, forcing some stretches of the Allied lines into retreat, I'd been sent to the front with a message warning Bishop he had a traitor among his staff. A traitor who might have even been the intelligence officer attached to his brigade. Soon after I'd delivered the missive, the temporary brigade headquarters Bishop had established near Bailleul, France, had blown up, sending me flying and scrambling my memory. For some time, I'd believed the explosion had been caused by a German shell, for a few minutes later that portion of the front had suffered a bombardment in earnest. However, with the help of a few other key witnesses, I'd recently realized the blast had not been caused by a shell, but a bomb placed within the HQ itself.

The Scot's eyes darted back and forth between me and Sidney. 'No' so much information as word that they've declined to reopen the investigation.'

I stiffened, the anger and frustration I found myself so often struggling to restrain of late bubbling just below the surface of my calm exterior. 'Despite the fact that there is now just *one* witness claiming the explosion was not caused by a bomb, and that witness was also the last person seen exiting the HQ moments before it exploded?' I wasn't certain how much the man before me actually knew of the inquiry, but I wasn't about to temper my words by speaking in vague terms when the issue was so important.

'They . . . they declined to accept the revised statement o' one o' the witnesses.'

'Why?' I snapped.

'They said it was unreliable.' His stare drifted to some spot between me and Sidney. 'That because . . . the woman had changed her mind it couldna be trusted.'

Based on the fact he couldn't look me in the eye it was clear he knew who the woman was despite C's maneuvering to try to keep my identity concealed. What wasn't clear was whether the Scot had figured this out on his own or if his commanding officers had discussed my involvement while reviewing the issue. After all, I had a number of detractors among the heads of the intelligence community – two in particular – and they and the officers in the War Office, in general, tended to believe women were overall unreliable agents, despite ample proof to the contrary.

My muscles tightened as I labored to remember my training and breathe evenly. Losing my temper with this subaltern would do me no good.

However, the rules for men were different.

'Never mind the fact that the change in this woman's testimony corroborates that of the testimonies already given by multiple witnesses,' Sidney countered sharply, his bearing shifting from that of the easygoing man-about-town he normally affected to the demeanor he must have presented to his men as a commanding officer at the Western Front. 'That her reasons for revising her statement are perfectly clear and understandable.'

The Scot flushed facing Sidney's withering set-down, but he was experienced enough to recognize the voice of command when he heard it. 'Aye, sir.'

I turned away, pressing a hand to my husband's arm to remind him this man was simply the messenger. And one who at least had the decency to tell us to our faces what others would have not.

I caught a glimpse of my grim expression in Etta's mirror. I'd lost some weight since my injury in December, and the hollows of my eyes and sharpness of my cheekbones appeared even more pronounced in the glare of the lights. The lack of answers, the lack of progress in both of our investigations was slowly eating away at me.

After taking a moment to stifle my disappointment, I turned back to the Scot, who stood anxiously waiting. 'You could have told all of this to Lord Ryde and avoided this awkward encounter,' I pointed out, narrowing my eyes in suspicion. 'So, why did you agree to meet with us?'

His Adam's apple bobbed up and down as he swallowed. 'Because this witness, the one who left the HQ shortly before it exploded, the one whose story contradicts the rest o' the witnesses . . .'

'Lieutenant James Smith,' I stated baldly, letting him know we were aware of the man's identity.

He hesitated a moment before nodding in confirmation. 'He came to the War Office two days past to provide an explanation for the discrepancy.'

I shared a look of surprise with Sidney before prompting the Scot to continue. 'And?'

'And I didna feel he gave a very good accounting of himself.' His mouth pursed in disapproval. 'All he truly did was disparage the other witnesses, especially the woman, and remind the officers o' the fruitlessness o' pursuin' the truth when the Germans' shells had destroyed all o' the evidence.'

'But other than disparaging them, how did he explain the fact that all the other witnesses reported the explosive was a bomb?' Sidney queried. 'And that he was the last to leave the HQ?'

The Scot's expression turned downright sour. 'He wasna pressed.'

Sidney turned to me, his face communicating the same cynicism mine did, the same ability to read between the lines. Lieutenant Smith wasn't pressed because someone had influenced the officers reviewing the file. Someone who was known to utilize Smith's abilities for his own purposes.

'Was Lord Ardmore part of this meeting?' I asked.

'Nay, but . . .'

I arched my eyebrows, urging him to overcome his sudden reluctance to continue.

'He met wi' one o' the officers shortly before.'

'Of course he did,' Sidney muttered under his breath.

'It was supposedly aboot naval deployments.'

This was a feeble excuse and the Scot seemed to know it. The look in his eyes begged us to explain, but I decided we'd already said too much. Max might trust the chap, but I didn't know him from Adam. However, that wouldn't stop me from pushing him for as much as I could get.

'You don't happen to know where we can find this Lieutenant Smith, do you?' Thus far we, nor C, had been able to gain access to his personnel record.

He glanced at Sidney, who stood quietly observing him, and then back. 'He gave his address as bein' in Wilton Terrace, but . . . I suspect it may be false.'

11

In all likelihood, he was right. Lieutenant Smith hadn't struck me as the type of man who resided in Belgravia, whether he could afford it or not. We would make inquiries, of course. Every lead must be followed, no matter how small. But I didn't expect to find him living there. It would be yet another false trail.

Ever conscious of the clock, I opened my mouth to thank him and send him on his way when Sidney suddenly spoke. 'Why are you helping us?'

I lifted my gaze to my husband's stern visage, somewhat surprised by the query. I'd learned long ago not to ask such questions of my transitory informants. It was too easy to lie, and those with the most significant information to offer often became unnerved by such close scrutiny. It was better to evaluate them on the content of their intelligence, and its corroboration with other sources.

However, the Scot seemed to have been anticipating just such a question. 'Because I respect Lord Ryde. And Lord Ryde respects you. I ken he wouldna be puttin' his neck oot askin' such questions just for anyone.'

A pulse of fear shot through me, for this was exactly what he was *not* supposed to be doing – risking his neck. Lord Ardmore had already proven to be ruthless in his aims. There was little doubt he'd had Max's father killed, along with at least nine other people we knew of despite our inability to find definitive proof of his culpability. Yet.

As such, the last thing I wanted was for Max or any of my other friends and colleagues to put their necks on the line by openly prodding the blackguard. Max had promised to be discreet. It was the only reason I'd acceded to his insistence on using his connections inside the War Office to gather information. But it seemed that the Scot was saying he'd done just the opposite.

'You served with him,' Sidney surmised, having further taken the man's measure while I stood there stifling my desire to throttle Max for placing himself at risk.

He nodded. 'At Divisional Headquarters.'

After Max had been injured in the shoulder and his father had pulled rank, having his son and heir transferred away from the battalion he commanded – the battalion in which Sidney had served – to become an adjutant to a major general safely behind the front lines.

'Then you understand how recklessly loyal he can be.'

The staff officer seemed much struck by this description for he grimaced. 'Aye.'

Sidney's stare was direct and intent. 'Don't let him take that loyalty too far.'

An understanding seemed to pass between the two men – one, to which, I wasn't opposed. 'Aye, sir.'

Sidney inclined his head just as the door to the corridor opened.

Goldy offered us an apologetic grin. 'Sorry for

the interruption, but Bruno just had to eject someone trying to sneak past him through the stage door, so you might want to wrap this up.'

The Scot's eyes widened, and with good reason. The bouncer might have evicted the man, but he'd likely not been working alone.

'I can hustle him back into the club through the kitchens,' Goldy assured us. 'Throw 'em off the scent.'

I nodded. 'Thank you.'

This expression of gratitude was meant for both men as the Scot moved to precede Etta's beau through the doorway, but not before he tossed one last glance my way.

'You two should lay low for a few minutes,' Goldy instructed. 'I'll be back after I have one of the men check the alley.'

With that he was gone, and I was free to pull the silver bangle from my wrist and hurl it at the chair on the opposite side of the room.

CHAPTER TWO

Sidney knew better than to say anything. Not when I was this irritated and flustered.

'Why are men such bloody beasts?!' I knew I was generalizing. After all there were as many men helping me as there were intent on putting me in my place, but at the moment the factions against me seemed to hold all the power and the least common sense. In fact, if Sir Basil Thomson – the newly appointed Director of Intelligence and a crony of Lord Ardmore's – and the men of his ilk had their way, all women's contributions to the war effort would be belittled and dismissed.

I crossed the room to sink down in the padded armchair, dropping my head into my hands as I tried to regain control of my temper.

'I'm sorry, darling,' Sidney said as he perched on the low table next to me. 'Shall I go down to the War Office and box their ears for you? They would probably take away my Victoria Cross, but it might be worth it if it knocked some sense into them.'

I scowled up at him, not finding his jest to be humorous in the least, but it was difficult to stay irritated with him when he was gazing back at me with such a consoling expression. He was already too handsome for his own good. Confronted with his dark hair, midnight blue eyes, square jaw, and rugged physique, it was all I could do to keep my wits about me when he became intent on charming me. However, at the moment, I was too riled.

'We've been blocked at every turn.' I gestured emphatically. '*Clearly* they don't care about uncovering the truth or obtaining justice for General Bishop and all those men.'

'Yes, but you know as well as I do that true justice is difficult to attain. And Smith isn't wrong. What evidence there might have been is long gone – destroyed by German shells or lost when the Jerries overran the area before we pushed them back. Is witness testimony enough when none of you actually saw him set the bomb?'

I gritted my teeth lest my first scathing retort slip past my lips and glared angrily at him.

He held up his hands as if to ward off my attack. 'I'm not saying anything you haven't already said yourself before. You knew Smith's guilt was going to be a tall order to prove.'

'Yes, but I hoped the War Office would at least want to reopen the investigation. I hoped they would at least want to *try*.'

He sighed, rubbing a hand over his jaw, releasing the scent of bay rum in his aftershave. 'Yes, there is that.' His expression turned pensive. 'But at least the effort wasn't a complete loss. Ardmore made a move to interfere, and I doubt he would have personally done so for just any of his minions.'

'Yes, but we already knew Smith worked for him. That he was more than a simple drudge. And it doesn't prove Ardmore had anything do with the bombing. Only that he doesn't want his man incarcerated.'

'Or beating his gums about what he knows.'

I tipped my head in concession. 'Regardless, I no longer see any way forward. Not when C can't even gain access to the full investigation file.'

Sidney didn't try to counter this, and I was glad he didn't offer me trite reassurances. Unless something drastic changed, we both knew we were at a dead end, and no amount of words could change that. Instead, he took hold of my hand, cradling it between his own and running his fingers over the black silk encasing my palm.

A rap on the door preluded Goldy's return, and I looked up to offer him a wan smile.

'We got the chap back to the floor,' he told us. 'Convinced one of the girls to make a fuss over him, so hopefully that'll draw the right people's attention.'

'Good thinking,' Sidney replied, pushing to his feet.

I could feel Goldy's eyes on me, searching, assessing, but he didn't ask the question I knew was foremost in his mind. And I knew Etta well enough to know she hadn't revealed to him anything she might have guessed at herself. That

17

I couldn't share exactly what I was doing now or what I'd done during the war at times felt like the height of ridiculousness, but there were other times when I fully appreciated the Official Secrets Act and the strict discretion we were to maintain.

'A taxi should be waiting for you in the mews where it dropped you off,' Goldy added as I retrieved my bangle from the chair cushion and joined the men in standing.

'Thank you, Goldy,' I told him sincerely, knowing from experience how difficult it was to be kept in the dark. 'How's Tim doing?' I asked, as Sidney fetched my aubergine wool coat with fur-trimmed rolled collar from Etta's wardrobe and draped it around my shoulders.

'Quite well. He seems very keen to learn.'

That was a relief to hear. My younger brother had been restless after returning from the war, needing a way to occupy his time that he would enjoy. When he'd confessed his desire to become a pilot – an aim that our mother had strictly forbidden after our brother Rob had been killed piloting an aeroplane at the Western Front in 1915 – Sidney and I had set about finding a way he could still be involved with aviation while not necessary stepping into a cockpit. At least, not immediately anyway. Goldy's family owned an aviation company that was investing in efforts to begin passenger aeroplane service to the continent and beyond, and he'd agreed to take Tim under his wing for the time being.

Goldy flashed me a wide grin. 'I've had him shadowing my cousin, who wanted to know if all the family is so annoyingly inquisitive.'

I couldn't help but smile at this assessment. 'Well, my oldest brother, Freddy, became a surgeon; Rob was attempting to build his own flying machine before he was out of short pants; and . . .' I cast him an arch smile. '. . . you've met me. So "annoyingly inquisitive" pretty much sums us up.'

He chuckled, offering Sidney the hand he always covered in a glove to hide the burns he'd suffered to the right side of his torso during his own plane crash during the war.

'Don't laugh. Just wait until you meet her sister,' my husband quipped.

Goldy turned to me. 'Is she coming to visit?'

'Over her summer holiday,' I replied, moving toward the door. 'That is, if she can manage to convince our mother to let her come.'

'Even odds, then,' Goldy guessed.

'Just.' I rose up on my toes to buss his cheek. 'Give Etta my love and my thanks.'

'I will.'

Sidney and I were still seated at the breakfast table the next day when we heard a knock on our flat's door.

My husband looked up at me over the newspaper he was perusing, his eyebrows lifting. 'Ryde is up and about early this morning.'

Taking a sip of my coffee, I glanced at the clock on the sideboard. 'I would hardly call ten o'clock early.' I narrowed my eyes playfully. 'After all, didn't you have to rise before dawn for morning stand-to during the war?'

'I made my subalterns do it.'

I rolled my eyes and shook my head, knowing full well Sidney would never have done such a thing, *if* he could even have gotten away with it. All soldiers and officers were required to take part in stand-to at dawn and dusk each day while serving in the trenches, positioned at the ready as if waiting or preparing for an attack, and Sidney had never been a slacker. I would more readily believe he'd been the first to rouse the men for their part, the first to place himself in any sort of necessary discomfort or danger to shield his men. I'd seen the way the men he'd commanded or served with respected him. It wasn't simply in deference to his rank. It was earned.

We heard the murmur of voices, and then Sadie Yarrow, our timid housekeeper, appeared in the doorway. 'Lord Ryde to see you.'

She knew better than to stand on ceremony where Max was concerned, and in fact he stood just beyond her shoulder, passing her with a nod as he entered the dining room.

I thanked Sadie, who lowered her heavily lashed eyes and hurried away.

'Now, what could possibly be bringing you to our door on this fine spring morning?' Sidney teased as he folded his newspaper and tossed it toward the center of the table.

Max all but ignored him, dropping a swift buss on my cheek before sinking into the chair next to mine. 'What did Curlew have to say?' His gray eyes were eager.

'Is that his name?' I replied, gesturing toward the coffee pot.

He nodded in response to my unspoken query. 'He didn't tell you?'

'No. Though, to be fair, I also didn't ask,' I admitted while I poured Max a cup of the dark java. 'I calculated that doing so would only make him jumpier.'

Max drank the bitter brew black just like Sidney, something my husband had never done before the war. I supposed it was a habit acquired from their time at the front, where you took your hot meals and drinks however you could get them. While I, on the other hand, had reacted quite differently to my time spent in German-occupied Belgium and northern France, liaising with our intelligence gathering networks at work there or on special assignment. The ersatz swill they'd been forced to drink in place of tea and coffee – such as roasted oat chaff or pea shells – had made me better appreciate the genuine article, as well as the cream and sugar which made it sweeter.

Max grimaced, either from the strength of the coffee or my description of Lieutenant Curlew. 'I was worried his nerves might get the best of him.

But at least he showed up. That's something. So what did he say?'

'That the War Office is officially declining to reopen the investigation.'

Max scowled. 'I learned that this morning.'

I frowned, wondering how he'd discovered such a thing. Given the classified nature of the inquiry, I knew it entailed him being rather more deeply involved than I wished.

'But surely that's not all?' he pressed.

Sidney's expression was watchful, letting me know I wasn't the only one who'd inferred rather more from Max's admission than our friend might have realized. 'He also said Lieutenant Smith had been allowed to meet with the officers in charge to explain himself, and they didn't press him for answers.'

'Probably because Lord Ardmore met with one of them shortly before Smith's meeting,' I added.

I didn't need to spell anything out for Max. He was fully aware of Ardmore's shadowy capabilities.

Max muttered a curse as he set down his cup, and then glanced up at me to utter an apology before returning his scrutiny to the geometric blue porcelain design. 'How can no one see him for who he is and what he's doing but us?'

I shouldn't have been surprised by the vehemence in his tone. After all, Ardmore had almost certainly arranged his father's murder. But I was. I suspected it was because I was so accustomed to his calm steadiness. However, over the past

22

months I'd begun to realize that his composure was as much of an act as my bravado. Something he'd hardened and perfected during the tumult of the war. Yet there were fractures, tiny faults which had begun to crack under the strain of this investigation and the lack of answers, of justice.

I reached out a hand to clasp his where it rested on the table, a consolation and an apology of sorts for my willingness to be fooled by the mask he affected when deep inside I knew the truth.

Sidney's gaze dipped to where mine clutched Max's, but he didn't address it. 'I suspect others know the truth as well. They're simply too afraid to do anything about it. Ardmore's tentacles run deep.'

They undeniably wound their way through the entire military intelligence community. C seemed to be the only director not held under his sway, and I suspected that was as much due to the fact that C was as eccentric as they came – riding about Whitehall on a child's scooter to accommodate his leg which had been amputated in a car accident at the start of the war. A false leg he took great delight in stabbing with a penknife to startle new recruits. As well as the fact that he took great pleasure in thwarting bureaucrats. Almost as much as he reveled in secrecy. That heightened instinct for privacy and concealment had served C and the foreign division of military intelligence well so far.

Max nodded, straightening in his chair, and I

released his hand. 'Then it's still down to us.' He tried to affix his usual artless grin to his face, but it didn't come so easily anymore.

Sidney removed his battered cigarette case from the inner pocket of his gray herringbone coat – a gift from me after our wedding, before he left for the front – and offered one to Max. He shook his head, extracting his own case filled with his own brand. I'd noted both men preferred Turkish blends, as most British did as opposed to the pungent American ones called 'stinkers,' but the smoke from Sidney's tobacco held a sweetness that was lacking in the more acidic aroma of Max's.

Max inhaled a deep drag and then settled back in his seat. 'So, what's our next step?'

'At the moment, I don't know,' I hated to admit. 'Ardmore has been quiet. Too quiet, in my opinion.' I exhaled past the tightness in my chest. 'Which makes me nervous.'

Sidney's eyes flashed with sympathy. 'I agree. He has a habit of causing trouble where and when we least expect it. But we've been expecting it for months now. So where does that leave us?'

Max tipped a fall of ash into the pewter dish near the center of the table. 'Perhaps if we stop expecting it . . .'

By the gruff sarcasm in his voice, I knew he was jesting, but I answered him, nonetheless.

'As if that's possible.' I pushed to my feet, crossing to the window to peer out at the skeletal trees lining Berkeley Square below. I watched as people bustled to and fro, bundled against the chill weather, completely oblivious to the conundrum we faced above them. Even the gold ormolu clock ticking merrily away on the sideboard ignored our plight and its implications.

'We'll simply have to redouble our efforts to locate those cylinders of phosgene and the Livens Projector we know Ardmore's men stole,' I stated as I turned to face Sidney and Max once again. 'They can't have used them yet, or we would have heard about it.'

'Yes, but Verity, honestly, what hope have we of finding them when C's contacts haven't been able to?' Max pointed out. His dark butterscotch hair was ruffled as if he'd been running his hands through it while my back was turned.

'I know it seems improbable, but what choice do we have? We have to at least try.'

Sidney sat forward to stub out his fag. 'Ver's right. We have to try. Between the three of us I imagine we have a fair number of our own contacts we can call on.' His expression was grave. 'Do you still believe they've been taken to Ireland?'

I nibbled my thumb nail as I considered his question. Given the fact that we strongly suspected the cylinders had been stolen by an Irish ship crew, Ardmore's own history and connections to that country, and the ongoing unrest from the Irish's revolt against British rule, it still seemed to me the likeliest solution. 'I do.'

25

'Then I know a few Irish officers I can write. They might be able to tell us something useful.'

'But will they?'

We both turned to Max in question.

'If they've joined the Republicans, then I imagine they'll take your request to heart. They certainly won't want to see gas used against their own men. But that doesn't mean they'll share what they know. Not when they could just as easily steal the canisters and use them against British soldiers.' His brow furrowed. 'And if they're Loyalists, they might decide the Irish rebels deserve it. There are a number of Englishmen who would say so.'

'Don't tell me you're in that number?' I asked aghast.

His eyes widened, seeming surprised and hurt I should have to ask. 'No. I would never wish to see phosgene used on anyone.' He shook his head sadly. 'I don't have to support the rebellion to agree the use of phosgene would be contemptible.'

'Forgive me, Max,' I replied chastened. 'I should never have doubted you, even for a moment.' I pressed a hand to one of my temples. 'I'm simply concerned, and frustrated, and . . .'

'It's all right, Ver,' he murmured. His eyes were soft with understanding.

'I suspect we're all a bit on edge,' Sidney interjected, and then frowned down at his empty cup. 'And the Irish situation isn't as straightforward as it would seem.'

I was much struck by this remark, especially

coming from my husband, but I hadn't time to contemplate it further before he moved on.

'But to answer your question, Ryde, I believe I know these men well enough to recognize they would want to help prevent a gas attack against *either* side. Better to have the gas out of both combatants' hands, and out of Ireland, than risk the possibility of it being used.' His gaze briefly met mine. 'The more men we have looking for those cylinders, the more likely we are to find them.'

I knew he was thinking of Alec Xavier. Alec was a fellow intelligence agent who had spent most of the war, and several years before it, embedded in the German Army as an officer. Our history was both colorful and turbulent, but for better or worse, we understood each other in ways others from outside the service could never hope to. And I cared for the scamp. Ever since I'd learned in November that he'd been sent to Ireland to infiltrate the IRA and Michael Collins's inner circle, I'd been worrying about him. The fact that he was also attempting to find out if the phosgene cylinders Ardmore's men had stolen had been transported to Ireland only doubled that worry, for I well knew how an agent's involvement in more than one objective doubled the risk of their discovery.

But Max was not aware of Alec's current location. Alec had already risked much by telling me, and the fewer people who knew, the better.

Max nodded in acceptance as he took one last drag of his cigarette before stubbing it out. 'Did you see any of Ardmore's men at the club?'

I sank back into my chair, reaching for the coffee to pour myself another cup. 'After we helped the lieutenant "disappear," a man tried to sneak backstage. He might have been one of Ardmore's men, or he might simply have been trying to see Etta. We learned later that she had just returned backstage moments before to prepare for her next set. What of you?' I asked, spooning sugar into my cup. 'Were you followed?'

'I can't say for certain. But there were a number of suspicious-looking men loitering about outside the Empire Club with the photographers.'

Because they weren't allowed inside. That's why we'd chosen to send Max to that particular club. The exclusivity of its membership made it seem like the perfect place to arrange a clandestine meeting. However, I was more than certain some of Ardmore's men were numbered in the ranks of the upper classes. As Max's next words proved.

'And I saw Lucas Willoughby.'

I quickly lowered my cup from my lips. 'Captain Lucas Willoughby? Of Naval Intelligence?'

'The very same.'

I frowned, recalling our run-in with Willoughby during an investigation last autumn. During the war, he'd served as a Naval Intelligence officer within the Royal Naval Air Service and later the

Royal Air Force, once the RNAS and Royal Flying Corps had been merged into the RAF. But last October, he'd been working for Ardmore, and intent on obstructing our inquiry. However, he'd also saved our lives, thwarting the ambush we were driving into by dropping practice bombs on our opponents from his Ninak aeroplane.

'Then he was there at Ardmore's bidding,' Sidney declared.

'Undoubtedly,' Max agreed.

I reached up to fiddle with the gold chain draped over my pale green voile blouse. 'I suppose there's no way to know for certain how much Ardmore has deduced, but to be safe, it would be best to steer clear of Curlew for the moment.' Which hopefully meant he would be steering clear of the War Office entirely.

'But don't ignore him,' Sidney added, sliding one hand into the pocket of his trousers. 'That would be even more suspicious.'

'I already thought of that,' Max replied, a vee forming between his brows at our inference that he didn't know what he was about. 'I exchanged greetings with him this morning, but nothing more.'

Then he *had* been to the War Office before coming here. I'd suspected as much. It was on the tip of my tongue to remind him that then he needn't go back, but I bit it back, instead changing topics. 'Then perhaps you'd like to accompany us to Wilton Terrace. Curlew said Lieutenant Smith had given that address as the one where he was staying, but Sidney and I have our doubts.'

'I'm at your disposal.' The intent gleam in his eyes as he spoke those words made me flush, and I was forced to turn away to hide my reaction.

It had been nearly a year since I'd still believed Sidney to be dead – killed during the war – and I'd allowed feelings to develop between me and Max, though we'd never acted on them. But every once in a while a look or word from him would remind me and stir the memories to life again.

I loved Sidney, and we were both determined to make our marriage work. In fact, we'd come a long way since last June, when he first returned to me, and the secrets and years of separation had threatened to destroy any hope of our remaining together. But that didn't mean I didn't also still care for Max. Such a connection couldn't be completely severed simply because it would be more convenient if it did. Not when the man involved was as kind and good as Max. I knew nothing more would come of it. Just as Sidney knew. Max was our friend and partner in this investigation, nothing more.

'Shall we, then?' Sidney prompted, coming to my rescue.

He slid out my chair and I turned to look up at him as I stood. To any casual outsider, he would appear unruffled, but I could tell that he'd witnessed my response. I pressed a hand to the turned collar of his gray coat over his heart, refusing to feel guilty for something I couldn't control, something that wasn't entirely my fault. His hand covered mine briefly, gently at first, and then with more pressure, telling me he wasn't letting me go. When he began to pull away, I turned my hand over, grasping his wrist, telling him I wasn't letting him go either.

CHAPTER THREE

Sidney and I had been home for less than an hour – our visit to Wilton Terrace as much of a waste of time as we'd suspected it would be – when the telephone rang. I abandoned my contemplation of the ornate plaster medallions on the ceiling, hoping that the hostess for tonight's dinner party was calling to cancel. As much as I normally enjoyed such engagements, I found myself wearied by the prospect of making light conversation when so many things weighed on my mind. Of course, I had carried on during the war doing just such a thing and under even heavier circumstances, but at least then there had been a purpose to it. A reason to listen to this matron prattle or that gentleman boast, hoping to glean any information that might be combined with the intelligence we already knew to paint a clearer picture of a situation. Now, it was mostly just noise.

Nimble's clumping footsteps could be heard crossing the flat to the entrance hall before he answered the phone in his deep tones. Sidney's valet and former batman listened for a moment before asking the person to hold, and then he clumped his way back down the corridor. I sighed. It must have been for Sidney, for I soon heard his lighter tread emerge from his study.

I remained where I was, shamelessly eavesdropping.

'This is Kent.' He listened. 'What can I do for you, Capitaine Marcisieux?'

My ears perked up, hearing the French rank.

'Yes, I served in France.' There was a note of confusion in his voice which matched my own. 'No, I don't believe I know—' He broke off, as if the Frenchman had interrupted him. A hint of steel entered his voice. 'Why are you asking me this?' He paused. 'I *do* have a right to know.' Another pause. 'As a British citizen, my even speaking to you is a courtesy,' he retorted sharply. His growing hostility made it clear that the man he was speaking to wasn't precisely ingratiating himself with my husband. 'You do that. But don't count on my returning your next call to hear your apology.'

I sat up at this defiant declaration, which sounded distinctly like he was calling the man's bluff.

He listened for a long time. Through the doorway I could see him clutching the base and the receiver of the telephone in separate hands and scowling into the mirror above the bureau where the phone normally rested. 'Yes, but what has any of this to do with me?' he finally answered impatiently.

Whatever the Frenchman's answer was, it had

a transforming effect on Sidney. His back straightened and his frown slackened, though I could tell he was no happier to hear this part of the conversation than what had come before. He exhaled in exasperation. 'She was an informant,' he admitted. 'Helped to uncover a network of traitors. Perhaps you read about it in the papers,' he quipped dryly.

He pivoted to find me watching him at the same time I realized what he was talking about. The only network of traitors he had exposed had been the one partially embedded in his own battalion. His friend and fellow officer, Walter Ponsonby, had passed traitorous intelligence sent to him by his fiancée in coded letters, which he then handed off to a woman posing as his mistress in France. When Sidney had become suspicious and begun investigating the matter, Walter had shot him, leaving him for dead in the confusion of the German's big push in the spring of 1918. But Sidney had survived, albeit in hiding, and then allowed almost everyone – including me – to continue believing he was dead so that he could pursue the proof he needed to catch the traitors and see them punished. A feat he wasn't able to accomplish until last June, when he'd finally revealed to me that he was still alive, needing my help to break a code.

The story had been splashed all over the newspapers in Britain and abroad – *the dashing war hero and his intrepid wife striving against all odds and*

34

braving tremendous danger to unmask the dastardly villains being too great a tale to pass up. It was part of the reason for our celebrity, and why our photographs were so often included in the society pages – which was both a potential boon and also a trial for our ongoing investigations.

But if this French captain was calling about a female informant, one who had helped Sidney uncover the traitors, then there was only one woman I could think of. From the look in my husband's eyes, he could tell I'd realized it as well.

'She's adamant?' he asked, still staring at me. 'Well, I don't know why. I'm hardly in a position to negotiate for her, or to speak on behalf of the British government.'

The furrow returned to his brow. 'I had a thirty-minute conversation with Miss Baverel . . . well, it was really more of an interrogation, but regardless, I've only spoken with her once. So, I haven't the least idea why she would believe me trustworthy.'

Ah, but Sidney sold himself short there. For I could tell that most people concluded that he was worthy of their trust within two minutes flat. He was purely the type of man others liked and who wanted to like them in return. It was partly his natural confidence and competence, though his good looks obviously didn't hurt, but it was also in the way he interacted with others, in the way he listened. It had been no wonder why he'd made such an exemplary officer.

'Give me a few hours—' He broke off momentarily again, his scowl returning. 'I understand you're in a difficult position, give me a few hours and I'll get back to you. At this location?' He picked up the pencil and jotted down whatever the man told him on the writing pad kept by the telephone for messages.

He rang off, hanging the receiver back on its switch hook with less vehemence than I'd expected. He stood staring down at the paper before him for a moment, seeming to gather himself, before moving toward the drawing room. Sliding my legs off the sofa, I sat taller, waiting for Sidney to speak.

'As I'm sure you heard, that was Capitaine Marcisieux. He's with the Provost Gendarmerie.' Who were essentially the equivalent of the British Military Police. 'Though I gather he also serves in the Gendarmerie during peacetime as a sort of inspector.' He sank down on the emeraldine sofa beside me, turning to meet my expectant gaze. 'Apparently, they've detained a Miss Adele Baverel for looting, but they discovered she already has a record. She was arrested more than once during the war on suspicion of collaborating with the enemy.'

'And you know this Miss Baverel?' I replied carefully, allowing Sidney to control the flow of the retelling.

He nodded once in confirmation. 'But not as Miss Baverel. When I met her she went by the name Dupré.' His eyes searched my face, his lips curling wryly at the corner. 'I know you've already guessed it. She's the woman who posed as Ponsonby's mistress in Suzanne on the Somme. She gave me his last coded message she'd squirreled away before she was arrested. The message I asked you to decrypt at Umbersea.'

I exhaled, realizing I'd been holding my breath, waiting for him to confirm my suspicions. 'Yes, I put two and two together. But what does her arrest have to do with you now?'

Something flickered in his eyes, something very much like misgiving. 'Capitaine Marcisieux says she's refusing to speak to anyone but me.'

My eyes widened in incredulity.

'That if she can talk to me, she'll confess all. Otherwise, she'll say nothing.'

'And by "all," I assume she's talking about more than simply her most recent looting charges.'

His eyebrows arched. 'Presumably. Marcisieux believes she knows the identities and possible locations of other collaborators.'

Like all the Allied countries, France was eager to root out those who had collaborated with the enemy against their fellow countrymen and see them punished. And if there wasn't enough evidence to prosecute them, that didn't mean the allegations alone wouldn't at least see them convicted in the court of public opinion, justified or not. In Miss Baverel's case, we at least already knew she was guilty. There was no ambiguity there. But that didn't mean the people she might name were. She wouldn't be the first person to point the finger at others in order to obtain a lighter punishment.

'You've met her. Do you think she's telling the truth? Do you think it's possible she knows more?'

'Oh, I'm certain she knows more,' he replied with more confidence than I expected. 'I only dragged out of her what I could, along with that coded message, because she was so furious with Walter for leaving her high and dry when she was arrested by the French that first time in 1917. But there was definitely more.' He turned to the side. 'I merely chose to overlook it because I was so fixated on catching the traitor in my battalion not whatever schemes she was involved in then.'

I remembered how consumed he'd been with uncovering the traitor and exposing him. So consumed that he'd allowed me to believe he was dead for fifteen months. So consumed that even when he'd returned he'd been harsh and rigidly focused. That obsession had almost cost me my life, and nearly ruined any chance of our repairing our marriage.

I knew now that he regretted his bloody single-mindedness, if not his pursuit of justice, not only for himself but also all of the men he'd lost. Some of whose deaths might have been laid at Walter's and his coconspirator's feet. But it seemed now Sidney also regretted not pressing Miss Baverel for more information or pursuing those other schemes she might have been part of.

'Would she have told you about them at the time?' I asked, striving to lessen some of his guilt.

I could tell from the look in his eyes that the answer was 'no,' even if he didn't say the word.

'Could you have exposed her without exposing yourself?' I already knew the answer to this was negative as well, but I waited for him to acknowledge it.

He frowned, as if agitated at my trying to console him with logic. 'I'm sure there was something I could have done.'

'Maybe,' I conceded. 'But maybe not.' I lifted my gaze, tracing the pattern of the pomegranate damask wallpaper over his shoulder. 'Sometimes we have to accept our limitations and be content with the battles we can win.' My eyes locked with his. 'And forgive ourselves for those we cannot.' I tilted my head. 'Or do you think I should have pressed harder every Belgian citizen I thought wasn't telling me everything?'

'That's different, Ver,' he answered gruffly. 'You were a British spy in a country occupied by Germans. They could have denounced you to the Secret Police.'

'And what would have happened to you had you been exposed?' I challenged, knowing he was fully aware that if he'd been discovered, he would have been arrested for desertion. Without the proof he'd been seeking, his accusations of treason and being shot by a fellow British officer would be considered the ravings of a shell-shocked coward. I slid closer to him, softening my tone. 'Your situation was no less delicate.'

His mouth was still stamped in a mulish line, so when all he replied was a begrudging 'Maybe,' I considered it a victory.

Reaching up, I straightened the lapels of his gray coat. 'What do you want to do?'

He exhaled an aggrieved sigh, pushing to his feet. 'I don't *want* to do anything.' He wandered toward the sideboard, but then seemed to think better of pouring himself a drink. Instead, he turned to one of the tall Georgian-style windows, lifting his arm above him to brace it against the frame as he leaned forward to look out.

I studied his pensive profile, knowing he had more to say. I just needed to give him time to find the words. His muscles were taut as he wrestled with his thoughts, and I couldn't help but admire the strong line of his back.

He huffed. 'I feel like I have to go. I *need* to. After all, the men in my battalion aren't the only ones who deserve justice.'

I crossed the room to join him, not speaking until I was standing beside him, sunshine warming my skin. 'I can understand why you would rather not travel to France. I assume Miss Baverel has been detained somewhere near the front.'

'Amiens.'

Which had seen its share of the damage, especially in 1918, though not to the extent of other cities and villages closer to the front for the duration of the war.

'Marcisieux says they intend to transfer her to Paris in three days' time.'

I nodded, wondering if it might not be better to wait then, though I doubted that was what the French captain intended. For I had seen firsthand how difficult it had been for Sidney to return to the wasteland that was still the Western Front during our investigation the previous July. Amiens would be nothing compared to the utter devastation of Ypres, but it was still certain to arouse some unwelcome memories. However, I didn't think that was what was troubling him.

'So, what's giving you qualms?' I asked.

He turned his head to look at me, the bright sunlight casting half his face in light and half in shadow. His jaw was tight with unspoken thoughts.

'I can tell when you're uneasy about something, and I don't think it's merely about returning to France.'

He lowered his arm, tucking his hands into the pockets of his trousers as his gaze drifted back toward the view outside the window. His eyes narrowed into the glare of the brilliant blue sky. 'Miss Baverel . . . she was . . .'

For a moment, my stomach clenched, worrying he was going to say something I didn't want to hear, something that could never be taken back.

'Sly. Crafty. With her, I had the feeling I could only trust half of what she said. And half of that was merely admitted as a distraction.' He glanced at me as if to see if I understood what he meant.

My stomach settled. At least, mostly. 'She's been trained,' I surmised, realizing what he was trying to convey.

He nodded. 'That, or she's natural at deception. But . . . I suspect it's the former.'

'By whom?' I posited. 'The Germans?'

Sidney gave a shallow shrug of his shoulders. 'I suppose they're the likeliest suspects, seeing as she was helping courier intelligence to them.'

'Then . . . you don't trust whatever she plans to tell you?' I moved a half step closer. 'You think she has ulterior motives for insisting on speaking to you?'

'Oh, I *know* she has ulterior motives,' he remarked with a humorless laugh. 'She'll want me to broker a deal. Transfer to British custody and clemency from the death penalty in exchange for whatever nonsense she proposes to gas us with.'

'Then you think it would be better not to let her swing the lead?'

He turned to face me more directly. 'If she makes her pitch and the French buy it, whether we believe her or not, do you honestly think they're going to let it go? They'll push it *and* my participation in securing it up to the highest levels of the British government if they have to.'

'I see what you mean. She's using you as a pawn.'

His shoulders slumped and the anger scoring his brow faded. 'But what if she *does* have something important to tell me? Something of actual use? How can I chance not hearing it if it will bring justice to others?'

'Sidney, darling,' I murmured, pressing one hand to his chest while I trailed my fingers over his jaw with the other. I could feel his stubble just beginning to emerge. That he was racked with uncertainty and some level of remorse was obvious. All the men who had returned from the war felt some degree of guilt for having done so when so many others had not, and a responsibility to honor the fallen in whatever ways they could, but at times Sidney's was acute. I knew this was partly to do with his rank as an officer, and the hundreds if not thousands of men he'd commanded who had been wounded or killed, and partly the fact that I'd learned from Max that the commanding officers had made Sidney rally the troops, forcing him to wield the trust and rapport he held with the men to bolster them for battle, sending many of them on to their deaths.

But I also sensed there was more. Yes, Sidney had been through the hell of the trenches, of open battle – many times, in fact. He had survived the Somme, for heaven's sake, which was already a byword for carnage and destruction – the bloodiest battle of the war, and for little gain. But something had happened in 1917. Something that had impacted him radically. Whether it was the cumulative effect of the trauma of three years of war or a single event, I couldn't say. All I knew was that he hadn't been the same since.

Seeing the pain buried in his eyes, my heart constricted, and I knew I would do anything to ease it. I arched my chin determinedly. 'Then you'll just have to take someone with you who's been trained to beat Miss Baverel at her own game.'

The strain in his features slackened. 'And by "someone," I presume you mean *you*?'

I gave him a confident smirk. 'Who better? Between the two of us, I'm sure we can sniff out her lies. She wouldn't be the first spy, or spy-catcher for that matter, I've run rings around to outwit.'

His eyes searched mine, perhaps sensing the flutter of nerves I hid behind my smile. After all, no one was infallible. Something I'd been reminded of all too pointedly several months prior when I'd failed to recognize the dangerous lengths a former neighbor would go to in order to take revenge and impose his own justice. Something I wouldn't soon forget, for my shoulder still twinged and ached where he'd shot me. But I wasn't about to admit my doubts to Sidney. Not when he needed this bluff.

His arm wrapped around me, drawing me closer. 'You're certain?'

'Well, you didn't think I was going to let you go alone, did you?' I pressed my thumb to the shallow cleft in his chin. 'In any case, I know you.

You won't be able to live with the possibility she might have had something valuable to tell us. So, let's find out if she does.'

'You're right.' His lips curled into a grim smile. 'I suppose it *is* the only option we have. I'll ring Marcisieux back and let him know we'll be arriving in Amiens late tomorrow.'

I looked at the clock on the fireplace mantel. 'Did you mean to catch the evening train to Dover?'

His face still looked pained. 'Better to have it over and done with.'

'Then I'll instruct Sadie and Nimble to begin packing our bags. But cheer up, darling. At least you won't be crossing the Channel on a troop carrier.'

He grimaced. 'That will be a welcome change.'

I snuggled in close, offering him a coy look. 'And I promise not to snore like Sergeant McCoy.'

A genuine smile broke out across his face, warming me from the inside. 'Told you about him, did I?'

I grinned. 'I think you wrote it in one of your letters. How his snores echoed through the hull so badly, one of the colonels in your convoy ordered him to remain awake lest his noise alert listening U-boats to your presence.'

Sidney chuckled. 'Do you ever forget anything?'

'Not when it comes from you.'

A look of tenderness entered his deep blue eyes – one that was devoid of the raw ache of uncertainty previously stamped there. His gaze dipped to my lips. 'Then let me give you another memory you won't forget.'

And he did.

CHAPTER FOUR

'You never did tell me how you managed to track Miss Baverel down,' I told Sidney as the train bearing us from Calais neared Amiens.

He didn't respond immediately, having been lost in seeming contemplation of the passing country-side. The nearer to Amiens we'd drawn, the quieter he'd become, and I couldn't help but wonder at his withdrawal and the furrow in his brow. The simplest explanation was our surroundings. Despite our distance from the destruction of the trenches on the Western Front, and the signing of the peace treaty nine months earlier, the evidence of the war was still everywhere. In the discarded equipment and slag heaps along the siding, in the soldiers standing at passing stations, in the faces of the people who were worn out and discontent. And the nearer we drew to the devastated lands, the worse it was certain to become.

But I also couldn't help but wonder if Sidney's silence had as much to do with the task before us as his memories of the war. After all, he'd confessed how reluctant he was to speak to this Miss Baverel, and I doubted his feelings had changed in a mere twenty-four hours. It seemed in our best interests for me to find out why.

He turned his head and, finding me watching him expectantly, blinked his eyes rapidly. 'What was that, darling?'

'Miss Baverel. How did you find her?'

He adjusted the homburg hat on his head, shifting position in his seat so that he faced me more fully. 'I managed to discover the name and location of a woman who had visited her in Suzanne, and after surveilling her for months, trailed her to a house outside Arras where Miss Baverel was living.'

'And you disguised yourself as a peddler the entire time?' I posited carefully, not having dared to venture any further questions about the fifteen months he'd allowed others to believe him dead after our initial discussion of it. Then I'd been too shocked, and afterward too frightened of what would happen if I prodded too closely at the wound to our marriage.

'Among other things,' he admitted vaguely, his attention straying back to the green and yellow fields beyond the window glass. 'Whatever was necessary to get by and not draw notice.'

I nodded in understanding, even though he was no longer looking at me. Hadn't I done much the same thing whenever I ventured over the electrified fence into German-occupied Belgium, attempting to blend in however I could?

Brushing a speck of lint from the sleeve of my Parisian blue traveling ensemble, I adjusted the fit of my coat, attempting to keep the tone of my voice offhand. 'What is she like?'

However, Sidney wasn't fooled. He turned to look at me squarely, his eyebrows arching sardonically.

'What?' I retorted. 'I can't help it if my curiosity is piqued. After all, it's not every day that one meets a woman brazen enough to be caught spying for the Germans and then demand for a British war hero's help.'

He tipped his head to the side, seeming to give the matter some thought. 'She's . . . elegant, droll, manipulative.' He shrugged. 'Exactly what you'd suspect from a woman in such a position.'

I swallowed a sigh, realizing I was never going to get anything useful from my husband. He was too preoccupied with whatever was troubling him to give the matter any greater thought than that. So, I relented, joining him in his scrutiny of the passing scenery.

We could feel the train slowing as the buildings grew closer together until we encountered an unexpected sight. Bands of barbed wire entanglements stretched off into the distance away from the track, drooping and twisted at several points. I realized this had once been part of the outer defenses of Amiens. After all, the city had been an important Allied rail hub, and a vital British logistics center in the rear of the Allied front.

Hundreds of thousands, if not millions, of troops as well as supplies had been transported back and forth on these rail lines during the war. Which had made defending Amiens from attacks – within and without – the highest priority. After all, acts of sabotage were not unheard of, especially when civilians faced heavy privations, as this part of France had done.

The train rolled on into the city, leaving the ramshackle defenses behind. It would only be a matter of time before the fortifications were taken down or scavenged, as other parts of the barricades had likely been. Though heaven knew, this part of Europe certainly wasn't suffering from a shortage of barbed wire.

We soon arrived at the temporary railway station and disembarked. The city's grand old station, built during the middle of the last century, had been razed to the ground during the bombardment in 1918 when the Germans' final push had brought the city within range of their big guns. Much of the city had also suffered from the shelling, we discovered as the cab we hailed carried us through the brick streets. However, astonishingly the cathedral had somehow survived. It towered over the surrounding buildings, all the more visible in the streets lined with rubble held back by old wooden boards.

The devastation was higgledy-piggledy. Here a block would stand almost untouched, while next door the buildings lay in ruins. As we weaved our way through the streets to our hotel, I couldn't help but wonder if upon hearing Sidney's British accent, the driver had chosen to take us on the scenic route, so to speak. He needn't have bothered. We'd both seen worse. Though I could feel the tension radiating through my husband's arm next to mine.

Since our arrival, Sidney and I had easily slipped into speaking French, both of us being fluent in the language, as much of the nobility and gentry were. It was practically a requisite for the educated, moneyed classes, though things were changing. But alone in our hotel room, Sidney lapsed back into English as he leaned against the open door leading out to the balcony. Beyond him I could see the green of the square opposite, a welcome bit of color even if many of the trees still lacked leaves.

I glanced up at him from time to time as I stored my few garments in the clothespress, hoping to prevent them from wrinkling. Normally such a job would be left to a lady's maid, but I'd grown accustomed to doing for myself during the war and after, especially when we traveled. I'd hired one fresh-faced girl in January, but within weeks we'd realized neither of us was the right fit for the other. Since then, I'd not been willing to make the effort to hire someone else. Not when Mrs Yarrow took care of my clothes and the few other duties I was willing to relinquish while we were in London. It being a short trip, Sidney had elected to leave Nimble behind as well.

It was clear there was a great deal on Sidney's mind, though he seemed content to keep his thoughts to himself. So, his next remark came as a surprise.

'I stayed here once during the war, you know.'

I nearly slammed my fingers in the drawer at the admission. 'You did?'

He peered over his shoulder at me before returning to the view. 'We often came to Amiens when we were given a day or two of leave. Too short to return to Blighty, but long enough for a bath, a shave, and a few good meals.' He nodded toward something in the distance as I crossed to him. 'Stayed at the Hôtel du Rhin a time or two, as well.' A smile quirked the corner of his lips. 'There was a walled garden behind it with a small pond where a stork and a gull lived. They were the oddest companions. If the stork strutted across the grass, the gull had to keep pace. And they *hated* aeroplanes. Whenever the Jerries would fly in our direction, they would hear the throb of their engines long before we could detect it, and the stork would point his beak skyward and clatter it together – rat-tat-tat-tat – like a machine gun.' He grinned outright. 'All of us officers were dashed fond of that bird.'

I listened intently, struggling to master my emotions lest he notice how his words had affected me. It was the most he'd shared about his life during the war in a long time, if ever. And spontaneously given, rather than me having to drag it out of him. I didn't want to break the spell.

His smile vanished. 'The Hôtel du Rhin was destroyed during the bombardment, but some press correspondents transported the birds to safer lodgings farther down the line. Little good it did, for the old stork died soon after. Last I heard they were going to stuff him and display him.' His voice had grown tight, and I couldn't tell whether he disapproved of this, or he was merely suppressing his feelings.

The breeze lifted the dark curling hair that had fallen across his brow and brought with it the scent of approaching rain. The pavement would be damp by nightfall.

His eyes narrowed briefly as he continued to stare out into the amber-tinged light of afternoon. 'I wonder how many of the other hotels, and American bars, and patisseries we visited during our leaves are still standing,' he contemplated morosely before turning his head to look at me. 'There was one café that served lemon ices, and every time I passed it, I would think of you and whether I would ever have the chance to take you there.'

My throat was clogged with emotion, but I managed to choke out a response. 'We can go look for it now, if you like.'

For a moment, I thought he was going to say yes, but then his eyes dimmed, and he seemed to retreat behind the wall he threw up whenever the discussion veered too close to a subject he didn't want to face. 'Maybe later.' He looked at the sky to the west where clouds could be seen gathering. 'There's still several hours until nightfall. I wonder if perhaps we shouldn't pay a visit to Captain Marcisieux first.'

I searched his features, recognizing the taut line of his brow, the rigid posture of his shoulders for what they were – nerves. Even the insouciant pose, with his hands tucked into the pockets of his trousers, was all in aid of masking his obvious anxiety. If visiting this gendarmerie officer would help ease his concern, then I was all for it.

'Better to have it over and done with it, right?' I replied, echoing his statement from the day before. 'Just give me a moment to change.'

A quarter of an hour later, we set off on foot, an umbrella tucked under Sidney's arm. With him dressed in a smart striped navy blue suit, and me in a chic Prussian blue walking ensemble and mauve roll-brimmed hat with netting, we might have been mistaken for a couple on a promenade to the park except for our determined stride. Sidney had set a brisk pace, his concentration on the conversation to come, and it was all I could do to keep up.

Fortunately, the gendarmerie wasn't far, and we were quickly shown into the provost's office. It seemed he'd been waiting for us. Or at least, Sidney. The lines around his mouth tautened as I was introduced.

Captain Marcisieux was rather spare in stature – his eyes being almost level with mine – and as if to compensate for it, his posture was rigidly correct, as was every other part of him. His uniform of dark and light blue was crisply ironed, the multiple cords – aiguilettes – expertly draped. A trim mustache perched above his upper lip, and even his hair was severely styled, copious amounts of pomade holding it in place. It was impossible to tell its true color, the Brilliantine rendering it a muddy medium brown.

Given his appearance and unhappy reaction to my presence, I could easily gauge his personality. And rather absurdly, the knowledge that I faced yet another tight-lipped, disapproving gentleman gave me the urge to reach up and ruffle his hair simply to see what his reaction would be.

As if sensing this impulse, Sidney pressed his hand to the small of my back and guided me toward one of the chairs sitting before the provost's desk. The chair was one of two unpadded armchairs, their hard wooden seats likely meant to inspire people not to linger. Though, to be fair, much of the space was rather Spartan. Even the captain's desk was empty save for a small pile of papers in a box at one corner and a single picture frame turned away from me.

'I am thankful you did not dawdle in coming here,' he informed Sidney in English.

Sidney replied in French, telling the man we were content to converse in their language. 'Yes, well, your tone implied the matter was rather urgent.' I didn't miss the wry undertone to his words, but from the lack of reaction from Marcisieux, it appeared he had. 'I take it, then, that Mademoiselle Baverel is being held here.'

'Yes. We can take you to speak with her in a few moments.' The door opened while he was speaking, and he nodded once to the man who entered, but did not address or introduce him. The other man took up a position beside the door, standing more or less at attention, while the captain continued speaking. The newcomer's pale eyes shifted to me, calmly assessing me, before returning to the captain.

'But first I wanted to speak to you about what your intentions are.' Marcisieux folded his hands before him on his desk. 'How do you intend to proceed?'

'You said she insisted on speaking with me,' he replied insouciantly as he extracted his cigarette case from his coat pocket. 'May I?'

The captain waved his permission.

'So, I *intend* to let her speak. I won't know how to proceed until I hear what she has to say.' He lit his fag, taking a deep breath and glaring through the stream of smoke he exhaled at the provost. 'Or was there a particular tack you wished me to take?' The look in his eyes and the tone of his voice made it clear he wasn't going to play anybody's fool.

'We need whatever information you can get from her, however you can get it. Particularly names.'

56

However you can get it. That little addend didn't sit well with me. I scrutinized the captain with new eyes, wondering just what methods he was willing to use, and whether he intended to use them if we didn't succeed.

'She may ask for some assurances before she freely gives up any such information.' Sidney arched a single eyebrow. 'Are you prepared to accept British interference?'

'If it gets me the names, then yes.'

The silence stretched as Sidney and Marcisieux eyed each other steadily, their gazes never wavering even as my husband took another drag of his cigarette.

'You do realize there's no guarantee the names or the information she gives us will be legitimate,' Sidney pointed out as he leaned forward to tip his ash into the dish at the corner of the desk.

'You let us worry about that,' the provost snapped. 'Your only concern is to convince her to talk.'

Though he didn't react, I knew that my husband would be as unimpressed as I was with this response. But rather than challenge it when we could just as easily circumvent it if necessary, Sidney merely nodded. 'Let's get this over with, then.'

Captain Marcisieux pushed back his chair to rise. 'I will escort you to our interrogation chamber. Your wife may remain here.'

Sidney stubbed out the remainder of his fag. 'You misunderstand. Mrs Kent will be joining me.'

The provost bristled. 'Monsieur, that is unacceptable. To allow a *woman* to take part in such an interview . . . No, it cannot be allowed.'

'Then I'm afraid you've wasted all of our time.'

His eyes darted to me where I now stood beside my husband and back. 'You would refuse to interview Mademoiselle Baverel simply because we denied your wife access?'

'I would.'

'But monsieur, there are procedures.'

Sidney shrugged one shoulder. 'Make an exception.'

Marcisieux seemed horrified by the prospect, muttering almost to himself. 'This is highly irregular. Highly irregular.'

'We hear that a lot,' Sidney quipped, and I was forced to bite back a smile. My heart was already buoyed by my husband's defense of me and his insistence I take part. I suspected it helped that we held the upper hand, but I knew that even if that weren't the case, he would have stood his ground.

I turned to look at the man standing next to the door, curious how he'd reacted to this display, but if he held any opinion on the matter, it didn't show. His uniform was similar to the gendarmerie's, but not entirely the same. I found myself wondering if perhaps he was from a different department or unit. Whatever the case, judging from his age and his cool collection, he was no raw recruit.

58

The provost grumbled under his breath, and then gestured for us to follow him. 'Come along, then.' He bustled us through the door the other man held open and then down the corridor. Abruptly halting before a door near the end, he thrust it open to allow us to precede him inside.

If I'd thought Marcisieux's office was spare, this space was considerably more so. A table and three chairs were all that the walls, a sickly shade of green, surrounded. That, and a second doorway leading into a closet with a small desk and a chair. I realized then that the other man had followed us into the room. He cast me a stoic glare before entering the closet.

'Lieutenant Charlaix will take notes, so that you will have no need to,' the captain told us as he turned to go. 'Mademoiselle Baverel will be escorted in momentarily.'

I scrutinized the wall that stood between us and Charlaix's concealed position. On one hand, I could appreciate the cleverness of such a setup. It would be easy to forget someone sat on the opposite side of the wall listening – if, in fact, the suspect realized it at all. But I was also leery of the other man's presence. There was something about him that was out of place, and I had begun to suspect he was much more than the lieutenant he was meant to portray. Given that, I didn't like the idea of him listening in on our conversation with Miss Baverel, particularly without the benefit of my being able to analyze his reactions.

It appeared Sidney was of a similar opinion, for he followed my stare, shaking his head as if to warn me not to speak of anything consequential while we might be overheard. I nodded, letting him know I understood.

Fortunately, we hadn't long to wait for the arrival of our honored guest. The door opened and a young officer escorted a woman dressed in a frock of merlot crepe toward the chair on the opposite side of the table. Her brown bob had certainly seen better days, but that did not detract from her beauty. Nor did the dark circles under her eyes. If anything, they made her appear more sympathetic. The young officer's gentle treatment of her, and the melting smile she offered him in thanks as he withdrew, seemed to confirm this.

Her regard veered to Sidney, and she offered him the same smile before speaking in a low, mellow voice in French. 'Monsieur Kent. Lovely to see you again.'

'I believe you promised me you were going to stay out of trouble,' he replied pointedly in response.

'Yes, well, I never *was* very good at keeping my promises.' She then turned to me. 'And this is Madame Kent, I presume.' Her eyes inspected me – analyzing, assessing, until I felt rather like a specimen in a jar.

I arched my eyebrows, letting her know I wasn't about to be intimidated.

She gave a light laugh. 'I had a feeling I would like you. The wife of Monsieur Kent . . . well, she must be something.' Her languid posture altered, leaning toward Sidney, and her eyes glinted with mischief. 'Did you tell her about us?'

CHAPTER FIVE

Iadmit her words jolted me, but I wasn't about to let her see it. Nor was I going to believe the implication she'd meant to make. Not when her features were alive with barely concealed malice, and Sidney was so unruffled.

'What there is to tell,' he replied in a low, sardonic tone.

'Are you sure about that?' she countered, undeterred. She leaned closer, reaching her arm across the table as if to touch him, but stopped just short. 'Remember that place we met?'

'That squalid little house where you were squatting.'

Her mouth formed a pretty pout. 'No one was using it. But that's not what I meant.' Her gaze slid to me where I calmly sat regarding her.

'I *know* what you meant to imply, but my wife isn't foolish enough to fall for such a ploy.'

Her eyes narrowed as if to verify this and then she sighed, sinking abruptly back in her chair as she crossed her arms over her chest. 'Very well.'

I was perhaps most surprised by the ease of her capitulation, but then, I remembered she was hoping to gain something from us that was far more valuable than merely getting a rise out of me.

'Now, you're wasting time. So, tell us, Mademoiselle Baverel . . .' Sidney paused to scrutinize her. 'That *is* your real name?'

She shrugged one shoulder. 'It's as good as any other. But *please*, call me Adele. I insist.'

'Mademoiselle Baverel,' Sidney began again pointedly.

She heaved an aggrieved sigh so loud the guard standing outside the door likely heard it.

A muscle ticked at the corner of Sidney's eye, and I was forced to bite the inside of my cheek, lest I smile at the evidence that Miss Baverel's outrageous behavior was getting to him. Had she not been a traitor, and had she not just tried to convince me she'd once been my husband's lover, we might have been friends.

'You insisted Capitaine Marcisieux send for me. That I was the only person you would speak to. So . . .' He held up his hands. 'Here I am. What have you to say?'

We sat in silence for several moments, waiting for her to enlighten us. But contradictorily, now that she'd been given the opening to speak, she seemed unable to find the words. Or perhaps she didn't know where to begin.

She sat very still, seemingly unperturbed. That is, until I recognized she was counting her breaths, in and out, steady and slow. It was a tactic I'd been taught to employ when my nerves threatened to get the best of me, although with much more stealth and finesse. It seemed probable that someone had instructed her, but that the training had been rushed and incomplete. When she did finally open her mouth, it was to utilize another trick.

'May I have a cigarette? I know you must have one.' She shot a glare at the door. 'They took mine when they locked me in that cell.'

The fag would provide her a distraction for her hands, and a plausible reason for any pauses where she might have to weigh her answers or concoct lies before she spoke. It also tested Sidney's goodwill. But even knowing all this, I did not object when my husband pulled his cigarette case from his pocket. For as much as her smoking could hide, it could also reveal, and I had a strong hunch that whatever slapdash training she'd received, it was not enough to smooth over any such fumbles.

She offered Sidney another melting look as he lit her fag for her, but did not follow it up with a smile when he remained unaffected. Inhaling a deep drag, she tilted her head upward to blow the smoke into the air. 'Did they tell you why I was arrested?'

He didn't answer, deducing she was merely making an opening to speak.

'Looting.' She gave a short humorless laugh. 'Really? Me, a looter?' She shook her head angrily and took another drag. 'It's all balderdash, of course. Émile's doing. *He* put those items in my cupboard and called the gendarme. And all because I'd told him he was a tedious lover. Well, he *was!*' She scowled at the floor. 'But now, here I am. Facing much more than charges of looting.'

She lapsed back into silence, and it seemed we might have to prompt her again, when suddenly her mouth twisted into a nasty sneer. 'Men, bah!' Her blazing eyes shifted to me. 'They judge us, but never understand us. One minute they expect us to fall at their feet, beholden to them for our every need and their every whim, and the next they abandon us to fend for ourselves. And the sins they write in our black book are treble what is written in their own.' Her elbow plunked down on the table as she leaned toward me. 'Tell me this, is a sin done out of necessity truly a sin at all? And what of a sin done to avoid a greater one?' Her eyes hardened as she stared into the distance beyond my shoulder. 'I know it must be better than a sin of pure lust and greed.'

All this talk of sins was making my head spin, but I thought I could decipher among her tangle of words what she was trying to say. 'What was the sin you were trying to avoid?'

Her eyes focused on me again, and her mouth puckered as if she'd tasted something sour. 'You may not realize it, having spent the war safely tucked away in London,' she began scornfully, of course not knowing that my war had been far more adventurous than that, 'but there are few

65

options for women caught up in the chaos of invasion. Our homes and livelihoods destroyed; our friends killed. We do what we must to survive.' Her voice sharpened with anger. 'And when I grew tired of spreading my legs for barely enough to afford a loaf of bread, I jumped at the first opportunity I was given.'

'To courier messages for Walter Ponsonby?' I clarified.

'Yes.' She paused, knowing the impact her next words would have. 'Among others.'

I straightened, my gaze seeking out Sidney's at this confirmation of our suspicions.

'Yes, there were others.' Her eyes danced lively, deriving satisfaction out of shocking us. But it was short-lived, her tone darkening again. 'But I only did it so I could stop playing the whore for all the Tommies. Some of them with wives and sweethearts back home worrying themselves sick over them, and all the while they're swiving the likes of me.'

Having spent time in the German-occupied areas of Belgium and northern France, I'd seen directly the toll that war had on women, especially those whose husbands had been killed or were on the opposite side of the front, fighting in the Belgian Army. And if they had children to feed or no family to fend for them, so much the worse. Many of them had been forced to do things they would never have even considered except for their own and their little ones' survival.

So, I was not without empathy for Miss Baverel's situation.

However, she had not been trapped inside the Germans' occupation zone. She'd had other options. Finding work in one of the cities and villages farther back from the line, catering to the troops and in constant need of more labor for their cafés and shops. Moving out of the war zone entirely. Yes, it might have been difficult, but not impossible. Whoring and turning traitor had not been her only two options.

'I knew what I was doing was wrong,' she confessed after taking a long drag from her cigarette before tipping the ashes onto the floor. 'But I never thought I was hurting anyone. Not really. I was just playing postman.'

If she'd thought to justify herself and engage our sympathies, she'd chosen the wrong way to go about it, for Sidney's shoulders stiffened in outrage at her attempt to pass the blame. 'Except the secrets you happened to courier cost hundreds, if not thousands of men's lives. You can pretend all you want, but that won't wash the bloodstains from your hands.'

His words seemed to unsettle her, for her hand trembled as she lifted the fag to her lips again.

Feeling the waves of fury still rolling off Sidney, I decided it was time to change the subject. 'You said there were others you couriered for,' I prompted her. 'Who?'

She drew one last deep inhalation from the

cigarette and her head came up. 'I'm not giving you names. Not until I make it clear what I want in exchange.' She dropped the cigarette to the floor, grinding it out with the heel of her shoe.

'Is that the reason you sent for me, then?' Sidney snapped, his temper barely leashed. There was a palpable tension in the air about him, as if he might lash out at any moment. 'To barter a deal? Then, I'm afraid you've wasted all of our time.' It was the same threat he'd wielded so skillfully against Captain Marcisieux, and it worked to the same effect.

'It is *one* of the reasons I insisted on speaking to you,' Miss Baverel replied swiftly before he could rise from his seat. 'I will come to the others if you will but listen.'

He crossed his arms over his chest. 'The clock is ticking.'

Her brow puckered in irritation.

'If not their names,' I interceded, 'then what *can* you share with us? Were they working for the same network?'

'Part of Helen Crawford's scheme? In a manner of speaking, I suppose.' Seeing my look of disbelief, her eyebrows arched in mild annoyance. 'Yes, I read the newspaper articles about your exploits. So even though I spoke the truth to your husband eighteen odd months ago, when I told him I didn't know exactly who I was working for, I recognized who Helen and Walter must be.'

I waved this away, more focused on the second

part. 'What do you mean by, *in a manner of speaking*?'

'Well, you didn't honestly believe Helen was in charge of that operation, did you?' she stated, looking back and forth between us. I turned to meet Sidney's gaze as she continued to speak. 'She didn't have the connections within Germany and France to pull that off.'

That had been one of the details I had been least satisfied with, but after unmasking Helen, Walter, and their other conspirators, our involvement in the affair had been complete. We had handed over the investigation and what evidence we had to the authorities to continue. In his confession, Walter had made it sound as if Helen had direct contacts with German Intelligence, who had arranged the courier route for the intelligence she gathered from unsuspecting high-ranked men in the British government, but perhaps this was wrong. He could have either been mistaken or outright lied.

'Then who was—'

She shook her head, cutting off this question.

I exhaled in exasperation. 'Right. No names. But how do we know what you're telling us is true? After all, making shadowy accusations is hardly proof of anything, and can just as easily be retracted.'

Her fingers drummed against the table as she considered this point. I noted that her nails had been bitten to the quick. Whatever ease and

69

confidence Miss Baverel was feigning, it was not genuinely felt. Her scrutiny slid toward the wall behind which lay the closet where Lieutenant Charlaix was concealed. She'd given no indication earlier that she'd realized it was there, but this seemed proof that she was more conscious of it than we'd realized.

I glanced toward it significantly, attempting to gauge how much of her reticence was due to the other man in the room, so to speak. When I turned back, her dark gaze met and held my own, and what I saw reflected there for but a brief moment was naked fear. Whether of Charlaix in particular, her incarceration in general, or the execution which awaited her if the charges of treason were proved, I couldn't be sure. Perhaps all three. But I felt certain that raw emotion had not been faked.

She blinked rapidly and it was gone, tucked away behind her audacious façade, but I knew the truth of what I'd seen.

'I carried other messages from different sources through this same route,' she finally admitted. 'Sources Helen and Walter never mentioned. Sources who used a different code than they did.'

They'd not admitted it, no, but it was still possible Helen had used other soldiers to transport her coded missives to Miss Baverel. After all, she'd met Walter through a Lonely Soldier column: the adverts some soldiers took out in English newspapers in order to solicit letters and parcels from any girls back home who might take pity on them. In the best of circumstances, these were placed with the purest of intentions, for there was nothing so dreary as never receiving a letter or parcel in the post at the front. Though in Walter's case, it had been done as more of a lark. One that had turned out to be one of the worst decisions of his life.

In any case, there was no reason Helen couldn't have written to other 'lonely soldiers,' culling and grooming them to find the ones most likely to be bribed and persuaded, unwittingly or not, to commit treason. Although, the greater number of people involved, the greater the risk of discovery. And having Walter so neatly under her thumb that he'd proposed marriage, I wasn't sure Helen would have taken the risk of continuing to involve others.

'So, you think someone other than Helen was coordinating this system from London?' I clarified.

'I don't just think it, I know it,' she stated firmly.

'But how . . .?'

'Because he's still doing it.'

I felt a tingle at the nape of my neck, as I always did when I realized I was about to learn something important. My breath quickened as I studied the other woman closely, intent on making certain I didn't miss any indications that she was lying. 'You're still a courier.' It wasn't a question, but a statement, as I suspected she would never confirm it directly anyway.

She clasped her hands before her on the table, choosing her words with care. 'There are still transfers of information going on. Not necessarily by the same routes. And not very often to Germany. But they are occurring all the same.'

I found that her specification about Germany's current role increased the veracity of this confession, for Germany's intelligence network – perhaps the most advanced of all the wartime agencies – was now in shambles. Not everyone was aware of this, but she was.

'How?' Sidney asked.

'I will not give you specifics. Not until we have a deal.'

His eyes narrowed.

'*But* I have hidden proof of what I speak. It is well concealed. They will not find it among the things they've taken from my home – not my paintings, or my sofa cushions, or my red leather portfolio, or my figurines. No.' She waved her hand. 'It is safe as houses' – she tilted her head – 'or at least as safe as one could be in Belgium during the war. Until I choose to retrieve it.'

I looked at Sidney, unsure what she was rambling about.

'Or I send others to do so.' She scrutinized us each in turn as if for this mission. 'But I do not know if I can trust you.' Her bobbed hair swung forward, partially concealing her face and the smile she flashed us. It seemed to me she was giving us the razz, revealing her last statement for the lie it was. Perhaps because of Lieutenant Charlaix's presence in the closet. After all, it was clear she didn't trust the French. Not if she was counting on an Englishman to help her broker a deal with them.

But there was also a growing frenzy to her words and movements, making them appear erratic in nature. Even now, she was using what was left of her gnawed nails to pick at her cuticles. Part of me wondered if this was a deliberate ploy, her feigning instability, but another part of me was not so cynical.

Before either of us could form a response, she tipped her head back and laughed. 'I can just imagine their agitation over what I've said. They will try to drag more information about its location from me, but I will say no more. I have already said too much.'

Sidney was watchful, plainly wondering some of the same things I was about Miss Baverel. 'Then what is this deal you hope to make?'

She straightened to her best posture, flattening her hands against the table. 'I will reveal all the names of people involved with these networks, both past and present. All the names of people I know, at any rate. Be they French or British or of another nationality. And I will share all the details about how the courier service worked and where the information was transported across and around enemy lines. I will also disclose the hidden location of my proof.' She dipped her head forward in emphasis. 'I will do *all* this . . . in exchange for parole in the United States.'

This was a contingency neither of us had anticipated.

'Not Britain?' Sidney replied, the destination we had been expecting.

'No,' she snapped so vehemently I was taken aback. She inhaled, gathering herself before she continued. 'No, not Britain. If the United States is not amenable, then possibly Spain or Switzerland.' Both of whom had remained neutral throughout the conflict. 'But nowhere else.'

It was clear, even if nothing else was, that Miss Baverel was frightened of something or someone in Britain, and she wanted to be as far away from it or them and their reach as possible. But what or who was she running from? The power behind Helen and the other networks she spoke of?

An image of Lord Ardmore flashed through my mind. For he was the only person I knew of whose reach and influence could penetrate so far, and who she might fear her testimony would never bring down. She might not know his real name, but she evidently knew such a figure existed, and that he was well insulated from the ramifications of his machinations. The trail of evidence always ended before it reached him. At least, thus far. Though I couldn't help but wonder if this proof she'd concealed might change that.

'You understand I haven't the power to arrange such a thing, if it's even possible,' Sidney warned her. 'There are many parties that will have to be involved in such a negotiation.'

'Maybe not, but you have influence,' she refuted. 'And as I understand it, you rarely use it.'

I frowned. How could she know how often he used it?

'I'm asking you to use it now.' She leaned forward, staring intently at him. 'It doesn't take a genius to see that justice means a great deal to you. Justice for the men who served with you, and justice for those who still serve. After all, you were once willing to throw everything else away to attain it.'

Her words pierced like a knife, recalling memories I would sooner forget. She was right. Sidney had been willing to risk it all – our marriage, our future, his very life – to obtain justice for the soldiers who'd been betrayed by Walter and the others. It had been a near thing, almost costing me *my* life before he changed course, choosing love over vengeance. But that desire for justice was still strong within him. It was part and parcel of the tangle of emotions he felt about the war.

'I can help you accomplish that. I'll . . .' She swallowed as her gaze darted to me. 'I'll even tell you what I know about the bombing outside Bailleul.'

I straightened in shock, having expected her to say anything but that. I'd been prepared to disgruntledly accept that the full truth about the explosion of General Bishop's temporary HQ would never be brought to light, and yet here Miss Baverel was telling me she held information about that very event. But what could she possibly know, and how? Had she been involved?

'But I won't tell you *anything* until I have assurances,' she reiterated before I could speak, her mutinous expression making that very clear.

Swallowing the questions piling up on my tongue, I turned to Sidney, unsurprised by the black look he'd aimed at the other woman. If there was one thing Sidney hated more than anything in the world it was to be manipulated. He had anticipated Miss Baverel had dragged him here to pull his strings, but being here, facing her across the table and hearing all the intelligence she promised, and yet would not give up until she'd secured her own aims . . . It was all far more difficult to stomach. I wasn't certain whether he would even be capable of making a civil response, and my suspicions seemed to be confirmed when he suddenly pushed back his chair and stalked out of the room.

Miss Baverel's eyes widened in alarm.

But I refused to offer her the reassurances she sought. Not when her behavior and motives were purely selfish, and she seemingly felt no compunction in using us like pawns. Perhaps the information she could provide would expose other traitors and allow the authorities to halt ongoing treasonous activities, but that didn't exonerate her of her wrongdoing. Nor did it wash the bitter taste of her duplicity from my mouth.

I rose more slowly from my chair. 'You've

overplayed your hand, mademoiselle. A little remorse would go a long way.'

Her eyes flashed. 'Even if it's feigned?'

I arched a single eyebrow, telling her how unimpressed I was by her display of defiance. 'I suppose we'll never know, will we?'

'You . . . you're just going to walk away?' she demanded to know as I turned to do just that.

I stared back at her in open aggravation. 'Did you really expect anything else?' I shook my head disdainfully. 'For a woman who hasn't yet proven the worth of her intelligence, you're certainly making a lot of demands.'

'I suppose you won't know until it's too late.'

I paused with my hand on the door handle. Her words sounded like a threat, but the tone of her voice had been far from it. In fact, if I wasn't very much mistaken, it was tinged with despair. But I refused to look back, lest her expression sway me. I needed to find Sidney and together we could decide how to proceed.

After all, Miss Baverel wasn't going anywhere. Not this evening anyway. There was time enough to speak with her again after she'd spent another night in her cell, pondering the consequences of her actions. Perhaps tomorrow she would be a bit humbler and more contrite. And now that Sidney knew what exactly he faced, he could better keep his temper in check. Unlike during the war, time was on our side.

Or so I thought.

CHAPTER SIX

Sidney was quiet as we strolled back to the Grand Hôtel de L'Univers, rain pattering against the umbrella he held over our heads. Though tempted to pepper him with questions, I knew I needed to give him time to turn over everything we learned, and to come to grips with his residual anger. Nothing made him less communicative than when he was miffed. Talking to him now would only yield grunts and monosyllabic answers.

Given the weather, we elected to dine at our hotel, but returned to our room to change into our evening clothes. The concierge had told us there would be music and dancing, and I was hopeful good food would cajole Sidney into a better mood. At least, one light enough to coax him to take a turn or two about the floor with me. There were few things I enjoyed more than dancing with my husband, but we'd had little opportunity as of late to do so.

I was struggling with the buttons at the back of my periwinkle blue gown when I heard Sidney return from the adjoining *en suite*. His footsteps halted and then advanced toward me as I huffed in frustration. Intricate fastenings in difficult-to-reach places were one of the tasks I most missed having a lady's maid to perform, especially since being shot. The muscles in my left shoulder twinged when I strained them in odd ways.

'Allow me,' Sidney said, brushing my hands aside.

I kneaded the aching muscles of my shoulder as his fingers deftly inched their way up my back, fastening the buttons.

'Is it troubling you?' he asked in concern.

'Only when I try to contort myself into unnatural positions,' I quipped, wanting to set his mind at ease.

When he was finished, I draped the matching capelet in sheer gauze around my shoulders, pivoting so he could see all of me. 'Will I do?'

His eyes warmed, and I felt the thrill of his admiration clear down to my toes. 'Always,' he declared with a private little smile, drawing me toward him.

I reached up to adjust his bow tie, reveling in the tingles of attraction that arced between us, but not allowing his mouth to find mine. If we started kissing, I feared we would never reach the dining room, and I was famished. But all thought of food temporarily fled when he broached his next question.

'What did you think of her?'

I looked up into his deep blue eyes, trying to

gauge whether he was truly ready for this conversation. 'Well, she was certainly bold and audacious.' I narrowed my eyes. 'But I sensed genuine fear in her, as well.' I stepped back, turning to pace a tight line back and forth as I thought back over our conversation with Miss Baverel. 'She'd received some sort of training, but it was slapdash at best, or perhaps incomplete. That suggests to me that she wasn't directly employed by any intelligence gathering agencies. They would never have sent such a reckless and ill-equipped agent into the field. No, she was far more likely recruited by a shadowy, unofficial network, and given very rudimentary instructions on how to proceed.'

'So, she was recruited by someone with training, someone who knew what he – or she – was about, but didn't have the time or interest in ensuring his recruit was fully trained,' Sidney summarized.

I turned to point at him. 'Precisely. Based on Walter's confession about the situation and what he knew of it, I assumed that person was a German agent. That Helen's contact with German Intelligence had given her instructions on how to access the letterbox Miss Baverel posted. Figuring out how to get the information she acquired for them to that letterbox was Helen's task, but from Miss Baverel onward the courier network was the Germans' doing. However, now I have my doubts.'

'Because the recruiter didn't finish her training?'

'That, and because she claims the network is still in use when everyone who knows anything knows that the Germans' agency is in shambles.' I paused, planting my hands on my hips. 'And what was all that about being as safe as houses and her rambling list of effects? In one breath she was claiming she didn't trust us, but in the next she seemed to be indicating the opposite.'

Sidney crossed one arm over his chest and lifted the other to his chin in thought. 'She did seem rather . . . erratic at one point, didn't she? I would have wondered if she was under the influence of some kind of drug had I thought she could have gained access to it. But then a few seconds later she seemed stable.'

'Do you believe she actually has hidden proof of everything she claimed?' I asked, coming to the heart of the matter. 'Do you believe she truly knows all she claims to? Or that whatever she tells us will be legitimate?'

A deep furrow formed in his brow as he turned toward the rain-darkened windows. I crossed the room to close the drapes as he mulled over the matter. 'That is the question I've been asking myself since walking away from her,' he admitted. 'And the answer is still . . .' He lifted his hands as if in defeat. 'I don't know. *Is* she capable of lying and making all or part of this up in order to save her own neck? Yes, if she's desperate enough.'

'And how much more desperate can you get than when you're facing the prospect of the guillotine?'

Sidney nodded. 'But that doesn't necessarily mean that she's lying. She could just as easily be telling us the truth.' He scowled. 'We may never know for certain until she speaks. And she won't speak until we meet her *demands*.' He practically spit the last word.

I understood his rage and disgust. Given what she'd done and the people she'd help hurt, it was justified. But I tried to look at the matter from another angle, to be more objective than the resentment churning in my own gut would have me be.

'While her attitude and lack of obvious remorse leave much to be desired,' I began begrudgingly, moving back toward him, 'I suppose if we imagine ourselves in her position, it's easier to comprehend her terms. She's thinking of her survival, and the only way she can guarantee it is by escaping the country. Being released from the gendarmes isn't enough. I'm sure she's witnessed the viciousness enacted by her fellow citizens when a person is even *suspected* of collaborating with the enemy. The authorities seem more than happy to make such a thing known and then turn a blind eye.'

'Yes, but to America?' he scoffed. 'Or Spain or Switzerland?' he added, seeing that I was about to remind him of that.

'America is far away and large enough to lose herself in, to shed her old identity. And Spain and Switzerland were neutrals.'

'Then why not Holland?' Another neutral.

'I suspect because it's sandwiched between the

belligerent countries, with Germany on one side, and Belgium, France, and Britain on the other. She must know, given her history, the authorities would never agree to such a relocation.' I narrowed my eyes in consideration. 'Though, by that measure, Switzerland would be just as bad.' And yet, she'd still included it as an option. Which meant there must be another reason Holland was unpalatable to her.

Sidney grumbled reluctantly, evidently not having pondered the geography involved. 'I was surprised when she didn't ask to be given amnesty in Britain. That's what I expected her to bargain for.'

'Me too,' I admitted, brushing a piece of lint from the shoulder of his black evening coat, avoiding his gaze. 'But *if* there was truly someone else in charge of Helen's network and others like it, someone still running such operations, and she suspected they lived in Britain . . .' I lifted my eyes to his, trusting he would grasp the significance of what I was saying. 'Then I would want to stay as far away as possible from them as well.'

I felt his quick inhalation beneath my hand. 'Ardmore.'

I nodded. 'Of course, there's no way to know for sure.' My lips twisted bitterly. 'There never is with Ardmore. But this bears all his hallmarks, and he undoubtedly knew Helen Crawford and her father.'

'And what of Miss Baverel's mention of the bombing outside Bailleul?'

'Yes, that caught my attention as well. As I'm certain she knew it would. But how? Who informed her of its significance to me?'

I could tell from the way his pupils widened that he'd not grasped the ramifications. 'Someone has been feeding her information about us.'

'I think we have to assume that's the case. But why? And when?' I frowned, not liking the direction these implications were leading me. 'It's almost as if someone knew she would be arrested, and that she would send for you.'

The situation was well beyond baffling, and steadily becoming more and more troubling. Was this entire matter some sort of ploy? But to what end? And was Miss Baverel part of it or merely an unwilling pawn? Was she following a script laid out for her or trying to best the chess master at his own game?

My earlier hunger had all but vanished, my stomach being too twisted with dread and uncertainty. As if sensing this, or perhaps seeking comfort for himself, Sidney pulled me closer, pressing his lips to my forehead below the gold headband holding back my auburn waves. He spoke against my skin. 'How do you want to proceed?'

I inhaled deeply, filling my lungs with the scent of his cologne and the starch of his collar, forcing my thoughts away from speculations about the unsettling things we didn't yet have answers to and focusing on strategy. 'I think we must make it clear that we need more proof, more assurances that the intelligence she claims to possess is legitimate. That as a show of good faith she needs to share something significant with us.' He lifted his head. 'If we can corroborate whatever she chooses to reveal with an independent source, then we'll agree to present her terms to the French and British authorities.'

'Presuming Captain Marcisieux hasn't already made a bargain with her,' Sidney retorted wryly.

'Yes, I thought of that. But then why ask you here? She could have negotiated directly with the gendarmes all along.'

'True. But perhaps she needed our clout.'

'Maybe.' I didn't even attempt to hide the doubt in my voice, because I didn't believe for even a second that the explanation was as simple as that. 'Regardless, I suppose we'll discover in the morning whether Marcisieux has made such a move and if Miss Baverel has accepted it.' Such a possibility left me feeling vaguely nauseous, for then we might never discover what the intelligence she claimed to hold happened to be, or if it connected to Ardmore.

Sidney's fingers touched my chin, recapturing my attention. 'And if they haven't come to an agreement, we'll proceed as you suggest.' He grimaced. 'Much as I *despise* the idea of being used to help her evade punishment, I recognize we can't in good conscience walk away from her offer. Far more justice may be obtained from her testimony than would be done by her merely being sentenced to death or imprisonment.'

I offered him a commiserating smile, letting him know I also felt the sting of accepting such a truth. Much of intelligence gathering in general was accepting that there were few total victories, few clear choices of right and wrong. Everything was shaded in gray. One had to make judgment calls, constantly wagering possible sacrifices versus gains. Sometimes you got it right, and sometimes you got it wrong. But whatever the outcome, you had to swallow the guilt and disgust such decisions and compromises at times wrought.

There was no need to explain this to Sidney, for war was much the same. I knew he'd had his fill of guilt and disgust as well. Though, with the war being over, he was supposed to be done with all of that. However, Miss Baverel's request had dragged him back into the mire.

'Come,' I urged him. 'Let's have a nice dinner, and do some dancing, and forget all this 'til tomorrow.' An ability, I imagined, we'd both found to be critical during the war – snatching moments of rest and peace wherever we could. I offered him a gentle smile, repeating the beginning of a Bible verse my father had often quoted when my mother or any of his children started fretting or borrowing trouble. 'Sufficient unto the day—'

'Is the evil thereof,' Sidney finished for me, his expression softening. 'You're right. It'll keep.' He tugged me toward the door. 'Come on, then. The concierge recommended their roasted lamb, and I know from experience how delicious their profiteroles with Chantilly cream are.' His eyes glinted with teasing, for he knew how much I enjoyed sweets.

Already tasting the light and buttery pastries melting in my mouth, I looped my arm through Sidney's to hasten him through the door and out into the corridor. He tipped his head back and laughed.

The next morning dawned bright and sunny, with rays of light slanting across our balcony and warming the stone and iron. We'd both dawdled in our toilette, reluctant to return to weightier matters when the sky was such a brilliant Delft Blue and the coffee brought on our breakfast tray so rich and dark. But the world would not wait for us, and the time we'd thought was on our side proved to be false.

I had just finished fastening my earrings when there was a rather insistent knock on the door. Sidney dropped the news-paper he'd been idly perusing on the bed and went to answer it.

'My apologies, monsieur, but the aspirant who delivered this said it must be brought to you immediately,' the porter told him.

Sidney thanked him, passing him a few coins in exchange for the message.

'Rather impatient, isn't he?' I remarked dryly, as I turned to watch him close the door before he unfolded it. Captain Marcisieux was obviously a man who didn't like to be kept waiting. That he'd sent a junior officer to summon us like tardy schoolchildren didn't really surprise me.

But the look that transformed Sidney's face as he read made it clear this wasn't a simple truancy notice.

'What is it?' I asked in alarm, edging closer.

'Fetch your coat and hat,' he declared as he reached for his own, shrugging into the black wool. 'We're leaving now.'

I followed his directive, snatching my aubergine coat and tam hat from the bed with unsteady hands. 'Sidney, what's happened? Why the urgency?'

His expression when he turned to look at me was grim. 'Miss Baverel has hanged herself.'

CHAPTER SEVEN

To say I was shocked would have been putting it mildly. I simply hadn't considered such a possibility. That Miss Baverel should kill herself seemed inexplicable, perplexing . . . Uncharacteristic.

She had not struck me as the type to give way to despair. Her sense of self, her bravado seemed too strong. Not to mention the fact that she was close to brokering a deal for her release. Yes, we had left her without reassurances, but she must have recognized that wasn't the end.

'Are they certain it was suicide?' I murmured as we strode through the hotel doors out onto the sun-drenched pavement of Amiens.

'The letter was brief and to the point,' Sidney replied. 'But I presume Marcisieux will have answers for us.'

A junior officer was waiting for us when we arrived, escorting us down to a lower level of the building, where presumably the prisoners' cells were housed. The captain stood just outside the door, speaking with Lieutenant Charlaix, and the look he fastened on me as we approached

89

was the sort reserved for the lowliest of scum. This was my first clue that something else was going on, and I realized we would have to tread carefully.

'We came as soon as we received your note. What's happened?' Sidney asked, turning to peer into the open cell.

The space was spare and gray, with little to recommend it other than its cleanliness. Miss Baverel's body lay on the tile floor before a small cot which appeared to have been pushed to the middle of the room, directly below a large beam.

'As you can see, Mademoiselle Baverel has hanged herself,' Marcisieux retorted sharply. 'But that is not why I have asked you here.' His dark eyes bored into mine. 'Come and see how.' He gestured for us to precede him into the cell, and while instinct screamed at me not to do so, not to be cornered in a room where they might slam the door, I knew we could hardly decline. His eyes narrowed at my brief hesitation, as if deducing my thoughts.

Coaxing myself to take even breaths, I forced my feet forward, slowly circling Miss Baverel's supine form. Someone had closed her eyes, but her face was very pale. A yellow scarf decorated with splashes of red, green, and black was still draped around her neck, though it had been loosened. By the ragged state of one end of the fabric, I could tell they'd had to cut her down.

I searched her face for congestion and petechiae,

as a physician in the Netherlands had once instructed me would be present had a victim been killed by manual or ligature strangulation rather than a hanging, but I didn't see any. However, her head listed to the side at an odd angle, raising my suspicions, though before I could voice any questions, the captain revealed the source of his fury.

'Recognize the scarf, Madame Kent?'

My gaze snapped to his, startled by the whip crack of his voice, and then returned to the article in question. 'No.' I leaned over to try to scrutinize it more closely, wondering if he was asking about the designer. But I should have known better.

'You should. As *you* gave it to her.'

I straightened in astonishment. 'Why on earth would I do such a thing?'

He gestured toward the corpse in that manner the French have of making their point without words.

'So she could hang herself? You cannot be serious.' I scowled, able to tell that he was. Perfectly. 'What conceivable reason could I have for doing such a thing?' I scoffed.

He clasped his arms behind his back as if he'd been waiting for me to ask this very question. 'I do not know, Madame Kent. Perhaps she had information you did not wish her to share. Information about you.' His bulging eyes shifted to Sidney. 'Or your husband.'

'Now *that* is ridiculous,' I retorted.

'Is it?' he countered. 'You were insistent that you

91

be allowed to speak with her. You even contrived a moment alone with her at the end.'

Sidney stiffened in outrage. 'Now, see here, *I'm* the one who lost my temper. I chose to step out rather than do something I would later regret.'

'I would hardly call it *contrived*,' I muttered dryly, eyeing Lieutenant Charlaix, who had stood silently brooding through this exchange. 'And I wasn't exactly alone.'

'No, but Charlaix could not *see* you. Giving you ample opportunity to pass her the scarf,' Marcisieux charged.

'Except I *didn't*.'

'So, you say, but Mademoiselle Baverel did not have such an article in her possession until *after* your visit. We would have confiscated it otherwise. She could not have hidden it.'

'And yet, if what you say is true, she managed to smuggle it back to her cell yesterday evening without anyone noticing, so how can you be certain she hadn't already been keeping it concealed from you?'

'No!' He shook his head, slicing his hand through the air. 'Impossible. It is a woman's scarf, and you gave it to her.'

I would have growled in frustration if not for the realization that this man could arrest me on such a trumped-up charge, and there was very little I could do to stop him. The chances of him keeping me here were miniscule. The British government would never stand for such a thing.

But in the meantime, while the governments wrangled over the matter, who knew what would happen.

I exhaled in aggravation through my nostrils, turning to study the contents of the room again. My scrutiny fell on the bedding. 'It doesn't make any sense. If Mademoiselle Baverel intended to hang herself, she could have used the sheets at any time. Or possibly her stockings,' I added, gesturing to her legs. Though it was debatable whether they would have been long enough or strong enough.

'You're simply being stubborn,' Sidney challenged. 'You haven't the slightest proof my wife gave Mademoiselle Baverel this scarf because she *didn't*. And as for the reason I insisted she join me for the interview, it was because I wanted my wife's objective opinion. Mademoiselle Baverel is a woman accustomed to using her wiles on men to manipulate them. You cannot pretend this is not true. I decided eliciting a female's opinion of her and her claims could prove invaluable.' What he didn't say, but was made abundantly clear by the tone of his voice, was that Marcisieux should have pondered the same notion.

However, my attention was divided, the awkward angle of her head once again drawing my eye and my suspicions. I knelt beside the body.

'Madame, what are you doing?' the captain protested as I reached out to peer beneath the scarf and then to feel. 'I must ask that you stop that at once.'

'Her neck has been snapped!'

'Yes,' he replied impatiently. 'That happens sometimes. A hangman's fracture. Please step away, Madame.'

I glanced upward at the beam, ignoring him. 'But not from such a short drop. She didn't weigh enough to generate enough force to snap her neck with such a short drop. And look here.' I pointed at the neck. 'The bruising and abrasions from the scarf are horizontal.' The markings were faint, but suggestive. 'If she died from hanging, they should angle across her neck toward the side where the knot was tied.'

The captain's face flushed such a brilliant shade of crimson even Charlaix seemed to take a half step backward, lest he be injured in the impending explosion. 'Monsieur Kent!' he barked, never removing his livid stare from me. 'Please remove your wife from the premises before I lock her up for obstruction. I do not appreciate the likes of some' – he sniffed – 'pampered society woman questioning the Provost Gendarmerie as if we do not know what we are about. Keep her and her presumptions far from my sight, lest I change my mind.'

I glared back at him uncowed, but I knew when it was best to hold my tongue, and this was one of those occasions. However, that did not mean this matter was closed. Not by a long shot.

I turned to proceed my husband through the door, though not before I noted the consideration reflected in Lieutenant Charlaix's pale blue eyes. The same as I noted his confident stance and the fact that he was standing shoulder to shoulder with the captain, rather than slightly behind. This man was definitely not what he seemed, but I had little time to consider what that meant before I swept out the door.

Sidney caught up with me at the staircase, linking his arm with mine and escorting me from the building. He turned our steps north toward the cathedral and the River Somme. The Palais de Justice stood to our left, its Corinthian columns and white stone damaged but standing, while across the street a maison lay in complete ruins. What remained of that once great house appeared poised to crumble at any moment, making the fences blocking access from the boulevard all the more vital.

A playful breeze tumbled crumbling old leaves down the brick streets and ruffled the hair peeking out from beneath the brim of my woolen embroidered tam hat. It brought with it the scent of the river and the promise of spring, born of the buds just beginning to show on the tips of the trees. My steps slowed as we reached the Cathédrale Notre-Dame d'Amiens, its massive heights soaring above us as if to pierce the heavens. I was overwhelmed by its size, and even unwillingly awed, struggling to hold on to my affront and anger in the face of such grandiosity. I had visited Westminster Abbey and the York Minster. I had stood before and within grand cathedrals, but this building seemed to dwarf those in comparison.

Perhaps it was due more to the shock of still finding it standing when everything else of even half its height had been destroyed during the war. I'd heard that the pope had interceded directly with the Germans to save it from their shells during the 1918 bombardment. The stained glass windows had been removed for their preservation and brick protections had been constructed to try to shield the building from damage, but nothing short of the Germans' deliberately directing their guns away from such a tempting target could have saved it.

Even with its colorful window glass still missing and the protections still in the process of being removed, it was an impressive sight, and Sidney guided me toward a bench facing the ornate chevet and its radiating chapels. To our left, across the Place Saint-Michel, we could see the bare branches of chestnut and linden trees waving in the breeze above the wall in which a portal had been built – complete with columns topped with Tuscan capitals and two stone lions – through which you could reach the park.

'Well, that was unexpected.'

I looked up, uncertain if he'd made this rather eloquent understatement in jest, but he appeared in earnest. 'That's putting it mildly,' I remarked drolly.

'Just to be clear, you don't own such a scarf. So, it couldn't have fallen out of or been stolen from your bag?' The look I turned toward him must have spoken for itself. 'I'm not accusing you of anything. I simply want to understand all the factors at play. If that scarf was taken from you, then the problem is somewhat thornier.'

'It wasn't mine,' I replied, as calmly as I was able. 'Though I understand what you're saying. If the scarf had happened to be in my luggage it would mean someone had gone through our things.'

'So where did it come from?' he posited, propping his ankle over his opposite knee as he leaned deeper into the bench. 'Did she have it with her all along, or did someone else bring it to her?'

'I'm more concerned with the fact that her neck was snapped *before* she was hoisted up to look like she'd hanged herself.'

Sidney turned to look at me. 'You're certain?'

'Yes,' I stated unflinchingly. The evidence was too clear. Evidence Marcisieux should have seen as well. That is, if he hadn't been so determined to paint me the villain.

His expression was grim. 'Then Capitaine Marcisieux seems to have been on the right track about one thing. *Someone* wanted to silence her. Just not us.'

I crossed my arms over my chest. 'And after he

97

practically tossed us from the building, it's going to be difficult to find out whether Miss Baverel had any visitors last night, let alone learn anything else pertinent to the matter.'

'It couldn't have been a visitor.'

The taut tone of Sidney's voice made me look up.

'They would never have been allowed inside her cell, and certainly not left alone with her.'

He was right. They could never have killed her, strung her up, and escaped undetected. 'Then . . .'

He nodded, answering my unspoken question. 'It had to be a gendarme, or another official who has access to the prisoners.'

It was much worse than I'd realized.

'Who?' I posited. 'Marcisieux?'

Sidney's eyes narrowed in consideration. 'I don't think so.'

'Then, perhaps, Lieutenant Charlaix?' I frowned. 'From the first, I've sensed that he's more than he seems.'

'I suspect his rank is at least equal to Marcisieux's, if not greater.'

'You noticed that as well?'

He nodded slowly. 'It's in the way he holds himself. He managed to mind his tongue and follow directions, but his mannerism wasn't convincing.'

I joined Sidney in his study of the statue of Peter the Hermit at the center of Place Saint-Michel; one arm clutched a rosary to its chest while the other lifted a small cross. He seemed oddly captivated by it, though I couldn't understand why. It wasn't particularly beautiful or inspiring. But when he next spoke, it wasn't clear if he'd been seeing the figure at all.

'Whoever Charlaix is, it seems clear that Marcisieux is aware of the truth. Which makes me less inclined to believe he's our culprit.' He inhaled audibly, tipping his head back to look up at the spires of the cathedral. 'There must be dozens of officers in and out of that building every day. It could be any one of them.'

'Or someone masquerading as a gendarme.'

He tipped his head toward me, conceding my point. 'Though I haven't the foggiest idea how we can discover such a thing now that Marcisieux has booted us from the building. I wouldn't be surprised if he doesn't drive us from Amiens as well if we don't leave quickly enough for his liking.'

I shifted to face him more directly. 'All right, then, what of the claims Miss Baverel made, the intelligence she promised to reveal?' I arched my eyebrows. 'Do we believe her now?'

He reached up to rub a hand over the back of his neck. 'I must admit, I am more inclined to do so. Unfair as that might be.'

'She made a living trading in secrets and spying for the enemy, by her own admission,' I reminded him, pressing a hand to his arm. 'It's no one's fault but her own that we should question her integrity.' I squeezed his arm, making sure he took these words to heart. I was not going to allow him to have one more death on his conscience. 'But I agree. And if someone was willing to take the risk of killing her in the bowels of the gendarmerie, then they must have feared what she might reveal.'

He scowled. 'And now that they've killed her, we may never know what that was.'

I bit the corner of my lip, thinking back over our conversation with the woman. 'Maybe. Or maybe not.'

He looked to me with interest.

'Do you remember when she was rambling on about paintings and sofa cushions, and the proof she'd hidden being safe as houses?'

'Yes. She said no one would ever be able to find it ex-cept her.'

'No, she said it was safe until she chose to retrieve it. Or . . .' I leaned closer. '. . . she sent others to do so.'

He frowned. 'That was merely the opening gambit to her brokering a deal. Of course, once the agreement was struck, she'd tell us where to retrieve it.'

'Hmm . . . but I wonder if perhaps that's merely how she wanted it to *sound*.'

I could practically see the thoughts flickering through his deep blue eyes as he reviewed the interview in his mind.

'Recall, she was perfectly aware that Charlaix was listening in. She indicated it. *Just* as she indicated with that flashing smile she hid behind the fall of her hair that she was lying when she said she wasn't certain she could trust us.'

He turned sideways to face me more fully, draping his arm across the back of the bench as his features grew more animated. 'Then you think she was trying to communicate some of those secrets to us all along?'

'Or at least the location of this hidden proof so we could learn it ourselves.'

He straightened, gazing up at the cathedral while he struggled to maintain his composure. 'But then . . . where does that leave us? For I didn't grasp any of her clues.'

I smirked. 'Oh, I think you did. More than you realize.'

He opened his mouth to argue, so I continued before he could speak. '*Remember that place we met?*'

His eyes flashed with recognition. 'Then she wasn't trying to imply we'd been lovers?'

My smile widened. 'Oh, I'm certain she was.' I eyed him narrowly. 'Should I have pressed her on that?'

His brow lowered briefly in affront, but I must not have sufficiently concealed my amusement, for one corner of his lips quirked upward and he shook his head in acknowledgment of my teasing.

I chucked him playfully beneath the chin like my older brother, Freddy, often did to me. 'But that's not the sole point she was trying to make.'

The hand resting on the back of the bench lifted toward my shoulder and his fingers began to toy with the auburn curls arranged near my jaw. 'Then you think she deliberately meant to send us to the place I met her?'

My thoughts sobered as I recalled Miss Baverel's nerves, and the erratic behavior she'd displayed. 'I think that she was aware of the danger she was in. Much more aware than we were. And that she was trying to communicate something to us . . . as a last resort.' My gaze dipped to the tweed of his waistcoat, picturing in my mind her too bright smile and her agitated plucking at her cuticles. *'But I will say no more. I have already said too much.'*

Sidney's chest rose and fell as he took a deep breath, drawing my eyes back to his face. 'Then I suppose we're headed to Arras.' A furrow formed between his brows. 'And we'll need a motorcar.'

The journey to Amiens from London was made swiftest by train and ferry, so we'd never considered taking Sidney's beloved Pierce-Arrow. Not when we'd anticipated we would be returning to London in but a day or two. However, now I could see that he wished we had.

'I've a friend who lives nearby. He owes me a favor.' He lowered his arm, pushing to his feet, and then turned to offer me his hand. 'I'll give him a ring when we return to the hotel.'

I allowed him to pull me up, linking my arm with his. 'But before we set off toward the north, let's begin by taking a look at Miss Baverel's lodgings here. I know she claimed the gendarmes would find nothing there, but let's take a look regardless. We might find something that will help us uncover who her current contacts are.'

Sidney bustled me across the street. 'Do you know where it is?'

'I might have seen her name and address scrawled across a file on top of Capitaine Marcisieux's desk.'

He turned his head to look at me. '*Did* you, now?'

I shrugged.

'All right, then. But let's be quick about it.' He glanced down a narrow cross street as we hurried by. 'The gendarmes are bound to be watching the place, and we don't want to give them any greater reason to detain us than they think they already have.'

CHAPTER EIGHT

In the end, we needn't have bothered. Whether by the gendarmes or someone else, Miss Baverel's flat had already been searched, and not gently. Everything in the two rooms had been upended. Clothes, papers, and other assorted items littered the surfaces, while drawers had been left haphazardly open. Even the mattress had been split down the middle, allowing feathers to spill out.

My heart sank at the sight of the mess, but I waded into the detritus anyway, carefully picking my way around a chipped mug, a handkerchief, and a hairbrush. I paused in the beam of sunlight that slanted through the curtains, casting a ray across the worn wooden boards. Bending over, I lifted aside a silk blouse to find a hand mirror lying next to a tarnished silver box tipped on its side, spilling its contents – a pair of glass earrings and a faux pearl necklace. I swiveled to the left and then the right, gazing around me at the peeling wallpaper and the water stain on the ceiling above, before letting the blouse fall from my fingertips.

'There's nothing here,' I declared. 'Nothing that

can help us, in any case.' The gendarmes had undoubtedly already taken anything that might appear suspicious or contain pertinent information. I might not be a fan of Captain Marcisieux or his shortsightedness when it came to Miss Baverel's murder, but in his duties with the Provost Gendarmerie he unquestionably knew what he was doing. He would not want his superiors or the counterintelligence officers at *Section de Centralisation du Renseignement*, or SCR, to have reason to criticize his evidence collection. Especially not when he had to explain how the prisoner and potential informant had died while in his custody.

Sidney tossed the watercolor whose frame he'd been examining back down on the sideboard where he'd found it. 'Agreed.' His gaze swept over the scattered debris. 'If there *is* anything of value to us, it wouldn't be worth the time or the risk to search for it.'

As if in response to this comment, a floorboard in the corridor outside creaked. Our eyes flew to the open door before meeting in silent communication. Someone was standing just outside, listening, and while it might just be a nosy neighbor, neither of us wanted to take that chance. Sidney gestured for me to keep talking as he stealthily began to pick his way across the floor, bending over to retrieve the broken leg of a table as he moved and hefting it in his hand like a cricket bat.

105

'Then I guess there's nothing more we can do. We'll simply have to return to London.' I tried to make it look like I was staring at the corner behind the door while all the while I was scrutinizing the shadows on the landing beyond. I sighed audibly. 'I suppose this was a wasted trip.'

'Oh, I wouldn't say that,' a suave voice answered me in English from the doorway a moment before Lieutenant Charlaix appeared. His pale eyes scrutinized me before shifting to Sidney. 'You will have no need of that, Monsieur Kent. I merely wish to talk.'

'You followed us,' Sidney charged, still holding tight to the makeshift cudgel.

'Now why would I need to do that when I could deduce that at some point you would come here?'

His posture was relaxed and unthreatening, his hands tucked into his trouser pockets. However, I sensed the watchfulness, the seemingly effortless vigilance that had marked some of my colleagues with the Secret Service. Charlaix wanted to appear like nothing more than a confident officer of the gendarmerie. He even sported their uniform of dark and light blue, much of his light brown hair concealed by his kepi hat. But I was more certain than ever that he was not.

I narrowed my eyes before asking in French, 'Who are you, really?'

'In English, please,' he responded, a faint nasality to his accent. He peered over his shoulder. 'These walls are thin, and I do not wish to alarm the

106

neighbors.' He looked at Sidney again when neither of us rushed to fill the silence, seeming to weigh his words before responding to my query. 'My name *is* Gabriel Charlaix, but I'm not a lieutenant in the Gerdarmerie.' He paused as if for dramatic effect. 'I am an agent with the SCR.'

As soon as the words left his mouth, I felt that I should have already suspected as much, and given a bit more time, I was sure I would have eventually drawn that conclusion. As such, his revelation did not have the impact that perhaps he'd hoped for.

Sidney lowered the table leg to his side. 'Then you would have taken custody of Mademoiselle Baverel when she was transported to Paris,' he deduced, apparently also aware of SCR's role as France's counterintelligence unit.

'Yes. When Capitaine Marcisieux informed us of Mademoiselle Baverel's insistence that she would speak only to you, I was dispatched to observe.'

Sidney gestured to his uniform. 'So, why the subterfuge? Why not simply inform us who you were?'

'That would seemingly be easier, no?' he replied with a sheepish shrug. 'But I was merely following orders.'

'Orders to learn as much as he could about *us*, as well,' I interjected, not fooled by his charade for even a moment.

But rather than the shame he should have felt for trying to gas us, his eyes glinted at me with begrudging approval. 'You are a fortunate man, Monsieur Kent. Had I a wife as clever as yours, I would recruit her as well.'

Sidney frowned at the man's mistaken assumption but was quick enough to grasp it would be better to let it stand rather than reveal the fact that he had matters backward. *I* was the agent and my husband my recruit, of sorts. However, Charlaix did not need to know this. Not when we couldn't be sure of his motives, or if he could even be trusted. Let him think what he wished.

'Why are you here now? In Mademoiselle Baverel's quarters,' Sidney clarified, turning the subject away from me. He spread his hands, motioning to the mess. 'Clearly it's already been searched.'

'Not by me. That was the gendarmes' doing.' His lips tightened as he surveyed the damage. 'Evidently they lack a certain finesse. But to answer your question, I'm here because I believe you are right.' He turned to me. 'Mademoiselle Baverel did not kill herself. Someone else helped her to it.'

I arched my eyebrows. 'Someone?'

A dimple formed in his right cheek as his lips quirked into the semblance of a smile. '*Oui.* Likely someone among the gendarmerie.'

'Now why would they do such a thing?' Sidney remarked with scornful flippancy as I picked my way around the piles of debris toward the men.

'Because she knew something they did not want

her to reveal. Perhaps something that would implicate them.' He tipped his head. 'Or they were bribed to do so by someone who would be implicated.' His gaze sharpened. 'Both scenarios I'm certain you've already deduced.'

I paused some feet from him, crossing my arms over my chest. 'Then why didn't you say something when Marcisieux was busy accusing me of aiding the woman's suicide?'

'The capitaine lacks imagination. And . . . I suspect . . . someone has placed this particular bee in his bonnet.' He shook his head. 'He will not let go of it easily. Rumor is his wife left him some months ago for another man, so . . .' He shrugged.

'So, he thinks all women are faithless and untrustworthy,' I finished for him. I scoffed, turning away. And men accused women of flawed judgment and bias.

'Particularly if he has what he thinks to be evidence of their guilt.'

The dashed scarf. An item he would never be able to prove anyone had ever seen in my possession, but a jury of men would undoubtedly leap to the same conclusion Marcisieux had implicated.

'Then he will not investigate further?' I asked over my shoulder.

'It is doubtful.'

'Will you?' Sidney demanded to know.

'I will try. But I'm not sure that my superiors

109

will be any easier to convince than Capitaine Marcisieux. After all, what is an easier scenario to swallow? That a British woman gave the prisoner a scarf, which she then used to kill herself? Or that someone within the gendarmerie killed her to keep their secrets safe?'

Sidney tossed the table leg off to the side. 'What of the evidence?'

Charlaix dipped his head in acknowledgment. 'That is the sticking point. But not all men place as much confidence in the evidence as they should.'

'I should think the possibility that a member of the Provost Gendarmerie had secrets an enemy collaborator might reveal would be far more concerning than if a British woman passed that woman a scarf to enable her suicide. But I am not a man, so what do I know?' I pronounced scathingly. 'But you still haven't told us why you're here. Not really.' I sidled another step closer, perhaps recklessly endangering the fiction he believed about my and Sidney's roles, but there was something about this man that had started to rub me like a blister. He was placating us and making a great show of pretending to be on our side without actually telling us anything we didn't already know. 'You're not here to ask for our help or to promise justice, so why have you come?'

This close, I could see that his eyes were as much gray as blue – the coloring of his uniform bringing out the latter – and that his conciliatory manner was as much a façade as his clothing.

'I'm here to tell you that someone tried to visit Mademoiselle Baverel three days before your arrival,' he answered more sternly. 'And interestingly enough, he was British.'

Sidney and I shared a look of mutual apprehension.

'After her death, I thought it pertinent to look more closely into the matter. The desk officer recognized his accent, and even extracted his name, though I cannot be certain it was his real one.'

The hairs on the back of my neck stood up at this proclamation, for I felt certain I knew what he was about to say.

'He claimed to be a Lieutenant James Smith, lately of the Royal Fusiliers, but as I understand it, Smith is a very common name in England.'

I looked at Sidney again, curious what he had made of this new information, but his face gave nothing away.

'Yes, it is,' he told Charlaix. 'As is James.'

'Then the name may not be helpful to you, but it was something I thought you should know, regardless. Particularly as you set off to look for this proof Mademoiselle Baverel claimed she'd hidden.'

My eyes darted back to the Frenchman, having been caught off guard.

His lips curled into a tight smile, having enjoyed surprising us. 'That is why you're here, isn't it? And where you are going?' He did not seem to

111

expect a response, instead backing toward the door. 'I do hope you intend to share whatever it is with us, if you find it.' He turned then to go, lifting his hand in farewell. 'Happy hunting.'

I stared at the door through which he'd disappeared, momentarily robbed of speech.

'I do believe he intends for us to do the work for him,' Sidney muttered, recovering more quickly.

'In all fairness, it's not a bad plan,' I murmured. 'After all, he must realize that we know more than he does.' I frowned. 'Though it would have been helpful to get a look at whatever information the French have on Adele Baverel in their files.'

We stood silently contemplating the matter, perhaps both wondering if my assumption was true. Did we know more than the SCR or were they toying with us?

'So, Lieutenant Smith attempted to visit Miss Baverel,' Sidney remarked, making his way over to my side. His voice dripped with cynicism. 'That can't be a coincidence.'

'No. Not when she claimed to know something about the explosion.'

His gaze wavered over my features. 'I wonder where Lieutenant Smith is now, and if he gave up on visiting Miss Baverel so easily.'

I recognized the implication he was making, and it made me uneasy. Had Smith found a way into her cell, either on his own or with help from someone in the gendarmerie? Had he killed her? And if so, why? And at whose instigation? His own or someone else's? Someone like Lord Ardmore. What *had* Miss Baverel known about the bombing?

Taking a bracing breath, I focused my thoughts on what could be done rather than the disquiet clamoring at the back of my mind. A disquiet that could only be soothed by facts. And facts could only be attained by action.

'We need more information,' I told Sidney as I strode toward the door. 'First of all, we need to know if Charlaix is a legitimate agent of the SCR, or else all of his claims are, at best, rubbish, and at worst, he's deliberately misleading us.' I lowered my voice as we reached the landing and began descending the scuffed and worn stairs. The space reeked of cooked cabbage, as if it had permeated the very wood, and I tried not to breathe through my nose. 'And we need to find out if we can trace Lieutenant Smith's movements. Which train and ferry he took and when.' This was all information that I trusted Kathleen Silvernickel, C's secretary, could unearth for us, so long as C agreed to it. I paused at the base of the stairs to look up at Sidney. 'I find it interesting that he didn't attempt to disguise his name. Did he not know we would be called in, or did he not care?'

'Or did he *want* us to recognize him?' he proposed with an ironic lift to his eyebrows.

'Yes, that, too.'

He opened the outer door and we exited onto the street, turning our steps down the narrow pavement toward the nearest tramline that would take us back to the center of the city at Place Gambetta. The structures here were crowded close together and, like the rest of the city, the destruction from the shells random. At one building, which appeared to have been shorn cleanly in two, I was both horrified and amused to see two children's heads peering down at us from the edge of a room whose outer and left wall had been neatly cut away, leaving half a room, complete with moldering chairs and even pictures hanging on the wall. They grinned and waved, blithely ignorant of the precariousness of their situation. When the door to the room suddenly burst open behind them, I was relieved to watch them scramble backward in the face of their mother's wrath.

'Don't pretend you wouldn't have done the very same thing in their situation,' Sidney teased, and I was forced to admit he was right. I had been a mischievous child. But I wasn't going to let it pass entirely without comment.

'At Freddy's or even *your* instigation.'

'You can't blame me. I wasn't such a troublesome influence on you until the ripe age of seventeen and a half.'

'What about the summer you visited when I was eleven?'

'Any trouble we got you in that year would have been Freddy's doing. Or your own.' His eyes twinkled, clearly recalling how I'd dangled after him – hopelessly besotted.

'What about that time I took a dunking in the

river? I distinctly remember you telling Freddy that any girl who could cross on those stepping-stones was a real goer.' His shoulders shook in silent laughter, so I poked him in the shoulder. 'And you were looking directly at me when you said it.'

He held up his hand. 'I maintain my innocence.'

I rolled my eyes and turned away; my cheeks flushed with color not only in aggravation but also residual embarrassment over the way I had thoroughly made a cake of myself in front of Sidney that summer.

His arm slid around my waist, pulling me closer. 'That was the first and the last time I egged you on, even when Freddy begged me to. The pained look on your face when you stood up in the middle of the river went straight to my heart.'

I peered sideways at him, seeing the earnestness reflected in his eyes.

'I couldn't bear to see it again.' He smiled tightly. 'At sixteen, I might have thought of your eleven-year-old self as just Freddy's kid sister, but I didn't want to see you hurt.'

I reached across my body to press my hand to his heart, believing him. If Sidney was anything, he was kind, to his core. Even at the darkest moment of our marriage, when I'd discovered he was alive and that he'd allowed me to believe him dead for fifteen months while he single-mindedly pursued the traitors Miss Baverel had acted as courier for, I'd still known that he hadn't set out

115

to deliberately hurt me, though he had. Deeply. If for even a moment I'd truly believed it had been intentional, I didn't think we would be here now.

The familiar clang of the tram's bell pierced the afternoon air, and we hastened to catch it. Locating an open space near the back, Sidney sank down on the wooden bench beside me as we looked out the window at the city passing by. The space was close and warm in the spring sun, and I was grateful for the cologne wafting from Sidney's skin, keeping my nose turned toward it so that it could drown out the stench of must and metal, and the unwashed body of at least one of our fellow passengers.

'I've had a thought.' He lowered his head to murmur as we rolled past a café advertising ices. 'I wonder if Walter knows anything useful about Miss Baverel. She *did* pose as his mistress, acting as the courier to whom he delivered Helen's missives. Maybe they were more intimate than either of them has admitted.'

I could tell from the tautness of his features that it had not been easy for him to suggest such a thing. After all, Walter had been the one to shoot him and leave him for dead during the Germans' assault when he feared Sidney had gotten too close to the truth.

'Maybe,' I replied evenly. 'It might be worth asking.' I couldn't help wondering if Helen or Felix Halbert also might have known something, but if so, they'd already taken it to their graves, having

116

been executed for their treasonous activities and the murders they'd committed last June. Walter had only been granted a reprieve because of his turning King's evidence.

'I wonder . . . I wonder if Ryde might be prevailed upon to visit him.'

I looked up into his eyes, knowing that had been almost as difficult a suggestion as the other. 'I'm sure he would.' The question, for me, was whether he *should*.

Max had already stuck his neck out for us and our inquiries a number of times, and all while knowing Ardmore had killed his father. The last thing I wanted to do was paint an even larger target on Max's back. And yet, he was our best option, our greatest ally, and I knew he would not take kindly to being coddled or excluded. As a woman, I knew the feeling all too well. So, despite my fear, I realized I had too much respect for him to deny him his chance to be involved, particularly now that we suspected Ardmore lurked somewhere in the background of these shadowy events.

'Then I'll ask him,' Sidney declared, though there was still a question in his eyes.

I dipped my head once in agreement. 'But tell him to take Crispin or George with him,' I cautioned. 'He should have someone to watch his back.'

'Crispin,' he stated, glancing toward the front of the tram. 'Bentnick may be brilliant with numbers and cracking codes, but I doubt he's good with his fists.'

'Heavens! I hope it doesn't come to that.' But he was right. George was not a fighter.

'No, but that is why we're sending them. And while Crispin's hearing may be damaged from his time as an artillery officer, his eyes are still good and his fists quick.' He cast me a chiding look. 'After all, you *did* put those to good use just the other night.'

'I was putting his *acting* skills to good use,' I retorted. After all, they weren't supposed to actually pummel each other when we'd needed a distraction at Grafton Galleries, just make it look as if they were.

Sidney snorted. 'Crispin wouldn't know the difference.'

I turned to him in surprise.

'My point is . . . Crispin's the man for this job. Not Bentnick. It would be a mistake to imagine otherwise.'

'No, you're right. I just . . .' I inhaled, cutting off my words and my worries, and then nodded decisively. 'They should be prepared for all eventualities.'

Sidney's eyes softened with understanding, recognizing my unspoken fears. 'They'll be fine, darling.'

'Of course they will,' I answered with false aplomb.

Or else I wasn't sure I would ever forgive myself.

CHAPTER NINE

If one had thought the haphazard damage to Amiens was bad, the destruction in Arras was far worse. Positioned just half a dozen miles from the front line for much of the war, within reach of the Germans' big guns, nearly eighty percent of the city had been razed to the ground, including its famous belfry, cathedral, and city hall. Even many of the buildings still standing were naught but burnt-out shells and far too precarious to inhabit. Perched on a plateau as it was, Arras had borne the brunt of numerous battles as the Germans tried again and again to take it, but it had never fallen.

As the verdant fields through which we'd been driving slowly began to give way to churned earth and beheaded trees, Sidney explained that part of the reason for this was the medieval tunnels beneath the city that had been expanded and linked by the Kiwis – the troops' affectionate term for soldiers from New Zealand. This enabled the combined British forces to shelter from bombardments, as well as move fresh troops, supplies, and the wounded up and down the front – even as far as the front line – in relative safety.

As we drew near the former front, I studied him out of the corner of my eyes for signs of strain. Some moments before he'd lit a cigarette, often a sign of his mounting anxiety, but his hands remained loose on the driving wheel of the Vauxhall D-Type he'd managed to borrow from his friend. It was undoubtedly a former staff motorcar, used to transport the red-cap officers from one of the divisions of the British Army. I wondered, but didn't ask, how exactly this friend had acquired it. Based on style and speed, it certainly wasn't up to Sidney's standards, but it was sturdy, comfortable, and proven reliable.

The dirt road before us was cleared, though lined periodically with piles of rubble waiting to be scavenged or carted away. Here and there, structures dotted the landscape, those that had been spared a direct hit from a shell. As we entered the village of Achicourt on the outskirts of Arras, the number of buildings still standing increased, as well as the devastation. Nothing taller than two stories had been spared.

'A windmill used to stand there,' Sidney told me, pointing toward a rise in the distance. 'Beyond the railway tracks. We would pass it on our way up the communication trenches. At least, until the summer of '17, when the Jerries finished it off.'

The motorcar slowed as we entered the village

proper – or rather what was left of it. Here along the narrow River Crinchon sat a number of streets lined with buildings that had been spared much of the damage. But when we approached the village square, I audibly gasped.

Sidney glanced over at me. 'It's quite a sight, isn't it?'

'What happened?' I asked, staring around me in shock. Even amidst a landscape that had suffered so much devastation, the degree of destruction suffered by this one small village square categorized an entire new level of catastrophic. The buildings closest to the center had been reduced to nothing but scattered bits of tiny rubble, while beyond them the next edifices had been decimated down to the lowest portion of their walls. The circle of structures beyond those – the ones that were still standing – appeared to be but hollow shells of pockmarked stone, broken glass, and collapsed roofs. And over everything lay a level of searing and scorching that could only indicate there had been some sort of intense fire.

'There were a large number of artillery batteries stationed in the surrounding area, and one night when a convoy of lorries was moving artillery through the village, the Germans decided Achicourt would make an excellent target.'

My stomach clenched at what I knew was coming.

His voice sharpened and his fingers flexed around the driving wheel. 'What's worse, there was some sort of obstruction in the road, causing a traffic jam. Something the military police were *supposed* to prevent by sending the trucks in different directions if the obstruction couldn't be removed. But for whatever the reason, the muddle happened, and at the worst possible time. At least one of the lorries took a direct hit from a German shell, and soon all twenty transports were burning. One rifleman told me the resulting explosion was the loudest he'd heard in the entire war, followed by yet an even louder blast.' He shook his head. 'Apparently, there were also ammo dumps in several of the adjoining buildings.' His expression was bleak. 'As well as men billeted.'

'Good God!'

He nodded, realizing there was no need to explain further. 'The explosions went on for another twelve to eighteen hours.'

I pressed my hand to my face as we turned, leaving behind the site of so much death and ruin. But something about the incident needled at my brain. After several moments of silence, I ventured a question, prodding at it. 'When was this? The explosions?'

He tilted his head in thought. 'Must have been the spring of '17. Likely April. Why?'

I frowned. 'Was it normal for so much ammunition to be stored all in one place? In the middle of a town?'

'There wasn't any other place *to* store it. And had the lorries not caught fire, strung out through the village, it's doubtful it would have spread as it did.'

I bit my lip, uncertain whether I should voice my uneasy suspicions.

However, Sidney knew better than to believe my questions were mere idle curiosity. 'What? Are you suggesting it was planned? That it was sabotage?'

Hearing his skepticism, I turned to face him. 'Well, think about it. The traffic jam just *happened* to occur when the ammunition convoy was passing through the heart of the village on a night when the Germans just *happened* to decide to shell it. What was the obstruction that caused this muddle in the first place? And why didn't the military police remove the obstruction or do a better job of directing the traffic?' I cast him a cynical look. 'It seems awfully coincidental that all of these things broke down at the same time.'

'Yes, but war is chaos. I could describe a dozen similar circumstances, when the factors leading to the catastrophe simply don't seem to add up, and yet the vast majority of them were caused by the natural fallacy of men and nature, not deliberate human error.'

I had to grant him that. If there was anything I'd learned from the four-years-long conflict it was that war was unpredictable. The normal rules of calculation, estimation, and prediction too often did not apply.

'*Although,*' he amended, 'I do admit that in this instance it does seem a shade more suspect.

Especially knowing that Miss Baverel's friend resided here at the time, if not Miss Baverel herself.' The 'friend' whose movements had led him to her location at the end of the war. 'But unless Miss Baverel has left some sort of evidence or a confession regarding the incident, I don't think there will ever be a way to know for sure.'

Sidney stopped the Vauxhall along the side of the street near a junction with a narrower lane, one down which the motorcar was unlikely to fit. 'This is it. She lived in a cramped room on the left, about midway down the mews before it intersects with the broader avenue on the other side.'

'Not exactly an auspicious address, but then again, one takes what quarters one can get when nearly half the town is uninhabitable.'

'And many of the buildings that are were serving as billets for the British army.'

'That, too.' I took a bracing breath before reaching for the door handle. 'Shall we?'

The morning sun was warm and bright, but here in the narrow lane it could not penetrate between the crowded buildings, which cast a shroud over the entire scene. Here and there, I spied crumbled masonry, but by and large these buildings seemed to have escaped the shells and bullets. The musty odor of mold and things that had too long lay damp assailed our nostrils as the spring temperatures thawed the earth and the other living things clinging to or nestled in the buildings. It was not the most pleasant of places to call home.

I stepped with care around the muddiest bits of broken brick as we slowly made our way to the door of Miss Baverel's former residence. 'Someone else must be living there now. I wonder if they'll let us look around.'

Sidney did not respond, his concentration seeming solely fixed on the dark door to the left. It looked as if it had once been painted a cheery red or purple which had since faded to a dreary brown. Otherwise, the façade surrounding it was unremarkable, blending in with the other abodes. The windows were streaked with grime, old cobwebs clinging to the corners, and I guessed they hadn't been washed since the beginning of the war.

My husband lifted his hand to knock, and to our surprise, the door swung inward with a creak. He glanced at me in question, before reaching out to push the door a little wider. '*Bonjour! Est-ce que quelqu'un est à la maison? Vous allez bien?*' When no one answered, he inched his way inside.

The interior was dark and, from what I could see of its contents, dusty. An old chair had been overturned near the window, and a box sat on the shelf of an open wooden cupboard – its wood thick and gnarled – but otherwise the space appeared empty. Sidney reached into the pocket of his coat to extract his lighter, holding the flame out in front of him, but it didn't reveal anything further hidden in the deeper shadows.

I slowly crossed to the chair, intending to right

it until I realized one of the legs was broken. Behind me, Sidney opened and closed the two lower cupboard doors before advancing to the far corners and then turned back to face me.

'This is where you met Miss Baverel?'

'Yes.' He lowered his arm, allowing the flame to flicker out. 'It was soon after the Armistice. The soldiers were leaving, and people were beginning to return to what was left of their ruined homes and villages. I suspect Miss Baverel moved on herself soon after to somewhere larger. Somewhere she could lose herself in the crowd. Somewhere like Amiens.'

I agreed, for if I'd been in her shoes, I would have done the same. 'Then why did she send us here?' I spun in a circle to look around me. 'What were we supposed to find?'

'I don't know.' His gaze drifted to the black smudge near the ceiling. 'I suppose we could start knocking on the walls and the floorboards, but I doubt we'll find anything.'

I shook my head, concurring with the futility of such an act. If Miss Baverel had left anything here, it was long gone. 'Maybe we were wrong. Maybe she didn't mean to send us here,' I remarked, turning away. Except I felt certain she had been trying to communicate *something* to us when we met with her, something more than what she'd seemed to be saying on the surface.

The floor groaned as Sidney moved to stand at my back, resting his hands on my shoulders.

'Maybe, but it was worth a try. After all, whatever proof she had must be hidden somewhere.' He paused. 'Unless she lied about that and there is no proof.' He sighed heavily, his gust of breath rustling the hair curling against one side of my neck. 'If there's one thing I can say about Miss Baverel, nothing is ever as one expects.'

My lips quirked wryly as my eyes, which had been staring unseeing at the grimy window, finally focused on what was beyond it. I straightened, moving a step closer to read the words painted on the brick. 'Did she ever mention Furnes?'

He followed me, stooping slightly to see the advertisement for a bakery located in the Flemish city of Furnes through the streaked glass. Could this be what she'd wanted us to see?

'Maybe. I'm not sure.' His words were slow and considered as if he was sifting back through the memories of their conversation. 'Actually, yes.'

I swiveled to look over my shoulder at him.

'Yes, I think she did. Somehow she knew I'd been at Passchendaele.'

I couldn't withhold my startled reaction, though the shutters that suddenly dropped behind Sidney's eyes made me wish I had.

There were a few battles and place names from the war which required no explanation, for the names themselves had become imbued with the extreme horror, and death, and devastation that had happened there. Passchendaele was one of them. And yet I'd never known Sidney had been there. He'd not breathed a word of it and somehow I'd missed it in the newspaper reports and rolls of honor which would undoubtedly have listed his battalion's mass number of casualties.

'Good heavens, Sidney!' I gasped. 'You were on the Somme *and* at Passchendaele?'

'Yes, well, at least I wasn't at Verdun.'

The jest fell flat, my alarm at the savagery he'd lived through too great. 'How did I not know this?'

'I'd been temporarily transferred to another battalion.' He shrugged one shoulder. 'It happened from time to time to patch holes in the command. By this point in the war there were green lads with barely six months of service under their belt commanding entire companies. One went where one was told.'

'Yes, but—'

'And Miss Baverel somehow knew, or inferred, that I'd been there,' he hastened to add, cutting off any further questions from me. 'Which led her to mention Furnes, where apparently she'd been living at the time.'

I had so much more I wanted to ask, so much more I wanted to say, but it was clear Sidney did not wish to discuss it. His jaw was set, and his eyes had taken on a mulish gleam. Given our surroundings and our need for direction, I decided to allow the matter to drop. At least, temporarily. But I was not going to ignore it forever, no matter how stubborn he became.

128

'Then maybe that's why she sent us here,' I suggested. 'To ultimately send us to Furnes.'

'It's as good a guess as we have.'

I narrowed my eyes at the sign. 'And Furnes is in Belgium. In the small area beyond the Yser that never fell under the Germans' occupation.'

Sidney straightened. '*As safe as one could be in Belgium during the war*,' he replied, quoting something else Miss Baverel had said during our interview that I hadn't understood at the time.

'Exactly.'

'Then I guess we're headed north. If we hurry, we might make it to Furnes by nightfall.'

He crossed the floor toward the door, holding it wide for me to exit before closing it after us and making certain it firmly latched. The lane was no brighter than when we'd first traversed it, but it seemed so compared to the deep shadows of the abandoned room. Even so, I struggled to step with care around the ruts and puddles, at one point rolling my ankle and stumbling into Sidney.

It was at that moment that we heard a loud crack, which seemed to echo off the buildings around us, and then a ping of something striking the dirt not far from where we stood.

I stiffened. 'Was that . . .?'

'A gunshot,' Sidney finished for me. 'Move!'

CHAPTER TEN

We dashed down the lane, heedless of the muck, our only aim being speed. There were no angles or doorways, no places to shelter. Even if there was, we couldn't be certain which direction the shot had come from, not with the rapport off the stone buildings hindering our ability to trace the origin of the gunfire. I flinched at the crack of the second shot, though my fear was more for Sidney than myself, as his arm remained wrapped around me, his body shielding me from behind.

We ducked behind the bulk of the Vauxhall just as a third shot struck the dark green frame. Sidney helped to boost me into the rear seat, ordering me to keep my head down. I heard him scramble about and the engine start as I untangled myself from my skirts, praying he was following the same orders he'd given me. Then I was thrown backward as we accelerated forward, the wheels spinning slightly in the loose dirt before gaining traction. I risked a glimpse behind me over the rolled top, seeing villagers anxiously peeking through their doors to watch us pass. There was no sign of the shooter.

My heart still pounding in my chest, I sat upright and leaned forward to speak with Sidney as he braked at an intersection and then turned left.

'Are you injured?' he asked me first.

'No,' I gasped. 'You?'

He shook his head firmly, his mouth set in a firm line and his eyes intent on the road.

'What was that?' I demanded in bewildered alarm.

'I don't know, but I'm putting some distance between us and whoever that was, so sit back. I'll stop when I think it's safe they haven't followed us.'

I sank into the deep leather seat, wrapping my arms around myself as I huddled against the chill of the wind whipping past my cheeks and the residual fear pumping through my veins. I hadn't a clue where we were, but I trusted that Sidney knew what he was doing. Eventually he appeared to settle on a road aiming more or less due north toward Béthune. Before the war we might have driven directly through Arras and then Lens, but that latter city had been completely destroyed.

At a safe junction, he pulled off to the side, the rear wheels sliding as he pulled hard on the hand lever. He helped me clamber into the front seat next to him and then pulled me into a tight embrace. Burying my head in the junction of his neck and shoulders, I breathed deeply of the scent of his skin, feeling some of the tension that had been racking me since our close call begin to loosen.

As he released me, his hands slid down over my arms and back, as if to verify for himself that I hadn't been hit. 'If you hadn't stumbled . . .'

He left the sentence unfinished, but I nodded, understanding what he meant. 'Where was the shooter firing from?' I asked. 'The upper floor?'

'Or the rooftop. Either way, it's clear he followed us. Or was lying in wait.' Sidney scowled, and though he didn't voice his suspicions aloud, I could easily guess them.

'You think Miss Baverel sent us into a trap?'

'Who else knew where we were going?'

'Anyone with any inkling of an idea of how stubborn we are when it comes to uncovering the truth could have followed us,' I pointed out, trying to be rational. 'Charlaix was certainly aware we weren't going to let the matter drop, and who knows who he told. Or who else might have figured that out on their own.' I peered over my shoulder in the direction we'd come. There was nothing but dormant fields and the occasional barn as far as the eye could see. The winter grass waved in the wind. 'Or perhaps it was someone who knew Miss Baverel well and had suspected where she'd send us.'

A light leapt in Sidney's eyes as he grasped my implication. 'Lieutenant Smith.'

'He *was* a sniper with the Royal Fusiliers.'

'And he attempted to visit Miss Baverel some days past.'

I adjusted the roll collar of my coat. 'Maybe he

was sent to silence her, to clear up whatever mess her arrest had created.'

'Including us.'

I looked up into Sidney's solemn face, seeing the concern and outrage stamped across his features. 'Yes.' I frowned. 'Though, not five months ago at Littlemote, Ardmore had Smith use his sniper skills to save me. Why would he now decide I was expendable?'

'Perhaps we're too close to the truth,' was his easy response. His eyebrows arched. 'Who knows in how many ways the situation has changed. It would be a mistake to think Ardmore will preserve your life indefinitely. In the end, we *are* his enemies.'

He was right. For all we knew, the status quo might have altered significantly, and the reasons Ardmore had been content to see me still breathing had vanished. To assume anything else would be fatal.

Sidney looked behind us before pulling back out onto the road. 'Whatever the case, one thing seems clear: We're not the only ones who believe Miss Baverel had something worth hiding, and we're not the only ones in pursuit of it.' His shoulders tensed. 'But here's hoping we're the only ones who know to look in Furnes.'

We arrived in Furnes – or Veurne, as the Flemish residents preferred to call it – as the dying rays of the sun were setting behind the city's Gothic belfry.

Furnes was a beautiful old medieval town, one that had long prospered from trade with England. It had passed the war in relative safety nestled within the pocket of northwest Belgium that had remained unconquered by the invading Germans. Tucked safely out of reach of the Germans by the deliberate flooding of the canals connected to the North Sea and the River Yser, it had faced little threat of invasion for much of the conflict, and had served as the headquarters of the Belgium Army. As such, her graceful old buildings still stood, including the ancient church of St Walburga, the massive tower of St Nicholas Church, and the *Landhuis*, or city hall.

Sidney found us a hotel just off the Grote Markt, the central market square. Many of the buildings in that plaza were Renaissance-style, built from the light-colored bricks made locally. Anxious to hear if Kathleen had learned anything, I placed a telephone call to her while he checked us in. Kathleen picked up almost immediately.

'Darling, you called just in the nick of time. I was about to step out,' she declared breezily, letting me know there was someone in the room with her who she didn't want to realize she was speaking with me. 'Let me get that number for you.' I heard the muffled sound of a voice and then Kathleen seeing them off before she returned to the line. 'If they ever put *that man* in charge, I'm retiring,' she groused, leaving me in no doubt who 'that man' was.

Only Major Davis could cause such vexation, especially among the female staff, whom he believed to be witless and unnecessary. I'd had more than my fair share of run-ins with the pig before *and after* I'd been officially demobilized from the service, and I still suspected he was doing whatever he could to tarnish my name.

'Let's see here. I have that information you requested. There is an agent by the name of Charlaix with the SCR. He's a Belgian from Soignies.' A village near Mons. 'And apparently liaised on cases between the Belgian and French Armies during the war.'

That was what had struck me about his accent, though it had been very subtle. Had I not spent time in Belgium during the war I might not have recognized it at all. I didn't know that the man's Belgian origins were in any way pertinent to our current interactions, but I filed the information away for future reference. The crucial thing at the moment was the legitimacy of his claims to work for the SCR.

'What of our friend JS?' I asked, knowing she would understand I was asking about James Smith.

'Yes, we were able to confirm that he sailed for Calais six days ago. Beyond that, we're still waiting for more information.'

Then Smith *was* in France, and so could have been the man who'd attempted to visit Miss Baverel. He also could have been the man who'd killed her and shot at us that morning.

135

'Where are you now?' Kathleen inquired.

'Furnes, following up with a friend.' There was no need to say anything further. She would know what I truly meant. I gave her the name of our hotel in case she needed to contact us.

'I need you to take a call tomorrow morning.'

My attention had wandered to a couple waiting in the lobby outside the partition where I sat cradling the phone, but it snapped back to Kathleen with this proclamation.

'I'll arrange it with the local authorities. I imagine there's a city hall.'

'Yes. The *Landhuis*.' I could hear her pen scratching across a piece of paper.

'Can you be there at 9:30?'

'Yes, I'll be there.'

We rung off and I slowly stepped from the booth, nodding to the couple while my thoughts were busily pondering this new development. The only reason Kathleen would arrange such a call was to ensure it was secure. And the only reason she would do that was if she had information to relay that she needed to be certain could not be intercepted. What that could be, I didn't know, but given the fact I'd been shot at just that morning I wasn't anticipating it to be anything good.

The following morning at a quarter after nine, Sidney and I presented ourselves at the stately *Landhuis*, and were greeted by the burgomaster and various other officials. Apparently being

136

granted the use of one of their telephone lines for official business with a branch of the British government was cause for great interest. Despite the evident curiosity shining in their eyes, they did not broach etiquette by asking what the matter was about. However, given the fact some of them recognized us – our reputations having preceded us – I suspected the speculations to soon run rampant.

We were shown into an elegant chamber far grander than the usual setting for making or receiving a simple phone call. Sidney stood with his hands in his pockets, gazing up at the painting on the ceiling. It depicted some sort of event from Flemish history, perhaps the Battle of the Golden Spurs, but before I could give it more than a cursory glimpse the telephone began to ring. I perched in a gilded Louis Quatorze chair next to a matching desk and pulled the base of the phone closer to me before picking up the receiver.

'Hello. This is Mrs Kent speaking.'

'Verity, it's good to hear your voice!'

The gravelly voice was not one I'd been expecting to hear, but a smile curled my lips, nonetheless. 'C, how are you getting on?'

Sidney's attention darted abruptly to me, knowing that C was none other than Mansfield Smith-Cumming, the chief of the Secret Intelligence Service – the name the Foreign Intelligence Service had only recently settled on for itself after being known by half a dozen different titles since its inception and throughout the war.

'Quite well, quite well, my dear. Did they look sharp for you this morning? I imagine all the dignitaries turned out in their full regalia.'

C had always derived a great deal of amusement from the pomp and circumstance that some officials insisted upon.

'They practically formed a receiving line.'

He chuckled. 'Well, much as I'd love to chat, I'm sure you're aware that's not the reason I arranged this call.' His tone sobered, though it never lost its warmth. 'We've encountered a bit of a problem, and you are just the woman to figure it out.'

I found myself straightening in my chair even though he couldn't see me, as always, won over by the confidence he expressed in me.

'About three weeks ago, a young lawyer by the name of Jacques Offerman was murdered on a train between Amsterdam and the Hague. The Dutch police have been investigating and they believe the shooting to be simply a matter of revenge. However, what they're not aware of is Offerman's connection to British Intelligence, or the sensitive nature of the documents stolen from his portfolio.'

'What did Offerman do for us, sir?'

'He was a Belgian refugee. One with enough skills to land a job inside one of the Dutch ministries.'

I understood, then. There was no need to spell it out for me. Offerman had passed intelligence from this ministry onto the British, something that the Dutch would never have tolerated. As a neutral country constantly walking the tightrope of diplomacy to stay out of the war, they'd struck a compromise by turning a blind eye to the activities of the Germans' and Allied nations' intelligence agencies, *so long as* they were directed at each other and not the Netherlands. They were rigid in controlling their own interests – something no one could fault them for – and had mobilized their own intelligence service to keep an eye on the spies in their midst. If they uncovered proof that the British had planted a spy in one of their ministries, diplomatic relations between the nations would be strained.

'There's more. The stolen documents also contain details about the sinking of a German vessel, the *Renate Leonhardt*, during the war, including the truth of its foundering, as well its real cargo.' C paused, and I knew he wasn't going to tell me they'd been transporting something as innocuous as coal or even munitions. 'Gold. Possibly even the Kaiser's own. Offerman was investigating the matter for us.'

Sidney couldn't hear C, but from the manner in which he watched me so intently, it was clear my own tension had been communicated to him.

'Verity, if those documents come to light, not only will the Dutch discover we had an informant inside their government who tipped us off to the sailing and cargo of the *Renate Leonhardt*, but there will also be a mass exodus of people to the crash site, trying to salvage that gold. The entire matter will become an international incident, and an embarrassment to the British government, as well as our intelligence division. I don't have to tell you what a coup this would be to Sir Basil Thomson.'

Thomson, as Director of Intelligence at the Home Office, had been trying to bring the foreign intelligence division more tightly under his control since his appointment to the new post last year. Thus far, C had been able to outmaneuver him, successfully arguing that in order to do its job properly, the Secret Intelligence Service must be able to maintain its autonomy to operate with the utmost secrecy. But a debacle like this could very well undermine all those efforts, and I happened to agree with C. While oversight was necessary, too many cooks spoiled the broth. Or in this case, spilled it.

'I can't send anyone officially, you understand,' he continued, the connection crackling and popping as he spoke. 'Not without risking Thomson finding out. I had a man on the ground, but there's been some complications. I need you to look into the matter for me.'

I'd known this moment would come. After all, when I'd come to C for help with a troubling matter involving a former fellow agent in Belgium last July and agreed to work with him in an unofficial capacity, I'd known that someday he would come to me requiring assistance. That our cooperation would have to be a two-way street. And given all that C had done for me, and all the faith and trust he'd placed in me over the years, I knew I couldn't turn him down. Not when his neck might very well be on the line. Not when the men who wanted to see him – *us* – fail were Thomson, and more than likely his shadowy friend Lord Ardmore.

So, in the end, there was only one thing I could say. 'Of course. Who can supply me with the details?'

Sidney shifted in the chair he'd taken beside mine, recalling me to his presence, and I felt a pulse of guilt for not conferring with him first. But I also knew that if he were in my shoes, faced with a plea from his former commanding officer, his response would be the same.

'T will meet with you in Rotterdam. You know the address.' He inhaled deeply and I could picture him in my mind's eye, leaning back in his chair, puffing on his pipe. 'But what of this other matter that brought you to Furnes? Have you uncovered anything?'

I filled him in briefly on what we'd learned about Miss Baverel and our quest for her hidden proof.

'Yes, intriguing,' he ruminated, his quick mind grasping the implications of the things I hadn't said. 'Take the day to finish what you need to, and then continue on to Rotterdam. I'll telegraph T to expect you tomorrow evening.'

As we rung off, Sidney sat staring at me expectantly, waiting for me to explain what I had just agreed to. I felt slightly overwhelmed, as I always did upon first learning about my next assignment, my mind scrambling to assimilate everything I'd just discovered. Filling my lungs with air, I let it out slowly, forcing myself to focus on the most immediate task. 'Tomorrow we're leaving for Rotterdam.'

Quickly, I informed him of everything that C had said, and all the inferences in between. I could tell from the deep furrow between Sidney's brows that he wasn't exactly pleased with this alteration in our plans. But rather than answering me when I'd finished, he pushed to his feet to cross toward one of the tall windows overlooking the square.

During the war, the Belgian Army had used it as a parade ground. Their King Albert I had stood not far from here when he decorated those soldiers who merited it on special occasions. He'd been tremendously popular among his people, choosing to be stranded in this small corner of his country which remained free rather than surrender to the Germans. He'd acted as commander of the Belgian Army throughout the conflict, refusing to allow his troops to be integrated into the corps of the British or French Armies, lest Belgium's sovereignty and independence be brought into question.

142

His defiance and his will to fight for his country had fueled his people's, and fostered a remarkable spirit of patriotism that had seen them through the horrors and deprivations of the war.

Though it wasn't easy, I forced myself to wait quietly as he absorbed everything I'd told him. If he had questions, he would ask them. My yammering on would only annoy him.

When he finally turned to face me, he pushed his coat aside so that he could prop his hands on his hips and gazed back across the marble floor at me resignedly. 'I suppose we have no choice in the matter. Though I do wish you would have consulted me first.'

'Darling, had we been in London, I would have done so,' I replied. 'But we're hundreds of miles away in a foreign country on an unreliable telephone connection. I had seconds to give him a response, not minutes.' I tilted my head. 'Tell me you wouldn't have done the same.'

He grimaced, still struggling with himself, but then nodded. 'Then I suppose if we've only got the day here, we'd best locate Miss Baverel's former lodgings, and swiftly.'

I could tell he wasn't completely reconciled yet to our taking up this investigation of the lawyer's death for C, but I trusted he would accept it in time. If later that evening he still needed coaxing, we could address it then. For now, it was best to focus on where Miss Baverel had hidden her proof.

I crossed to the heavy wooden double doors,

opening them to find the man who had escorted us there – a secretary of some kind – standing on the other side.

'Were you able to complete your call?' he asked politely.

'Yes, thank you. How can I find out the address of a former resident? Are there any records we can search?'

His eyes glinted with curiosity, but he was too well trained to question such a request. 'Of course, madam. If you give me the name, I will find out for you.'

'Adele Baverel.'

'Or she may have gone by the name Dupré,' Sidney interjected, reminding me that was what he'd known her as before four days ago.

He dipped his head once in understanding. 'If you would wait in the parlor, I will have tea brought to you while I get that information for you.'

And so we passed a pleasant half hour, sipping tea, and further scrutinizing the sumptuous décor in the chamber. I felt a pulse of sadness at the realization that so many similar rooms and buildings in nearby cities in Belgium and France had been destroyed during the war. It was more the loss of that beauty and craftsmanship molded by gifted human hands that I mourned than the objects themselves. The labors of those who had toiled seemingly in insignificance to carve a chair or construct a church steeple had lived on long after their craftsmen had been largely forgotten. Perhaps the laborers' names had been known to but a few, perhaps they had never made it into the pages of a book, but the legacy of their hands, the sweat of their brows had been poured into the very foundations of those buildings, some of which were close to a thousand years old. It was yet another reminder that nothing of human invention was permanent. Especially our frail human bodies.

I wasn't certain how long it would take for the secretary to find the information we sought. I supposed it depended on how organized their records were and how accomplished their clerks. However, as the clock ticked past the half hour, I began to wonder if there was a problem. For all we knew, Miss Baverel had gone by a different name when she lived in Furnes. Or perhaps she'd resided with someone else as a guest and her name had never been registered.

When I changed seating positions for approximately the fifth time in as many minutes, Sidney reached out to clasp my hand, offering me a reassuring smile.

'I doubt combing the streets for someone who knew her will yield quicker results,' he chided.

I gave a huff of laughter at my failed patience. 'It would also be far from subtle.'

The curl of his lips acknowledged this.

When the door opened over his shoulder, I released his hand and sat taller, watching as the secretary advanced into the room.

'Here you are,' he declared as if he'd been searching for us and not an address. 'I apologize for the delay. We couldn't find an Adele Baverel or an Adele Dupré. But we did find an Adélaide Dupré. Could that be her?'

I glanced at Sidney. 'Yes, I suspect it could.'

'Then she resided with a Simone Lemaire in Klaverstraat.' He handed me a piece of paper on which he'd written this information and I thanked him.

'That's the friend of hers I mentioned,' Sidney leaned down to murmur as we exited the room. 'The one I followed to Miss Baverel's lodgings in Achicourt.'

I stared down at the address written on the scrap of foolscap, finding this fact to be interesting. 'I wonder if she's still living here.' And what she might be able to tell us.

CHAPTER ELEVEN

Klaverstraat being just a few blocks south of the Grote Markt, Sidney and I elected to walk, and were soon glad we'd chosen to do so. The streets in this part of Furnes were narrow with little room for parking, and the buildings faced with flat brick façades in varying shades of muted red, gray, and mustard yellow. Here and there a door was painted a brighter color, or a roofline formed an interesting angle, but otherwise the presentation remained neat and relatively uniform, albeit monotonous.

However, this changed the moment we stepped through the arched brick opening which led beneath two adjoining buildings to the dwellings accessed from the mews beyond. The hidden courtyard into which we emerged was both more colorful and chaotic. Dormant plants and vines climbed the walls in several places, their buds just beginning to show in the midst of the twining branches, while piles of clutter filled two of the corners. The walls had been repaired with a higgledy-piggledy assortment of bricks, creating a makeshift patchwork of hues and textures.

We found the door to the dwelling we were searching for easily enough, sandwiched between a cluster of pipes and a window with a small web-shaped crack in the lower right corner. But rather than approach it directly, we hung back in the shadows, surveilling our surroundings. Given the shots that had been fired at us in Achicourt, we were justifiably hesitant to step out into the open, lest we discover too late that the shooter had figured out where we were going. A group of children played on the opposite side of the court-yard, kicking a ball. One would hope this fact would deter Lieutenant Smith or whoever our adversary was if they were somewhere nearby watching us, but we couldn't count on that.

After several minutes of close scrutiny of the roofs and windows, we both felt safe in assuming the shooter was not here, and slowly made our way toward the door, keeping to the perimeter of the courtyard. A gust of wind kicked up the dirt, whirling it across the bricks before our feet. We halted just outside the door, and Sidney signaled for me to wait, moving closer to the window to see if he could see anything or anyone inside, but the curtains blocked most of the view. Our ears strained for the sound of voices, but if there were any, they were drowned out by the chattering laughter of the children behind us.

He nodded, and I lifted my hand to knock, hoping this Simone Lemaire was home and that she would be willing to speak with us. There was always the chance that the records were wrong and she didn't live here anymore, but gaining access to these lodgings was our best hope of finding whatever Miss Baverel had hidden. *If* she had hidden anything. There was still the possibility this was nothing more than a wild-goose chase, but I lived in hope.

At the sound of approaching footsteps, I turned to Sidney, my eyebrows arching at the realization that the tread was too heavy to be a woman's. Perhaps Miss Lemaire had a husband or a lover, a brother even. My lips parted to ask him what he knew of the woman from the time he'd spent trailing her, trying to locate Miss Baverel, but the door opened before I could speak.

The face it revealed was not one I'd anticipated. A fact that must have been perfectly obvious based on the smirk that stretched across his lips.

'Mrs Kent, how lovely to see you again,' Captain Lucas Willoughby proclaimed in flawless French. His gaze shifted to Sidney. 'As well as your husband.'

The appearance of a petite blond woman staring out at us anxiously from the corridor behind him spurred me into speech. 'What are *you* doing here?' I demanded of him.

'Why, waiting for you, of course.'

This response shocked me almost more than his appearance, and his mocking laughter as he turned away, leaving the door open for us to follow him inside, made my stomach twist in dread. He didn't even pause to see if we would follow, instead wrapping his arm around the waist of the woman I presumed to be Miss Lemaire to usher her back into a room off to the right. Her eyes darted over her shoulder to meet mine just before the pair disappeared from sight.

I stood transfixed a moment longer, feeling at a loss on how to proceed. The warm hand that Sidney pressed against the small of my back was all that propelled me forward. Though I no longer had the foggiest idea what we would find.

I was under no illusions that Captain Willoughby was there to assist us. Just because his aviation derring-do and practice bombs had helped save us from a dangerous situation during our last encounter did not make him any sort of ally. He had served with Naval Intelligence during the war, and now worked for Lord Ardmore, and not just as some low-level thug in his shadowy organization, but at a much higher rank. While he'd not committed murder during that previous inquiry, his involvement *had* precipitated the events that had brought it about while he searched for the phosgene gas canisters concealed on the property – part of the stash Ardmore had contrived to steal for purposes yet unknown.

I also could not forget that Willoughby's partner in that effort had been Lieutenant Smith. The man who we suspected of bombing General Bishop's headquarters in April 1918. The man who had tried to visit Miss Baverel at the gendarmerie several days before her neck was snapped. And the man who had perhaps put his sniper training to good use just the day before when we were shot at in Achicourt.

As such, I half expected to find Smith waiting for us as we followed Willoughby and the woman into the room. Apparently, Sidney was entertaining the same thought, for I heard the rustle of fabric as he reached behind him to extract the Luger tucked into the waistband beneath his coat. I stepped in front of him to conceal the movement, wary of what we were walking into.

A swift survey of the room revealed no Smith, but that didn't mean he wasn't somewhere in the house. Accordingly, Sidney and I moved away from the door, positioning a wall at our backs, lest someone attempt to sneak up behind us. The chamber was little more than a parlor fitted with a sofa and a chair, both upholstered in a pastoral toile that had clearly seen better days. The walls were painted a garish shade of persimmon and the rug was worn and much too small for the space.

Captain Willoughby stood with one hand resting negligently against the corner of the sofa, and one ankle crossed over the other. He wore a thin, brown-plaid suit rather than a military uniform. I noted his sun-bleached hair had darkened over the British winter, and his skin tan had faded.

In stark contrast to his carefree persona, the

151

woman beside him gripped the back of the chair before her as it were some sort of shield, though who she felt the need to protect herself from – us or Willoughby – I couldn't say. She was softly feminine and attractive, though it was evident her best days were already behind her. Deprivation and hardship had a way of etching itself onto one's face, and this woman's showed the wear, despite the fact she couldn't have been older than thirty.

'Miss Lemaire, I presume?' I asked, hoping by addressing her first I could both put her at ease and find my footing again after Willoughby had pulled the rug out from under me.

'*Oui*,' she replied timidly before peering uncertainly at the captain, making me wonder if she'd been ordered to keep quiet.

'I understand Mademoiselle Baverel – or is it Dupré? – is a friend of yours,' I persisted. 'My condolences on your loss.'

She blinked rapidly as her eyes filled with tears. '*Merci.*'

'I see she laid her breadcrumbs well,' Willoughby interjected, still wearing that smug smirk. 'For here you are.'

'I would say too well,' I retorted. 'Or else you wouldn't be here also.'

He laughed lightly. 'My dear Mrs Kent, who do you think told her to lead you here?'

I stiffened, searching his features for some indication he was bluffing.

'Yes, Mrs Kent, I'm telling you the truth,' he

taunted. 'Mademoiselle Baverel was acting under *my* instructions.'

And by 'my' I knew he really meant Lord Ardmore's.

'But why would he . . .?' I began to ask as Willoughby rounded the sofa and sank down in the cushions, propping one ankle over the opposite knee.

'To distract you,' he replied before I could finish. 'To get you away from Britain.'

I felt as if I'd been slapped. For if he was telling the truth, then Ardmore must have had a very strong reason for wanting us out of Britain, and I could think of only two possibilities. The first threatened to bring me to my knees as I scrambled to recall when Sidney had last spoken to Max over the telephone. We'd not been able to reach him the evening before, but his butler hadn't sounded worried.

The other possibility was less personal, but no less alarming. Had the phosgene cylinders been hidden somewhere under our very noses and Ardmore had needed to smuggle them out? Or perhaps put them to use? I had been so certain they'd already been taken to Ireland, but maybe I was wrong. I'd not read the latest news from London in the papers this morning. I glanced at Sidney. And neither had he. We'd been running late.

'Then you're telling us everything Mademoiselle Baverel told us was a lie?' Sidney's voice was taut with skepticism. 'That it was merely some story to keep us preoccupied?'

Willoughby spread his hands out, palms up, as if that was answer enough.

'And her death?' I asked, my own doubts beginning to trickle in. 'What was that?'

'Just a simple suicide,' he replied carelessly.

Miss Lemaire sobbed, but he ignored her.

'As she was instructed.'

Except Miss Baverel had not struck me as the type of woman who would kill herself, especially not because she was *told* to do so. She'd seemed cunning and resourceful, a woman who didn't give up easily and would attempt to turn every opportunity to her advantage. Despite her agitation, she had seemed far from defeated when we'd spoken with her. Could she really have hidden her intentions so well?

'Why?' I queried. 'Why would she go through with such a thing?'

Willoughby's expression lost much of its insouciance. 'Because she had no choice.'

'There's always a choice,' I refuted angrily.

He arched a single eyebrow. 'Is there?'

I recognized what game he was playing, for he'd learned it from the best. After all, Lord Ardmore didn't simply aim to outwit his opponents, but to corrupt and demoralize them. To turn them against themselves, against their very morals. He'd done as much to Max's father and countless others before killing them. And Willoughby was implying he'd done the same to Miss Baverel, but with such skill that she'd actually killed herself.

Except the evidence proved otherwise. And facts – unlike people – didn't lie. She couldn't have snapped her neck. Someone else had done that.

I decided for the moment to play his game, to find out what I could. 'What did he hold over her?'

His eyes glinted in satisfaction at my asking the question he'd clearly wanted me to, and then he turned to the side as if to pretend it mattered little to him. 'I don't know exactly. But I *am* aware that there's evidence she sent a bit of precious cargo west to Caen some years ago.'

Miss Lemaire gave a little gasp, drawing our attention.

'A bit of cargo that requires . . . regular maintenance,' he continued, in case we hadn't caught his implication.

An implication that it seemed Miss Lemaire knew nothing about it. This was something I found difficult to believe. Miss Baverel might have been a private person, but she couldn't have kept the existence of a child concealed from everyone. Could Miss Lemaire truly not have known? Or was Captain Willoughby once again lying?

I crossed my arms over my chest, stating the matter bluntly. 'So you threatened to harm her child unless she convinced us to come to France, and once that was achieved then killed herself?'

He shrugged. 'Something like that.'

Sidney's jaw clenched at the callousness of his reply.

Miss Lemaire pressed a hand to her mouth as if she might be ill.

'Leave the room if you're going to be sick,' Willoughby snapped, his smooth persona slipping.

'Then why did Lieutenant Smith attempt to see Miss Baverel a few days ago?' I countered, attempting to wedge a crowbar into that crack.

Miss Lemaire's footsteps slowed as she moved toward the door, evidently recognizing the name. However, the look Willoughby turned back to me was tinged with confusion.

'Why did he shoot at us just yesterday in Achincourt?'

His eyes widened the tiniest of fractions, telling me this news had caught him off guard, though he pretended not. He bared his teeth in a smile that did not quite reach his eyes. 'Why, to make you even more determined to find this place.'

'Then he's not waiting in the next room to give his aim another try?' Sidney jibed.

But Willoughby had become more acclimated to the shock of the news we'd delivered about Lieutenant Smith, his sangfroid returning. 'Now, you're not thinking. You're the Kents! You can't simply be shot and left for dead or made to disappear. It would draw too much attention. There would be inquiries and inquests, and reporters swarming all over the place, asking *far* too many questions. It would be the biggest story of the new decade.' He chuckled. 'No, no. The death of a war hero and his beautiful wife would require much more delicate handling.'

The air was charged with the quiet menace of such a statement.

'Now.' He pushed to his feet. 'If you'll excuse me, I've told you all I can,' he declared as if he'd done us a great favor. 'But I have other pressing matters to attend to.' He held his hand out toward the door, telling us to leave.

Such a move left me off balance, for while I wanted to demand more answers, it was evident he wouldn't give them to us. Not that I even knew what to ask in the first place. I would be stabbing in the dark for the most part. The fact was, I hadn't seen this twist coming, and so I hadn't been prepared for this confrontation. My thoughts felt jumbled and scattered, and I didn't have enough information to be able to catch Willoughby out in his lies. Perhaps if he were a civilian my disorientation wouldn't have mattered so much, but Willoughby was trained. He knew the tricks of the trade as well as I did, and so foiling him would be infinitely harder.

In the end, there was nothing for it but for us to do as he asked and retreat, and we soon found ourselves back outside in the courtyard where the children still kicked their ball. Sidney laced his arm through mine as we strode around the perimeter, conscious of the doors and windows we passed. We didn't attempt to speak, perhaps neither of us being capable of it in that moment. However, one last surprise awaited us.

With one last look over my shoulder, I allowed Sidney to guide me into the tunnel leading under the buildings and out to Klaverstraat. There, cowering against one of the walls, stood Miss Lemaire, her arms wrapped around herself defensively. At our appearance, she straightened and then hastened closer. 'Is it true?' she murmured in French. 'Is Adele truly dead?'

'I'm afraid so,' I told her.

She turned her head to the side, staring unseeing at the opposite wall, visibly trying to master her emotions.

'But we don't believe she killed herself.'

Her eyes flew back to mine, round with shock and then fright as she comprehended what that meant. Her gaze darted over my shoulder, as if afraid she would find Captain Willoughby watching us. She had risked more than she realized by sneaking out to intercept us, and as such, time was of the essence.

'It is true that she left us breadcrumbs, leading us to your door. But we think it was for a greater purpose than to merely distract us. Can you think of any reason why she would have done so?'

She shook her head.

'Did she live here with you? Did she leave anything behind?'

Her blue eyes were wide in her pale face. 'She

did live here with me, for a time. But that was over a year ago. And I don't remember her leaving anything behind.'

Which didn't mean she hadn't, but if it had truly been more than a year ago, I struggled to believe it was this proof she spoke of.

'Will you search where you can? Check the floorboards and the walls,' Sidney instructed. 'And let us know if you find anything.' He gave her the direction of our hotel. 'We'll be there until the morning.'

She nodded in agreement, but I wasn't about to send her back to her house without some explanation as to what was going on, even if she had been an enemy informant like Miss Baverel.

'Are you in danger from Captain Willoughby?'

She seemed surprised by the question. 'I don't know,' she admitted hesitantly. 'He hasn't hurt me yet. Not since he pushed his way into my house yesterday. I don't think he would make the effort.' Her chest rose and fell as she took a swift breath. 'Unless I displeased him.' The implication being clear. She needed to return soon.

'Do you think Captain Willoughby was speaking the truth? Did Miss Baverel have a child?' I asked, having wondered at her initial reaction to this news.

Miss Lemaire's eyes flooded with tears. 'If she did, she didn't tell me, and we told each other everything.' She sniffed, swiping at her damp cheeks. 'Or at least, I thought we did.' She sniffled

159

again, turning to Sidney. 'She even told me about you.'

His eyebrows raised.

'How decent you were to her.' She hugged herself tighter. 'Most men aren't, you know. When you've been forced to make your living as we have, you learn that quickly. That's why I'm here.' Her anxious gaze flicked toward the end of the tunnel behind us, reminding us again of the risk she was taking.

'Is there anything else you can tell us? Anything that might help?' I hastened to say, feeling uneasy for her. Willoughby didn't seem prone to casual violence, but then I didn't really know him. For all I knew he could be a vicious bastard.

'You said a Lieutenant Smith tried to see her? That he . . . he shot at you?' she voiced timidly. 'Well, they were lovers. For a time.'

The hairs on the back of my neck stood up at this unexpected pronouncement.

'Adele, she . . . she even thought he might propose to her at one point. But I think that was just wishful thinking.'

'When was this?' I asked, curious about the timing.

'Oh, about two years ago, maybe. The war wasn't yet ended.'

My eyes met Sidney's. The explosion of General Bishop's temporary HQ had happened about two years ago. That might explain how Miss Baverel had known something about it. After all, we knew Lieutenant Smith had been inside the HQ moments before it had blown up.

'But when I saw her about a month ago, she told me she was seeing him again. On the side,' Miss Lemaire continued. 'And when she said she was taking a trip and would be out of the country for a time, I wondered if he might be accompanying her.'

A trip? 'Where were they going?' I pried.

'I don't know. Truly.' She shrugged uncomfortably. 'She never said.' She began to back away. 'I need to get back before . . .'

She didn't need to finish that sentence and I waved her along, telling her so. 'Thank you.'

She dipped her head once and then hurried away. I wondered for a moment if we should follow her to make sure Willoughby didn't harm her, but then I realized that if he spied us doing so, it might only make matters worse. Sidney also seemed conflicted, but then he voiced a question that had also been troubling me.

'When she said she'd been forced to make a living the same as Miss Baverel, I wonder precisely what she meant.'

Had she been referring to how Miss Baverel took lovers? Or had she also implicated herself as an enemy informant? I'd suspected the latter, and that raised some serious questions.

'She might be lying,' he said. 'About Lieutenant Smith. About not finding anything. Willoughby might have put her up to it.'

He was right. She could be lying about it all. Except my instincts were telling me differently. 'I don't think so.'

He turned to look down at me, but rather than argue he merely nodded. 'I don't think so either.'

His hand stole into mine as we continued to the end of the tunnel, pausing to look in both directions down Klaverstraat before setting off toward the hotel. Given the dangers we'd already faced, I was none too fond of these old narrow streets, where the verge of the pavement ended flush against the buildings. There were no front gardens or stoops to jump behind. No obstructions whatsoever. Should someone decide to shoot at us or, heaven forbid, if a motorcar should come barreling down the lane toward us, there would be no place to cower for protection. Only a tunnel like the one we'd taken to reach the courtyard where Miss Lemaire resided every few hundred feet. As such, we increased our pace, lest Willoughby or Smith, or some unknown player, decide our deaths *were* worth the trouble.

My anxiety eased as we turned the corner into a wider thoroughfare lined with shops and cafés with tables set along the bricks outside their doors. 'Then if Miss Lemaire wasn't lying, what do you think of what she told us about Lieutenant Smith?'

'It certainly shines a new light on why he might have tried to visit her in jail,' he conceded.

'And why he might have shot at us. Do you think he blames us for her death?'

Sidney's brow furrowed beneath the brim of his hat. '*If* you believe Smith was truly in love with her. And *if* you believe Willoughby's assertion that they don't mean to kill us in such a haphazard way. Then I suppose it makes some sort of sense.' But I could tell he was dubious on both points.

I couldn't say that I blamed him. The one time I had met Smith face-to-face I had not been the least impressed. He'd been insolent and disrespectful, particularly toward women. Dodgy, that was how one maid had referred to him, and I'd had to agree. Not a man I would want to find myself alone in the dark with, for he would exploit it unpleasantly.

But Miss Baverel had told Miss Lemaire she'd believed he might propose marriage. This was something I struggled to believe. Had Miss Baverel been mistaken, or was my assessment of Lieutenant Smith faulty?

'One thing is for certain,' I said. 'Willoughby wasn't aware of Smith's movements. Though whether that means Smith is acting alone, or Ardmore didn't share Smith's orders with Willoughby, I don't know.' I peered about me as we crossed the next intersection, relieved to see that the other pedestrians didn't seem to be paying us the slightest attention. 'The more pertinent question is whether we believe the captain's other assertion.' I lowered my voice. 'Did Miss Baverel deliberately send us on this wild-goose chase to distract us?' I turned my head to meet Sidney's gaze. 'And if so, what exactly was she distracting us from?'

CHAPTER TWELVE

Sidney closed the door to our hotel room and turned the lock. As we'd neared the Grote Markt, the pedestrian traffic had increased, so by unspoken agreement, we'd postponed the remainder of our discussion until we were in private. Even so, he had not questioned me when I veered into one of the small alcoves set up in the hotel lobby for the guests' use of the telephone. I could see in his eyes that he knew exactly for whom I was most concerned.

However, Max's butler had informed me that he was once again unavailable. I feared I'd unsettled the fellow by demanding to know the details concerning the last time he'd seen his employer, but as that had been no more than an hour earlier at least I had been able to breathe easier knowing Max had not been harmed. At least, not yet.

Perhaps somewhat high-handedly, I'd ordered the butler to send a footman after Max and have him telephone us here as soon as earthly possible. He needed to be warned.

I circled our hotel room, checking behind the drapes and under the bed while Sidney peered into the *en suite*, but we quickly confirmed, to our relief, that we were alone. I sank down on the edge of the bed, pressing a hand to my silk blouse over my heart. After fetching the *Times* he'd requested be delivered on our breakfast tray but had been too rushed to open, Sidney sat beside me to flip through the pages. His eyes skimmed swiftly over the print, searching for anything alarming, anything that might be connected to Ardmore.

'You think Willoughby was being truthful, then?'

'As much as you do, hastening to call Max and interrogating his butler,' he retorted, softening his words by offering me a sheepish smile. 'I think we're both rattled.'

I inhaled past the tightness in my chest. 'You could say that.' I traced the medallion pattern of the carpet with my eyes. 'If Willoughby *was* being truthful, then Ardmore went to a great deal of trouble to get us away from London, from England.'

He turned another page, scanning the print. 'Which means his reason for doing so would have to be something he feared we would uncover and foil before it could be executed.'

'Something with the gas cylinders? An attempt on Max's life? Some attack that clearly bears his hallmarks?' I enumerated the possibilities. 'Though I can't think of anything we know enough about to be able to thwart.' Things had been quiet. Unsettlingly so. I had feared there was something we were missing. Was this it?

He hummed as if in agreement, and I looked

over to see if something in the paper had caught his eye. Then just as he was about to turn the page, a name leapt out at me.

I reached over to stop him, rumpling the paper. 'What's this?'

He read the lines along with me. It was some news out of Ireland. The body of John Charles Byrnes had been found in Dublin, killed by 'The Squad,' a group of men from the Irish Republican Army who'd been chosen specifically by Michael Collins to carry out assassinations of policemen, soldiers, and political figures not sympathetic to the republican cause. Through the end of the previous year, they'd already murdered over 150 men, and that number had continued to grow since then. It had been a lethally effective method of getting their point across.

Sidney frowned. 'Wasn't he the agent Thomson sent to infiltrate the IRA?'

'Yes. The one I told you was never going to fool them, that he would only end up dead.'

I derived no satisfaction from being proven right, only a cold lump of fear knowing that my friend and former agent, Alec Xavier, had separately been given the same task. I had far more faith in Alec than I'd ever had in Byrnes, but that didn't erase my worry. Alec was intelligent and coldly effective, but he was also reckless.

My husband wrapped his arm around my shoulders. 'Xavier knows how to take care of himself,' he tried to reassure me, clearly deducing the direction of my thoughts. 'There's no point in borrowing trouble.'

I swallowed. 'You're right. In any case, it has nothing to do with our current dilemma.' I straightened my shoulders, determined to push it from my mind. '*Did* Ardmore, through Willoughby or another of his henchmen, convince Miss Baverel to lie to the authorities and lure us over to France, and then commit suicide?'

Sidney set the newspaper aside. 'I think we can safely presume they at least spoke with her. Or else, why would they admit to such a thing? To knowing Miss Baverel and having a working relationship with her.' His eyebrows lifted. 'But that doesn't mean Miss Baverel stuck to their script, or that she didn't have proof of her fellow informants' crimes squirreled away somewhere.'

Pushing to my feet, I began pacing between the windows. 'We *know* that Miss Baverel didn't kill herself. The evidence that she was murdered is clear. So that much is certainly a lie.'

'Which leaves open the possibility that she *wasn't* lying to us. She might have agreed to Ardmore's demands, refusing to speak to anyone but me, but then once she had us before her, took advantage of our presence.' He tilted his head. 'It would also explain why, in exchange for her testimony, she wanted to go to America. She wanted to escape Ardmore's reach.'

'That does make sense. Miss Baverel is . . . *was* resourceful. She would undoubtedly have used whatever means were at her disposal.' I narrowed my eyes in thought. 'Then she never intended to commit suicide, which also fits with our assessment of her character. Rather she hoped to turn the situation to her advantage. But Ardmore foresaw that' – I turned to look at Sidney – 'or learned directly of her conversation with us from someone else and then made certain she was silenced.'

'You're thinking of Charlaix,' Sidney surmised.

'He *did* listen in on our entire conversation with her from the concealment of that closet.'

Sidney pushed to his feet. 'Yes, but he also undoubtedly reported it to others, including Capitaine Marcisieux. So, any number of people might have known about the proof she claimed she hid and her desire to go to America.' He crossed toward one of the windows, opening it about a foot. Fresh air came rushing in, along with birdsong and the soft drone of voices from the square below. 'Plus, you'll recall, Charlaix came to *us*, and willingly revealed his role with the SCR. He needn't have done that, nor shared what he knew about Lieutenant Smith's attempted visit and his own suspicions about Miss Baverel's death.' He extracted a fag from the case he pulled from his coat. 'If he was working for Ardmore, I struggle to see why his doing either of those things would in any way be to their advantage.'

He had a valid point. One I pondered for a moment while he lit his cigarette before I shook my head. 'We're straying from the point. Let's assume that one of Ardmore's men *did* approach Miss Baverel. That they convinced her to insist on speaking to you, knowing I would tag along, and used her child as leverage to force her to do so.' I halted, frowning. 'The child. Wouldn't Miss Baverel be afraid of what would happen to him or her if she defied Ardmore? Wouldn't she have wished to take them with her to America?'

He shrugged. 'Maybe she didn't believe Ardmore would really harm the child, and intended to send for them after she arrived. Or maybe she decided the child would be better off without her.'

An icy shard lodged in my chest at the idea of risking a child's life in such a manner, of abandoning them. But Miss Baverel had been facing an unfathomable choice: commit suicide or gamble that Ardmore would not follow through on whatever his threats had been.

'Or maybe Willoughby was bluffing,' Sidney added, exhaling a plume of smoke. 'Maybe there was no child, but he thought telling us there was would better convince us of Miss Baverel's motives to follow Ardmore's directives. After all, Miss Lemaire – who by all appearances seems to have been the closest of friends to Miss Baverel – didn't know of the child's existence.'

I nodded. 'But we should at least try to find out if it's true. For the child's sake, if not for our investigation. Though I doubt they'll be found in Caen. Willoughby was probably lying about that.'

'That's something Charlaix would be able to help us with.' Sidney reached for the pewter ashtray on an adjoining table, setting it on the window ledge where he tipped his ashes into it. 'He would have the resources.'

'Yes, let's ask him,' I agreed after a brief pause. If nothing else it might test his loyalty.

'But back to your earlier point, if Ardmore's men approached Miss Baverel, then either they'd worked with her before or at least knew *of* her and her work as an informant. And if they were the ones to plant the idea of her insisting on speaking to me, then Ardmore must have had a very good reason for wanting us out of England.'

Feeling a renewed pulse of anxiety, I glanced at the door, wishing one of the hotel staff would knock with a message that Max had returned my call. 'And yet, we don't know what that reason is.' My gaze met Sidney's. 'Should we be racing back to London or is it already too late?'

'What of your investigation for C?'

I pressed a hand to my forehead. 'Blast! How could I forget that?' I turned abruptly away and then back toward him. 'But if Ardmore is up to something, surely that should take precedence.' Except C was counting on me to find whoever had killed this Belgian lawyer and taken his papers, and stop them from making any of the information public. How could I let him down when he'd placed such faith in me?

'But we don't know that Ardmore actually is up to something.'

I blinked at Sidney in disbelief. 'You think Willoughby was lying about that as well?'

He took one last drag of his cigarette before stubbing it out. 'I think that it's possible. And until we have any actual evidence Ardmore had reason to want us out of England, I think we should proceed as planned.'

However, I was having more of a difficult time letting it go. 'But why? Why go to the trouble of tracking us down to tell us these lies and risk revealing their direct involvement with Miss Baverel?' But I realized I already knew the answer to my question. 'To stop us from searching.'

Sidney nodded solemnly. 'And if that's their real motive, then whatever proof Miss Baverel hid must be incredibly damaging. Damaging to Ardmore,' he specified.

Heaven only knew what that could be, but my fingers twitched just at the thought of holding it. 'Then we *have* to find it.'

'Yes. But where do we go from here?' he asked, moving to stand closer to me. 'If it's not at the home she shared with Miss Lemaire, then where were we meant to look?'

I scrutinized the diamond pattern of his tie. 'Maybe we weren't supposed to find it there. Maybe Miss Lemaire was supposed to be able to tell us something that would direct us where to look.'

His posture straightened as he remembered something. 'The trip she took with Smith.'

'Yes!'

He frowned. 'Except Miss Lemaire didn't know where they'd gone.'

'But maybe we can find out. If they traveled using their own names.'

The corner of Sidney's lips quirked. 'Another favor to ask of Charlaix.'

He was our best bet for uncovering the information we sought, and quickly.

'I'll place a call to him and let him know he can reach us in Rotterdam. Just as soon as we hear—'

As if on cue, there was a knock on the door. I turned toward it with a start, but he laid a reassuring hand on my arm and moved to answer it for me. I heard his softly worded '*Danke*,' but didn't bother to correct him. Essentially, Flemish was a dialect of Dutch, and Dutch was similar to German, but they were distinctly different languages. So, while Sidney's reply had been in German, I was sure the Flemish hotel clerk had understood what he meant. In any case, my attention was riveted instead to the note in Sidney's hand.

'Max returned your call.'

'Oh, thank heavens,' I exclaimed in relief, joining him by the door. 'Then let's go speak with him, and then Charlaix.'

Max answered for himself on the second ring.

'Verity, is everything all right? Prescott said you sounded rather overset.'

I laughed a trifle breathlessly. 'I would say that's an understatement. We're all right here. I was merely anxious to hear that you're well.' My eyes lifted to meet Sidney's as he stood beside me in the alcove, listening. 'We've had a bit of a development.' I briefly explained Willoughby's claims and our concern that it might have something to do with him.

'No, I'm hale and hearty,' he replied. 'Could he have been referring to something else?'

'Quite possibly,' I admitted. 'But we wanted to warn you to take extra precautions, nonetheless. I know you're intimately aware of how underhanded and ruthless Ardmore can be.' After all, he'd managed to poison Max's father to death without being even in his proximity. 'So don't let your guard down. Please,' I added, allowing him to hear my genuine concern for his safety.

'Of course,' he replied warmly. 'And you both, as well.'

'Ask him if he's spoken to Ponsonby,' Sidney murmured.

Max must have heard him, for he replied without my prompting. 'I saw him yesterday. Looks rather worn down, the poor chap. Not that he doesn't deserve the lot that's befallen him. But he seems much chastened.'

Sidney's jaw was tight. I suspected that was difficult to hear, even knowing Walter Ponsonby had been the one to shoot him and leave him for dead. But Walter had also been one of his closest friends, his best man at our wedding, and those bonds of attachment and affection were difficult to sever completely.

'I asked him about Miss Baverel, and he told me he'd known her as Miss Dupré. That they met for the first time at Miss Crawford's instigation. That Miss Crawford had told him Miss Dupré was a school friend, though he could immediately tell this wasn't true.'

'And yet he continued to meet with her and forward the coded correspondence Miss Crawford sent in the letters she wrote to him at the front?' I remarked scornfully, as ever, disappointed with Walter and unimpressed with his excuses.

'Yes.' Max's derisive tone told me he was in agreement. 'He claimed he didn't know much about Miss Dupré other than what she chose to tell him about herself, and that was also suspect. Although, he did learn one thing rather by accident, apparently while in bed with her.'

Despite the fact he'd sworn to us that he'd never slept with her, though I wasn't truly surprised to hear he'd lied about this.

A burst of static drowned out the beginning of his next statement. '. . . woke her from a nightmare and she lashed out at him. Accused the British of being heartless monsters. Said the soldiers who she'd begged to take her daughter when the Germans invaded refused to do so, and because of them the girl had been killed by enemy fire.'

Sidney and I shared a look. This must have occurred during the first months of the war, when the front had constantly been in motion, mostly in the wrong direction for the Belgians, French, and British, as the massive German Army continued to push north and westward, swinging in a giant arc toward Paris. The Germans had moved with ruthless speed, sometimes making the smaller Allied forces scramble to retreat, lest they be captured, leaving injured men and equipment behind. As for the citizens caught up in the terror of the invasion and the battles and skirmishes fought to stop it, there was little the armies could do except to urge them to flee faster. Even if a platoon of soldiers had wished to take a child with them, they couldn't have. The most they could have done was take the child to the nearest road strung with refugees and hope someone among the throng would take her into their care.

'And he thought Miss Dupré was being truthful on this point?' I clarified.

'He said her voice and her face were too raw not to be genuine,' Max replied.

Then this sounded like confirmation that Miss Baverel/Dupré had, at least, at one point had a child. But if her daughter had died in the late summer of 1914, then she couldn't have been used as leverage against Miss Baverel now. Unless there was still some part of this equation we weren't understanding.

176

'Did Walter say where Miss Dupré had lived before the war?' I asked.

'He didn't. And I didn't think to ask him. But I can return. Or send him a telegram,' he amended, already anticipating my insistence that he stay far away from Walter, given our ignorance of Ardmore's intentions.

'Yes, do that.'

I tipped the mouthpiece toward Sidney as he spoke. 'Did Ponsonby know anything about Lord Ardmore?'

'He said he didn't, and he denied any knowledge of the bombing either. Frankly, I believed him. Ponsonby might be a lot of things, but he's never been a good liar when confronted with a direct question.'

Max was no fool, and he'd served as Walter's commanding officer for some time during the war. If he was inclined to believe him, then so was I.

'Take care of yourself,' I told him, having to bite my tongue to hold back the needless words of caution crowding into the back of my throat as we prepared to ring off. Max knew how to look after himself. I had to trust that.

'The same to you,' he said. 'Let me know when you reach Rotterdam.'

I replaced the receiver on the switch hook, passing the telephone to Sidney. His eyes were soft with understanding. 'Don't fret, Ver. He knows what he's doing.'

I nodded, having told myself the same thing. If only I could believe it.

His eyes narrowed in determination as he picked up the receiver. 'Now, let's see if we can track down Charlaix.'

CHAPTER THIRTEEN

Considering the damage done to the devastated swath of Belgium and France that had made up the Western Front, particularly the flooded Yser plain immediately to the east of Furnes – damage it would take years, if not decades, to clean up and set to rights – Sidney and I elected to circumvent it by traveling to Rotterdam by ship rather than motorcar. We abandoned the Vauxhall at Dunkirk, from where Sidney's friend had told him he would have no trouble fetching it, and boarded the ferry. The seas were relatively calm, yet it still took us the better part of the day to reach our destination.

I felt an odd sense of déjà vu upon entering the port and disembarking. I hadn't returned to Rotterdam since the war, since my last assignment here had been completed in October 1918, though I had made the ferry crossing from Harwich often enough during the final two years of the conflict. Little, if anything, had changed. The Netherlands having remained neutral throughout the war, the country had seen little destruction except from the occasional bomb

179

dropped off course by an Allied aeroplane. Any harm done to its shipping fleets – which had admittedly taken a beating despite its neutrality – had been swiftly remedied, and its commercial might in shipping had rapidly regained traction since the end of Germany's U-boat warfare and Britain's blockade.

In Holland, water seemed to be everywhere, and Rotterdam was no exception. Interlinking canals lined with trees spread out all over the city, intersecting with streets, and connecting to the Maas River at its center. Even the air felt moist, caressing – or nipping – one's cheeks as it blew in from the North Sea. Fortunately, today the wind and temperatures were mild, but I knew from experience how slicing the wind could be in this flat country.

We booked a room at a hotel on Willemsplein which had been infested by German agents during the war for obvious reasons. The food and accommodations were superb, and its proximity to much of the city's amenities convenient. It was also just a short walk from T's office – the headquarters for British Intelligence during the war. A fact the Germans had been well aware of, just as we had known they were working out of their consul. The war being over and Germany's intelligence agency in shambles, this was no longer a concern.

Sidney tried again to contact Agent Charlaix with the French *Section de Centralisation du*

Renseignement. When he'd telephoned the Amiens gendarmerie the previous afternoon, he'd been directed to call the central office in Paris. They had taken a message and promised to pass it along to Charlaix. Sidney's second attempt yielded no better results, but he did learn that Charlaix had received his first message, and so should receive his second informing him where he could contact us.

'T is likely waiting for us,' I informed Sidney when he returned from the lobby. I had changed into a honey brown dress and red picture hat, and freshened my appearance. I glanced at the ormolu clock perched on the room's clothespress. 'Though I don't anticipate him waiting much longer.'

Richard B. Tinsley was a private citizen, after all, and one with ample means and powerful friends. As such, C had to tread carefully where he was concerned. A former merchant marine officer, T was managing director of the Uranium Steamboat Company. He'd had a working relationship with C before the war, but when hostilities had broken out and all of his company's ships were confiscated by the British government for troop transport, he'd agreed to head and house British Intelligence's central office in Holland.

Under T's able leadership, the Rotterdam office had quickly became the Secret Service's largest and most important network. Thanks to his shrewd handling of the Dutch authorities, and the collaborative relationships he'd developed with men like François van 't Sant with GS III (Dutch Intelligence), we rarely experienced problems with the various branches of the Dutch police, and when we did, T went to battle for us, whether the interference came from Holland, the Belgian authorities, or our own British War Office.

I had not often interacted with T during my time in Holland as a field agent, reporting to Captain Henry Landau instead. In truth, I had not spent much time inside the large building on the Boompjes which comprised our head-quarters. Since I was moving in and out of occupied Belgium, my identity and likeness needed to remain unknown to the Germans, who rigidly monitored our HQ. Instead, upon my arrival in Rotterdam, I would telephone the number given to me and be directed via code to one of our various safehouses, where I would receive my instructions or relay the intelligence I'd gathered to Landau.

However, I had gotten to know T rather well during my time working as an analyst and secretary for C. I'd read and collated T's reports, and even taken notes during the few times he and C had spoken directly. So, I was well aware of what to expect from the man.

The fellow guarding the entrance to T's building was unknown to me, but he'd evidently been awaiting our arrival. He ushered us inside and up to the first floor. T's office occupied nearly the entire level, and we arrived to find him standing next to one of the windows looking out over the water where the sun was beginning to set. He was a short man with broad shoulders. His ruddy complexion and wide stance I attributed to his time as a ship's officer, and his small piercing eyes to his tendency to cut straight to the heart of a matter.

When he turned to see me, a look of what I was flattered to think was pleasure flashed in his eyes. 'Mrs Kent, I trust your journey was uneventful.' One corner of his mouth curled at this feeble jest, a reminder of the danger every ship had faced when sailing the northern seas during the war.

'Yes,' I replied. 'We shall all have to grow accustomed to the tedium of such a crossing once again.'

He offered Sidney his hand. 'And you must be Mr Kent. Heard about your Victoria Cross. Good show.' Before my husband could reply, he turned to address me again. 'You might have passed Miss McNeill in the street. She was rather sorry to have missed you.'

During the war, Eileen McNeill had typed the espionage reports from agents behind enemy lines, including mine.

'I'll have to stop in just to see her,' I said, envisioning her wide grin and riotously curly hair. 'Does she still have a fondness for *stroopwafels*?' Something all of Holland seemed to share, though many had to go without this sweet treat when food shortages gripped the country late in the war.

'But of course,' he replied, his steps moving toward his desk on the other side of the room.

'Then I'll have to bring her one.'

A pair of deep leather chairs more suited to a man of Sidney's height were positioned before T's bureau plat desk decorated to imitate red and gold Chinese lacquer. On my first visit to his office, I'd deduced that T was a man of eclectic, but highly selective taste. He cared less for the overall appearance of a space than for specific pieces. The result of which was a higgledy-piggledy jumble of old and new, expensive and cheap, exquisite and dowdy. Such as his writing desk and these armchairs.

'Now,' he declared, folding his hands before him. 'As usual, I suspect C has told you the bare minimum.'

I arranged the pillows at my back so that I wouldn't sink too deeply into the chair cushions. 'You know him well.'

He offered me a private little smile. 'I do. Then, I suspect you may at least know that the matter involves the murder of one of our informants – a promising young lawyer and Belgian refugee named Jacques Offerman. These are the facts I've been able to glean from my contacts with the police,' he began, and then laid the details out for us.

On the Saturday evening in question, Offerman had boarded the express train at Amsterdam Central Station at 7:15 p.m., bound for the

Hague. His birthday was the following day, and he was going to spend it with his parents, as he typically did. At 8:36 p.m., the porter opened the door of the first-class compartment for a woman boarding at the Hollandsche Spoor station to discover a body lying on the ground covered by a coat. The porter thought the passenger was drunk, and so warned the conductor and the substation chief. But when they attempted to rouse the man, they discovered blood pouring from multiple wounds and two copper shell casings on the floor. No gun was found. The body was removed from the compartment and the train continued on its route. It was not examined further until several hours later when it was stored at the depot in Rotterdam.

A doctor was called in to examine the body at the Rijswijkschen Road police station and discovered three gunshot wounds – one each to the chest, left forearm, and under the collarbone. The nature and angle of these injuries, in addition to the gun not being found, definitively ruled out any possibility of suicide. The man's wallet containing ten guilders was found on the body, but his identification papers were missing. Though fortunately a number of business cards tucked into a pocket of the wallet helped to reveal his identity as Jacques Offerman. A fact his parents later confirmed. Meanwhile, the police in Rotterdam examined the train compartment again and found the third shell casing, as well as a crumpled paper bag from a sandwich store with a single piece of shrimp in it.

'The conductor and substation chief missed a crumpled paper bag?' I asked doubtfully, unclear how such a thing could be overlooked in their initial inspection of the compartment as they removed the body.

T's cynical expression told me he'd had the same question. 'They claimed they were in a hurry.'

'The Dutch do like their trains to be punctual,' Sidney quipped dryly.

'Upon questioning the conductor at the Amsterdam station where Offerman boarded, they discovered two other passengers had been seated in the first-class compartment with him. The first was a lady in her midtwenties, who disembarked at Haarlem, and the second a man, who has become the focus of the police's inquiry. The woman – a nurse – came forward as soon as she saw the notice in the newspapers and described the other passenger as being a man of substantial stature with dark blond hair and a thick mustache, wearing a gabardine raincoat and a limp, brown hat with a round dent in it.'

'Quite specific,' I remarked.

T nodded once. 'We shall come to that.'

Exactly what that meant, I didn't know, but it evidently wasn't good.

'She said that the man settled down to sleep, with no luggage of any kind, while Offerman sat in his corner of the compartment reading. She

186

says they were both engaged in the same activities when she got off the train.'

'Then given her statement, the police must believe the murder happened between Haarlem, where the nurse disembarked, and Hollandsche Spoor, where the body was found,' I deduced.

'The police have narrowed it down even further, for a woman came forward claiming she saw two men struggling on the train at Leiden.'

'While it was stopped at the station? Then why didn't she say—'

He shook his head, cutting me off.

It took me a moment to realize what he was refuting. 'She saw them while the train was passing? How could she be certain of such a thing?'

He arched his eyebrows. 'I wondered the same. But the police appear to take her seriously.' He shrugged one shoulder. 'Of course, they've also been chasing down any number of other ridiculous stories. The murder has caused quite the sensation here in Holland, given it happened in the first-class compartment of a moving train, and the perpetrator seems to have vanished into thin air. 'Twas the lead story in all the newspapers for the past fortnight, and updates on the investigation progress are still posted daily. So, the police have been inundated with tips from Spiritualist mediums claiming to have received messages from the deceased.' T's voice dripped with scorn. 'As well as a number of well-meaning members of the public who've placed significance on the most trivial of details they noticed about fellow passengers. People dashing to catch their trains. Men without a hat.' He leaned into this last pronouncement.

I frowned in confusion. 'Had they found a hat they believed the killer had left behind?'

'No, but one traveler from Delft claimed he'd seen a man jump out of the train bareheaded and run for the exit, which the newspapers widely reported on. As a result, the police have been inundated with tips about just such a man, as well as various hats purportedly found near train stations.' He shook his head before drawling, 'Apparently the number of men who lose their hat in Holland is quite astonishing.'

'And let me guess, none of the hats turned in match that distinctive description given by the nurse?'

'None that I'm aware of. In any case, a musician came forward to say he'd been the man seen hatless running to catch his next train on the evening of the incident. That he'd tucked his hat under his arm along with his violin. So that line of inquiry is closed.'

T leaned forward, clasping his hands on his desk. 'The point is, in addition to their own fumbling, the police have also been forced to chase down a spate of false starts. It's no wonder they haven't made much headway in solving the murder – especially not knowing what we do.'

I glanced at Sidney. 'Yes, C mentioned that Offerman was one of our own.'

'He was a crucial informant. One we *don't* want the Dutch government finding out about or we'll have a serious headache on our hands. Both from the Dutch and Thomson.' The way T said his name, with a snide curl to his lips, told me he was no greater a fan of the Director of Intelligence than C. 'Hence your presence.' He pressed his finger to the felt surface of the desk. 'The night he was murdered, Offerman was transporting documents from an investigation he'd been conducting on our behalf to the Hague to be handed off. But when his body was found, not only were his identification papers missing, but the red leather portfolio he'd been carrying with him was empty. The documents it had contained were gone.'

I straightened at these words, wondering why they sounded so familiar. Both men turned to me in interest.

'You've thought of something,' T said.

'No. Maybe.' I turned to Sidney, curious whether he'd noted anything in particular either, but he gazed back at me unruffled. 'I don't know,' I exhaled.

T continued to stare at me as if expecting me to continue, but I truly didn't know what to say.

'Did the police fingerprint the compartment?' Sidney asked, drawing his attention.

'No. Too many sets of prints. And the nurse claimed the other man was wearing gloves, so it was unlikely to do them any good anyway.' He swiped his hand to the side. 'Any further questions you have about the murder investigation you can ask the police yourselves. I've used my influence with Van 't Sant and Chief Commissioner Versteeg to gain access to the investigation.'

Van 't Sant had been T's main contact with Dutch Intelligence at GS III during the war and had continued to be an ally despite his appointment to Chief of Police at Utrecht. There were long-held rumors that the man was aiming for a position of even greater power, namely Versteeg's current job as chief commissioner of the Hague, and given his connections with the royal family he would probably get it.

'You have a meeting with Inspector Van de Pol tomorrow morning,' T explained, giving us directions to the location before cautioning us. 'Be forewarned. I had to imply that an acquaintance of yours met a similar fate a few years back and you were curious about any similarities between the cases. That when a war hero and heir to a marquessate like Sidney Kent requests something, you find a way to accommodate them.'

'Then I trust we'll find this Inspector Van de Pol in an extremely cooperative state of mind,' Sidney drawled sarcastically.

This brought a brief smile to T's face. 'Quite right.'

'What of your initial contact?' I asked. 'C said you'd had a man on the ground, but there were complications. Is there anything he can share with us?'

T scowled. 'It's doubtful. The fellow was a policeman, and he was initially assigned to the investigation.' His voice hardened. 'But then he got himself suspended for drunk and disorderliness. So, I'm not sure anything he could tell you should be trusted.'

It was clear how displeased he was by this turn of events. After all, having a man on the inside, as it were, of the investigation was ideal. Even with T exerting his influence, as outsiders there was only so much the Dutch police would share with us. And only so much of our interference they would allow.

'Now.' He sat forward as if to rise. 'What I need to relay to you is the pertinent details of the investigation Offerman was undertaking for us. That of the *Renate Leonhardt*. But first . . .' He pushed to his feet. 'Dinner, I think.'

CHAPTER FOURTEEN

As if on cue, the door to T's office opened and a pair of men entered carrying a table, which they set before the massive hearth surrounded by sculpted marble with ornamental flourishes. A hundred years prior, the Boompjes had been the noblest street in the city, lined with the opulent residences of its wealthiest citizens. But throughout the nineteenth century the street had seen a shift to more commercial use as the ease and speed of transport allowed the elite to retreat permanently to their country houses on the outskirts of the city. I suspected this fireplace was a holdover from that earlier time.

In short order, the table was joined by chairs, and then plates, cutlery, and a meal of thick beef steaks covered in rich gravy, *zuurkoolstampot* – a sauerkraut and potato mash – and *kapucijnerschotel* – Dutch peas with apples and bacon. The latter two dishes were traditional Dutch fare, but the steaks were certainly a nod to T's Britishness. T had never been a man to do things by halves.

One of the men finished by lighting a fire in the hearth before they both slipped away, and we took our seats at the table. Parched, i lifted my glass to take an experimental sip, finding it filled with a fragrant genever-based punch, heavy on the genever – a dutch spirit similar to gin, as it was flavored with juniper berries, but instead distilled from malt wine and various botanicals. While i wasn't one to turn down a good gin punch, i recognized i would need to pace myself while imbibing this concoction, or i would wind up under the table.

sometime later, with our stomachs pleasantly full and our bodies warmed with genever, T returned to the matter at hand. 'The *Renate Leonhardt*,' he declared by way of transition after popping one last date into his mouth from the plate of fruit and Reypenaer cheese – a crumbly aged Gouda – which had been served as dessert, 'was a German ship which was torpedoed by one of our destroyers and sank off the coast of Den Helder in August 1917.' He raised a finger. 'But first, it was part of a rather notorious event a month earlier at Bergen aan Zee.'

I set my cup down and pushed it out of reach as my head was beginning to feel a bit muzzy. 'I remember that. The British shelled a convoy of ships in the German merchant navy loaded with coal en route to Sweden. Four ships were captured, four escaped, and two were wrecked on the Dutch coast in order to evade apprehension. But what created an international incident were the English shells that landed inland at Bergen and Warmenhuizen.'

T nodded. 'The episode caused a bit of a diplomatic crisis between Britain and the Netherlands. We'd attacked inside Dutch coastal waters and damaged a few buildings and killed some cows. Not to mention the Dutch lives lost on the two ships who wrecked rather than being captured, but they knew what they were getting into by joining a German crew and trying to transport supplies to our enemy during wartime.' He tipped his glass back, emptying it before continuing. 'It took a great deal of money and finesse to smooth that one over.'

'Then I take it that the *Renate Leonhardt* was one of the two ships which were wrecked,' Sidney surmised, having turned in his chair so that one elbow was propped along its back.

'It was taken to Amsterdam to be repaired. Then it was towed out past IJmuiden, where it set sail, steaming north again, close to the coast, and ran into a sandbar at the Schulpengat near Den Helder.'

My eyes widened. First a shelling and subsequent beaching, and then running into a sandbar? One would have thought the crew would have had second thoughts about the fortunes of sailing on such a vessel.

'The tugboats pulled the ship free at high tide and they set off again, only to be torpedoed almost the moment they exited territorial waters.' He leaned forward intently. 'I tell you all this to explain the amount of time that passed between leaving Dutch coastal waters and another incident which occurred in IJmuiden two days before. Some of the crew from the *Leonhardt* died, but others were rescued by the Dutch navy. One of them was a stoker who claimed that, in the night hours before the ship departed from IJmuiden, several small boxes were brought on board by the ship's officers and hidden under a quantity of cocoa butter. The crew was told not to interfere, but the stoker said he'd seen inside one of the boxes, and that it was filled to the brim with gold.'

My gaze met Sidney's across the table, curious what he'd thought of this tale.

'Was the stoker another of your informants?' he asked.

T sat back. 'No, but we had another man on site who heard as much from him and was also able to corroborate the information through another source. He transmitted the intelligence to us, and we were able to convey it to the Royal Navy so that they were in place at the right moment to intercept.' He reached into his coat pocket to remove his cigarette case. 'We couldn't know for certain it was true, of course, but we certainly weren't going to allow the ship to slip by on the chance that it might be.' After extracting a fag for himself, he offered one to me and then Sidney, but we both declined.

'Then that was what Offerman was investigating?' I replied. 'The veracity of these claims?'

T inhaled a drag of his cigarette and nodded.

'As you can imagine, the stoker's story has captured the public's attention, especially now that the war is over and one is no longer in danger of being blown sky-high by a torpedo or a mine. Supposedly there was fifty-five million guilders in gold loaded onto the *Leonhardt*.'

Sidney gave a low whistle at the amount.

'And now it's sitting at the bottom of the North Sea, ripe for the plucking. If one can find it. The currents along that part of the coast are ferocious, and always shifting and moving the sand about. What was visible of the wreck for a short time has long since disappeared under the waves and the sand. It would be quite the undertaking to recover it.'

'But perhaps worth it if the amount of gold reported to be there actually *is* sitting at the bottom of the sea,' Sidney remarked, crossing his arms over his chest. The challenge had made an impression on him. I could see the wheels turning in his head as he tried to work out the best way to go about such an undertaking. Such a quandary would be irresistible to him.

'Yes. As long as someone else isn't likely to swoop in and attempt to claim it.'

'So Offerman wasn't just trying to ascertain if the gold was real, but also where it had come from,' I said, holding myself very still, lest the room begin to spin from the genever punch.

T tipped his cigarette toward me. 'Precisely.'

'What's the prevailing theory?' my husband

asked, though his eyes remained on me. Clearly, he'd taken some note of my partially pickled state.

T sighed. 'That the gold was the Kaiser's. That he feared Germany's imminent defeat, and so with the Dutch royal family's assistance planned to transfer part of the German gold stock to Sweden.'

I supposed this made some sense. After all, the war had not been going well for either side of the conflict in the summer of 1917. And everyone had known that Holland's beloved Queen Wilhelmina, while ostensibly remaining neutral like her country, actually favored Germany. Her husband was German-born, after all, and she'd granted asylum to the Kaiser himself just days before the Armistice was signed, and denied all subsequent demands made by the Allies that he be handed over to be tried for his war crimes. Though, truth be told, none of the Allied countries truly wanted her to relent. Not when prosecuting and executing the former emperor would create a dangerous precedent they weren't certain they wanted to make.

'Another theory is that the gold was stolen from the occupied countries,' T said.

Which would bring a swarm of claims from Belgium, France, and even Luxembourg – both from their governments and private citizens.

'Those are the two most widespread and credible hypotheses, and Offerman was using sources both from inside Germany and within the Hague to uncover what he could.'

'Sources who, in addition to Offerman, you don't wish to come to light,' I summarized.

He stubbed out his cigarette in the gravy drippings on his plate. 'Precisely.'

But Sidney seemed to be contemplating another matter as he picked up his glass to take another drink. 'Why would the Germans risk such a thing when they knew we were patrolling so heavily off the Dutch coast? Wouldn't it have been smarter to take the gold across land to the Baltic coast, and then across the sea to Sweden? It would be a shorter sea crossing.'

T interlaced his fingers over his stomach. 'I have no answer to that except that perhaps the Germans gambled that, after the Bergen Incident, we would be more hesitant to attack merchant ships, and so the *Renate Leonhardt* was likely to continue the remainder of her voyage unmolested.' He shrugged. 'I'm afraid that's all I can tell you. Offerman didn't share the names of his contacts with us, though I would wager they were included in that portfolio. Now, do you have any questions for me?'

My thoughts snagged on that word again. Portfolio. Who had I recently heard mention one? Was it even relevant?

I looked up as Sidney spoke, his eyes once again watching me closely. 'How can we be certain these papers haven't already passed into government hands or out of the country entirely?'

'We can't,' T admitted. 'Though it's a good bet they haven't, or else I would have at least heard whisperings about it, if not outright accusations. However, rumors *have* begun to circulate that the missing papers had something to do with the *Renate Leonhardt*. With her location and contents. We can only speculate these were started by whoever took the papers in the first place in hopes they would stir up interest. Perhaps in preparation of whatever their next step will be. We would prefer to find them before whatever that next step is takes place.'

He pushed back from the table, signaling our meeting was at an end. 'Where are you staying?'

'The Maas Hotel,' I replied.

He grinned and shook his head. 'Landau. He's the one who recommended it to you, isn't he?' he asked, but then continued to speak before I could answer. 'Did I ever tell you how the green lad stayed there on his first night in Holland? He'd had no idea the place was practically swarming with German agents. Nearly mucked up his first assignment before it was even begun.'

I smiled politely, having heard Captain Landau tell the story himself multiple times, and with much more charm.

'Then I'll know where to contact you.' T shook Sidney's hand before taking hold of mine, patting the back of it with his other. 'Keep me apprised of what you uncover.'

I assured him we would before accepting Sidney's arm to steady me as we exited. Without it, I'm not certain I could have walked straight.

'That gin has gone straight to your head,' he remarked in concern as we made our way down the stairs.

'It has,' I admitted. 'Though I don't recall genever having such an effect on me before. Not after only two glasses.' I sighed, having to focus rather hard on putting one foot in front of the other. 'Wait, I take that back. It happened once. After I returned from an assignment. I was dog tired, and after writing my report and answering Landau's questions he offered me a drink. Thought it would help calm my nerves. But it went straight to my head. Just like now.' I could hear that I was rambling, perhaps even slurring my words, but Sidney didn't try to stop me. 'We were at one of our safehouses, not far from Landau's place on the Heemraadssingel, and when he saw how corked I was, he decided he'd better risk taking me back to his rooms. Nothing happened.' I raised my head to clarify, fearing he would presume otherwise given the fact that I'd slept with another colleague – Alec Xavier – in a different safehouse after helping him escape Belgium during the months when I'd believed Sidney was dead.

'I didn't think anything had,' my husband replied calmly, guiding me through the door and out into the street. Lamplight illuminated the brick street and reflected off the dark water, streaming golden trails over the rippling surface.

'Landau was a complete gentleman,' I assured him. 'He just didn't think I should be left unattended in such a state in the safehouse.' I broke off as something occurred to me. 'Safehouse. Safe house,' I repeated. 'Safe as houses.'

'Verity . . .'

I gasped, nearly falling over as I whirled to face him when the heel of my shoe caught in a crevice between the bricks. 'Sidney, I remember what I couldn't remember. The red leather portfolio! That was one of the things Miss Baverel mentioned when she talked about how she'd hidden the proof. The portfolio was part of her list of things the police had supposedly taken from her house.'

His face transformed in recognition and then misgiving as his hands clasped my arms to steady me. 'And she specified a red leather portfolio, didn't she?'

An object that, while not exactly unusual, was certainly not common.

'Surely that can't be a coincidence? It would simply be too . . . bizarre.'

I tried to recall the other items in her list – paintings, sofa cushions, and figurines. Those were all rather generic descriptions, and yet she'd been specific about the portfolio.

'Yes, but she said the police had seized it,' he pointed out, turning our steps once again toward our hotel. 'While Offerman's portfolio was left with his body. Only the contents were taken. So they couldn't be one and the same.'

I breathed in the damp air deeply, trying to clear the fog from my brain. 'But I don't think she meant to imply that she had it. I think she merely meant to draw attention to it. And do so in a way that wouldn't immediately rouse Charlaix's interest while he was listening in the closet behind us, or that of the gendarmerie.'

Sidney's brow furrowed as he considered this. 'It's possible,' he granted, though he sounded far from convinced. 'But if so, that would mean our two investigations are connected. That . . .' He seemed to balk at stating his next thought, so I finished it for him.

'That Miss Baverel had something to do with Offerman's death and the theft of those papers. That perhaps that was the reason for the trip she and Lieutenant Smith took some weeks ago. The one Miss Lemaire alluded to. The timing would be about right.'

I fell silent, allowing Sidney to brood on these things for a short time, waiting for him to speak. Our footsteps sounded overloud in the stillness of the evening, each clack and crackle of dirt underfoot audible. A ferry plied silently past on the river, headed downstream toward the Hook, where the waterways flowed northwest from Rotterdam to meet the North Sea.

'We can't make any assumptions on such slim proof,' he finally replied.

'Of course not,' I agreed. 'But we also can't dismiss the possibility. After all, it seems certain that Miss Baverel and Lieutenant James Smith had some sort of relationship. And if she saw him less than a month ago, then he easily could have told her what he knew about me, about my past and present association with the Secret Service. She might have assumed I would be asked to investigate Offerman's death, or that I would at least hear about some of the details of the case – namely that red leather portfolio.' I pressed in closer to his side, tightening my arm where it draped around his back. 'None of that is a stretch of the imagination.'

His arm wrapped around me and pulled me nearer as well. 'No, it's not.' His jaw set. 'All right, then. We'll keep an open mind. After all, if the papers taken from Offerman's portfolio include proof of his and other Dutch citizens' involvement with British Intelligence – information that could harm C and the foreign intelligence division's autonomy – then that seems like something Lord Ardmore would want to get his hands on.'

I nodded in agreement, but then frowned. 'Except, if Ardmore's men were behind the murder and robbery, then wouldn't he already have the papers? After all, it occurred three weeks ago. What would have stopped his men from taking the papers to him then?'

'What's to say they haven't?' Sidney's eyebrows

arched. 'You know as well as I do that Ardmore likes to toy with his victims. Maybe he already has the papers and is simply waiting for the right time to reveal them.'

'And getting a good laugh at watching all of us scramble to retrieve them.' I scowled. 'Yes, that does sound like him.' My eyes narrowed into the distance. 'But then why was Lieutenant Smith shooting at us? And why was Willoughby sniffing about Miss Baverel's friends and former residences?' I turned to look up at him. 'I know he claimed Miss Baverel's asking for you was all a ruse to get us out of England. That he was there to flaunt it in our faces. But something isn't adding up.'

Ardmore didn't do anything without a reason. While it was true he enjoyed playing with his victims, he also didn't take unnecessary risks. Sending Willoughby to France certainly seemed like that. Why not leave us chasing our tails a little longer, then drop a hint of what he'd done after we returned to London? That was much more his style. And if he was the one to deliver the suggestion, all the better, because then he got to watch my reaction.

'Then maybe they're not related.' Sidney guided me around a puddle. 'Maybe Ardmore has nothing to do with Offerman's death and we're simply grasping at straws. We won't know until we have more information.'

'Well, we have our meeting with Inspector Van

de Pol tomorrow, and then I'd like to speak with this nurse who shared the carriage with Offerman and the unknown man.'

'I'd also like to speak to the porter and the conductor. I know the police are focused on this unidentified man, but I can't help but wonder about these railway workers. After all, a train is their natural habitat. They pass through the carriages all but unnoticed because passengers expect them to be there.'

'That's a good point.'

'The second man could have left the train soon after the woman. We only have the porter's and conductor's word for it that they don't know where or when he departed. They might be lying because they slipped into the compartment to kill Offerman and then slipped out again without raising anyone's suspicions.'

'A definite possibility.' I lifted my finger. 'We should also gather up what newspapers we can. Sometimes newspapermen have surprisingly useful insights. Specifically, I'd like to know how swiftly the rumor began that Offerman's missing papers were about the *Renate Leonhardt*.'

Sidney waited until another couple passed us with a nod before replying. 'You think someone else knew about the papers and believed they would lead them to the gold wreck.'

'Maybe. Although, it doesn't seem to be any great secret where the wreck is located. At least, in a general sense. The trick seems to be getting to it. But the timing of when those rumors began might reveal something nonetheless.'

We paused before the bridge spanning the Leuvehaven canal. Some of the city's canals were spanned by immense – but nonetheless attractive – drawbridges, while those bridges that were most frequently crossed were more permanent, boasting but a three-foot-wide plank opening on hinges at the center through which the masts of vessels fitted with sails could pass through. This bridge was a type of the latter construction.

I leaned against the railing and turned to gaze south across the New Maas at the massive Holland America building lit with lights and crowned by a green copper roof. The scaffolding surrounding it suggested it was being expanded once again, and no wonder. As much as ever, people were clambering to escape the devastation wrought by four years of want and war and cross the ocean to America in search of a better life.

Had the killer also been searching for a better life, thinking that if he had the documents in Offerman's portfolio about the gold wreck he might be able to alter his fate? If so, he might have come from anywhere in Europe. Thus far we hadn't heard anyone claim they'd heard the mystery man speak. He might have been Belgian, or Polish, or even German. T had said some of Offerman's contacts were German.

'I'm going to write to Captain Landau,' I said. 'You might recall I told you he's stationed in

Berlin.' In thanks for his service during the war, C had given him one of the more plum assignments after he'd helped liquidate our intelligence assets in Belgium and seen those who deserved compensation paid and sometimes decorated. In Berlin, Landau now ostensibly worked as a passport control officer for the diplomatic service, which provided him both a cover and diplomatic immunity. But that wasn't all he did.

'I'm curious whether he ever worked with Offerman when he was stationed here in Rotterdam,' I explained. Landau was more likely than T to have interacted with the lawyer directly. 'But I'm most interested in whether Landau had contact with Offerman recently. If Offerman visited any of his contacts in Germany, Landau might know who they are.'

'If we could find out exactly what was in Offerman's report, it might change our perception of who our suspects should be. After all, rumors begun after the fact aren't always accurate. We need to know who was aware of Offerman's report and its contents *before* he was killed.'

I sighed, leaning into him. 'Then it sounds like we have a plan, and our work cut out for us.'

'Yes, but it'll keep until tomorrow,' he murmured, tipping my face upward so that he could see into my eyes. 'You're feeling steadier?'

'I suspect the air helped,' I replied, asserting my prerogative as his wife to remain firmly in his arms rather than stepping back to stand on my own two feet. 'Though it would probably be best if I avoided imbibing any more genever punch from here out.'

'Or at least any served by T.'

'But this is nice,' I remarked, snuggling closer, grateful for the warmth of Sidney's body as the breeze off the water picked up, nipping my flushed cheeks.

His features softened. 'It is.' Then a roguish glint lit his eyes. 'There's only one thing I can think of that would make it nicer,' he murmured before his mouth met mine. My husband had always been an excellent kisser, and this evening's demonstration of his skill did not disappoint. I didn't know whether it was the genever punch, or his effect on me – maybe a combination of both – but when he pulled back it took some time for the world to settle right side up again.

'You're right,' I finally managed to reply. 'That *was* nicer.'

'Then perhaps we should take that nicer out of this cold breeze and back to our hotel.'

'Hmmm,' I hummed in response, allowing him to guide me toward the bridge.

It was only several steps later that I turned to look at the far shore and saw a man watching us. From this distance in the darkness, I had no hope of seeing his face, especially not with his collar up and his hat pulled low, but there was no doubt in my mind he'd been observing us. The realization sent a jolt down my spine.

However, when I looked for him again, seconds later, after we'd passed another couple, he was no longer there. Tugging Sidney's arm, I moved closer to the railing to see if he'd somehow passed beneath the bridge, but the embankment was empty.

CHAPTER FIFTEEN

T he following morning, we took the train to the Hague and presented ourselves at the Rijswijkschen Road police station at the time arranged. However, from the manner in which we were left waiting in an interview room for almost an hour, it was clear just how cooperative Inspector Van de Pol intended to be. There could have been a break in the investigation, an urgent matter that needed to be handled, and I might have given him the benefit of the doubt that this was the case, had he not been speaking to his colleague when he opened the door.

'Yes, give me five minutes with these British busybodies and I'll meet you at the Peacock,' he declared in Dutch. At least, that was the rough equivalent. He evidently wasn't expecting either of us to speak the language.

I schooled my features so as not to give away his blunder until I wished to do so, but from the manner in which Sidney glanced my way it must have been evident, at least to him, that whatever the policeman had said, it was not complimentary.

The inspector was a fair man, with hair the color

of winter wheat turning gray at the temples and skin so pale one could see the veins through it. His browbone was pronounced, making his blue-gray eyes appear more sunken than they really were, and his lips were thin, and made all the thinner by the barely restrained annoyance stamped across his features as he offered Sidney his hand before sinking into the chair across the table.

'Mr and Mrs Kent,' he declared flatly in English. 'I understand you have questions for me about our investigation into Jacques Offerman's death.'

'Thank you for seeing us,' Sidney replied. 'We understand you must be a very busy man.' There was a subtle edge to his voice, one that the ear couldn't help but pick up on, and yet was unclear whether it was meant in scolding, especially when his expression remained so pleasant.

In response, the inspector's gaze sharpened, searching his face, though he couldn't defend himself without sounding churlish.

In any case, we had a part to play, and Sidney adjusted his approach accordingly. 'We've already reviewed most of the particulars of your case. We simply wish to clarify a few details.'

This wasn't a lie. Besides the briefing we'd received from T the previous evening, we'd spent much of the morning reading every newspaper and magazine we could lay our hands on – from Rotterdam, the Hague, and Amsterdam – in an effort to bone up on all the developments in the investigation. Much of the reports merely rehashed the facts already known, but some of them made some pertinent discoveries or posited interesting suppositions of their own. Then there were the salacious rumors, which while unproven still might hold a whiff of truth to them.

'We understand that one motive for the crime you're considering involves his work as a lawyer. That he was killed either out of revenge or anger, perhaps by a disgruntled client or the losing party of a dispute. But you seem to have ruled out that possibility.' Sidney's voice lifted at the end, even though his statement wasn't really a question.

'Yes, it seems unlikely,' Inspector Van de Pol supplied blandly.

'Then you don't believe the papers taken from his portfolio were work related?'

'They may have been, but as far as his employer knew, he wasn't working on anything worth killing for.'

'His employer . . . that would be Mr Van Grych?' Sidney clarified, deliberately lulling the inspector into a stupor. We'd discovered that Offerman had left the ministry where he'd been employed during the war to work for a private firm in Amsterdam.

Van de Pol pulled his watch from his pocket. 'Yes.'

'What of the possibility that the papers were personal in nature? Love letters, perhaps. From a work-related affair or another individual.'

This captured Van de Pol's attention, for he lifted his eyes to scrutinize Sidney, his lips pursing again.

212

Sidney leaned into that displeasure. 'Pieces of correspondence that an individual might fear being made public.'

'You've been reading the papers, I see,' the inspector derided. 'The scandal rags, isn't that what you call them? Rumor mills?'

'That doesn't mean they're not true. Or parts of them,' Sidney pointed out.

He scowled, but my husband was undaunted. 'We know the police seized his personal correspondence from his home, so if anyone is in a position to know it's you. Are any of the rumors true?'

But Van de Pol was not going to be pressured so easily. 'Was your friend also of that persuasion?'

He was referring to the acquaintance of ours that had supposedly met a similar fate – the reason T had given for our curiosity about Offerman's death.

They stared at each other in rigid silence for several moments before Sidney replied. 'He was single.' Which was, of course, an outright lie, as there was no friend, but it allowed him to let Van de Pol believe whatever he wished.

The inspector hesitated a few more seconds before gruffly relenting. 'There is some indication that Mr Offerman was . . . leading a double life.'

Which was as much of a confirmation as we were likely to get. At least from someone with the police.

The newspapers had buzzed with salacious

rumors about Offerman's private life and his preference for men, most of which I took with a grain
of salt. However, it wasn't enough for the newspapermen that he'd favored men – a fact alone
that condemned him to keep secrets because of
society's views on the matter. They'd also tried to
link him to some rather notorious actors and other
public figures whose activities weren't so harmless.
Thus far, such proof seemed slim, and I found
their efforts to cast aspersion on his character to
be both offensive and obstructive.

To be honest, when I'd first read the papers'
rampant speculations, I was surprised T hadn't
at least mentioned them to us. After all, in order
to find Offerman's killer, we needed to seek out
his connections so we could figure out how the
culprit had learned his habits, his routines. Just
as we needed to rule out other avenues of motive.
C's and T's certainty that Offerman had been
murdered for the documents he carried in his
portfolio didn't make it true. He might have been
slain for another reason, and the contents of the
portfolio taken because the killer believed they
contained personal correspondence, or in an
effort to confuse the authorities.

'Then is it possible a spurned or jealous lover
– or the family member of such a person – was
the killer?' Sidney pressed, reverting to his earlier
question.

'We haven't discarded the possibility,' Van de Pol
admitted begrudgingly. 'But we do not have a

suspect who fits that scenario, nor does it seem like the manner in which someone with such a motive would go about it. It was rather risky to murder him on an enclosed, moving train. Easier to accost him in the street or at his home.'

Sidney and I had wondered about this ourselves. The murder *had* been risky. What if someone on the train had heard the shots and come to investigate? What if someone had seen the perpetrator leaving the compartment? There weren't many places one could hide on a moving train.

'Then if not love letters, what do you think was taken from the portfolio?' Sidney asked, having finally worked around to the question we actually wanted to ask, hoping he would be lulled into being frank with us.

It didn't work. Or not entirely.

'Unlike the newspapers, I'm not about to publicly speculate on such matters.' Van de Pol leaned toward us. 'And before you ask, no, I don't think he possessed documents relating to a gold wreck.' His eyes narrowed. 'Though I could see how it would be in Britain's best interest to make everyone think that the reason they sunk the *Renate Leonhardt* was because it was full of German gold.'

Then the police were leaning toward the idea that the claims of gold on the *Leonhardt* were invented by the British. If that was the case, then they must not have yet stumbled across anything to the contrary. Which meant that if anyone in Offerman's circle of friends and coworkers had known about his investigation, they hadn't shared that with the authorities.

'Now, if that's all . . .' he stated, beginning to rise.

'It's not, actually,' I told him in Dutch.

He blinked down at me.

'The woman who shared the compartment with Mr Offerman. We understand that Miss . . .' I trailed off, hoping he would still be too startled by my grasp of the Dutch language to mind his tongue.

'De Boer,' he obliged, choking on the 'r' as he realized too late what he'd done.

I plowed forward as if I hadn't noticed anything out of the ordinary. 'That she identified one of your suspects as being the other man in the carriage. That she was certain it was him.'

'Yes, we were optimistic for a time that we'd caught the culprit,' he retorted, his face flushed with irritation. 'But the fellow had a solid alibi and multiple witnesses to it. He couldn't have been our man.'

I turned to Sidney, reverting to English. 'Was there anything else?'

The identities of the porter and conductor would be easy enough to discover at the train station, and Offerman's address had been listed in the newspapers, giving us the location of his landlady. A number of his friends had also been listed, as well as his parents. And now that we had the nurse's last name and city of residence, we

216

should be able to track her down with relative ease as well.

Sidney shook his head. 'That about covers it.'

'Thank you for your help,' I told the inspector with perhaps too sweet a smile. 'We certainly don't want to keep you from your friend at the Peacock any longer.'

He glared back at me a moment longer before a smile suddenly cracked one corner of his lips and he shook his head. It was good to see he at least had a sense of humor. 'Where did you learn to speak Dutch like that?'

'From a Dutchman,' I replied cheekily, rising to my feet.

The inspector looked as if he didn't know whether to laugh or be annoyed by such a response. But then he hit a little too close to home. 'During the war?'

Sidney joined us in standing, sliding his hands into the pockets of his trousers. 'Ver's a veritable polyglot. Hears a language once and can just about repeat it verbatim.'

This was an exaggeration, but I appreciated his coming to my rescue, nonetheless.

'It's how I learned Italian,' I admitted. From the mother-in-law of the owner of the music shop nearest to the village where I'd grown up. I'd developed a habit of visiting with her each week following my piano lesson with her daughter, and within a few months we were conversing fluently.

217

French I'd learned from our French tutor, and German from my father and great-aunt.

However, the look in Van de Pol's eyes said he wasn't distracted by this banter. 'Well, good luck with the investigation into your *friend's* death. I do hope if you learn anything pertinent, you'll share it with us. And a word of advice,' he added before turning to go. 'Steer clear of Commissioner Besseling. He's rather . . .' He seemed to search for the right word before settling on 'Territorial.'

Two minutes later we were back out on the street, though when I peered back at the police station it was to find Inspector Van de Pol watching us from the steps.

Sidney followed my gaze, and then scanned the remainder of our surroundings. 'You haven't seen the man you saw watching us on the bridge last night again this morning, have you?'

'No. I told you I would tell you the moment I did,' I answered a bit testily. 'Or at least signal you.'

His reaction last night when I'd told him about the man had been swift and furious. Despite the fact that I'd hardly had time to tell him before the man had disappeared, he continued to harangue me for not speaking up sooner. We'd decided that if the man had truly been following us, it must be Lieutenant Smith, and so were naturally leery of finding ourselves in his crosshairs again.

'Well, pardon me for trying to prevent you from taking another bullet.'

I glowered at him for dragging my misadventure from December into the matter. My shoulder was healing quite well, except for a few aches and pains when I exerted it. 'If we return to Rotterdam in time, I'll stop by to see Eileen and find out if Smith is even in Holland. If he's traveling under his own name, he should be listed on the documents they receive from the Dutch at the border crossings.'

'And if he's not traveling under his name?'

'Then I haven't the foggiest,' I snapped, tugging at his arm. 'Slow down.'

He complied, adjusting his ground-eating stride to one that was more manageable for me, being a foot shorter.

'Where are we off to in such a hurry?'

'The Hollandsche Spoor station to see if we can locate that porter and conductor before the good inspector informs them not to speak with us.'

'He didn't buy that ridiculous tail T concocted for us for longer than a minute, if that,' I agreed.

'I hope T wasn't often charged with devising your covers.'

I snorted. 'Not unless we *wanted* to be caught.'

Sidney turned to me in surprise. 'Did you?'

'Not me.' I looked toward the canal we walked alongside. A trio of boys had set paper boats on its surface and were now watching them race. The wind was stiffer today, though not as slicing as it might have been. 'But there were instances when it was done to test the German Secret

219

Police's resources and methods.' I didn't explain further, and he didn't ask.

'Well, Inspector Van de Pol is undoubtedly aware we're investigating Offerman, though we can only hope he won't figure out exactly why. At least, not before we have those papers in C's hands.' His voice was tight, as it always was whenever we'd been speaking of my service during the war, of the risks I'd run, without his knowledge I was doing so. 'Speed is our greatest ally at the moment.'

'Tomorrow we should take the train to Amsterdam and Haarlem.'

He nodded. 'Fortunately, the newspaper and magazine reports of the police investigation have cleared some avenues of inquiry off our list.'

Like the sandwich bag with its single piece of shrimp. It had been traced back to a restaurant on the Damrak in Amsterdam, and the staff and manager questioned. Their Saturdays were always busy, and they couldn't recall anything more than that they had sold several shrimp rolls to different customers on the day in question. In truth, I wasn't sure the bag wasn't a false trail anyway, as the conductor and substation chief had missed it upon their first search of the carriage before letting it carry on with the express train. The bag could have ended up in the compartment *after* the body was removed.

'And Inspector Van de Pol cleared a few others,' I remarked as we waited at the corner for the traffic to clear. I pulled the roll collar of my coat

220

tighter at my throat against the chill. 'It seems doubtful that Offerman was killed by either a disgruntled client or a spurned lover, despite the allegations being printed in the press.' I lowered my voice as another pedestrian stopped behind us. 'Which makes it all the more likely C is right. He *was* killed for that report.' Tidying those suspicions out of the way allowed us to focus on one theory.

The policeman directing traffic blew his whistle, and those of us waiting to cross prepared to step out into the road. But at that moment, I heard the revving of an engine and held Sidney back as I stared down the road in the direction of the noise to see a black motorcar bearing down on us. Unfortunately, the man next to him was more impatient and stepped out into the road before the policeman had even signaled to us. Sidney reached out to pull the man back by his shoulders just as the motorcar swerved toward us, narrowly missing the man as it roared past to the piercing shrills of the policeman's whistle.

Everyone around us exclaimed in alarm and anger, and even the policeman turned to curse at the swiftly retreating vehicle. I could only stand there visibly shaken, wishing I'd gotten a better look at the driver. It was a man, there was little doubt of that. Or a woman in man's clothing. But beyond that, everything had happened so quickly, I hadn't caught more than a passing glance of a dark coat and hat pulled low.

It was impossible to know for certain, but given

the way the driver had veered toward us, it seemed a safe bet that the motorcar had been aiming for me and Sidney. My husband seemed to think so as well, for as soon as he'd ensured the man was unharmed and nodded to his exclamation of gratitude, he hustled me across the intersection and along the pavement as far from oncoming traffic as possible. Then he diverged onto a narrow lane which led between several buildings. One too small for a vehicle to fit.

'Did you get a good look at the driver?' I asked him now that my heart had slowed, and he was no longer bustling me forward.

He shook his head, his brow lowered thunderously. 'But I know you must be thinking the same thing I am.'

'Smith?'

'He *is* the person most likely to have shot at us at Achicourt.'

'That's true.'

Hearing the reticence in my voice, Sidney turned his glare on me. 'Don't tell me you think there's more than one person trying to kill us?'

'No, you're right. He makes the most sense. It's just . . .' I frowned at the pavement, trying to find the words to express my uncertainty. 'Does this confirm that the two investigations are related?' I looked up at him. 'Or does someone merely want us to think they are?'

Sidney considered this. 'You're thinking of Captain Willoughby.'

I linked my arm through his, holding tight to the strength of his upper arm. 'I don't yet understand his role in all of this, but we *do* know that two days ago he was in Furnes, and that he wasn't being entirely truthful with us.'

'I suppose it's feasible he might have discovered where we were going and followed us,' he conceded. 'But the same could be said of Smith.'

'Maybe. But we haven't actually seen Lieutenant Smith,' I remarked, finally hitting upon the matter that was troubling me. 'Though we *have* had his presence in France and his connection to Miss Baverel confirmed by two separate individuals – Agent Charlaix and Miss Lemaire – and I don't think they were lying.'

'We should also consider Smith's proclivity for committing murder at a removed distance. He's a sniper, for goodness' sakes. *And* he planted that pencil detonator bomb and coolly walked away. Firing at us from a rooftop and attempting to strike us with a motorcar seem to fit his modus operandi.'

'Yes, but his other kills were also carefully planned and executed. That attempt with the motorcar was rather slapdash. And the police will now be looking for that motorcar, so it'll have to be ditched. If the policeman got a better look at his face than we did, they'll be looking for him as well.'

We came upon a black cat perched on the lid of a metal can. He sat watching us intently through slitted yellow eyes. As we passed, he jumped down, padding ahead of us several feet, as if to lead us down the dusty path with weeds sprouting between the cracks in the bricks.

'I'll grant you that,' Sidney replied. 'It wasn't his usual style.' Sidney dipped his head to avoid the low-hanging branch of a thin rowan tree which had taken root against one wall, and then cast me a jaded stare 'But that may only mean he's growing desperate.'

Which was no less dangerous than his planned attacks and left us ever on our guards against the next attempt.

My shoulders squared as the busy thoroughfare came into sight at the end of the lane. Opposite it stood the train station. 'Well, whatever the case, one thing is clear: Someone is trying to harm us, and the best way to figure out who that is and why is by finding out who killed Jacques Offerman and took his papers.'

Sidney agreed. 'Then let's hope this conductor has some answers for us.'

CHAPTER SIXTEEN

Our hopes were rather swiftly dashed. Not because we couldn't locate the conductor, who we managed to intercept ending his shift, though the porter would not be on duty again until the next day. But rather because the conductor had plainly been advised by the police or a representative with the railway not to answer any such questions.

'I cannot help you,' the slight gentleman with a Van Dyck beard repeated in English for the third time as he hurried along the crowded platform while we hastened to keep pace.

'You cannot, or you will not?' Sidney pressed.

The conductor rounded abruptly to face us with a huff, forcing others to go around us. 'I cannot.' But then his eyes narrowed, scrutinizing us from head to toe, taking in our expensive, well-tailored clothing and careful grooming. 'You are not reporters.'

'No.'

His expression turned suspicious. 'Then what could your interest be in this?'

'An acquaintance of ours was killed in similar

circumstances some time ago, and we are trying to determine whether they could have been committed by the same individual,' Sidney explained, sticking to the story T had manufactured, even ridiculous as it sounded.

'Then why aren't the police investigating the link?' the conductor challenged.

'They've dismissed it as unlikely. Rather prematurely, we think.'

It was clear the man didn't know what to make of us, but when he was jostled from behind by a man, he was jolted from his indecision, shaking his head. 'I'm sorry. I cannot help you.'

'But what of the bag from the sandwich shop?' I hastened to say as he turned to go.

He glared at me, bristling like a hedgehog.

I adjusted my words accordingly. 'The newspapers suggest you and your colleague missed it, but I struggle to believe such a thing.'

His proverbial quills lowered, and his eyes seemed to reassess me once again. 'We did not miss it because it was not there,' he stated succinctly. 'I admit we failed to locate the third shell casing, but that is surely more understandable, as it had become wedged between the wall and the floorboard beneath the seat, and we were being pressured by our superiors to remove the body and send the express on before it fell too far behind schedule. Also, we are not policemen, and I can assure you, such a task is not part of my normal duties.'

This man had been affronted by the insinuations made to his intellect, and I strove to reassure him. 'Of course not. It would be the height of folly to expect anyone who has not been specifically trained to do better. I'm sure anyone with a modicum of intelligence has the wit to see that.'

'Oh, well, yes.' He tugged down on his coat. 'I would like to think so.'

'How do *you* think the sandwich bag came to be in the compartment?'

'It must have happened after the carriage was uncoupled at Rotterdam station, for it certainly did not happen on my watch. Not that I'm saying it was done intentionally,' he hastened to say. 'But not everyone is as conscientious these days.' He looked to the left and then the right, as if thinking of someone in particular. 'These young men returning from service.' He shook his head. 'Got used to dawdling on the job.'

My gaze shifted to Sidney in concern, but he seemed to take this comment in stride.

It was easy to forget that even though they had not taken part in the war as a belligerent, in order to maintain their neutrality, the Dutch had still been forced to field a substantial standing army relative to the size of their country. Dutch troops had been stationed near every border, including along the sea, to act as a deterrent and to prevent the incursion of any of the warring factions. They'd also positioned a large portion of troops behind the carefully prepared inundations dubbed

'Fortress Holland.' These engineering works could be flooded in the event of an invasion, creating a formidable barrier between the heart of the country, including the major cities, and any encroaching force. However, unlike the warring nations, the Dutch army had suffered from boredom and a decided lack of support from its populace over the necessity and cost of maintaining such a large military.

'Do you think that's how the mystery man slipped out unseen?' I asked. 'Someone dawdling?'

But this question seemed to cause him great discomfort. 'There are a number of ways he could have slipped past. He . . . he might have jumped the platform and already had a return ticket to Amsterdam. It's even conceivable that he might have jumped out between stations when the train was slowing or picking up speed.' Both such scenarios had been mentioned in the press. The conductor began to back away. 'No, I . . . I really cannot say more than that. I cannot. Though I'm sorry for your friend.'

Then before we could detain him further, he hurried away, leaving us standing like a stone in the midst of a great stream as the crowds flowed around us.

'Why did my mentioning the unknown third passenger discomfort him?' I queried aloud softly as we watched him weave between bodies before disappearing from sight.

'Perhaps he's not as ignorant of who the man

may be as he'd like us to believe,' Sidney postulated with his hands tucked into the pockets of his black wool coat.

I was wondering the same thing. 'He knows something he isn't telling us,' I concurred.

He turned to me with a teasing smile. 'Though he told us much more than he intended to.' He glanced back in the direction the conductor had gone. 'Next time, I suggest we visit him at his home.' I didn't ask how he intended to find out where he lived, for the typist he'd spoken to in the station office had seemed highly susceptible to tall, dark, handsome men. She'd told him everything he'd asked her, and obviously wished he'd ask her more.

'He might be more willing to talk if he was certain he wouldn't be overheard.' Sidney's eyes twinkled. 'And I'll let you be the one to do the charming.'

I rolled my eyes. 'He simply didn't want to be thought of as being stupid.'

'Something you realized much quicker than I. Hence, the charm.'

I arched my eyebrows. 'Because I tell people what they want to hear?'

He leaned closer. 'No, because you treat people how they wish to be treated.' His deep blue eyes peered into mine. 'You see to the heart of them, to the heart of how they want to be seen, even when that conflicts with who they truly are.'

I realized he was including himself in that

statement, and the earnestness in his voice and in the shimmering depths of his eyes made my heart twist. But how exactly did I see him that he didn't believe he truly was? I searched his face, but there was no easy answer waiting there for me. Only chariness and uncertainty – two emotions I was unaccustomed to associating with my strong, steadfast husband.

'Sometimes . . .' I admitted for the sake of honesty because he wasn't wrong. 'Sometimes I see that conflict, and it tells me more about a person than they realize.' I took a step closer, grasping the lapels of his coat. 'But sometimes' – I looked up into his eyes – 'I simply see them as they *are*.' My gaze bore into his, wanting him to accept the gravity of what I was saying. 'Even when that conflicts with who they *think* they are.'

Sidney's lips parted as if to argue, but then a man jostled him from behind as he brushed past, reminding us this wasn't the place for such a conversation.

'Well, I don't think there's any more to be learned here today,' he told me instead as he threaded his arm through mine and guided me down the platform. 'Other than the fact that this is a busy station. If it was even half as bustling at the time the express arrived the evening Offerman was killed, it seems entirely feasible to me that the mystery man could have slipped away unnoticed. Especially if he jumped the platform, as the conductor suggested.'

I hummed to myself doubtfully. 'I think that

would have drawn *someone's* attention, and that someone would have come forward by now, what with the murder being splashed all over the newspapers for the past three weeks.' I turned to watch a tall Nordic-looking fellow as he rushed past, trying to catch the train even now beginning to pull out of the station. 'It seems more probable to me that he took another train departing from the station. A smaller branch line or the *Hoektreinen*.' The Hook of Holland train. 'The papers noted that one departed for the Hook at nine fifteen and another at nine thirty that night. Which means the man could have caught the night ferry from those docks to England.'

'Which would make sense if that man was Lieutenant Smith.'

I acknowledged that I'd had the same thought. 'And if that's the case then Offerman's papers might already be in Ardmore's hands. We've already established that Ardmore is quite capable of sitting on such an acquisition, watching us all scurry about, trying to find them, while he waits for the perfect opportunity to employ them to his optimum benefit.' I frowned. 'But all of this is simply conjecture. We haven't a shred of proof.'

'Other than that motorcar trying to run us down earlier,' Sidney pointed out.

'Which also isn't proof because we didn't see the driver,' I reminded him. I shook my head. 'We have to stop looking at this as if we already know who the killer is or we're going to lose all objectivity and miss something important. The conductor might just as easily have grown uncomfortable for another reason.'

'True. But you can't tell me that the possibility that Smith and Ardmore are involved isn't preying on your mind?'

'Of course it is,' I snapped, startling a woman striding past me. I took a calming breath and lowered my voice before continuing. 'But I'm trying to keep an open mind.' I reached across my body with my free hand to poke him in the side. 'I need you to help me be impartial.'

'Duly noted.' His mouth flattened. 'Though I fear that asking for impartiality from me when someone seems determined to harm you is rather a tall order.'

I hugged his arm tighter to my body. 'Then we shall both simply have to keep each other impartial.' I glanced over my shoulder. 'And do a better job of concealing our movements.'

Sidney didn't require any further prodding, veering right to lead us on a winding course back to the platform where the train returning to Rotterdam would depart.

By the time our tram from the train station arrived back at the Maas Hotel, the sun had already sunk low in the sky behind a bank of leaden clouds moving in from the west. The streetlamps had yet to be lit, and long shadows cloaked the streets. Fortunately, the tramlines passed down

Willemsplein, directly in front of our hotel, so we only had to hurry to avoid the fat raindrops that had begun to fall from the sky – and any attempts on our lives – for about a hundred feet.

Once inside the brightly lit lobby, we shook the water from our coats before advancing toward the stairs. But before our feet had even touched the second tread, a familiar voice rang out from the adjacent parlor.

'Monsieur and Madame Kent!'

We turned as one to see Gabriel Charlaix advancing toward us looking cool and collected in a gray tweed suit. Sidney and I shared a speaking look, neither of us having expected to see the SCR agent again. As such, his sudden appearance was naturally suspicious, though we pasted on pleasant expressions, giving every indication that we were quite pleased to see him.

'Monsieur Charlaix, what a surprise,' I declared warmly, offering him my cheek in greeting as we bussed the air beside each other's faces.

'I was sent to Antwerp on a different matter, and when I discovered you were nearby in Rotterdam decided to pay you a visit.'

'You received my messages, then,' Sidney remarked as they shook hands.

'*Oui*, and I have some information for you, if you have a moment.' He peeked at his wristwatch. 'Then I'm afraid I have to return to Antwerp.'

Sensing no artifice in him, I consulted with Sidney in a glance. 'Of course.'

He led us across the parlor filled with accents of warm wood tones and the low hum of conversation to a table near the windows overlooking the street and the river beyond. The thick brocade drapes had not yet been drawn, which must have allowed Charlaix to see us exiting the tram. I made a mental note of this. If we were being followed, the man doing so – be it Smith or someone else – might be managing it right under our noses.

Lifting his hand to the passing waiter, Charlaix requested two more glasses before tipping the bottle of pinot gris at the center of the table back to show us the label. 'From my family's vineyard.' He grimaced. 'Or what used to be.'

I recognized the vineyard. It was set in the Walloon countryside of Belgium, southeast of Mons and not far from the border with France. A lovely, idyllic pastoral landscape. Or at least it had been before the war.

'Is there anything to salvage?' I asked soberly, grateful for the opening to ask him about his Belgian heritage, even if that reason was a rather sad one.

'Very little. What wasn't destroyed when the Germans marched in was burned when they left,' he replied bitterly. 'But my father and brother, they managed to find a few roots they could salvage. And my mother's family are French vintners near Alsace. Their vineyards survived. There is some small hope that with their help and

234

with careful nurturing of those surviving vines, in time, they can rebuild.'

I offered him a consoling smile, for there was nothing I could say to make it better.

He gently rolled the neck of the bottle between his fingers so that the label was tipped toward him. 'Much of the stores were wasted on the Bosche, but every once in a while one stumbles across an old bottle, such as this one.' He shrugged a shoulder toward the bar. 'Some German officer probably sent a few confiscated bottles to their compatriots here during the war, and this one was left behind unopened.' His lips stretched into a forced smile. 'Until now.'

The waiter returned and Charlaix poured for each of us. I tipped my glass to inhale the slightly spicy scent, hoping for the man's sake that it was good. Fortunately, my first taste confirmed I wouldn't need to lie.

'It's lovely,' I murmured in complete sincerity after savoring the rich, complex flavor.

He nodded, seeming gratified by my reaction.

'Do I detect some cinnamon and cloves?' Sidney took another sip. 'And maybe some ginger?'

Charlaix's expression softened with real pleasure. 'You have a refined palate, Monsieur Kent.'

'What I have are parents who are genuine wine connoisseurs,' he admitted with a self-deprecating twist to his mouth. 'Some of whose knowledge I couldn't help but absorb.'

He had admitted to me once in an unguarded

moment that wine was one of the only topics he could discuss with his parents that would hold their interest for long. As a consequence, he had rather mixed feelings on the subject, often eschewing wine for liquor or ale simply to avoid the complicated emotions vino dredged up. Not that he'd admitted to the last. This was something I'd merely inferred from his drinking habits and his usual avoidance of such topics of discussion. The fact that he'd spoken now of his parents at all surprised me.

Charlaix tipped his glass toward him. 'Then they would have much in common with my parents, who began to train us practically from the cradle. When I left to take my place with the army, my four-year-old niece could already taste the difference between a pinot gris, pinot blanc, and a riesling grape.'

'Were you with the army from the very beginning?' Sidney asked casually after taking another drink.

'At Liège.' Where the Germans had pounded the city's ring forts into submission to gain access to its rail lines and the River Meuse. 'And during the retreat to Antwerp and then across Flanders.' Into the small corner of the country where, with the help of the French and British, as well as their own savvy, they'd been able to halt the Germans' advance. And where they'd remained for the rest of the long, bloody conflict, cut off from home and family, who were left to suffer under the Germans' occupation.

None of these things needed to be said, for we all knew them. They were facts etched into our brains, dominos falling to trigger other even more calamitous events. If we allowed ourselves to continue to follow the cascading trail of wreckage forward, we would soon find ourselves emptying this bottle and then another and another, all in an effort to forget.

So instead, I determinedly change the subject. 'How did you come to be with the SCR?'

He lifted the bottle, pouring more into each of our glasses. 'I found myself working as a liaison with French Military Intelligence, and when the war ended, they offered me a position. Given the state of my family's prospects, I decided it would be best to accept.' This was stated plainly, but I knew it could not have been so easy. Not when the life he'd expected to live had been upended and destroyed by the war.

He took a deeper drink than the sips he'd taken before and then set his glass aside, folding his hands before him. 'But you did not agree to drink with me in order to hear my sad history, and I have a train to catch.' His pale blue gaze met each of ours directly. 'As I said, I received your messages, and I asked a colleague of mine in Caen to look into the possibility that Mademoiselle Baverel had placed a child somewhere in the vicinity – at an orphanage or via some sort of private adoption. It is something we should have researched before, but . . .' He shrugged. 'How could we have known? She certainly did not tell us of such a child.'

'Has he discovered anything?' I asked.

'Not yet. Not under the name Baverel or Dupré. That is her other known alias. But she may have used a different surname. One of which we are not yet aware. Rest assured, if she did, we will find the child.'

I nodded, my looming doubts over the veracity of Willoughby's claims about the child growing. 'You'll keep us apprised either way?'

'Of course.' He lowered his voice, leaning closer to us across the table while he surveyed the room behind us. 'As to your questions about the other matter. I can tell you that at the end of February, Mademoiselle Baverel traveled to the Hook and then on to Amsterdam. We were aware of that trip even before we took her into custody.'

My expression must have conveyed my curiosity for he confirmed.

'We've been monitoring her for some time.' He nodded to Sidney. 'And yes, she traveled in the company of a James Smith for at least part of that journey.' He sat back, frustration marring his brow. 'However, we lost track of them both some days after their arrival, and did not pick up Mademoiselle Baverel's trail again until she docked in Calais.'

'Where had the ship originated?' I asked, expecting him to say the Hook.

'Antwerp.'

I blinked in surprise. How had she gotten to Antwerp undetected? Had she used a false identity? Perhaps a disguise? And what was she doing there? Antwerp was a major port. Or at least, it had been before the war, and was steadily regaining its footing. Perhaps she'd merely gone there to catch a boat. But then what had she been doing between the SCR losing her tracks in Amsterdam and her boarding that ship in Antwerp?

Then my thoughts shifted, and my gaze sharpened as I recalled that Charlaix had said he'd come from Antwerp and would be returning there this evening. Was he searching for Miss Baverel's trail from that end? But before I could voice the question, he shook his head lightly.

'I cannot discuss my current assignment. I shouldn't even be divulging what I already have. But . . .' His lips pursed briefly in indecision before continuing. 'I sense that we may be on the same scent.'

What exactly this meant I couldn't say, not without disclosing more than *we* were allowed to. Except it was evident he believed we were still investigating Miss Baverel and following her movements. Whether he knew anything about Offerman's death and our suspicions about her potential involvement was debatable, and I wasn't ready to tip my hand to him even on the chance he was.

Sidney, on the other hand, appeared to have latched on to a different point. 'You said you knew

239

even before she'd been taken into custody that she'd traveled with a fellow named Smith. So surely when a man by the same name attempted to see her at the gendarmerie, it raised a red flag.'

'It did. Especially when he slipped the leash of the officer we detailed to follow him within an hour.' He arched a single eyebrow. 'But what you really want to know is why I didn't tell you about their trip when I informed you of Smith's attempted visit.'

'Well?'

'As I said, I have not been cleared to tell you any of this. And I would not have told you about their trip even now had you not asked me specifically about it.' He shrugged, holding up his hands in answer to the irritation stamped across Sidney's brow. 'It is simply how the game is played, monsieur. I do not make the rules, but I must follow them.' His regard swung to me. 'Your wife knows this well, I think.'

So, he'd finally deduced who the actual intelligence agent was. I wasn't surprised he'd worked it out. Charlaix was nothing if not clever. Though I admitted to a pulse of alarm as to what he intended to do with this information now that he possessed it. We'd already recognized that he was content to have us do his investigating for him. That's why he'd approached us in Miss Baverel's ransacked room, and that was probably what he was doing now. Perhaps he was even baiting me to solve it quicker than he could.

Whatever the case, his admission and the fervency that he didn't quite manage to mask left me uneasy.

But he *was* right about one thing: There were rules to follow. And one of them was that I was not about to either confirm or deny his assertion that I knew them. 'What of the investigation into Mademoiselle Baverel's death?'

The dimple in his right cheek appeared as he smiled at my deliberate avoidance of his assertion.

'Did you manage to convince them to take a closer look?' I pressed.

'I'm afraid not.' He shook his head. 'I told you Capitaine Marcisieux is stubborn. They've ruled it a suicide.'

I scowled. 'Then whoever killed her has gotten away with it.'

'They think they have. For now.'

My expression only darkened, for I knew precisely what he was doing. I was not going to be cajoled into taking responsibility for the fate of that investigation. Not when it was *his* and the French authorities' job to see that justice was done.

'Didn't you say you had a train to catch?' I provoked.

But this only drew a wider grin from him. 'I do. I'll just leave this bottle here for you to finish, then, shall I?' He rose from his seat, gathering up his coat before offering us a cheeky farewell and a wish for luck. '*Bonne chance!*'

'*Bonne chance*, my foot,' I scoffed once he'd left the room.

'His family does make good wine, though.'

I turned to glare at Sidney, who had finished his glass and was now pouring himself another.

He shrugged one shoulder. 'I'm not wrong.'

I rolled my eyes, shifting my stare to the now empty chair across from us.

My husband draped his arm over the back of my seat. 'You're just miffed because the fellow is currently able to play the game better than you.'

I snapped my head around incredulously, finding his face closer than I'd expected. Snagging the glass from his hands before he could take another drink, I clunked it on the table. 'And you've had too much to drink.'

His eyebrows raised. 'Do I look or even sound primed?'

I frowned, having to concede that he didn't, and I knew the signs. 'Then why are you so mellow about this?'

'Because, for the moment, there's nothing to be done about Charlaix. So he's not telling us everything. The man's a French intelligence agent,' he lowered his voice to mutter. 'You didn't really expect him to, did you? At least he shared the information we asked for.'

I huffed a breath, knowing he was right, but agitated all the same.

His hand lifted to knead the muscles at the back of my neck, knowing it would disarm me. 'The real question is . . . why are you so riled by it?'

I sat sullenly brooding, unsure I wanted to

242

answer him, but his silence and the gentle pressure of his fingers unwound some of the tension coiling inside me. 'The French . . .' I began reluctantly. 'They weren't always as cooperative as they could have been.'

In fact, they could be downright obstructive at times. Allies we might have been, but in intelligence gathering it often felt like we were in competition. The British had a leg up from the beginning because we'd already had somewhat of a presence in Holland and elsewhere, and we also had the funds to recruit and support the intelligence gathering networks within the occupied territories. One would have thought the French would have recognized this and been content to benefit from it, but instead it often seemed they resented it. And that had hindered us in more than one operation.

'It wasn't enough that we had the Germans and the German-sympathetic Dutch and Belgians to contend with, at times we also had to be wary of our own allies,' I grumbled.

Sidney considered this for a moment before speaking. 'Is there a particular instance?'

'None that I'd like to share. Not now.' I met his gaze wearily. 'Let's just say I'm rather fed up with the French's lack of cooperation.' I sighed. 'Though, to be fair, I'm sure we British weren't always as cooperative as we could have been either. Especially when we weren't certain our allies could keep the matter quiet.'

Upon entering the hotel, I'd been chilled from the damp and wind outside, so I'd opted to leave my wool coat and hat on. But in the heat of the parlor, I was beginning to feel smothered under all of my layers, so I got to the point. 'Charlaix knows much more than he's saying, and he's deliberately leading us on to his own ends, and frankly, I don't appreciate it.'

The look in Sidney's eyes was strikingly solemn. 'It's difficult to know which flank to protect when you don't know from which direction your enemy will be coming.'

There were times when military jargon certainly cut straight to the heart of a matter, but in this instance, I also couldn't help but wonder if it concealed as much as it elucidated. I searched his face, wishing that I knew what had brought that haunted look to his eyes. Wishing I knew the right questions to ask. But despite all my avowed charm and skill in making people talk, in these sorts of interactions with Sidney the words never came easy, and my abilities failed me. My blasted feelings got in the way.

'Sidney . . .' I began, but he had already rebuilt the walls between me and whatever memory from the war was plaguing him.

'You must be stifling in this coat,' he said, correctly interpreting why I'd tugged open the top buttons. He leaned closer, his breath stirring the hairs around my ears. 'Come upstairs and I'll help you remove it.'

I knew what this was. I knew because I'd employed it at times myself. It was a ploy to stop me from asking questions. For a moment, part of me considered resisting. But another part of me was just as eager to be distracted, to avoid the conversation I could barely begin and had no hope of convincing my stubborn husband to continue.

So I forced an arch smile to my lips in an effort to return his banter. 'Is that all you intend to remove?'

But Sidney wasn't fooled, and some of the playfulness slipped from his expression. He grasped my elbow, helping me to my feet as I plucked my tooled leather handbag from the table. 'Darling, I'll help you with anything you wish,' he murmured against the brim of my hat as he guided me around the tables and through the door.

I tipped my head to see past the rolled brim, noting the affectionate glint in his eyes. The knowledge that he knew his evasiveness unsettled me and that he regretted it did much to ease my concerns. At least he was openly acknowledging the effect his silence and secrecy had on me. It didn't change the fact that I would still have to be patient until he was ready to share, but it made it easier to endure.

'Is that so?' I teased as we began to climb the staircase, hope lifting my heart.

'You doubt my sincerity?' he asked, the mock outrage I heard in his voice only partly feigned.

I turned to look into his eyes, allowing him to

see my own earnestness. 'Oh, I don't doubt your sincerity.' My lips curled and my gaze skimmed lightly over his features before I turned to hurry up the remaining steps. 'Merely your intentions.'

He caught up with me at the top, draping his arm around my waist. 'But haven't my intentions been quite clear?' His voice dropped into silky tones as he guided me down the hall and around the corner to the door to our room. Crowding me up against it, he removed my hat, his lips finding the tender skin just behind my ear and making warmth pool at my center. 'I *intend* to get you out of these clothes.'

My skin flushed at the look in his eyes. 'Only if I can return the favor,' I replied huskily.

His answering smile could only be described as devilish as he slid the key into the door. 'Please do.'

CHAPTER SEVENTEEN

Happily, the night passed without any further incidents other than our own mutual intentions being played out. We woke to the sound of rain being flung against the windows by the wind and a heavy gray mist covering the river. It was the type of conditions the Dutch called dog weather for some reason unknown to me. Though seeing as the British had approximately thirty-seven ways to describe rain and forty-two ways to say gloomy – half of which also made little sense – I figured I had no room to criticize.

I was just summoning the impetus to rise from the warm cocoon of our bedding and prepare myself for the cold soaking we would endure once we ventured outside when there was a knock on the door.

Sidney groaned into his pillow. 'Tell Nimble to go away.'

'That's not Nimble, darling.'

He fell silent, taking a moment to recall we weren't at home in our flat in London, so the person rapping couldn't be his valet. Gathering himself, he pushed up onto his elbows and scrubbed his face with his hands. 'Right.' He turned to look at me and my heart flipped over seeing him in such a rumpled state. His normally restrained dark hair curled about his head in messy abandon, and his jaw was dusted with dark stubble.

He took one look at my likewise bare shoulders and thoroughly tumbled appearance and his lips curled into a rather pleased grin. 'I suppose I should get that.'

'Well, *I'm* certainly not going to answer the door in all my deshabille,' I retorted.

Just then there was a swoosh of sound. Clutching the covers to my chest, I sat upright to look toward the door while Sidney rolled onto his side and pushed up to do the same. On the floor just inside the door lay a white rectangle someone had slid underneath. My mind began to churn with the possibilities of who the sender might be, and so I began to separate the duvet from the sheet, wrapping it around me as I tried to rise from the bed.

'Stay, Ver,' Sidney urged, reaching for my arm, but I pulled from his grasp. 'Just leave it lay a little while longer,' he cajoled, collapsing back into the bed. 'I'll make it worth your while.'

I laughed. 'I'll be right back,' I assured him, scurrying across the carpet to collect the paper before diving back into bed.

My husband made short work of unwrapping me and readjusting the duvet so that it covered both of us while I struggled to keep the letter from his grasp.

'Sidney,' I scolded and then ruined it by giggling as his hands brushed up my sides. 'Just let me read it.'

He rolled me over, hovering above me. 'Only after I get a proper good morning kiss.'

'A proper one?'

He smiled. 'Or a thoroughly improper one. Your choice.'

I cupped his jaw, the bristles prickling my fingertips as his lips melted into mine for a long, leisurely kiss. One that I knew was meant to make me forget the missive in my other hand, but Sidney should have known better than to think he could drive it entirely from my mind. Not when we were in the midst of an investigation. Though for the sake of honesty, I had to admit it was more difficult than I'd anticipated.

'Much better,' he murmured when he pulled away, offering me a melting smile that I felt clear to the tips of my toes. He rolled over and clasped his hands together behind his head, offering me an impressive view of his physique as well as the puckered scar over his chest where he'd been shot in March 1918. A scar which nearly matched my own on my shoulder. 'Now, read that so you'll no longer be distracted when I crumple it up and toss it to the other side of the room.' His eyes glinted in almost a challenge, leaving me with no doubt he would do it.

I laughed. 'You have a one-track mind.'

'At present I do. So start reading,' he playfully growled.

I shook my head and unfolded the missive. But the words typed across the page wiped the humor from my face as I sat upright, scanning the few lines again. 'It's from T. He needs to see us urgently.' My gaze met Sidney's. 'The contents of the portfolio are being put up for auction.'

Less than an hour later we were hustled into T's office to find him once again staring broodingly out the window. Apparently, this was his preferred place to muse, as well as a good vantage from which to view the ships coming and going up the river, as well as the traffic in the street below. I was certain he'd seen us dash through the driving rain from the tram passing along the Boompjes to the building, but when he turned to look at us, his thoughts seemed to be somewhere else.

He blinked his small eyes several times, bringing us into focus, and then gestured toward the arrangement of chairs before his desk where we'd sat during our last meeting. 'You received my message.'

'Yes. What do you mean the contents of the portfolio are being put up for auction?' I queried, getting straight to the point.

'We've received word that a select number of individuals have been invited to bid on the papers taken from a . . . *former ministry clerk who recently*

250

met his demise on a train.' He arched his eyebrows indicatively.

'Plainly they're referring to Offerman.'

'The auctioneer promises the contents *expose the secret maneuverings and machinations of a world power in their quest for domination.*'

'He's using rather hyperbolic language, but I suppose one would if one was trying to stir interest and drive up the price.' I sat forward in my chair. 'When is this auction to take place?'

T clasped his hands before him on the desktop. 'Interested individuals have until five o'clock on Thursday afternoon to place their bid.'

'How are they supposed to place these bids?' Sidney asked.

'At a bank in Amsterdam. And yes, we already have men in place, surveilling everyone who goes in or out of the premises. Particularly those with an interest in a specific safety deposit box. So, I don't want either of you going anywhere near it,' he cautioned. 'Your faces are known, even here in Holland, and if the culprit or any of the bidders catch sight of you, they might hesitate to place or collect the bids.'

I looked at Sidney. 'All right. Then what *do* you want us to do?'

His voice hardened, displaying more of the bullying persona I had known he possessed, but had never been directly subjected to. 'I *want* you to figure out who this murdering auctioneer is *before* this auction ends. We've been granted a

251

reprieve of sorts. At least we know that Offerman's report hasn't yet been handed over to individuals we would prefer not to have access to it, but it's a short one. And I want you to take full advantage of that.'

So, this was his way of prodding us to move faster when we'd only just arrived on the scene, so to speak. I could appreciate his frustration, his sense of urgency. What I didn't appreciate was his taking it out on us.

'How did you learn of all this?' I scrutinized his tight jaw. 'One of the individuals offered a bid must have contacted you,' I guessed, and knew I'd hit the nail on the head when his already pugnacious scowl deepened.

'A reporter who has worked as an informant for us in the past.'

In exchange for exclusive information, no doubt. I didn't disparage the arrangement. I understood how intelligence gathering worked, especially during the war. But if the relationship was ongoing, I *was* curious what information we were exchanging with him now.

'Can you arrange a meeting with him for us?' I requested. 'He may be able to tell us more.'

Such as why the auctioneer had contacted a newspaperman, and whether he'd contacted other reporters. Was his goal to have the information circulated in print, to reach the maximum number of people as possible? Heaven knew, if a piece of news was salacious enough, the papers would be salivating for the chance to be the first to publish it. And the others would be scrambling to catch up, printing it the next day and racing to out-scoop the others as the story and its impact began to unfold. It would create a frenzy.

Or was there another reason this reporter had been contacted and singled out from his competitors? We wouldn't know until we spoke with him and discovered some of the other potential bidders.

'That's not necessary. He's already told me everything he knows.'

I frowned, not having expected to be rebuffed. 'Yes, but you know as well as I do that sometimes people think they've told you everything they know, but . . .'

T slapped his desk, startling me. 'I said he's told us everything! That line of inquiry is closed.'

I blinked at him in shock and consternation.

He scraped a hand down his face, exhaling in exasperation. 'Just . . . find the blasted documents before Thursday and destroy them.'

The sense of disquiet that had settled over me firmly took root.

'I thought C had need of the information contained in that report?' I ventured.

'No! Just destroy it. That's an order!' Then, as if truly noticing our bewildered reactions for the first time, he softened his stance. 'It's already caused us enough trouble.'

I didn't think I'd given any indication of the

stubborn resistance developing inside me, but perhaps T knew me better than I realized. Or perhaps he was paranoid. For his eyes suddenly narrowed as he reiterated his instructions even more pointedly. 'Don't even bother to read it. Just destroy it.'

'Yes, sir,' I replied, rising to my feet.

Sidney had been wise enough to remain silent through this exchange, though I could sense his simmering outrage as we exited T's office and passed through the outer office where several secretaries and typists were at work. Eileen McNeill looked up, catching my eye, and then shook her head minutely in warning before returning to her work. Upon our arrival, I had intended to stop to speak with her after our meeting with T. Despite the fact that I'd come empty-handed, still not having purchased the *stroopwafels* I'd intended to bring her, I knew Eileen would be happy to see me. But I sensed the tension running through everyone in the office. Apparently, Sidney and I weren't the only ones T had taken out his frustrations on. I would have to find another time or place to see Eileen.

Once in the lobby, we had to wait for a passing tram, making small talk with the burly doorman. But when we were safely squeezed into the trolley's packed confines, with Sidney clutching a handrail overhead with one hand while the other arm wrapped around me, our eyes met in mutual suspicion.

'What was that?' he murmured indignantly, his voice pitched low so we wouldn't be overheard.

'I don't know,' I admitted. 'But something isn't right.' I glowered at the knot in his amber yellow tie, trying to decide what our next step should be. We were supposed to take the train to Amsterdam today to look into Offerman's life there, but there was something more pressing we needed to do first. 'We're stopping by the telegraph office.' I arched my chin determinedly. 'There's a message I need to send.'

I could tell by the look in his eyes that he understood I meant to contact C. I was tempted to go back to the hotel and telephone him from there, but depending on his schedule, I knew an entire day might be wasted in waiting for him to return my call. If I contacted him by telegram, hopefully a reply would be waiting for me at the hotel when we returned this evening.

Given the weather and the crowded conditions on the trams, we were forced to withhold any further conversation until we were snugly situated in a first-class compartment of the express. It was a compartment much like Offerman had been killed in, and we'd hoped by retracing his route, albeit in reverse, we might gain some insight previously missed as to how the crime had been committed. For the moment, we had the space to ourselves, and so we wasted no time in comparing notes as the train began to pull away from the station, heading toward the Hague.

'I take it you found T's behavior even odder than I did?' Sidney began as I finished shaking out my mackintosh and hung it on the hook by the door.

'*First*, they're anxious to convey what an important report it is and how they need the intelligence it contains, and *now* T simply wants us to destroy it? And not only destroy it, but not *read* it before we destroy it?'

'Hmm, yes. I caught that, too.'

I sank down beside him on the bench. 'It makes me wonder, just what on earth is really in that report? I mean, we've already established that the contents are damaging to the British relationship with Holland, and C and T, in particular. Given those facts, naturally, they would be anxious to retrieve those papers. But . . .' I turned my hands palms up in my lap, struggling to give voice to the disquiet that had settled within me. 'Is all of this *truly* about the wreck of the *Renate Leonhardt* or is there something more?'

'You think there's something even more damaging to T in there?' Sidney queried, taking hold of one of my hands. 'Do you think *that's* why he was so adamant?'

'Maybe. I don't know.' I searched his face as if some of the answers I sought might be written there. 'But I think we should know precisely what C's directives are, and whether T altered them in any way.' I turned to peer out the rain-splattered window. 'Perhaps this auction merely

256

has him on edge. After all, T is as human as the rest of us.'

But even rationalizing that didn't unravel the knot that had formed in my gut. It didn't banish my certainty that lurking behind T's gruff anxiety had been a sense of genuine panic. And it didn't dispel the uneasy sensation that I was now no longer certain exactly who I could trust.

It felt a bit like being hurled back into the war, smuggled through the electrified fence into German-occupied Belgium again, and then left to find my way with just a few names and a memorized map to lead me to those who might be able to help me along the way. I'd grown somewhat immune to the terror during the conflict, much like the soldiers at the front, but that didn't mean it went away completely. At the most importune moment, it would suddenly rear its ugly head, and it was all I could do to beat it back, to not blow my cover, to not get myself or my comrades killed.

'What of this reporter he refused to share the identity of?' Sidney suggested, recalling me to the present. 'Should we try to uncover who he is?'

I turned to look at his face – at the aggravation etched across his brow and the determined set of his mouth. I wasn't alone anymore, I realized. I had Sidney. Sweet, protective Sidney, who had looked as if he'd wanted to draw T's cork, and would have done so had I asked him to.

The corners of his eyes crinkled in concern when I didn't respond, and I squeezed the hand that still held mine, reassuring him. 'Actually, I have a strong suspicion I already know who he is,' I admitted. 'And I think it would be quite beneficial to pay him a visit while we're in Amsterdam, regardless of T's opinion on the matter.'

The door opened and a young gentleman took a single step inside before stopping short. A look of uncertainty passed across his features, and I could guess what he was thinking. After all, the facts of Jacques Offerman's murder had been splashed all over the newspapers. Offerman had sat in a first-class compartment of a train with a man and a woman who were strangers to him, just as this young man was about to do. He couldn't help but compare the similarities.

I offered him a reassuring smile before asking Sidney to pass me the society column of the English newspaper he'd purchased at the station. There was nothing for it but to carry on, acting as normally as possible, and allow the young man to decide for himself whether he wished to sit in our carriage or find another seat. Eventually, he closed the door and settled on the bench closest to the exit. He took out a book, flipping a page periodically, but it was clear from his tense shoulders that he wasn't actually reading it.

Sidney and I resigned ourselves to making inconsequential small talk the rest of the journey, for the young man was listening, and if we tried to whisper I feared we'd give the poor fellow heart palpitations. In any case, we needed to be mindful of the route we traveled and the stations we passed between the Hague and Haarlem. The nurse, Miss de Boer, had disembarked at Haarlem, and *Het Vaderland* – a newspaper based in the Hague – had reported that the police believed the murder had happened between Leiden and the Hollandsche Spoor station, where the body had been found – a distance traveled in perhaps twenty minutes.

However, the stations between those stops, as well as the one at the university town of Leiden, were small, with fewer passengers getting on and off the train, which would make it easier for the porters and stationmasters to take note of those who did. No one at these stations had reported anything out of the ordinary, and now having seen them for myself, I struggled to imagine the killer being brazen enough to exit the train at any of those stops. Perhaps he might have slipped past without being detained that evening, but he would have been spotted and remembered.

The likeliest scenario still seemed to be that the murderer had left the compartment when it pulled into the Hague and exited the train before he could be noticed. Whether he'd jumped platforms – another risky maneuver – to take the train back to Amsterdam, taken the *Hoektreinen*, or simply walked out into the streets of the city, I didn't know. If the killer's plan all along had been to auction the papers they'd taken from Offerman's portfolio to the highest bidder, then it seemed doubtful they would want to draw further attention to themselves by leaving the country on a ship from the Hook that evening. However, if circumstances had forced them to alter their original intentions, then such a possibility could not be ruled out.

I stifled a pulse of frustration. My hope had been that by retracing Offerman's route matters would be made clearer, but it seemed the more data we gathered, the *further* we got from the truth. It was no wonder the police were stymied. Even knowing what important documents Offerman had carried, we still hadn't arrived at the truth of why the crime had been committed or how they'd escaped. If we didn't figure it out soon, those documents might be brought to light for all to see, C might be forced to retire, and Ardmore's grip on all of Britain's intelligence assets would be even more complete. The consequences were not to be borne. This was one murder that *had* to be solved.

CHAPTER EIGHTEEN

Jacques Offerman had lived in a set of rooms along the Rokin – a lovely little district near the center of Amsterdam. Tall brick houses lined the street paralleling the wide canal, across from which stood the impressive neoclassical façade of the Nederlandsche Bank. A few buildings to the north of Offerman's flat even stood the Arti et Amicitiae, the home of the Dutch artists' society. Unfortunately, the damp, blustery weather made it all but impossible to enjoy these surroundings.

His landlady – a nervous matron somewhere between the ages of forty and fifty – eyed us askance when we knocked on her door and informed her of the reason for our visit. I could hardly blame her. After the murder of her former tenant and everything that had been revealed about him in the press, particularly the wild speculations about his personal life, we couldn't have been the first people to appear on her doorstep trying to coax or bribe information out of her. Our assurances that the police were aware of our efforts also did little to console her. As such,

261

we stood in her chilly vestibule, dripping on her rug, rather than being invited into the cozy drawing room I could see just beyond her shoulder.

'His rooms have already been cleared.' She crossed her arms over her chest, shaking her head. 'Wouldn't have let you into them anyway.'

I'd anticipated as much. The murder *had* happened over three weeks ago, and she had a living to make.

'What about visitors?' I spoke in Dutch as she had, while Sidney looked on. 'Did he have friends who called on him? What about any strangers? Or people hanging about in the street watching the house?' Her stony expression compelled me to ask as much as I could, hoping something would induce her to share anything she knew before she drove us back out into the rain.

'I'll tell you the same thing I told the police. He had a man come to see him around three o'clock the day he died. Said he was his friend, but I'd never seen him before. Asked when Mr Offerman would return.' She shrugged a shoulder. 'But I didn't know.'

'What did this man look like?'

She tilted her head toward her shoulder. 'Handsome.' She flipped a hand at Sidney. 'But not like a film star. Smart suit. Sharp eyes. He knew better than to try to charm me.'

Smith *could* fit that description, but so could any number of other men.

'He spoke Dutch?'

She studied me with pursed lips, evidently finding my intelligence lacking. 'I would've said if he hadn't.'

I wished I knew whether the lieutenant could speak Dutch, for that might help us at least rule him out.

'I heard Mr Offerman in the stairwell returning to his flat around six o'clock,' she continued. 'He was speaking with someone who went up with him, but I don't know whether it was the man from earlier or someone different. I didn't see them, only heard them. Then around six thirty, I heard footsteps descending the stairs, and I presume that's when he departed with his friend. I never saw him again.'

She was probably right, for we knew he'd boarded the 7:15 express from Amsterdam Central Station, and he would have needed about thirty minutes to reach the train.

'As for any other . . . *visitors* . . .' Her mouth tightened in distaste. 'I don't know anything about that.'

It was clear she was referring to the insinuations made about Mr Offerman in the press. What wasn't clear was whether her disapproval was directed at his preference for men or the scurrilous accusations – as yet unproven – that had been bandied about in the gossip rags. Considering the fact that she was unlikely to know anything helpful about that part of his life, I chose to ignore the comment in hopes she might be able to direct me to someone who did.

'What of your other tenants? Were any of them friendly with Mr Offerman?'

'Only in passing.' She tilted her head again. 'Though you might try Mr Gevers. He was, I believe, a friend as well as a colleague.'

'Then they both worked for Mr Van Grych at his firm?'

'Yes.'

This was easily done, as we were paying a visit to Offerman's employer next. Hearing the bell of the tram coming down the street outside, we thanked his landlady and rushed to catch it.

The offices of L. van Grych, Jr were not far away, but unfortunately part of that distance could not be passed by tram. Instead, we had to strike out on foot from Dam Square in the direction of the Trippenhuis. By the time we reached the neat, narrow building in which the law offices were situated, we were more wet than dry. Only my mackintosh and Sidney's trench coat had kept us from being utterly soaked.

The advantage to our making such a bedraggled entrance was that we were welcomed in without question, swiftly divested of our outer garments, and set before a warm radiator to dry. We weren't asked to account for our presence until the secretary had returned to us with two warm cups of tea – a musky-sweet Darjeeling blend. I blew across my cup, content to let Sidney do the talking since we'd been addressed in English. It was to him that the secretary's eyes kept being drawn anyway.

'We're here to speak with Mr Van Grych, as well as Mr Gevers.'

Her brow pleated. 'May I ask what it is in regards to?'

'We're investigating a crime similar to what befell Mr Offerman and are attempting to compare all the similarities,' Sidney replied, correctly deducing that she had already made the obvious connection between the two names. 'But you must have also known him,' he added sympathetically. 'We're sorry for your loss.'

She seemed flustered. 'I . . . thank you. Mr Offerman was always very kind to me. He was quiet, didn't talk much, but he always had a smile for me, and even remembered my birthday.' She blinked rapidly, her eyes filling with tears. 'I'll just . . . I'll speak with Mr Van Grych.' She turned away before looking abruptly back at us, but she seemed unable to find the words to voice whatever she was thinking, for she dropped her gaze and bustled away.

We waited a number of minutes with nothing but the rain splattering against the window and the clock ticking on the wall to interrupt the silence. Wherever the secretary had gone to speak with her employer, it was on the far end of the building. We sat there so long that I began to wonder if they hoped we'd simply give up and leave. A foolhardy wish given the weather. It was much more comfortable in here than out in that slicing rain.

Finally, we heard the sound of footsteps approaching, and looked up to see two gentlemen entering the room. The older man with a trim white beard was evidently Mr Van Grych, and the younger man must be Mr Gevers, Offerman's friend. Of the two, he interested me most. He hovered almost in his employer's shadow, observing us while the older man spoke, but I didn't think this was done out of deference, but with a purpose. Perhaps he hoped to study us while we weren't yet studying him. Whatever the case, it was evident that behind his unassuming appearance lay an intelligent mind.

'We are all naturally very shaken by the death of Mr Offerman,' Mr Van Grych was saying. 'But I'm afraid there's nothing else left for me to say that I haven't already told the police.' His eyes narrowed and his head swiveled to scrutinize us, much like a barrister might do to a person in the witness box, I imagined. 'They *are* aware you're here?'

'We've been consulting with Inspector Van de Pol in Rotterdam,' Sidney replied, which wasn't precisely a lie, but I doubted this gentleman would appreciate the subtlety of such a nuance once he checked with the inspector, as he was bound to.

He nodded slowly, as if still trying to decide whether to believe us. Then he glanced over his shoulder at the other man. 'But Mr Gevers has agreed to speak with you *briefly*.'

There was no mistaking the emphasis he placed on that last word, and so I began to arrange the questions we most needed answered in my head while Mr Gevers led us down the corridor to his office. However, all this careful planning flew out the window when he rounded on us after closing the door. 'You're his contacts, aren't you?'

I was momentarily stunned – the reaction Mr Gevers had undoubtedly hoped for when he'd chosen this approach. 'Excuse me?' I finally managed to stammer.

'His contacts? His keepers, handlers . . .' He gestured with his hands. 'Whatever you call them?' His dark eyes bored into mine. 'He reported to you.'

I'd already noted the man's intelligence. His tactics now confirmed it. So I made a swift calculation.

'No,' I replied calmly. 'But we know who was.'

But rather than disarm him, this confirmation seemed to anger him further. His hands clenched into fists at his sides as he moved several steps closer. 'Then I'm right. Whatever he was doing for you British got him killed,' he hissed.

'He told you about that?' I countered, wondering just how much this man might know. And if Offerman had told Gevers about his work, whether he'd shared it with anyone else.

He stopped, his brow furrowing, and then

changed course to the opposite side of his desk. 'One evening, some months past, when he was deep in his cups.' His gaze lifted from the papers arranged over the felt top, as if he'd been interrupted in the midst of his work. 'He let slip that he'd supplied information to the British during the war.'

I struggled to mask my disapproval. Men like Sir Basil Thomson and Vernon Kell, the head of counterintelligence during the war, liked to talk about women being unsuitable for intelligence work because of our tendency to fall prey to our emotions and the illusions that intimacy inspired, but I found that British Intelligence faced far more danger from the loose lips of drunken men. After all, Sidney had first learned of my position with the agency from just such a sotted colleague. Because of the Official Secrets Act, I'd been forbidden from telling anyone about the real war work I'd undertaken, even my husband. And now I learned that Jacques Offerman was another embalmed, burbling owl.

'And what did you think about that?' I managed to reply, hoping to keep Mr Gevers talking while I sorted out my impressions.

He turned away, struggling with himself. 'I'm a good Dutch citizen. So my initial reaction was affront. But then I reminded myself that Offerman was Belgian. His country had been overrun by Germans, and he'd fled to Holland with his parents.' He braced himself on his desk. 'I knew

268

that he felt guilty, for not having joined the army, for not staying behind to help. Little good that would have done. He would have been deported to work in Germany, and likely died from the harsh conditions. He was not the hardiest of individuals.'

Offerman having been a young man, Gevers was likely right. Over the course of the war, the Germans had forcibly rounded up and deported more than a hundred thousand Belgians to work in Germany on their farms, in their factories, and even at the front. Many had died, and even more had returned with their health shattered. This practice was not only in defiance of the Hague Conventions, but had also caused an international incident between them and the Dutch, for the Dutch had promised the tens of thousands of Belgian refugees who had fled across the border into Holland at the start of the war that if they returned to Belgium nothing untoward would happen to them. Germany's actions had broken the Dutch's word.

Gevers sighed, sinking down into the chair behind his desk with a troubled frown. 'But he carried that guilt, and so it's not surprising that he would have sought the chance to alleviate it. I would have likely done the same,' he admitted as we sat in the chairs across from him.

I well understood the power of guilt in the face of one's nation's and neighbors' suffering. After all, that had been one of the chief motivators for the men and women inside the German-occupied areas who'd joined our intelligence gathering networks. They'd wanted the chance to do *something* to help defeat and oust their occupiers, and trapped within their snare there was little else they could do.

'Why didn't he return to Belgium after the war?' I asked, curious why a man who'd spied on behalf of his country had then elected not to return to it.

'He considered it. Even returned for a brief while. But their home near Mons had been destroyed, as had much of their village, and his parents were growing older and had elected to remain in the Hague, where they'd settled. In the end, he decided to stay here, at least for a time. I think he always planned to go back eventually. Perhaps after his parents passed.'

I nodded, recognizing it could not have been an easy decision. War had upended their lives permanently, and even if they'd returned to Belgium there was really no way to go back to the way things had been.

Sidney's fingers tapped the arms of his chair, revealing some of his agitation. 'Was Mr Offerman prone to . . . sharing such things, or were you simply that good of a friend?'

Mr Gevers's expression tightened. 'Not *that* kind of friend. Not that I cared.' His eyes narrowed. 'Do you?' he asked, perhaps worried we had some sort of moral axe to grind, or that we'd use

Offerman's personal life as an excuse to dismiss the man's death as warranted, as some in the press seemed to do.

The two men eyed each other levelly. 'Not if it doesn't have any bearing on our investigation. Not if he wasn't sharing secrets he shouldn't have been,' Sidney added, bringing him back around to the reason for his question.

Gevers seemed satisfied with this response. 'Offerman normally kept to himself, and he wasn't inclined to drink. Fortunately, it seems,' he muttered wryly. 'That's why I was so surprised when he let it slip. And he seemed embarrassed by the fact the next day when he asked me what he'd said and tried to explain himself. That's why I don't believe it ever happened again.'

'What did he try to explain?' I asked.

'What he meant, why he did it. But I told him he didn't need to explain. I thought I'd already worked out why he did it.' He frowned. 'Now I wish I'd let him talk. Perhaps he might have revealed some insight into why he was killed.' He looked up at us with snapping eyes. 'Or do you already know?'

'We have a suspicion, but we're not certain.'

'The papers.'

Dash, but he was intelligent.

'The ones taken from his portfolio. That's why, isn't it?' Gevers pressed.

'We're not sure.'

He scowled, and I wished I could be straight

271

with the man, but there was too much at risk, and Mr Gevers had not been thoroughly vetted. My instincts were telling me his intentions were genuine. He just wanted justice for his friend. But what if that justice was not in British Intelligence's best interest? Much as that idea repelled me, I couldn't give assurances I couldn't keep.

'What do you know about them?' I asked, curious whether Offerman had revealed anything about his report to Gevers.

'Nothing.' Based on his stony expression, I feared we'd learn nothing else from him, but then his lips pursed, and a deep vee formed between his brows. 'But something was troubling him.'

I straightened, sensing this might be important. 'What do you mean?'

'He was different the last few weeks before his death. Brooding. Unsettled. Offerman had always been quiet, but not in a gloomy, sour sort of way. He always seemed contented, but recently he'd seemed far from tranquil.' He reached into his desk drawer to extract a pack of cigarettes. 'Ever since he'd returned from Berlin.'

I waited silently while he lit his fag and took the first drag, not wishing to break his concentration.

'I thought at first it was merely anger and disgruntlement from being surrounded by the former enemy, being forced to interact with them and watch them go about their daily lives when a short time ago their soldiers had ransacked and

272

raped his country and killed and maimed his countrymen. Traveling there could not have been easy. But after a few days, I realized there was more to it than that.'

'Did you ask him about it?' Sidney asked, his voice sounding equally as intrigued by this perception.

'I tried, but he refused to elaborate.' Gevers leaned forward, knocking a fall of ash from his rapidly dwindling cigarette into the pewter dish at the front edge of his desk. 'All he said was that he'd learned something upsetting. Something that had made him rethink the choices he'd made, the loyalties he'd chosen.'

Sidney and I shared a long speaking look, neither of us seeming to know what to think, let alone how to respond to this revelation.

'I take it neither of you know what to make of that,' Gevers surmised.

When I turned to look at him, I noticed he looked paler than he had before. 'No. We don't,' I answered honestly, to which he inhaled a long drag. His hand shook slightly as he lowered the fag from his lips.

My mind struggled to piece together how the intelligence allegedly contained in the report would lead to Offerman making such a statement. Unless the two were unrelated. But we knew that he'd been sent to Germany to learn more about the gold that had purportedly sunk with the *Renate Leonhardt*, and now Gevers was telling us his demeanor had changed upon his return. It was difficult not to link the two matters.

I leaned forward, deciding to take a risk. 'What do you know of the *Renate Leonhardt*?'

Gevers tapped some more ash into the dish. 'The German ship that was sunk? The supposed gold wreck?' He shook his head. 'Not much. Nothing more than what the papers have reported.' His eyes darted between us. 'Are you telling me the papers contained in Offerman's portfolio *were* about the wreck?'

'We're not telling you anything, but it's one possibility that was suggested to us by someone we *thought* to be a reliable source.' I was swiftly revising that assessment, and it was a disconcerting insight.

'What of the people Offerman associated with?' Sidney spoke into the uneasy silence that had fallen. 'Were you aware of anyone new or disconcerting he'd become involved with?'

Gevers sighed, stubbing out his cigarette. 'I wish I had. That might have given the police some lead to follow.' He shook his head. 'But I didn't.' He spread his hands. 'I don't know anything more than I've told you.'

'Which was still a great deal,' I said, wanting to reassure this man in some small way. Gone was his defiance and anger, leaving behind only a conflicted, grieving man.

He clasped his hands together very carefully in front of him. 'I've read what they've printed about him in the papers, the aspersions they're casting on his character, but the man I knew wasn't like that. Yes, he may have preferred the company of men, and some people do not accept such things, but that does not make him a villain. He was a good citizen, a good lawyer, and a good friend.'

Gazing at the lines of sadness etching Mr Gevers's face, Offerman became truly human to me for the first time. He was no longer just a name, a victim, but a flesh and blood person who had loved and been loved in return. We had not spoken to Offerman's parents, of course, being warned they were old and frail, that the police had already questioned them, and that they knew nothing. But knowing that they, and Mr Gevers, and even the secretary, had been so affected by his death made my own conscience stir.

Yes, we had been asked to undertake this investigation in order to recover the report that had been stolen, but murder had been committed, too. Offerman deserved justice. That was as important, if not more, than recovering those documents.

'Thank you,' I told Gevers sincerely, though I knew it might not be clear exactly what I was thanking him for. 'I truly am sorry for your loss.'

He nodded, but I could tell his thoughts were elsewhere. Somewhere in the past, with his friend.

CHAPTER NINETEEN

Most of our remaining interviews in Amsterdam proved futile. Our conversation with the manager of the sandwich shop, from which the crumpled bag inside the train compartment had come, yielded no greater detail than the magazine article I'd read had already reported. It had seemed a dead end anyway, but worth following up on since the shop was located nearby on the Damrak.

While I warmed myself in a tea shop across the street, Sidney visited the police station where they had taken the correspondence they'd collected from Offerman's flat, on the chance they might let him view it. However, when he returned a short time later, I didn't think I'd ever seen him looking so discombobulated. Obviously, they'd turned him away, but apparently not before treating him like a degenerate and a pervert for even making the request.

'We misjudged that rather badly,' was all he would say. 'I should have taken you with me.' We'd thought they would balk at allowing a lady to read the letters, but at least if I was present, they might not have leapt to the wrong conclusion. Or at least not voiced the accusations out loud.

Fortunately, our next interviewee was far more accommodating. We tracked him down in the offices of *De Telegraaf*, one of the largest newspapers in the Netherlands, and one which had also expressed rather blatantly pro-Allied leanings during the war, thanks to its pro-Allied director, Hak Holdert, famed cartoonist Louis Raemaekers, and the man before us – its editor in chief, Johan 'Kick' Schröder. This, of course, had not gone over well with the Dutch government, who were attempting to tread the rather fine line of neutrality. Schröder's words and Raemaekers's images had helped turn public opinion not only in the Netherlands, but across much of the world, against the Germans. The graphic depictions of the Germans' treatment of the Belgians – some of which were exaggerated, though not all – had rapidly shifted sympathies to the Allies, and in particular Britain, who had, at least ostensibly, joined the war in order to safeguard Belgian neutrality. This, of course, incensed the Germans, and eventually led to Schröder's arrest in late 1915, when he was accused of voicing anti-German views in violation of the Netherlands' neutrality. But public opinion had been with Schröder, and the charges almost impossible to conclusively prove, so he had been acquitted in 1917.

I had never met Kick Schröder myself, but I was well aware of his larger-than-life persona. He had been a footballer and cricket player in his younger days – hence his nickname – but at fifty years of age now possessed a burly physique. His bushy head of hair, fiery beard, and temper to go along with it, had led to his second sobriquet – Barbarossa, after the notorious pirate.

Evidently, Schröder was also well aware of *our* reputations. He'd likely printed photographs and stories about our past exploits in *De Telegraaf*. He welcomed us into his rather cluttered office with a sweep of his arm. Every surface, save the four chairs, was covered in papers, books, and even boxes of type. Old cups with the dregs of tea jostled with pens and bottles of ink. From the looks of things, what the editor needed most was a bit of housekeeping.

'Heard rumblings that the two of you were sniffing about the Offerman murder, but I didn't believe it until now,' he declared as he sat behind his desk, plunking his hands down over a stack of papers and nearly upsetting a mug at the corner with his elbow.

'From whom did you hear that?' I asked in some surprise.

His eyes crinkled in a secretive little smile. 'Sources. *Now*, what brings you to my door? It wouldn't be a certain auction I informed the Brits about, would it?'

'An auction, really? Tell us more,' I drawled, deciding two could play this game.

He chuckled. 'I understand how it is. Must be

in your training, or your blood, for none of you can give it to me straight.' His gaze turned shrewd. 'For instance, if I asked you about your time here during the war, you'd only demur.'

I felt a pulse of uneasiness. The last thing I needed was a man like Barbarossa sniffing around in my past. But I merely crossed one knee over the other, settling deeper into my chair. 'I have—'

'No idea what I'm talking about. Yes, yes,' he finished for me. He stared down his rather hawkish nose at me, perhaps gauging how far he would have to push me to get me to break. Then his eyes drifted to Sidney, and I could see his brain making the calculations, recognizing from the hard expression on my husband's face that I was probably his weak point. I began to wonder if I'd made a grave error in coming here.

But then Schröder's pointed aggression faded as his shoulders lowered and the sharp glint faded from his eyes. Though by no means did I think he'd forgotten what he'd just learned. He'd simply filed it away for future reference or exploitation. Barbarossa, indeed.

He shuffled some papers on his desk until he found what he was looking for. 'I received this cable yesterday evening.'

Sidney leaned forward to take it from him before holding it out for both of us to read.

It laid out the details of the auction that T had already conveyed to us, but the bait was far more lurid and specific. In telegraphic shorthand, it essentially conveyed that the papers being auctioned would provide proof of betrayal at the highest levels of government. That they would expose the secret maneuverings and machinations of Britain and upend the world's understanding of the last two years of the war.

A pit formed in my stomach as I scanned the rest of the document, including the header and the origination and destination stamps, though I noted the sender's name was blacked out. 'This came by cable? From London?'

He nodded. 'From a colleague at a paper there.'

'Then you didn't receive an invitation to bid yourself?' Sidney verified.

'No.' He sat back, chuckling. 'No, I didn't. And I'm not likely to, given the things I published during the war.'

He was referring to his pro-British sympathies.

'Then your colleague certainly wasn't with one of Lord Northcliffe's or Lord Beaverbrook's newspapers,' I replied. Both men had contributed to the downfall of former Prime Minister Asquith and the promotion of Lloyd George to take his place, as well as held influential roles in creating propaganda for the government. As such, unless there had been a falling out among the men, they would not have wanted anything untoward to be revealed about Lloyd George's government during the final two years of the war.

Schröder neither confirmed nor denied this, but

I could tell from the twinkle in his eyes that my thinking wasn't entirely correct.

'Or perhaps he is, and that's why he sent this to you.' I peered at the telegram again. 'Did he share any suspicions as to who might be behind the auction?'

'He didn't. But obviously he thought the man was in Amsterdam, since the bank is also here. He'd heard rumblings that a number of reporters had been tempted to Holland by the promise of such a scoop.'

'And he hoped you'd stop it?'

He folded his hands over his rounded middle. 'Well, now, isn't that what you're trying to do?'

So that's why he'd informed T – to prevent the hand-off of such information. Or perhaps he was hoping to make an arrangement to acquire it himself, with the promise that any intelligence it contained would be published with delicacy, shaded to do damage to some but not others. But then why hadn't T told us everything indicated in the telegram? And why had he warned us away from Schröder?

The most obvious answer was that he hadn't wanted us to know everything, and that he'd been worried Schröder would tell us. Because the remainder of that threat didn't fit with the details we'd been given. How would the British sinking of the *Renate Leonhardt* reveal betrayal at the highest levels of government? And why would it upend the world's understanding of the final two years of the

281

war? The sinking of a single ship, and the revelation that a former Dutch ministry clerk had been supplying information to the British hardly amounted to a scandal of that proportion. Relations between Britain and Holland would be strained, and Sir Basil Thomson might very well use it as an excuse to oust C and subsume the Foreign Intelligence division under his mantle as Director of Intelligence for the Home Office, but by no means did it live up to the scandal advertised.

Was the auctioneer lying? Were the threats mere puffery meant to draw in higher bids? Was it simply a bit of scurrilous propaganda? Or were C and T intentionally misleading me and Sidney? Were they purposely not telling us all? Given the fact that T had ordered me just that morning to destroy the report without looking at it once we'd found it, I was suspicious of the latter.

The very idea made the pit in my stomach ache and my chest tighten with dread. When I had worked with the Secret Service during the war, I had known that I wasn't privy to every detail, but I'd never felt that I was being lied to. Not willfully and deliberately. But if C and T were telling me one thing when they knew another, and trying to keep that fact from me all while coercing me to do their bidding, then I didn't know where that left me. Did I blindly follow orders? Did I disobey? And what of all the assignments and instructions carried out during the war? Should I begin to question those, too?

Had it been possible to blame Ardmore for causing these sudden doubts, I would have, for this type of manipulation and malevolent influence was his stock in trade. But I couldn't. Not when C's and T's own words and actions were the impetus.

Maybe C's response to my earlier message about T's instructions would be more reassuring. Maybe he was unaware of the orders his section chief was giving.

I passed back the telegram, forcing my thoughts back on track lest Schröder notice my distress. 'If we are meant to stop it, have you learned anything since yesterday evening that might help us do so?'

'I've learned that Offerman recently returned from a trip to Berlin.' He arched his eyebrows. 'But perhaps you already knew that.' He paused, perhaps waiting for a reaction, but I wasn't about to give him one, and Sidney followed my example. 'I also learned that a number of his letters mention a Mr Wijsman from whom he obtained information. That he'd read some of his reports and found them particularly illuminating.'

I didn't ask how Schröder had gained access to Offerman's correspondence when Sidney had been sent away with a flea in his ear. Clearly, he had an informant on the police force. But I did puzzle over this Mr Wijsman. From the wording Schröder had shared, it might have been easy to assume he was a journalist, but the look in his eye and my own instincts told me his occupation was much different. Perhaps an agent with GS III – Dutch Intelligence.

I pushed to my feet, thanking him, but before I turned to go, I scrutinized the newspaperman where he still sat at his desk, stroking his red beard. 'You might extend us the courtesy of not announcing our presence in Holland for a few days.'

'I'll extend you the same courtesy we extended all combatants during the war.'

I narrowed my eyes, knowing full well that all Dutch newspapers had been forbidden from publishing information about all enemy forces, including aeroplanes, for only six hours after observation.

Schröder shrugged. 'I've got papers to sell.'

And stories about Sidney and I happened to sell heaps, particularly if the photograph was a good one. I spared a moment to wonder what image Schröder might have acquired, and then dismissed it from my thoughts. Whatever it was, he wouldn't be convinced to part with it, so why waste my breath.

Sidney took my arm after we'd rewrapped ourselves to face the weather and exited the building into a gust of rain. I'd suffered much worse from the elements during the war – and Sidney infinitely worse than me – but that did little to mitigate the disgruntlement I was beginning to feel at our having been made to traipse all over Holland in such wretched weather. Especially when our efforts forced us to face scoundrels like Schröder. But at least we were finished with Amsterdam. At least for today.

We clambered onto another tightly packed tram which reeked of damp wool and perspiration, taking it the short distance to Amsterdam Central Station, where we boarded the train bound west for Haarlem. If possible, the wind there was howling even harder, the raindrops striking us even sharper, all thanks to its proximity to the North Sea. Here there was no tram to bear us to Miss de Boer's door, only damp brick paved streets.

I had feared the nurse's house would be difficult to locate, or that she would not be home, but we found her easily enough in a street lined with tall, narrow buildings a few blocks from the train station. Sidney lifted his hand to knock on the cobalt blue door, but it opened before his fist could even connect with the wood. The woman pulling a dark oil-cloth cloak over her white nursing uniform stopped short at the sight of us. Her face had worn a slight scowl, as if she was no happier than us to be thrust out into this weather, but now her eyes beneath the brown fringe of her bangs and her white cap with veil were wide with shock and something very close to alarm. She turned away abruptly to shut the door, shielding her face from my view.

'Miss de Boer—' Sidney began, but she cut him off before he could continue.

'Don't tell me you're another of those benighted newspapermen,' she snapped in Dutch, tugging at her cloak and settling it more firmly over her shoulders. 'My name was supposed to remain confidential.'

It seemed we weren't the only ones who'd uncovered her identity as the woman who'd shared the train compartment with Offerman the night he was murdered.

'We're not reporters,' I said, hoping that by alerting her to my presence as a woman it might reassure her. But if anything, it only seemed to unsettle her further. 'But we wondered if we could ask you a few questions. We—'

'I'm sorry. I don't have time.' She pushed past us, backing down the pavement. 'I'm already late as it is.'

'Please,' I pleaded. 'We're investigating a similar crime, and . . .'

She startled like a frightened doe, her face blanching in the waning light. 'I . . . I have to go,' she stammered. 'I can't help you.'

I stared after her in consternation, taken aback by her reaction as she tore down the sidewalk as if we were the hounds of hell nipping at her heels.

'What just happened?' I murmured to Sidney.

'You frightened Miss Muffet away,' he quipped.

I turned to look at him. 'That *was* unusual, wasn't it? I mean . . . I can understand her aggravation at having her name leaked to the press, and

286

her desire for privacy, but she seemed *terrified*, and there are no similar crimes. We made that up.'

'None that we *know* of.'

'True.' I frowned. 'But wouldn't we have heard about them if there were. After all, Offerman's murder has been front-page news for weeks. The newspapers have been plumbing it for all it's worth. I can't imagine they would have missed such a connection, even one that's tenuous at best.'

'Probably not.'

I looked down the street in the direction Miss de Boer had disappeared. 'But still, she was most definitely terrified of *something*.' I only wished I knew what.

'Well, we're not going to figure it out standing around in this gale,' Sidney grumbled, pressing a hand to my back to urge me forward. 'Let's head back to the station. At least it'll be dry there while we wait for the next train.'

I couldn't argue with that.

Once I was settled on a bench in one corner of the recently refurbished station, dripping dry, Sidney went in search of some sort of sustenance. He returned a short time later with two cups of coffee to find me absorbed in studying the colored tiles adorning the walls depicting modes of transport.

'It was the best I could do,' he apologized unnecessarily as he passed me my cup, for I was simply grateful for something warm to wrap my hands around.

'I've been thinking about Miss de Boer,' I admitted as he settled beside me, draping an arm across the back of the bench behind me.

'About her rather extreme reaction?' He took a sip of his java and grimaced, either from the heat or the taste.

'Yes. She must know more than she's saying, and she's frightened by it. That's the only explanation I can think of.'

Sidney appeared to consider this for a moment. 'The question is what? And how can we convince her to tell us?'

'I don't know,' I admitted, and then sighed, pressing my fingers to my temple and rubbing them in a circle. It had been a tiring and frustrating day, and I wanted to do nothing more than change out of these wet clothes and curl up in a warm bed and go to sleep.

'It's troubling you, isn't it?'

I looked up to find my husband observing me, concern stamped across his brow.

'Everything we've learned today. The fact that what Schröder and Mr Gevers are describing don't seem to be the same thing as T, and even C, have led us to believe.'

I lowered my hand as the hollow pit that had opened up inside me throbbed in acknowledgment of his words. 'I would be lying if I didn't say yes.' I inhaled a bracing breath. 'But maybe C's response to my message will better explain.'

'Maybe,' he conceded, but he didn't sound nearly as hopeful as I would have liked.

'Have you managed to track down the porter?' I asked, wanting to avoid this discussion. At least until I'd received C's answer to my cable.

'Actually, yes.' He nodded his head toward the ticket office, where he must have spoken to someone when he went to fetch our coffees. 'He's scheduled to be working on the next train. We should be able to speak with him en route to Rotterdam.'

But the porter had nothing more to offer us, and for once I believed the witness. The poor man seemed harassed and exhausted, and entirely incapable of prevaricating. Yet his story did not deviate from what had already been reported to the police and in the press. In truth, I thought he was a bit haunted by what he'd seen.

Though discouraging, at least he was one potential suspect who had been present that night we could cross off our list. However, our return to Rotterdam without a clear understanding of the crime or a definitive suspect was still disheartening, to be sure.

CHAPTER TWENTY

There was one bright spot to our return to Rotterdam – the rain had ceased. We were relieved when we exited the train to be able to stroll to the tram stop without being drenched. The wind still sliced like a knife, but that was something I could endure as long as it didn't also fling water in my face.

Upon entering our hotel, I went straight to the desk to ask if I'd received any messages, and felt my spirits lift as I was handed a telegram which had been delivered earlier that day. However, my hopes were swiftly dashed as I tore open the envelope to read its contents.

FOLLOW T'S INSTRUCTIONS STOP HE HAS MY UTMOST CONFIDENCE

Sidney, reading over my shoulder, wrapped an arm around my waist, offering me what support and comfort he could. But nothing could halt the swell of wariness and uncertainty, and the sharp crest of alarm that suddenly surged up inside me, making it difficult for me to catch my breath.

I had trusted C since the moment I'd sat before him for an interview. Through countless difficult assignments and missions, I'd trusted his directives, his goals, his intentions. I had placed my and others' lives at risk, time and time again, and I'd carried out countless questionable acts of espionage in the name of my country – sometimes blindly – all because I believed in C.

But now, I knew he was lying to me – if not outright, then by omission. I could feel it in my bones. Those instincts that had carried me through the war and the year since were screaming at me. I couldn't shut them off. I couldn't turn away. They would not be silenced, and I didn't know how to move forward now. I didn't know how to reconcile this.

So it was deeply unfortunate that I should look up at that moment to find Lord Ardmore's man, Captain Willoughby, staring at me. I knew he had seen my pain, my distress, but rather than the delight I'd expected to see, compassion flickered across his features. He couldn't know the contents of the telegram, couldn't know what they were about. He must simply be reacting to my expression – a fact that was almost more difficult to bear.

Turning aside, I forced myself to take a deep breath, even though my lungs felt as if they couldn't expand to hold it, and fumbled to rearrange my face into a mask of careful indifference while Willoughby crossed the lobby toward us. I folded and tucked the telegram into my pocket just as he reached us.

'This weather isn't fit for man or beast,' he remarked as he drew closer, scrutinizing our appearance before his gaze landed squarely on my face. 'You both look like you could use a drink.'

It was kind of him to suggest the weather was the reason for my haggard countenance, but that only further increased my suspicions rather than lowering them. What was he doing here? We hadn't seen him since Furnes, and yet here he was, looking smart in a blue pinstripe suit. So what was he now doing in Rotterdam plaguing us? We needed to find out.

'Are you buying?' I countered, pushing past the fatigue that dragged at my bones and setting aside the misgivings roused by C's telegram.

'Of course.'

Willoughby turned to lead the way toward the parlor, where I could hear the tinkling notes of a piano being played.

Sidney threaded my arm through his and leaned down to whisper in my ear. 'Are you certain about this?'

I nodded, never removing my eyes from Willoughby's back, lest I falter in my resolve. I couldn't think about the rest now. I had to banish it from my mind and concentrate.

It being a later hour on a Saturday evening, we were greeted by a far different atmosphere from the previous evening when we'd joined Charlaix

292

for a glass of wine. Nearly all the tables were occupied by patrons, as were the seats along the polished wooden bar. The smoke from cigarettes and cigars created a light haze over many of the tables and filled the air with their scent. A piano player plunked out a jaunty tune while a few couples circled the open piece of carpet that served as a dance floor.

There were undoubtedly more men here than women, and the sight of a pair of men in military uniform made my steps falter slightly as a memory assailed me. I'd entered a parlor much like this one in Brussels once during the war, but the occupants hadn't largely been civilians but rather German officers. And I hadn't been clinging to Sidney's arm but my colleague Alec Xavier's. He'd been posing as a German officer, as he'd been doing for nearly six years, since even before the war began, and I was supposed to be his latest Belgian mistress. The fact that, an hour before making that entrance, I'd learned from one of the Germans over dinner that the field hospital where my older brother, Freddy, had been stationed as a Royal Army Medical Officer had been captured a few days before had only heightened the sense of déjà vu. Then, as now, I'd had to suppress my dread and anxiety and do my job. I'd had to pretend the other matter didn't exist.

Of course, I'd discovered later that my alarm had been unnecessary. Freddy had retreated to safety with the rest of the hospital's staff and patients before they were overrun. But I didn't think this outcome would be similar.

Willoughby managed to secure us a table equidistant from the piano and the rowdy patrons near the bar, and ordered us drinks as we took our seats. I wasn't surprised he was aware that my preferred libation was a gin rickey. It wasn't something I bothered to hide, and the man almost certainly would have done his research.

'So, what brings you to Rotterdam?' I asked, choosing to be direct.

However, Willoughby surprised me by outdoing me in this regard. 'You.'

I was momentarily at a loss for words, not having expected him to be so open about his intentions, and this brought a grin to his lips.

'Well, there's no real reason to beat around the bush, is there? You know it, and I know you know it.' He shrugged. 'So why not just call a spade a spade.'

'Yes, but *why* have we brought you to Rotterdam?' I queried, deciding to test this newfound willingness to be forthcoming.

Our drinks arrived then, and I arched a single eyebrow at him, letting him know I wasn't going to let him forget I'd asked this question. I accepted my gin rickey, sipping it with care given my empty stomach and the reaction I'd had to T's genever punch a few night's past. Sidney, on the other hand, didn't seem to harbor any such worries, downing half his pint of beer in two swallows.

Willoughby took a more leisurely swallow before answering. 'To tell you that I spoke with Lieutenant Smith.'

Once again, I was set back on my heels. Something he obviously enjoyed, his blue eyes twinkling.

'The lieutenant was rather besotted with Mademoiselle Baverel.' He draped his arm over the back of the chair next to him, offering a smile to a young woman passing our table. 'Turns out the chap has a heart after all, and a fondness for women as perverse and callous as he is. He lost his head. Thought you had something to do with her death.' His look acknowledged but didn't apologize for his associate's actions in shooting at us. 'He's been warned away.'

I found this confession to be interesting, but not particularly compelling. After all, another of Ardmore's men had gone rogue and tried to kill me contrary to Ardmore's instructions just five months prior. 'When did you speak with him?'

'Two days ago.'

'Where is he now?'

'Recalled to London. Beyond that, I don't know.'

It seemed noteworthy that he wasn't bothering to pretend that neither he nor Smith weren't operating under someone else's orders. We might not have spoken Ardmore's name, but we both conceded his role in this cat and mouse game we were playing with each other.

'Are you certain?' I pressed.

'Yes.'

'So Smith couldn't have been in, say, the Hague yesterday attempting to run us over with a motorcar?'

His pupils widened a fraction, telling me he'd been unaware of this. 'No.' He straightened slightly, revealing he was no longer quite as at ease as he wanted us to believe. 'He wouldn't disobey a direct order.'

'You don't sound so sure about that.'

His brow furrowed in annoyance. 'I am. The consequences . . . aren't worth risking.'

I'd seen firsthand how Ardmore handled disobedience, so I perceived all that was being left unspoken by that small waver in his voice. But it didn't explain why he was sharing all this with us. Why he was telling us that Smith had been called off.

Unless Ardmore wanted us to know he was still shielding us. That if he chose to rescind his protection orders, we would find ourselves in a precarious position rather swiftly. Perhaps all of this was not meant as a reassurance, but an implied threat. Get too close to the proof we sought, displease him, and whatever armor he'd placed – or wanted us to *think* he'd placed – between us and peril would be removed. That was the trouble with Ardmore. The line between fact and fiction was razor thin, particularly when it was his own men who were threatening us.

I slowly spun my glass with my fingers, leaving a ring of condensation on the tabletop, never removing my gaze from Willoughby's urbane features. He didn't squirm or fidget, but then I hadn't expected him to do so. As the impoverished orphaned great-grandson of a duke, he had been raised by a dowager aunt within spitting range of the aristocracy, but made to understand he would never be a part of it. Everything he'd achieved or earned had been through his own steely resolve and merit. It was something I would have respected, had he not fallen in with Lord Ardmore.

'Why else did you seek us out?' I asked.

He lifted his glass to take another drink. 'Who says there's anything more?'

I cast him a look that warned him not to treat me like a fool. Of course there was more.

His lips quirked in acknowledgment of this, though I didn't share his amusement. 'I merely wished to offer you a warning . . .' He held up a finger when Sidney lowered his drink to the table and loomed toward him. 'Or rather a bit of advice.'

I continued to glare at him, barely containing my annoyance. It hummed along my already frayed nerves.

'Be wary of the information others are telling you.' His eyes met mine intently, and his next words made the hair stand up on the back of my neck. 'Even those closest to you. For much of it is incomplete, if not outright lies.'

Hearing him reiterate the doubts I'd already been

entertaining was more than disquieting. It was downright disturbing. And yet this was Willoughby – Ardmore's man. I knew I couldn't trust him, or his intentions. My heart pounded in my ears and my skin flushed with repressed emotion, so I latched onto the only one that would stop me from dissolving into a quivering wreck in front of the enemy. Anger.

'Do you honestly expect us to believe you're now *helping* us? That you're some sort of *ally*?' Several heads swiveled our way at the sound of my raised voice, so I lowered it, leaning across the table toward him. 'We know that you lied about Miss Baverel's child.' We didn't know any such thing, but it was a good bet, and I was curious how he would react. 'Just as we know Smith was here in Holland with Mademoiselle Baverel a little over three weeks ago. And yet you still wish to pretend he wasn't aware of her movements immediately after, when she was *arrested*?'

'Ah, but Smith wasn't here in Holland three weeks ago,' Willoughby asserted calmly, saying nothing about my accusation about the child, which was rather telling in and of itself. His composure only enraged me further.

'His arrival was notated at the border,' I snapped.

'Perhaps his *name* was notated, but he wasn't there.' He spoke over me as I opened my mouth to object. 'He couldn't have been here because he was in London.'

This silenced me, for we already knew he had

been to London recently, in order to visit the War Office and reiterate his lies about the bombing of General Bishop's temporary headquarters. But that meeting had occurred a week and a half ago, allowing plenty of time for Smith to have traveled from Holland.

'Check with your sources. He was out and about, all over town. I'm sure they'll be able to corroborate it.'

I turned to meet Sidney's steady regard, not sure what to think. If Willoughby was telling us the truth, then Charlaix had lied. No, that wasn't quite right. Charlaix had simply told us someone claiming to be named Smith had entered Holland with Miss Baverel, and we all had assumed it must be the Smith in question, because who else could it be? So if Smith *had* been in London, if he hadn't been the Smith who traveled with Miss Baverel, then he couldn't be Jacques Offerman's killer.

My head swirled and I felt slightly nauseated, be it from fatigue, the gin rickey, or my own stupidity. All I knew was that everything seemed wrong side up. Including Willoughby, who was gazing at me with an expression that looked suspiciously like compassion.

I turned away, about to ask him to excuse me, when I realized that he hadn't flinched at the timing. He hadn't questioned why Miss Baverel and this Smith's presence in the Netherlands three weeks ago was important.

'You know why we're here,' I stated flatly.

He hesitated briefly before shrugging. 'Isn't it rather ob-vious?'

'Perhaps to those in our line of work,' I conceded. After all, the press had touted the possibility that the papers stolen from Offerman's portfolio pertained to the sinking of the *Renate Leonhardt* – a ship the British had sunk. I narrowed my eyes. But for all intents and purposes the investigation was a police matter, not one for Dutch or British Intelligence. 'How did you find out?'

'I have my sources the same as you.' He offered me an unctuous smile. 'There's no reason we can't cooperate when the situation merits it.'

Except I was all too conscious of what any such cooperation might mean, and I wasn't willing to accept the terms. 'I'll take that under advisement,' I replied in a dry voice. I scrutinized his neat appearance again. 'I take it you'll be drifting about Rotterdam, then?'

'For the foreseeable future.'

Lovely.

He reached his hand across the table, not quite touching mine. After all, my husband was seated next to me, glowering at him. 'So, if you should require any assistance . . .'

'Thanks. But I believe we'll manage.'

I managed to cross the room with my head still held high, but I was grateful for the arm Sidney had wrapped around my waist, steadying me, because I felt as fragile as glass and just as likely to shatter. When we reached our room, I dropped my coat, hat, and handbag on the floor and collapsed onto the bed, staring blankly at the ceiling. Sidney appeared in my line of sight a moment later, gazing down at me in concern.

'That was suspicious,' he finally murmured as he lifted one of my legs and began unlacing my boot.

I shifted my focus to him, too tired to even offer a token resistance to his playing lady's maid for me. 'Which part? The idea that Willoughby might actually be sharing information with us that could prove valuable? His suggestion that we might need to be wary of our allies? Or the fact that he appeared to deliver this message immediately after I received that cable from C?'

'All three.' He slid the first boot from my foot, dropping it on the floor by the bed with a *thunk*. 'But that doesn't mean his words weren't at least partly genuine.'

My mouth pursed in disfavor.

'Not that that makes him any more trustworthy, but . . . Willoughby is conflicted by you.'

I blinked at him in confusion. 'What do you mean?'

'Well . . .' He set to work on my second boot. 'I doubt he encountered many women while deployed with Naval Intelligence or in his time with Ardmore. You're an anomaly. And a lovely one at that. One with nerves of steel.'

I scoffed. 'I hardly put on a good show of that this evening.'

He removed my second boot, but retained hold of my foot. 'What you showed was that you're human, and then you gathered your pluck and gave him back as good as you got, if not more so.' He dropped the boot beside its mate and then slid his hands up my leg to unfasten the garter and roll my silk stocking down my leg, all while his eyes remained locked with mine. Heat gathered low inside me. 'Nerves of steel and seeming imperviousness are all well and good, but sometimes the realization that vulnerability and softness lie beneath them is a far headier influence.'

I swallowed as he released my second foot and returned to my first. My skin tingled at every point he touched, coming achingly alive as he removed that garter and then the stocking. It was a bit of a struggle to hold onto the strands of the conversation, but at least I was no longer feeling disgusted with myself. 'Maybe, but I'm under no illusion that whatever conflict Willoughby might be experiencing means he won't do Ardmore's bidding.'

'And what do we think *is* Ardmore's bidding?' he asked, sitting down on the edge of the bed, and bending forward to remove his own shoes.

I contemplated this. 'Finding out what we know, and . . .' I broke off, realizing the answer wasn't as simple as it seemed.

'If Smith was the mystery passenger on the train and he murdered Offerman and took the papers, then he was working at Ardmore's behest, and so

Ardmore should already have the papers. Whether or not he then decided to stage this auction to gain interest in those papers in order to see them published and the information disseminated without implicating himself, is a separate issue.' Sidney straightened, turning to me. 'The question is, does he have the papers or does he not? But Willoughby claims Smith wasn't in Holland when the murder occurred. That he was in London.'

I sat upright, reaching for Sidney's tie to loosen it. 'Willoughby could be lying.' I frowned. 'But I don't understand what the reasoning would be in doing so. He must know we're not going to take his word for it, that I am going to attempt to corroborate it. So unless his goal was simply to waste our time, he must recognize the truth will out, and his lie will change nothing.' Pulling his tie from his collar, I handed it to him. He promptly flung it, and my stockings, to the floor. I shook my head.

'Then let's suppose he wasn't lying,' Sidney speculated. 'That Smith isn't our culprit.'

'That doesn't preclude the possibility that Ardmore paid someone else to commit the murder, but I understand what you're proposing. What if Ardmore *doesn't* have the papers? What if he wasn't behind the murder?'

'Then that would leave us wondering not only who *did* kill Offerman, but also why Ardmore has sent Willoughby here to shadow us.'

I scrubbed my hands over my face and up into

303

my bobbed curls, which must look a fright after being rained upon and smashed under a hat all day. 'If Ardmore doesn't have the papers, then he knows about them, or at least has some suspicion about them. And if he knows *we're* here looking for them, then he must know there's some sort of significance to them.' C's actions in requesting us to investigate might very well have unwittingly tipped his hand to Ardmore about that. 'Consequently, he must be eager to obtain them for himself, and so he's sent Willoughby to either find them before we do or intercept them from us.'

Sidney's hand flourished sardonically. 'Hence this new spirit of cooperation and Willoughby sticking close by us.'

'But if not Smith, then *who* is the murderer? And who did Miss Baverel travel to Holland with? And why did they use the name Smith?' I demanded to know, growing frustrated with our ignorance. 'I mean, other than the obvious.' That it was the most common British surname and, therefore, unremarkable.

His eyes narrowed at the wall just below the landscape painting hanging there. 'I think someone is deliberately toying with us.' His eyebrows lifted and fell. 'That, or they're doing a hashed job of framing Smith.'

I flopped back on the bed again, pressing a hand to my forehead, struggling to make sense of matters through the fog permeating my head.

'Let's forget about Smith. After all, the facts didn't lead us to him. We were only trying to fit one of Ardmore's henchmen into the role and he seemed likeliest given the circumstances. So let's swipe him from our thoughts for now and concentrate on what we do know.'

'All right.' Sidney laid down beside me. 'We know Miss de Boer and a mystery man shared the train compartment with Offerman and were the last to see him alive.'

'And Miss de Boer was frightened of something when we tried to question her, but we don't know what. We should definitely pay her another visit.'

His dark hair rustled against the counterpane as he nodded once in agreement. 'We know that, according to the porter's and conductor's testimony, no one else could have entered the compartment between the time the train left Amsterdam and when the body was found in the Hague.'

'Except them.'

'Just so.'

I squinted at the ceiling. 'But how could they know that for certain? Couldn't *someone* have slipped past?'

'I wondered the same thing. But for now, let's assume that's true. Then we're left with three possible culprits.'

'Though we've already ruled out the porter, haven't we?'

'Yes, I'm nearly certain that chap is innocent.'

'Then either the mystery man or the conductor.'

Sidney's head rolled to the side to look at me. 'Who was also acting strangely when we spoke to him.'

I turned so that I was lying on my side, facing him. 'We should also speak to him again. At his home this time, like you suggested.'

He reached up to finger one of my auburn curls as it fell forward over my cheek. 'Sounds like we have our plan of action for the morning.' He turned toward the window. 'And hopefully there won't be more rain.'

'I should also pay a visit to Eileen.' First thing, before T arrived. 'I'm hoping she'll help us look into Smith's movements, be it Lieutenant Smith or another man. And I trust she'll let me put in a call to Kathleen about corroborating Willoughby's claims that Smith was in London.' C's secretary would know who to contact to find out that information.

Sidney's midnight blue eyes appraised me intently. 'Do you want to talk about that message in your coat pocket?' The telegram from C.

The hollow place inside me twinged, reminding me it was there, waiting for me to fall into it.

'Not particularly. At least, not now,' I told him.

He didn't press, and I was grateful for that. Instead, he took my face in his hands. 'Whenever you're ready.' He waited for me to acknowledge this and then brought my mouth to his in a kiss.

CHAPTER TWENTY-ONE

Despite my fatigue the evening before and the early hour I'd greeted the sun, I woke up feeling refreshed and reinvigorated. Our having boiled the disorder of the inquiry down to its essentials had given me new hope that we might actually be able to uncover the truth.

Unfortunately, I'd forgotten the day was Sunday, so a visit to Eileen was out of the question. She wouldn't be at the Boompjes office, and I didn't know her home address. Neither would Kathleen be at the Secret Intelligence Service's new London premises in Melbury Road near Holland Park, west of Kensington Palace. My queries for both ladies would have to wait until the following day.

On the train bound for the Hague, Sidney and I discovered Schröder had carried through with his warnings that we would appear in their paper. We weren't on the front page, but close enough. However, the draw of the article wasn't our capacities as investigators, but the photograph they'd included with it. A photograph I hadn't even been aware was being taken as we stood gazing into each other's eyes on the busy platform at the Hollandsche Spoor station. The short article accompanying it speculated about our presence in Holland, including a rather tongue-in-cheek inquiry about whether we were on the heels of another traitor or murderer, but it didn't state anything outright, for which I was relieved.

But the photograph appeared to have had the exact opposite effect on the conductor. At the sight of us standing on the doorstep of his narrow brick house in his respectable neighborhood several blocks from the station, his eyes nearly bulged out of his head. 'You cannot be here!' he exclaimed after flapping his arms to shoo us back and joining us on the doorstep. He darted a glance behind him and then shut the door with a decisive click. 'My wife, her heart is not so good, and this murder business has already upset her terribly.' He scowled. 'And then for a picture of the two of you in *my* station to appear in *De Telegraaf*.' His mustache fairly quivered with indignation. 'No, you must go.'

I eyed him shrewdly. 'We'll go, if you tell us what you're keeping from the police.'

His gaze darted to the left and then the right, confirming what I'd suspected. That he had just as little wish for us to be seen by his neighbors as his wife. 'I am not keeping anything from the police.'

'You are. Something about the mystery man. Perhaps you recognized him.'

308

His hands fisted at his sides. 'I know nothing about the mystery man. Now go.'

'Hmm. Then I suppose we shall have to continue strolling up and down your block.' I turned to Sidney, adjusting my gloves. 'I do so hope no one steps out to offer their assistance. That could be awkward.'

We had already stridden two steps to the south before he snapped, 'It's not about the mystery man.'

We pivoted to stare up at him expectantly.

Propping his hands on his hips, he puffed out an aggravated breath. 'It concerns the woman who stepped forward, claiming she was the other passenger in the compartment with Offerman and the other man.'

'The nurse from Haarlem?' I clarified.

He nodded. 'I saw her at the police station. Heard her giving her testimony.' His round eyes were grave. 'But she wasn't the woman I witnessed board the compartment in Amsterdam.'

'She wasn't?'

He shook his head.

I shared a look of surprise with Sidney. 'Then do you know the woman who did? Can you describe her?'

'She had brown hair. Same as that nurse. But it was a darker color, and shorter, and more . . .' he gestured toward his head as if uncertain how to describe it.

'Chic?'

He pointed at me. 'That! She was certainly a looker. And she had this way of smiling. Charmed everyone in her vicinity.'

Not Miss de Boer, then. Although I was sure she had a lovely smile, when she chose to use it, it was not the melting smile of a woman accustomed to wielding it to her advantage. But I knew a woman who was, and who had been in Holland on the days in question.

'Why haven't you told the police any of this?' Sidney asked.

'Because the woman knew all the particulars. She was respectable, and she made a point of telling the police that people often don't recognize her when she's not in her nursing uniform. How was I to counter that?'

He had a point. The police probably would have dismissed his claims as those of a muddled man who routinely saw hundreds of faces getting on and off the train every day. But he still should have made the effort.

'I take it you're thinking the same thing I am,' Sidney remarked as we walked away.

I nodded grimly. 'That we need to find out how well Miss de Boer knew Miss Baverel. And how much she knows about Offerman's murder.'

However, Miss de Boer did not want to speak with us.

When no one answered her door after Sidney rapped on it three times, he turned to scan our surroundings with a frown. 'Perhaps she's not home.'

But I had seen the curtain in the adjacent window twitch. 'Oh, she's here.' I stepped forward, raising my voice to be heard through the glass and wood. 'Miss de Boer, you really should open up and speak to us. We know you weren't on the train that night.'

Sidney nudged me and nodded toward a woman across the street who had stepped out on the pavement to eye us curiously.

'Or I could speak a bit louder – and in Dutch – so that your neighbors can hear.'

At this threat, the door was wrenched open. 'Stop that!' she hissed in French, confirming my suspicions that she spoke either English or French or German, for Miss Baverel spoke no Dutch.

'Then I suggest you invite us in, for we're not leaving until we have answers,' I replied, staring her down.

After a moment, her eyes dropped and she stepped back, allowing us to enter the small vestibule. She closed the door and locked it before leading the way into a small, serviceable parlor with few ornamentations. Rather than sit, she turned to face us, crossing her arms over her chest. 'What do you want?'

'Why did you lie and tell the police you were the woman who shared the train compartment with Mr Offerman on the night of his murder?'

She turned her head to the side, as if by not facing us she wouldn't have to admit what she'd done.

'Were you paid for the trouble . . . or blackmailed?'

Her shoulders hunched at the ugly word, and I knew I was on to something.

'Tell us and we might be able to help.'

She sniffed, lifting her hand to swipe at her cheek. It was then that I realized she was crying. Sidney and I waited silently, giving her time to gather herself before she spoke.

'Three weeks ago, on a Sunday morning much like this, a woman appeared on my doorstep.' She crossed toward a small table, reaching inside a drawer to extract a handkerchief. 'I didn't know who she was, but she seemed impossibly elegant.' Her red-rimmed gaze dipped to my own fashionable icy blue gown and leather boots. 'And she told me she had a . . . a *proposition* for me.' She fairly spat the word before her head dipped to the handkerchief she was now wringing in her hands. 'That if I did as I was instructed, she . . . she wouldn't reveal that I had secretly fed information to . . . to one of the belligerents during the war.'

'Which belligerent?' I pressed, though I could easily guess. After all, we were clearly British, and if she'd been sharing information with the Allies, she would have simply stated it, counting on our affinity.

I felt rather than saw Sidney stiffen beside me as he grasped this and some of its ramifications. If she had been feeding information to the Germans, then she must have had access to intelligence they wanted. Which meant she must have served in a hospital or a camp that treated Allied prisoners.

By the terms of their neutrality, the Dutch had been forced to maintain such camps for both the Allied and German soldiers who crossed over the Dutch border, either intentionally or by chance. This included sailors whose ships had been sunk, pilots whose aircraft had been downed, Allied soldiers who were caught escaping over the border from Belgium, and sometimes German deserters.

'I don't know how she'd discovered it,' she continued, ignoring my question, 'but I couldn't risk her sharing what she knew. I would lose my position if nothing else.'

'So you agreed to lie for her,' I prodded.

She nodded hesitantly. 'She said all I had to do was tell the police that *I* had been the one who'd traveled in the compartment with Mr Offerman from Amsterdam. That they would keep my identity confidential and no one else would know what I'd done.'

'And she supplied you with the information to convince them.'

'Didn't you stop to think that maybe you were helping a murderess to get away with her crime?' Sidney demanded harshly.

'No.' Her voice shook. 'It couldn't have been her. She said Mr Offerman was still alive when she exited the train. That she simply couldn't be caught up in the ugliness of the crime, but she

313

would tell me everything she would have told the police to help catch the killer.'

'And yet she just happened to know where you lived and that you'd supplied information to the Germans during the war,' I pointed out, hoping this statement and my skepticism would pierce through her wall of denial.

She flushed.

'So everything you told the police, all of that information came from this woman?'

She nodded.

'The timeline of events, the interaction – or lack thereof – between the two men, the description of the third passenger?'

'Yes.'

Which meant that all of it could be lies. Everything we thought we knew could be false.

My eyes narrowed. 'What of the suspect the police arrested? The man you identified from his photograph?'

She hunched deeper into her shoulders. 'He looked like the man she described.'

I couldn't halt my lip from curling in disgust. Thank goodness the man had possessed an iron-clad alibi.

'I thought I was helping,' she protested.

'By identifying a man you'd never actually seen? A man who would be arrested for murder based on your faulty testimony?'

She blanched. 'I had no reason to think the woman was lying.'

Except she had. Was she really blind to that fact or simply refusing to acknowledge it?

'Describe this woman. In detail,' I specified.

'She was about your height and had dark brown hair bobbed to about here.' She touched her neck beside her chin. 'Heavily lashed eyes, a wide mouth, pert nose, and a slightly pointed chin.'

This fit Miss Baverel to a T.

'And did she tell you anything about herself or where she was going?' I asked.

'No. She told me what to do and say and then left.'

I scrutinized her closely before glancing about the room. 'Did she give you anything or leave anything behind with you for safekeeping? And I would be *very* careful before you lie to us on this point,' I cautioned with a gimlet glare.

Her eyes widened, darting to Sidney – who I trusted appeared similarly intimidating – before returning to me. 'Just her train ticket and . . . a few guilders.'

I didn't ask her to specify how much 'a few' amounted to, I was more interested in discovering whether Miss Baverel had used this place to conceal Offerman's report or the evidence she'd spoken to us about in Amiens. But Miss de Boer, for all her faults, appeared in this instance to be telling the truth.

We excused ourselves, strolling through the sun-drenched streets of Haarlem back toward the train station. The skies today were a brilliant

315

blue with naught but a few white, fluffy clouds dotting the horizon far off to the west, over the North Sea. The chill wind still tugged at my toque hat and stung my cheeks, but this weather was a vast improvement over the previous day.

'What are you thinking?' Sidney queried as we rounded the corner to see the arched façade and rectangular towers of the station standing a block before us.

'I'm wondering if we've all had the timing wrong. If perhaps the murder took place before Haarlem, and Miss Baverel exited with Offerman's report tucked into her bag or her coat.'

'And the other man remained on board with the body?' Sidney replied doubtfully. 'Isn't that rather risky?'

'Maybe. Maybe not. Remember, the porter initially thought Offerman was simply a drunk who'd fallen asleep.'

He dipped his head, conceding this.

'It still would've taken a lot of nerve, but then killing a man in a closed compartment on a moving train already requires a great deal of daring.'

'Or stupidity.'

I offered him a weak smile in acknowledgment of this jest. 'And yet they've gotten away with it. Partly, I suspect, because of Miss Baverel's ruse. Everything the police know about the crime and the people involved could be a lie. Maybe Offerman did recognize the other man. Maybe they all interacted. Maybe they forced him to give them the report, Miss Baverel exited, and then the man killed him. Whatever the exact truth is, we don't know. Other than that Mr Offerman, Miss Baverel, and a second man boarded that first-class carriage in Amsterdam, Miss Baverel exited at Haarlem, and Offerman's body was found when the train reached the Hague.'

Sidney slid his hands into the pockets of his trousers. 'What makes you think that Miss Baverel left the train with the report?'

'Several things. For one, she left the train earlier than the men, and I have to believe that was for a reason – to remove the report, their main objective, lest they be discovered. It also allowed her to deflect suspicion from the female passenger and to instigate their ruse with Miss de Boer, but I think the chief purpose was to secure the report.'

I fell quiet, smiling at a passing young girl walking a very large dog. Or rather a very large dog walking a young girl. I doubted the child could exert any control over the canine should he choose to disobey.

'You'll also recall what Agent Charlaix told us about her movements,' I continued once we were beyond earshot. 'He said that when leaving Holland she'd taken a ship from Antwerp to Calais, though they didn't know how she'd gotten from Amsterdam to Antwerp. But I don't think that was the plan.'

Sidney took hold of my arm, guiding me around a streetlamp, which in my growing enthusiasm I'd almost collided with.

317

'I think the third passenger – the mystery man – took the *Hoektreinen*, as we've already hypothesized, and caught one of the night boats to England. Miss Baverel was supposed to take a ferry from IJmuiden to England to join him, but she didn't. Instead, she made her way across Holland and into Belgium either covertly or using an alternate identity.'

'You think she double-crossed him.' His brow furrowed, appearing to give this due consideration. 'She's certainly capable of it. But why would she risk such a thing?'

I shook my head. 'I don't know. Maybe she thought she could extort more money out of them. Maybe she sold it to a higher bidder.' I frowned as a more unsettling possibility occurred to me. 'Or maybe after looking at the report and reading whatever information it contained, she balked at passing it over to whoever hired her.'

Sidney turned to look at me, clearly following my trail of thought, but his response had to wait until we'd boarded the train. 'Mr Gevers did say that Offerman had told him he'd learned something upsetting,' he murmured close to my ear, lest the woman on the opposite side of the compartment overhear us. 'Something that had made him rethink the choices he'd made and the loyalties he'd adopted.'

I nestled closer to his side, grateful for the warmth of his arm wrapped around me, and the bay rum of his aftershave drowning out the

318

mild odor of fish permeating the carriage. 'And the telegram Schröder shared with us from his colleague about the auction claimed the papers contained proof of betrayal at the highest levels of government, a betrayal that would alter the world's understanding of the final two years of the war.'

'Verity, that doesn't sound, to me, like Offerman's report was about a gold wreck,' Sidney said, being the one finally brave enough to state outright the suspicions that had disturbed my thoughts with increasing urgency since our meeting with T the previous morning. '*Or* the repercussions from the disclosure that a Dutch ministry employee was sharing intelligence with the British.'

'I know,' I replied in a small voice and then closed my eyes, forcing myself to be courageous enough to face the rest. 'And I think C and T also know it.'

We sat silently, allowing the ramifications of this fact to settle around us. Sidney's arm tightened around me, recognizing the pain ricocheting through me, shredding me from the inside out. I had to force myself to inhale, to focus my thoughts and not give in to the despondency and disillusionment swamping me.

'Then they've been deliberately misleading us, and we have to ask ourselves why,' Sidney said softly while his hand massaged my hip.

I blinked open my eyes, staring blindly toward the view outside the window. 'The obvious answer is that they don't want us to know what the report

319

contains.' The sour taste of betrayal filled my mouth. 'That would also explain why T ordered me to destroy it when we found it rather than open it.'

'And if they don't want us to read it, then it must be bad.' Sidney's voice was taut with the same restrained emotion I was struggling with, and I turned to look up into his haunted eyes, knowing his brain was evoking and discarding dozens of possibilities, each one worse than the last. 'Ver, what could it be?' he pleaded on a sliver of sound.

But I had no answer for him. None but the same sort of unfounded phantasms my own mind was conjuring. The only real clue we had was that it had something to do with Offerman's trip to Germany. What had he learned there? What had he discovered?

I had sent a telegram to my former commanding officer, Captain Landau, in Berlin three days prior, asking him to uncover any information he could for me about Offerman's movements, but I'd yet to hear back from him. Perhaps it was time to prod him again.

'We have to find that report, Sidney. Not for C, but for us.'

I needed to know why they'd lied to us. Sidney needed to know. We'd both sacrificed nearly all, including each other, for our country. We needed to know what C and T were so intent on hiding from us.

CHAPTER TWENTY-TWO

'**W**here do we start?' Sidney asked as the train departed the next station. The woman who had been sharing our compartment had disembarked, and we no longer had to speak in whispers. 'If Miss Baverel took the papers, as you're suggesting, what did she do with them?'

I noted his features were no longer quite so haggard, the shock having worn off, but I still remained close by his side, seeking his comfort even as I gave him mine. 'Perhaps she hid them. Somewhere between here and Antwerp.'

'Like she hid the proof about other collaborators at work along the Western Front?' His voice was skeptical.

'Maybe they're one and the same, or hidden together,' I posited. 'Perhaps that's why she was really arrested. She was outed by the partner she'd betrayed. She *did* claim she'd been denounced to the authorities by a lover. More specifically, by Émile. Or did she mean "a rival"?' I arched my eyebrows in emphasis. 'That *is* one of the meanings of Émile. A rival.' I'd not considered it before, but now knowing what we did, how could we not?

Sidney nodded in thought before shaking his head in challenge. 'But what of the auction? Are you suggesting that's also a ruse?'

I turned to face him more fully. 'Maybe. Whoever is behind it doesn't seem to have offered up any proof that they actually have the documents they claim to. The auction could be the work of an opportunist seeking to profit from the rumors swirling in the newspapers about the documents taken from Offerman's portfolio.'

'Yes, but then wouldn't the auctioneer be claiming they contained information about the sinking of the *Renate Leonhardt*?'

I stilled.

'If this auctioneer is simply profiting from an opportunity in the press, how does he know that the documents aren't about the gold wreck?'

I pressed a hand to my temple. 'You're right. A swindler would know he could capture the interest of a more gullible breed of person by perpetuating the idea the documents give the location and specifics about a *gold wreck* rather than some nebulous claims about the maneuverings and manipulations of the British empire.' I tapped my leg, trying to see my way through to a solution. 'All right, then, maybe she *did* hide them, but someone found them.'

'Who? Her partner? Smith?'

'He's the likeliest player. And since the two seem

322

to have been lovers, he may have known about some of her hiding places.'

Sidney's head sank back against the seat. 'It's a better solution than I can come up with.'

It didn't quite fit all the known parameters, but it was close. However, I wasn't entirely satisfied, and I doubted I would be until we could prove Smith was in all the places we needed him to be to make the story fit. And I couldn't do that until I spoke with Eileen and Kathleen.

I tipped my head to the side, letting it rest on Sidney's shoulder. 'The question now is, where is Smith?' I felt Sidney shift to look down at me and lifted my head again to meet his gaze. 'Is he in London as Willoughby claimed? Or is he here, in Holland?'

We hadn't faced any direct threats to our lives for over forty-eight hours, but that didn't mean Smith wasn't somewhere nearby, biding his time.

Sidney's hand drifted to the pocket of his trench coat, and I knew he was fingering his Luger. I had never liked relying on guns. During the war, when my assignments had taken me over the electric fence into German-occupied Belgium, I'd not been allowed to take a pistol. The Belgians and French living under occupation were forbidden to have them, and the discovery of any such weapon would have resulted in my immediate arrest, followed by interrogation and the Germans' unpleasant third-degree methods. But perhaps it was time I started carrying the Webley I'd secreted away in my luggage on a more regular basis.

I was waiting for Eileen with a warm *stroopwafel* when she arrived at HQ the following morning. She immediately wrapped me in her lavender scent and then hurried me up to a small side office, correctly deducing that I was avoiding T. By necessity our visit was brief, but I was relieved to see her looking well, and she didn't even bat an eyelash at my request that she look into the recent movements of Lieutenant James Smith, lately with the Royal Fusiliers, as well as Adele Baverel, also known as Adele Dupré. She also patched me through to Kathleen in London, who agreed to attempt to corroborate Willoughby's claims and send her reply through Eileen.

Then Eileen hustled me out the back entrance with a warning. 'T's on a rampage about this one. I've never seen him this way before. I don't know exactly what all this is about.' The secretaries, clerks, and analysts rarely did – I remembered that much from my time seated on that side of the desk. 'But . . . be careful, Verity.' She clasped my hand briefly before shooing me on. 'And stay away until you've got something to report, or you're likely to get your nose bitten off.'

I took her words to heart, scurrying down the Boompjes before T caught sight of me.

Back at the hotel, I discovered Sidney was out, so I pulled my Webley pistol from my luggage and sat down to clean it. I knew Sidney preferred a Luger, despite the fact he'd had to make do with a British army–issued Webley during the war. The aim on the German Lugers *was* supposed to be superior. However, my brother Rob had given me the Webley a few months before his aeroplane had been shot down and he was killed. He'd also taught me how to fire it and care for it, cautioning that a poorly maintained weapon was as dangerous as a poorly aimed one. I'd taken this lesson to heart and derived a sort of comfort from performing the ritual – the last thing that my beloved brother had ever taught me. It made me feel closer to him somehow, at least temporarily.

Meanwhile, I allowed my mind to wander, and it was while doing so that I began to puzzle over the gun used to shoot Offerman. We hadn't yet considered the case from this angle, though the police had collected three shell casings from the scene. The papers had reported that they were labeled RAC 25, and that they came from the Remington Arms Company, an American machine factory. They'd also discovered that the casings were two to three years old, manufactured in 1917 or 1918, and were likely fired from a Colt automatic pistol.

It wasn't entirely surprising to be confronted with American shell casings fired from an American gun in Europe. After all, the Americans had entered the war in early 1917, and begun arriving in France early the next year in droves. But it *was* rare to find them in Holland, far from the Western Front. It was possible that a Dutchman possessed an American pistol. There were undoubtedly dozens who did. But it was unusual enough that it had led to hypotheses that the killer was foreign.

This fit with our own suspicions that Smith was the killer, but would Smith choose such a weapon? And if he did, would he really use two- to three-year-old ammunition? I was no gun expert, so the answer to that question was beyond me. But Sidney might know it. Perhaps the Colt was a superior weapon, something a sniper might choose as his sidearm even if the ammunition was slightly dated.

I jolted in surprise, lowering the rag I'd been using to wipe down my pistol as a realization dawned on me. Smith was a sniper. He was trained to kill with precision and accuracy. I'd seen the evidence of his skill firsthand when he'd executed a man with a single shot from a roof three hundred feet away. So, why had it taken him three shots to kill Offerman?

I knew a pistol was different from a sniper rifle, just as I knew killing someone at close range was different from killing someone from afar. But there had been no evidence in the carriage of a struggle or that Offerman had fought back. Yet the killer's aim had been rather poor. Offerman had been shot in the forearm and under the collarbone near the shoulder before the kill shot was made to his heart. Offerman had been seated in the corner of the carriage by the window, with nowhere to run. In such a scenario, the shot should have been easy for a man like Smith.

It didn't make any sense. And I told Sidney so the moment he returned.

From the furrows marring his brow, I could tell he was also flummoxed. 'Then Smith isn't the shooter?'

'I don't see how he can be.' I paused, biting my lip. 'Unless he was deliberately trying to muddy the waters. But why would he do so when he had already placed himself in a precarious situation? What if the shots had been heard? What if he couldn't get away cleanly?'

'I agree. That does seem doubtful.' He rubbed a hand over his jaw. 'But if not Smith, then who?'

I shook my head, returning to the notion I'd come up with before his return. 'Maybe Inspector Van de Pol can tell us more about the angle of the shots. Perhaps if we better understood it might not seem so implausible.'

Sidney agreed and we gathered our coats and hats and set off for the train station. However, we were waylaid in the lobby by the man behind the desk.

'Mrs Kent, this just came for you,' he said, holding out an envelope.

I thanked him and then stepped to the side to open it, already recognizing the handwriting on the outside. 'Eileen confirms the information that Charlaix already told us about an Adele Baverel and a James Smith entering Holland three and a half weeks ago.' I summarized aloud as I read. 'But she needs more time to delve deeper.' The next words I read made my heart still.

'Ver, what is it?' Sidney asked. My unease must have been evident.

'There's an addendum.' I tilted the page so he could read the words scrawled at the bottom.

Be advised. The suspect arrived at the Hook on a ship from England on 27/3. Whereabouts currently unknown.

Given the fact we knew Miss Baverel was dead – we had seen her with our own eyes – the suspect in question must be Smith.

Sidney's gaze met mine momentarily before turning to scan the occupants of the crowded lobby. 'So much for Willoughby's assertions.'

Except, with the clarity of rest and distance, I believed Willoughby had thought he was telling us the truth about Smith's current whereabouts. That Smith had been issued a warning and would stay put rather than incur Ardmore's wrath. So, if Smith was here now, then either Willoughby had been lied to, or Smith was willing to risk all that to accomplish whatever he'd come here to do. Given that fact, I wouldn't put anything past him, and that made Smith a very dangerous man.

I grasped my suede reticule, feeling the outline of the Webley I'd placed there before we left our room through the fabric.

'We'll need to proceed with caution,' Sidney murmured.

'I agree, but we can't simply halt the investigation.'

'We'll wait near the doors until the tram approaches.'

I tucked my arm loosely through his left arm – lest he need to draw his pistol with his right – and remained close by his side. Once on the tram, we found seats and settled in for the short ride to Rotterdam Central Station to catch the train to the Hague. The sky outside the tram windows was gray and threatening rain, though the wind was not as ferocious as it had been the past few days. However, the heavy clouds were deterrent enough to keep those who could remain inside off the street, and the number of passengers on the late-morning tram was few.

There was some sort of commotion as the tram-line veered right to pass to the east of the Westersingel canal and then the clang of bells as we were brought to a standstill. Sidney rose to his feet along with several of the other passengers to see what the problem was. Some began voicing their displeasure, so I had some inkling that it was no small matter.

'It appears a cart has spilled part of its load on the tram tracks,' Sidney grumbled.

I could hear the tram driver hollering at the carter, and a few others joined in.

Turning to survey the scene out the window, I noted the quiet flowing canal, and the trees bordering it. On the other side of the tram, the street was lined with Rotterdam's characteristic buildings constructed from small bricks varying slightly in shade and texture. It was a quiet area except for the passing trams, with few intersections and wide enough verges that the looking glasses which often projected from the sides of buildings, angled so that drivers could see the traffic going up and down the next cross street before they were upon it, were not needed.

The back of my neck prickled, and I straightened in alarm.

'Something isn't right,' Sidney murmured, sensing the same thing I had.

This wasn't the customary place for a cart accident. In fact, it was difficult to understand how one could have happened at all.

Unless it wasn't truly an accident.

My heart kicked in my chest. People had begun exiting the tram, and Sidney took hold of my hand, urging me to follow. All the while, we continued to scan our surroundings for something or someone suspicious.

We were partway through the door when the detonation occurred. I was hurled through the air, and the next thing I knew I was lying facedown on the brick pavement. There was a ringing in my ears, one that muffled the chaos that met my eyes as I blinked them open. The front of the tram was on fire. Smoke billowed from its doors, and the carter struggled to bring his rearing horse under control. People were running and screaming from the scene, while the bodies of others littered the street here and there.

I pushed up onto my elbows, trying to gather my wits, and had just caught sight of Sidney lying several feet away with his back to me, when a pair of arms grasped me under the armpits and began pulling me away from the carnage. I tried to speak, to ask them to help my husband, but I couldn't tell if any sound emerged. It wasn't until the arms dragged me into a neighboring building and slammed the door behind us that I realized they weren't aiding me.

By the time my brain had grasped what was happening and my limbs had gathered the energy to protest, I'd been dumped in a heap in the corner of the next room. A moment later a bucket of cold water was thrown in my face.

I gasped and spluttered, swiping away the wetness from my eyes. My cheekbone stung as I dragged my hand over it, and other parts of my body began to make their pain known, including my left shoulder where I'd taken a bullet nearly four months earlier. It screamed in pain as a pair of hands unceremoniously grabbed my upper arms and yanked me upright, shaking me.

'Who killed Adele?'

I stared, horrified, into Smith's snarling face.

'Who killed her? Tell me!' He shook me even harder. 'Tell me!'

I struggled to find my tongue, and when I didn't

do so fast enough, he backhanded me across the face.

I yelped in pain. 'I . . . I don't know.'

'Tell me!' he roared into my face.

I felt myself cracking as a whimper escaped my chest. 'Please, I don't know,' I sobbed. 'They . . . they wouldn't let us investigate.'

He glared down at me in righteous fury, and I was certain he was about to kill me, but instead he tossed me to the ground like I was so much rubbish.

I lay blubbering in the puddle of water from the bucket he'd dumped over me, trying to gather together the tatters of my self-control. My head spun and my thoughts kept fluttering away from me like tattered ribbons I couldn't grasp hold of. Finally I seized one and wrangled it to the ground with all my strength. Inhaling deeply, I pushed upright, seizing another ribbon and another, until I didn't feel like I was coming quite so unraveled. Even so, the remnants of my self-possession were naught but a ratty cloak I clutched around me as I turned to face Smith.

He had paced away from me, muttering foul curses, but now he rounded on me again. His sharp features were contorted with rage, but also grief. It was that emotion that I latched onto, reminding myself he was human and not a monster.

'Who killed Adele?' he demanded again with more control.

'I honestly don't know,' I told him. 'At first, we

thought it might be you,' I hastened to add. 'We know you tried to see her several days before she was killed.'

His eyes narrowed briefly. 'Aye, and I thought it was you when I saw you at the gendarmerie and then searching Adele's home.' His jaw ticked. 'But now that we both know the other is not responsible, who is?' he snapped.

'I wish I knew. But as I said, the gendarmes wouldn't let us investigate. My best guess is that it was one of them.' My voice sounded tinny to my ears but given the fact, a short while ago, I couldn't even hear that, I was relieved I could hear at all.

He grunted, his gaze dipping to my chest where my coat had come open and my sodden white silk blouse now did very little to conceal what was beneath. I yanked the sides of my coat closed, and he smirked. Apparently, his grief over Adele's death didn't prevent him from still being a lecher. However, his amusement was all too short-lived.

'The gendarmes wanted her to testify. They wanted the chance to lock up as many enemy collaborators as possible. It doesn't make sense for one of them to have killed her,' he argued.

'Maybe they realized she never meant to go through with it.'

But I could tell from the tightening of his features that he didn't know what I was talking about. Or perhaps he was pretending not to.

'Your colleague, Captain Willoughby, told us that Lord Ardmore instructed Miss Baverel to coax us to Amiens. To say whatever she needed to in order to convince us to come.'

The muscle in his jaw ticked, and I realized his bafflement was genuine.

'You didn't know?'

'No,' he bit out. He assessed me once again, and then his chin came up. 'But I knew Willoughby had been sent to Furnes to intercept you.' His lips curled mockingly. 'To undermine whatever Adele might have told you.' His disdain softened. 'Though I'm not entirely certain how you worked out you needed to visit Miss Lemaire. Not when I wasn't allowed to visit Adele to tell her that Willoughby was keeping her friend company, lest she forget herself.'

And reveal to us whatever secrets they wanted to remain hidden.

But if everything he was saying was true, then Miss Baverel hadn't lured us to France at Ardmore's urging. She'd asked for Sidney of her own volition, and upon learning of it, Ardmore had simply tried to turn that request to his advantage, and blunt whatever damage she might have wrought.

'You're certain Ardmore didn't contrive to have her arrested?' I queried, expressing my own doubts as well as trying to sow seeds of suspicion in him.

He hesitated a moment, and his eyes lifted to scrutinize the wall above my head, giving me a short time to search the space without his direct observation. We appeared to be in some sort of storeroom. Boxes and crates were stacked along the walls and the air smelled of dust and smoke, though I suspected at least the latter was coming from my own clothes. Gloomy sunlight filtered through two windows, both positioned too high above street level for anyone to peer inside.

Even more disturbing, I couldn't find my reticule. It must have flown from my hand during the blast and been left on the street. Which meant all the care I'd taken to clean my Webley this morning was for naught. Not when I didn't have it close to hand when I most needed it.

'Stop trying to confuse the matter,' Smith barked, recapturing my attention. 'I'm fairly certain I know who arranged her arrest, and it was not this . . . Ardmore you speak of.'

I glared at him, angry he was toying with me. He knew full well who I was talking about. It was stamped in his sneer and the scornful glint in his eyes.

'So if you know who arranged her arrest, then why aren't you interrogating them instead of setting off bombs in trams and injuring innocent bystanders simply so you can speak to me?' I demanded to know. I attempted to arch one of my eyebrows, but the movement hurt the muscles in my face too much. 'Another pencil detonator?' Just like the one we'd figured he used in the bombing of General Bishop's temporary HQ.

Smith neither confirmed nor denied this, but I

didn't really need him to. Instead, he flexed his fists at his sides and took a step closer, intent on intimidating me. It worked, too, but I had regained enough of my poise that I didn't shrink from his thunderous glower.

'Because I don't know his name.' He cracked his knuckles. 'Yet.' He enunciated the consonants precisely.

I frowned. 'And you think I do?'

'You *are* investigating his crime.'

'The Offerman murder?'

Having not just been blown off a tram step, his facial muscles appeared to be in good working order, allowing his brows to lift and crease in all sorts of insolent ways.

'Then you didn't travel with Miss Baverel to Holland three and a half weeks ago?'

'I did not.'

'But a James Smith is recorded arriving with her.'

'I'm well aware,' he practically growled. 'But it wasn't me.'

Then a thought occurred to me. 'Do you usually travel under your own name? Or an alias?'

That muscle in his jaw leaped again, telling me he was reaching the end of his tether, but he answered me regardless. 'I rarely bother with an alias, unless I sign my first name John instead of James. The surname Smith is so common, and who would believe I would use my own name if I'm intent on . . . mischief?' he finished, settling on the rather innocuous word to encompass all the murder and destruction he caused.

'Then maybe this man knows you well enough to know that. Or Miss Baverel told him.'

He clearly didn't like the idea of that last part, but I could tell that I'd given him something to chew over.

While he was lost in this contemplation, I shifted so that my feet were beneath me, which would make it easier to stand. The world spun slightly, but not enough that I didn't think I could make it out the door if given the opportunity.

The sound of loud knocking drew both of our attention to the front of the shop. Someone was trying to get inside, and hope surged inside me. I had to get out of here and get to Sidney. The hazy memory of him lying on the bricks unresponsive made my chest clutch in fear. But first I had to deal with Smith.

'Where are the documents they stole?' he demanded.

'You know about that?' I countered, stalling for time.

'Everyone knows his portfolio was emptied,' he snarled, looming over me. 'So where are they?'

'Do you think if we knew we'd still be bumbling all over Holland?' I snapped back, tired of being barked at.

His face reddened and his eyes glittered with violent intent, and my throat dried with terror as I realized I'd pushed back too hard. Had the second series of knocks and the shouts that followed not landed even harder than the first, I was certain I would not have walked out of that building of my own volition. But flight proved more important to Smith than punishing me, and he turned and fled up a staircase I hadn't seen hidden behind a stack of boxes.

I reached out to the nearest crate, pushing up onto my wobbly feet just as the outer door burst open with the splintering of wood. 'Back here,' I raised my voice to shout, and then grimaced. 'I'm back here,' I called out again, ignoring the pain in my head.

A moment later, two city policemen opened the door to the storeroom with truncheons raised.

'Upstairs,' I directed them. 'He fled up the stairs.'

They took off up the steps and Sidney rushed into the room. I gave a sharp cry of relief at the sight of him and grasped onto him tightly as he gathered me into his embrace.

He breathed an oath into my hair. 'When we couldn't find you, I feared the worst.'

I sobbed into his shoulder and began to shiver.

His hands lifted to my face, turning it up so that he could see me, gently swiping away some of the tears that were spilling down my cheeks. I could tell that he was assessing me for damage, much as I was assessing him. Fortunately, except for an abrasion on his forehead and the debris on his hair and clothing, he appeared to have escaped rather unscathed.

His hands dropped to my upper arms as his eyes flashed with concern. 'Ver, why are you wet?' There was no need to reply as his gaze dipped to the floor behind me, taking in the entire scene. I couldn't have responded anyway, for I was now shaking so badly that I couldn't have formed words if I tried.

He wrapped an arm around me to guide me toward the door. 'Come on. Let's get you out of here.'

CHAPTER TWENTY-THREE

Two hours later, having bathed, changed clothes, and had our wounds tended to, Sidney and I sat on the settee arranged before the hearth in our hotel room with a blaze lit before us. My nerves and body had only just stopped shaking – an aftereffect of the shock to my system once the immediate danger had passed. I'd experienced it once before after a similar explosion, though that one had been followed by a terrific shelling where I'd huddled in a trench for hours. I didn't miss the irony that Smith had been the cause of both incidents. Or at least the explosions. I supposed I couldn't blame him for the Jerries' bombardment.

The physician who had seen to my and Sidney's cuts, bumps, and scrapes had given me a couple of phospherine tablets to calm my nerves, much like the ones they'd given the soldiers in the trenches who'd become windy. In truth, I couldn't help but link the uncontrollable tremors I'd felt with the shell shock experienced by so many of our Tommies. My own encounter had given me a greater sympathy for their plight, having to suffer through night after night of such barrages, some-times for weeks on end, even when they were supposed to be at ease. It tore my heart apart all over again at the recognition of what those men had suffered. What they continued to suffer. Men like my husband.

I huddled closer to Sidney. The rain which had threatened that morning now drummed against the windows, and the fire cast a flickering light over the dim room. Gazing into the hearth, my thoughts drifted to the lone woman who hadn't survived the tram explosion. As I'd suspected, Smith had used another pencil detonator placed at the front of the tram. Boarding at the back, we'd failed to see him. He had, of course, arranged for the carter to block the tram tracks – though that carter claimed he'd had no idea what his true intentions were. Then Smith had set the detonator and exited the tram, crossing to the side of the street where he'd waited for his chance to grab me after the explosion.

It had been a daring and risky plan. And one executed with almost zero concern for the loss to human life. I used the qualifier 'almost' because Smith seemed to have calculated the precise amount of the charge so that it disabled the tram and injured those in a nearby radius but did not completely destroy the trolley or everything in its path. The woman who had been killed had been standing within a few feet of the bag containing the bomb. However, I credited this mitigating factor to the reality that Smith had needed information from me, and so had not wanted the blast to kill me outright.

That Smith had gotten away – escaping onto the roof and across the adjoining buildings – did not surprise me. He had clearly plotted the entire matter ahead of time, down to every detail, including having that bucket of cold water at hand to dowse me with, snapping me from my stupor in the wake of the explosion. However, that did not lessen my fury. Had it taken Sidney and the police but a few more minutes to realize where Smith had dragged me, he might have killed me. I held no illusions about what he was capable of, despite Willoughby's assertions that he'd been warned not to harm me.

Though after seeing Willoughby's face in the lobby of the hotel upon our return, I held no further doubts that warning *had* in truth been issued. His expression had been bleak and angry, and more than a little apprehensive. I suspected the latter had as much to do with the fact that he would be the one who would have to report Smith's defiance to Ardmore as any worry for whatever the repercussions would be to Smith.

Sidney's head was bowed, his cheek resting on my forehead. After I'd finished relaying everything Smith had told me, he'd fallen into this silent revery, turning over the information in his mind. I'd been content to let him do so, for I'd had my

342

own reflections to ponder, but now I was anxious to hear what he thought.

'Do you believe him?' I finally prodded.

His chest rose and fell as he inhaled. 'That he didn't kill Miss Baverel?'

'That, and the rest.'

'Well . . . it seems odd to me that he would go to such lengths to interrogate you and then allow you to escape if he'd murdered her himself.' I could hear the strain in his voice as he struggled to be impartial. 'You said his wrath and anguish seemed genuine?'

'Yes, very much so.'

'Then I think we can at least absolve him of that crime, but the other . . .'

His voice trailed away, and I straightened so that I could see his expression in the dancing firelight. 'You find *that* less convincing.'

'Honestly' – he blew out a long, exasperated breath – 'I don't know *what* to think. He's our best suspect, and yet your insight about the shooting rings true. Smith isn't the type of assassin to do shoddy work. Today only proved that. He's calculating and precise.'

I had to agree. With minimal effort, I could think of a dozen different ways Smith could have gone about killing Offerman and stealing his papers that would have been less perilous to his possible discovery. A small amount of reconnaissance would have shown him that the route Offerman took from the train station at the Hague to his parents' house was quiet and deserted on a Saturday evening. He could have ambushed him then with less fuss and had a much easier escape.

'The one thing that *does* seem certain is that Smith is interested in Offerman's papers,' Sidney said.

I reached up to smooth the edges of the plaster the physician had affixed to a cut beside his right eyebrow. 'It makes sense if he thinks those are what got her killed, if he thinks she concealed them.'

'Or if she double-crossed him and he's intent on retrieving them for Ardmore,' he countered cynically.

'Yes,' I replied in a subdued voice. For that was the problem. We could make either scenario fit if we twisted the factors we didn't know to fit it. 'Then he let me live in hopes I would lead him to them.' Either on his own behalf or Ardmore's.

I could feel Sidney studying me in worry and turned to look at him. 'There's no need to beat around the bush,' I stated as calmly as I could, refusing to pretend the threat I'd faced today hadn't been critical. The bomb had stunned and disarmed me. I'd been unable to bring any of my training or natural wits to bear against Smith, being too befuddled to recognize up from down let alone defend myself mentally or physically. In those first minutes immediately after the blast I'd been utterly powerless in every way.

A tremor passed through me at the memory, and Sidney's hand lifted to cup my jaw, avoiding the abrasion to my cheek. 'Ver,' he murmured in an agonized voice.

I lifted my hand to grip his wrist, urging him to halt whatever he was about to say. 'Don't,' I choked out past the lump in my throat. The experience had been terrifying, yes, but putting that into words wouldn't make it less so. And neither would smothering it in pandering platitudes. It was simply something I was going to have to learn to accept. The body and the mind had limits.

I offered him a tight smile and what reassurance I could before returning to my point. 'So we need to be as prepared as we can be to confront him again.' I adjusted positions, gritting my teeth at the twinge in my left shoulder. 'He's certainly not going home now.'

'Then maybe we should.'

This quiet pronouncement surprised me. 'You can't mean that?' I replied.

'Why can't I?' he demanded. 'We've both just been blown up. We're battered and not in our best form.'

'A few scrapes and bruises . . .'

'It's more than that, Verity, and you know it.' His glare dipped to my shoulder. 'You were shot four months ago. You weren't entirely healed and now you've reinjured it. And my hip is hurting like the devil,' he growled, lest I argue further about the extent of our injuries.

'All right, but that doesn't mean we should stop. We *can't* stop. Not now.'

'Why not?'

I spluttered in aggravation. 'Because . . . because recovering these papers is too important—'

'More important than our lives?'

The grief and torment reflected in his eyes brought me up short.

He reached out to grip my hands. 'I almost lost you in Yorkshire, Ver. I watched you bleed out on that chapel floor before my very eyes.'

'That's a bit of an exaggeration.'

The look he shot back at me made me wish I could snatch those words back. Exaggeration or not, I *had* been seriously injured, and had our situations been reversed I would have been just as upset.

'When I woke up lying on the ground after that explosion today, and I lifted my head and couldn't find you, I could only imagine the worst.'

I flushed hot and then cold, my hands tightening around Sidney's as I relived my own fear of the moment I'd looked over to find him unresponsive and then been dragged away before I could go to him.

He stared down at our joined hands, seeming to gather his words. 'I understand that recovering these documents is important. I understand that you find purpose and meaning in continuing this intelligence work. I do, as well. I just . . . I'm not sure it's worth our lives anymore.' His face paled, making his features stand out in stark relief. 'I lost *enough* friends to the war, watched *enough* men die.' He inhaled sharply through his nostrils. 'I don't owe my country anything more. I definitely don't owe them my *wife*.'

I could hardly argue with that. I didn't *want* to argue with it. But a part of me still balked at the idea of abandoning this investigation when it felt as if we were close to solving it. It was partly my nature to never leave anything unfinished, and partly the obligation I felt to C and even T, despite the suspicions I now harbored about them. But it was mostly my heightened awareness of how drastically the events of the past could affect the future.

I closed my eyes against the tears threatening, bowing my head to press my cheek to his. 'I hear you, Sidney. I even agree,' I admitted softly. 'I just worry what our failure to procure those documents might mean.' I lifted my head to meet his gaze. 'I don't want to later regret that we didn't persevere. Should they be as damaging as we fear, should Ardmore consolidate more power . . . well, not only do I worry our lives might become more difficult, but I also fear we might look back and despise ourselves for walking away.'

Sidney had no ready answer for this. At least, none he could make in the three seconds between my finishing speaking and the knock on the door. He went to answer it while I brushed the wetness from the corners of my eyes and adjusted my skirts, lest I give the bellboy we anticipated a glimpse of more than my ankles.

However, when Sidney opened the door, it was not the hotel page who came striding in uninvited, but T. Clearly, he'd heard about the bombing, or he would never have darkened our doorstep, his hat and shoulders damp with rain, but rather summoned us to him.

'Word of the explosion is all over Rotterdam.' He stopped short at the sight of me, his eyes widening at the contusion on my cheek and the bandage peeking out at the wrist of my blouse. 'And the abduction of a woman from the scene. There are even rumors circulating that the intrepid Mr and Mrs Kent were among the injured parties.'

I sighed. If that was true, then the newspapers were certain to print it, and it would only be a matter of time before the London papers picked it up as well. I would have to call my family, as well as our friends, lest they begin to worry. This was one of those times when being a celebrity was a nuisance.

T's beady eyes narrowed. 'But I suppose all of the Netherlands, if not the world, knows you're in South Holland right now.' Apparently whatever sympathy he might have felt at our being injured was short-lived if he was already preparing to take us to task for Schröder's rather innocuous article. Before he could move on to berate us for visiting *De Telegraaf*'s editor in chief against his express orders not to, I pushed to my feet, cradling my left arm for maximum effect.

'Darling, my sling,' I told Sidney, who was

scowling at T's back as if he was contemplating tossing the man out on his rear end. His eyes met mine, deducing my ploy.

'The doctor and I warned you to take it easy, dearest. No one could blame you for resting under the circumstances.' That this last comment was directed at the other man in the room was almost too obvious.

Sidney draped the cloth over my head and helped me to adjust it to fit correctly, all the while wisely keeping his tight expression turned away from T. From the few glances I'd snuck of him over my husband's shoulder, I could tell he wasn't as devoid of compassion as he'd first seemed. His ruddy cheeks had blanched, and he averted his face until Sidney had finished.

Once I'd settled myself on the settee again, with a pillow propped under my arm, he cleared his throat. 'Did you recognize the fellow who did this?'

I filled him in on the same particulars I'd already relayed to the Rotterdam police, but while I'd told the Dutch that Smith had abducted me for ransom, and then abandoned me when I'd feigned a greater injury than I'd suffered, I told T the truth. Minus a few details. For example, T didn't know that both Eileen and Agent Charlaix with the French SCR had shared information with us about Smith's movements. I also conveniently left out several of the facts we'd learned about Miss Baverel. I reasoned that T wasn't telling us all, and until we discovered what he and C were concealing from us, I had a right to conceal what I wished from them.

Had the war still been on, or had I still been officially employed by the Secret Intelligence Service, this argument would not have sufficed. My absolute loyalty and submission to their orders had been demanded by the oath I'd taken. But C had been the one to demobilize and then not reinstate me, not the other way around. He had chosen to keep me in this shadowy role. As such, there were no definite rules, and so I decided this was the stance I would take.

T peppered me with questions, some of which I deflected or redirected with my normal ease. A fact that further calmed my rattled nerves. Whatever inhibited state I'd temporarily found myself in after the explosion, at least my mental faculties had fully returned.

When he finished, he pushed to his feet, casting another long look over my drawn features. 'Take what time you need,' he surprised me by saying. His hands fidgeted at his sides. 'But . . . be mindful that the clock is ticking.' Now, that was the T I knew.

Sidney waited until he'd shut the door behind him. 'They'll just have to hope the men they've had monitoring that bank in Amsterdam are up to the challenge,' he stated with finality, as if we'd already decided we were abandoning the search and returning to London.

I remained silent, allowing him to think what he wished. The auction deadline wasn't until Thursday. We could afford to take the remainder of the day to weigh our options. There would still be three days left to search if we chose to remain.

I'd been honest with Sidney. I did fear we would regret not seeing this through. But I also harbored an equal dread that if something happened to either of us, the other would live to regret that we had. If only there was some sort of clear indication as to what course of action was the best to take.

That indication came the next morning.

CHAPTER TWENTY-FOUR

'Y ou're *certain* this is wise?' Sidney asked for perhaps the sixth time that morning as we hurried across the bridge over the Heemraadsingel canal.

'Yes,' I repeated, wrapping my aubergine coat around me and stifling my exasperation. I knew my husband was only concerned for our safety.

This part of Rotterdam was largely residential, so the streets were quiet at this hour on a chill Tuesday morning. In fact, other than the clicking of the wheels of a passing bicyclist and the chiming of the bells from the nearby Cathedral of St Lawrence, there was little to disturb the silence save our footfalls on the brick streets.

We'd taken all of twenty steps before Sidney fretted again. 'You're sure this isn't a trick?'

I rounded on him abruptly at the edge of the canal. 'Sidney,' I gasped, grasping hold of his arms. 'We've been over this. The message was from Landau. I'm certain of it.'

'Someone else couldn't have discovered his code and used it?'

'No,' I stated firmly, not about to let his doubts

sway me. By the time the war had ended, I'd been intimately familiar with all the codes Captain Henry Landau preferred. Not only that, I'd known the manner in which he organized his thoughts, the way he turned a phrase like the back of my hand. 'There is no way someone faked this message,' I assured him. 'Why he came to Rotterdam to speak with us, and why he's summoning us to a secret rendezvous in code, I don't yet know. But I suspect that will all be revealed shortly.' I lowered my chin to glare up at him. '*If* we ever *reach* the rendezvous.'

A deep vee formed between Sidney's brow, telling me he was no more reassured than before, but seeing as we were practically on the doorstep of Landau's former lodgings, I hoped he'd accept the time for dithering was at an end.

Taking his arm, I pulled him toward the tidy brick building sandwiched between two larger structures overlooking the canal. I'd been to Landau's flat just once, for the Germans had known precisely where he lived, and it would have been too dangerous for me to be seen entering or exiting on a regular basis. His rooms occupied much of the second story, opening onto a mews at the back. We entered the narrow stairwell, which smelled strongly of tobacco, much as I remembered from my previous visit, and quickly climbed the steps.

I wasn't entirely certain what to expect when we reached Landau's door, for I anticipated his flat

353

had been leased to another individual when he'd moved to Brussels in November 1918. But when I rapped on the door, we were greeted by none other than Landau himself. He flashed us a wide grin and flourished his hands as if making a grand entrance, but his amusement swiftly faded at the sight of my face.

'Good heavens, Ver,' he exclaimed as I stepped forward to greet him, kissing the air beside his cheek on alternating sides. 'What's this?' he asked, touching the skin below my contusion. 'Have you been in an accident?'

'An explosion,' Sidney stated flatly.

Landau turned to him in surprise, offering him his hand to shake. 'Truly?'

'I'm afraid so,' I replied.

His eyes lost much of their luster. 'Then I'm glad I came.'

I shared a look with Sidney, curious what that meant. But first things first.

He ushered us inside. 'I'm afraid it's not as comfortable as it once was, but at least we'll have some privacy.'

Gone were the worn but cozy furnishings that had once filled the flat, replaced by a quartet of simple ladderback chairs and a table with one mismatched leg. What the space was currently used for I could only guess, and we had more pressing questions to be answered.

'I was surprised to receive your note yesterday evening,' I admitted as the men allowed me to choose my seat first, providing the opening for him to explain.

'Yes, well, what I'm about to relay to you is better done in person.'

He sank down in the chair across from me and scrubbed a hand over the lower half of his face, as if deciding where to begin. He looked tired, with dark circles around his eyes. They competed for one's attention with his slightly misshapen nose and his large ears that protruded from the sides of his head. I was reminded that Landau had never been a particularly attractive fellow, though his quick mind and sharp wit often made you forget this fact.

'You asked me to trace the movements of Jacques Offerman when he visited Berlin some weeks ago,' he began, pressing his hands together before him. 'Well, he paid some rather interesting calls.'

'To whom?' I asked.

'Theobald von Bethmann Hollweg and Johann Heinrich von Bernstorff.'

I stiffened in surprise. 'The former German chancellor, and the ambassador to the United States?'

'The very same.'

Bethmann had served as chancellor of Germany until he'd been ousted in July of 1917. He was a figure who was highly unpopular in Britain, for many believed he'd helped orchestrate the cascade of catastrophic failings of diplomacy during the summer of 1914 that led to the war. Meanwhile,

Bernstorff had served as the German ambassador to the strategically important United States until he was recalled in February 1917 when the Americans broke off diplomatic relations after Germany resumed unrestricted submarine warfare. This had been quickly followed by the United States' entry into the war on the side of the Allies. Bernstorff also happened to be much hated by the British *and* Americans as a spy and saboteur.

'He also spoke to Kurt Riezler and Arthur Zimmerman, among others.'

Two other German political figures – Bethmann's chief advisor and his last Secretary of Foreign Affairs, respectively.

'What on earth do any of them have to do with the sinking of the *Renate Leonhardt* and the Kaiser's gold?' Sidney demanded to know, echoing my thoughts.

'I don't know that they do,' Landau admitted. 'Especially not Bernstorff and Zimmerman.'

'Then . . . you think his meetings were about something else? That *this investigation* is about something else?' I asked.

'Maybe.'

Something clearly troubled him. Something related to these interviews. And yet he struggled to give voice to the suspicions he harbored. Landau had always been cool and considered. That was one of the things that had made him such a successful agent and commanding officer. He knew when to keep a piece of intelligence private and when to reveal it, and he was ever conscious of the political implications at play. So when he voiced an opinion or posited a theory, I knew they were worth heeding and considering.

I watched him closely, weighing how much to share. 'T is being cagey,' I finally told him, knowing he'd interacted directly with the head of Rotterdam station far more often than I had. 'One moment he's telling us to do whatever it takes to track down a set of stolen documents, and the next he's refusing to share information and ordering us to destroy any evidence we uncover before we're certain they're even the items we're looking for. Is that normal?'

I could already tell from his expression that it wasn't, but I waited to hear his answer. 'No. T can be as enigmatic as the rest of us. We are, after all, a rather secretive bunch.' He grimaced self-deprecatingly, and then shook his head. 'But I've never known him to vacillate so widely. Not about a matter he claims is so important.'

The room was cold without heat or a fire, and I wrapped my arms around myself to conserve warmth. 'Then what do you think is really happening?'

Landau studied my face again and then Sidney's, his features tight with strain. 'Have you been given any clues as to what this report could be about? Any indications?'

It was obvious he knew something, and the fact that he still needed another nudge before sharing it set me further on edge. For if he was this hesitant to give voice to his suspicions, then they must be awful indeed.

'Offerman's friend told us that he'd learned something upsetting on his trip to Germany,' Sidney replied, finding his voice before I could. 'That something had made him rethink the choices he'd made, the loyalties he'd chosen.'

Landau's eyes dropped to where his hands now rested flat against the table.

'That doesn't make me think of a sunken ship or lost gold,' Sidney stated pointedly.

'And neither do the words of the person claiming to now possess that report and offering it up for auction to the highest bidder,' I added. 'Alleging it will *prove betrayal at the highest levels of government* and *upend the world's understanding of the last two years of the war.*'

'No, it doesn't,' Landau admitted gravely before sitting back in his chair and again scraping a hand over his face. He appeared to be bracing for something, and that made me brace as well. 'You're both aware that there were some overtures made by Germany and Austria-Hungary in late 1916 to open peace talks?'

Sidney scowled. 'I remember the proclamation they made just before Christmas. The one that defiantly offered no peace terms.' And thus was promptly rejected.

But Landau remained reserved. 'You might also be aware that both sides hoped the Americans, in

358

the form of President Wilson, might broker such a peace. Something similar to what former president Roosevelt did for Russia and Japan back in 1905.'

Sidney stilled, perhaps not knowing this detail. 'I know Wilson fancied himself a peacemaker, but his speeches and letters did little more than express high ideals rather than offering concrete solutions.'

He was right. Publicly, Wilson had done little to facilitate a tangible road to peace, but I was also aware that there had been far more private wrangling and discussions, at least with the British. I'd read, analyzed, and collated some of C's reports from William Wiseman – one of his men in Washington – so I'd known about some of the delicate debates taking place. However, I was also acutely aware I'd never been privy to the entire picture. Something that hadn't bothered me until now.

I met Landau's gaze directly, knowing whatever he was about to say next would not be easy to hear. I could see in the depths of his eyes the confirmation of that fact.

'There were rumors – just rumors, mind you,' he cautioned, though I knew perfectly well that if he was repeating them then they must be quite credible, 'that it was Chancellor Bethmann who approached President Wilson through Germany's Ambassador Bernstorff and asked him to begin a mediation among the belligerents to discuss peace negotiations. That Germany was willing to settle for terms amenable to Britain, Belgium, and France, including the immediate evacuation of German troops from Belgium and the restoration of its sovereignty.'

Sidney and I both sat in stunned silence for a moment before my husband surged forward in his seat, stabbing the scarred table with his finger. 'Of course they say so *now*, when two more *years* of that godforsaken war stand between us and that moment. But they failed to make aware their willingness to capitulate to the Allies when it might have done a bit of good. We can't have been expected to read their bloody minds.'

'The rumors also say that these terms were communicated to Wilson.' Landau paused. 'And that the British government was aware of them.'

Sidney scoffed. 'How?'

Landau's eyes darted toward me, recognizing I would know far more about the viability of such a claim than even him.

'At the start of the war, we cut the Germans' telegraph cables in the North Sea,' I explained. 'Given that, and the fact we controlled most of the seas and the other telegraph lines around the world, it was difficult for Germany to communicate with countries like the United States. Their only options were to either send dispatches by clandestine courier or via a U-boat surfacing off the coast – both of which take a great deal of time – or to do so by coded telegrams sent by circuitous routes through neutral countries. For example, we

360

know the Swedes would let them insert these codes into their diplomatic traffic sent through Buenos Aires to Washington.' I tipped my head to the side. 'Upon occasion, the United States would also agree to transmit especially urgent messages through their own cable to the American embassy in Berlin, as long as they were assured the message was not about the war.' I broke off, suddenly hesitant to continue.

Sidney's brow furrowed. 'And we know all this because . . .'

'We were intercepting all their telegrams.' I grimaced. 'Even the Americans'.' It hadn't been sporting, not when both Sweden and the United States had been neutrals. But there was a war going on, and we'd needed to utilize every resource possible to discover what the Germans were up to. I inhaled deeply, forcing myself to admit the rest. 'And for the most part, we were able to decrypt their messages. From time to time they would switch out their diplomatic code, but we were always able to break it again in a relatively short amount of time.'

He breathed an oath. 'Then we were reading most of their messages.'

I nodded and turned to Landau, my stomach churning as I answered what he had silently been asking me. 'So, in theory, it's possible . . . that we knew. If those rumors you referred to are true, that is.'

Sidney sank back in his chair, pressing his hand

to his mouth, clearly as sick at heart as I was at the very idea that the war might have ended in late 1916 or even January 1917. Any chance of such peace talks must have ended when the Germans resumed unrestricted submarine warfare on February 1, 1917, which had severed diplomatic relations between the United States and Germany and set the Americans on the path to declaring war. I closed my eyes, struggling to grapple with the thought of all the lives that might have been saved. All the soldiers on the battlefields, of seamen sunk on ships. All the civilians killed by shells or ravaged by starvation and devastation. Not to mention the Spanish influenza carried home by returning troops. Would Russia have fallen into its bloody civil war? What of the tattered economies of much of Europe which left many countries also vulnerable to bloodshed and revolution? Might they have been salvaged more swiftly? And what of the pain, anger, disgust, and disillusionment felt by so many? Where would they lead us in the years to come?

I gritted my teeth, pulling the reins to halt my stampeding thoughts lest the horror they inspired run away from me. '*If* these rumors are true,' I stated as evenly as I could manage, 'and *if* Offerman uncovered proof . . .' I swallowed. 'If that proof was made public . . .'

'All hell would break loose,' Sidney finished for me.

Landau's eyes were wide with the seriousness of

what we were contemplating. 'There would be a tremendous uproar. One the likes of which I can't even contemplate.' He clasped his hands together so tightly his knuckles turned white. 'Our government is already fragile. Not as fragile as Germany's. But something like this, the discovery that peace might have been made two years earlier than when the war ended and the same goals achieved without the additional millions of lives lost in 1917 and 1918. It could cause a revolution.'

Sidney rose from his chair, turning to pace a few steps away. His hands fisted at his sides and his back was rigid. Clearly, he was struggling to grapple with the possibility that he'd continued fighting for fifteen months or longer after it all could have ended. How could he not be contemplating all the men he'd lost in that time, all the friends who had died? Whatever had happened in late 1917 that had marked him so profoundly would not have happened. He would never have been shot and left for dead by one of his closest friends. He would never have needed to feign his death or been separated from me. He would have gotten two years of his life back. It was almost too shocking and painful to fathom.

'But it's just a rumor!' Sidney rounded on us to exclaim. His eyes were almost wild, and the skin seemed stretched taut over the bones of his face. 'We don't have proof. And if Offerman had any, it couldn't have simply come from Bethmann and Bernstorff. Their word alone can't be trusted.'

Part of his vehemence was a result of the hatred sown by the British press for both men, but he was right. The Germans' word alone would not have made Offerman himself or his report dangerous. Offerman would have needed confirmation from a British source that they knew of the Germans' intentions.

'We need to find that report,' I declared. 'It's the only way we'll know if he found proof from the Allies.'

I watched the series of emotions that played across Sidney's features. The realization that we *couldn't* abandon all this and return home. The dread of what that would mean if the worst proved true. He, as much if not more than me, *needed* to know the truth.

Had Landau not been there I would have gone to Sidney and wrapped my arms around him, trying to blunt some of the anguish he felt, but I knew he would not appreciate the gesture in front of an audience. Not when he was already battling to restrain his emotions.

'Well, be careful,' Landau warned us quietly. 'If this report is as damning as we fear, then C and T have good reason not to want it to see the light of day. And if they suspect you're not as committed to following orders as they wish . . .' He reached across the table to touch my hand. 'Ver, they could prove just as dangerous to you as whoever else is pursuing it.' His voice was stark. 'There's a reason they inhabit the positions they do. They can be ruthless, too.'

A shiver trembled down my spine. 'We'll be cautious,' I assured him, though I didn't know how. Not when the number of people we could trust had now narrowed considerably.

CHAPTER TWENTY-FIVE

That wariness remained with us as we made our way back to the hotel, only to be accosted yet again by someone lying in wait for us. Something I was growing rather tired of. This time it was Agent Charlaix with the French SCR.

'I heard about the bomb,' he murmured as he hastened over to us from where he'd been seated near one of the windows overlooking the street. His gaze skimmed over the contusion on my cheek and my arm cradled in the sleeve of my coat, as my shoulder had begun to ache. 'And I feared it might have something to do with your investigation.'

A brief scrutiny of the room showed me that Captain Willoughby wasn't there, but that didn't mean he wasn't lurking nearby.

Charlaix's demeanor expressed the appropriate amount of concern and remorse, and yet I couldn't help but question his presence. He seemed to be unusually well informed of our circumstances for a man who was supposed to be pursuing his own investigation in Antwerp.

I must not have done an adequate job of concealing my suspicion, for he drew us aside. 'I asked a colleague of mine stationed here in Rotterdam to keep me apprised of your situation.'

I arched my eyebrows in keen aggravation, and he held up his hands in defense before I'd even said a word.

'I know, I know. I overstepped. But . . . I was afraid something like this might happen.'

'Why?'

He reached up to rub the back of his neck with his hand, stalling for time.

I narrowed my eyes as Sidney crowded in closer at my back, straightening to his full height. 'Why?' I reiterated.

He exhaled resignedly. 'We have reason to believe that Mademoiselle Baverel may have been in possession of the report you're searching for when she was in Antwerp.'

I turned to look up at Sidney as Charlaix continued.

'One of the people she was in contact with while she was there claims Mademoiselle Baverel was very particular about a small portfolio she was carrying, keeping it on her person at all times. I was instructed to retrieve it, believing that it contained the proof she referred to when she spoke with you in Amiens. But now . . . I'm not so sure.'

'How long have you known about this portfolio she possessed in Antwerp?' Sidney demanded to know.

Guilt flashed in Charlaix's eyes. 'Nearly a week.'

Sidney scoffed angrily and turned away.

'I was not authorized to tell you. I still haven't been,' he pleaded with me, perhaps hoping that I would be more empathetic than my husband.

But I was tired of being lied to and manipulated by even our allies.

'Who was this contact?' I countered, and then pressed on even as each question was met with silence. 'When did they last see her with the port-folio? What did they think she did with it?'

Charlaix's face flushed with regret. 'I'm not authorized to tell you.'

I nodded once, and then turned on my heel to follow my husband. Perhaps I was unfairly taking out my frustrations on Charlaix because he happened to be the final straw, but in that moment I didn't care. He certainly wasn't innocent, and my head ached too much to try to sort out the difference.

We had nearly reached our hotel room when the hotel page caught up with us in the corridor.

'Pardon, Madame!' He gasped for breath. 'But this was delivered for you this morning, along with these.'

My eyes widened at the sight of the floral arrangement he lofted in one hand, passing me an envelope with the other.

'Shall I place them in your room?' he asked.

'I can do that,' Sidney volunteered, taking the vase from him while I thanked the young man as he hurried back to his station.

368

'Who on earth . . .?' I began, wondering which of our friends had made such a gesture.

Sidney opened our room door before following me inside. I gestured for him to set the arrangement of roses and lilies on the sideboard. These blooms surely cost a pretty penny, for they must have been grown in a hothouse. Ignoring the letter for a moment, I plucked the card from the bouquet, and flipped it over to read the message. What I saw written there made me drop it as if I'd been stung.

'What is it?' My husband picked up the card to read it, and his face transformed into a ferocious scowl.

BEST WISHES ON A SWIFT RECOVERY
ARDMORE

'I can't tell if this is a taunt, a jest, or in earnest,' I admitted, having had several moments to process the discovery that Lord Ardmore had sent me flowers.

'Perhaps all three.'

'Yes.'

Evidently Willoughby had informed him of Smith's attack. But while the card expressed his condolences, it didn't explain precisely what they were for. Willoughby claimed that Smith had been warned away from me, but I trusted that about as much as I trusted anything Ardmore said.

'Shall I toss them into the fire?' Sidney offered as I continued to stare guardedly at the flowers.

'Leave them for the moment,' I answered, forcing myself to turn away. Crossing to the sofa, I sat and broke open the seal on the envelope, the familiar handwriting on the outside having already told me who it was from. I trusted this one wouldn't bite.

Sidney perched on the arm of the settee next to me, waiting as I perused Eileen's missive. 'What does it say?' he asked when I finished.

'Eileen is confirming Miss Baverel's movements, which appear to be the same as Charlaix already told us.' I studied the short list of dates and locations again, lifting my finger to point at one near the middle. 'Though she managed to find the place where Miss Baverel crossed over into Belgium on her way to Antwerp.' A location Charlaix hadn't known. Or at least hadn't shared with us.

'What is it?' he asked as I continued to frown at the page.

The name of the village had leapt out at me, and the tingle at the base of my neck told me my instincts weren't wrong. But still I wanted to verify it before I said anything more. 'I need a map.' I sat forward, glancing about the room as if an atlas might be handily sitting by. 'Ring down to the front desk,' I told Sidney. 'See if they have one we can borrow.'

Rather than ring and wait for the porter, he hurried down to the lobby himself, returning a few minutes later with the book tucked under his arm. We set it on the table between us, flipping the pages until we came to southern Holland, specifically its border with Belgium. My finger trailed across the map to the spot where the Belgian villages of Minderhout and Hoogstraten abutted the Dutch border.

Before I could even speak, Sidney had already stumbled upon the same question I had been contemplating. 'If she was coming from Rotterdam or Amsterdam, why didn't she cross the border near Strijbeek? That would have been the most direct route.'

'You're right. If she was coming from those places, it doesn't make sense.'

The village of Minderhout lay ten kilometers farther south than Strijbeek. The only reason it touched Holland at all was because of the strange delineations of the Belgian-Dutch border. East of Strijbeek, the border abruptly dipped south, then swung west to encapsulate a narrow pocket of land before turning back toward the east.

'But I don't think she was coming from Rotterdam or Amsterdam.' I looked up at him, unable to hide the thrill of discovery now pulsing through my veins. 'I think she was coming from here.' I stabbed the map about ten kilometers to the east of Minderhout.

Sidney leaned closer to read. 'Baarle-Hertog?'

I nodded. 'A Belgian municipality which just happens to be surrounded by Holland.'

He straightened in surprise, following my line of logic. 'Then . . .'

'It was *as safe as one could be in Belgium during the war,*' I finished for him, quoting Miss Baverel. Because in order to reach Baarle-Hertog, one had to cross a thin slice of the Netherlands, and the Germans could not do this without compromising Dutch neutrality. This meant that Baarle-Hertog was the only place in Belgium east of the River Yser and the Western Front not occupied by Germans. Though that didn't stop German spies from infiltrating it, or the Dutch from sealing off the Belgian enclave with barbed wire fences in late 1915 in order to prevent such clandestine activity by the Germans and the Allies. But not before the British had already set up a wireless telegraphy station there, enabling us to intercept German communications.

'I completely forgot about the enclave until now, but it makes complete sense that it would be the place Miss Baverel was referring to.' I circled the village with my finger. 'Not only that, but it's just fifty kilometers or so from Antwerp, where we know she boarded the ferry back to France. Eileen's discovery that she crossed the border at Minderhout seems to all but confirm it.' I stabbed the map again. '*This* is where we need to go. If Miss Baverel had proof hidden about other enemy collaborators, if she had the report she and her partner stole from Mr Offerman, then *this* is where she hid them.'

Sidney nodded in agreement. 'Have you been there before?'

'No.'

His gaze sharpened, hearing the tension that had tightened my voice.

'I tended to avoid the area of Belgium nearest to Antwerp. That's where German Intelligence based their headquarters and training school inside Belgium. That's where many of their deadliest agents were located.' I shook my head. 'It was too thick with them for my blood.'

He didn't speak, but I could tell by his very stillness that my words had unsettled him. Confronting the risks I had taken during the war – unbeknownst to him at the time – was never easy for him. Just as it was never easy for me to learn about his.

I searched his features, recalling the distress he'd exhibited earlier that morning. 'It must have been troubling for you to learn everything we did from Landau,' I broached carefully, wary of him brushing my concern aside.

He didn't look away, but I could feel him withdrawing. 'It must have troubled you as well.'

'Yes, but . . . our situations were different. What I lost during the final two years of the war was different from what you lost.'

He turned aside. 'Yes, well, at the moment we're still chasing a rumor. Unless that changes' – his throat muscles worked as he swallowed – 'it's useless to speculate.'

373

He was right, and yet I knew he'd not stopped speculating since that morning. That our discussion had loosened the earth around something he'd long kept buried. It was only a matter of time before all the soil eroded away.

Obeying his wishes, I didn't press. But it didn't stop me from worrying.

'I suspect we'll need a motorcar,' Sidney said, turning the subject.

I joined him in standing. 'Yes, and I'd like to place a call to London to touch base with Kathleen. If Smith follows us, as he'll undoubtedly try to do, I'd like to know whether what he and Willoughby said is true. Was he in London when Offerman was murdered or not? It won't make him any less dangerous,' I conceded as I tucked my hands into the pockets of my blue serge skirt, 'but it will at least tell us where he stands.'

Sidney's brow darkened. 'And whether we're still searching for Offerman's killer.'

The lowering skies when we set off the following morning in a slightly battered Citroën Sidney had managed to borrow were not auspicious to our quest. By the time we crossed the Hollandsch Diep, it was raining, and when we reached the outskirts of Breda, the wind was gusting with such force it rocked the little motorcar. Fortunately, by the time we drove into Baarle-Hertog, the gale had slackened, though not the rain.

Upon first glance, Baarle-Hertog and the Dutch village that abutted it – Baarle-Nassau – appeared much like any other Flemish village. Pretty redbrick buildings and two tall church steeples were surrounded by dormant fields and the occasional scrubby tuft of a tree. However, most villages didn't have their streets, and in some case buildings, divided by an international border. I suspected this fact had meant very little until the war. Then it had made all the difference in the world, between besieged and free, belligerent and neutral, potential friend and foe.

We parked the motorcar near St Remigius Church and climbed out, surveying the businesses lining the road and keeping our eyes peeled for any sign of Smith or Willoughby. The road from Breda had been flat and narrow, and not well travelled, but just because we hadn't seen anyone following us didn't mean they hadn't. Part of me also wondered whether we might find Agent Charlaix wandering these streets. He'd claimed his current assignment was in Antwerp, but he might have been lying. He might just as easily have already beat us here.

The fact of the matter was that I was disinclined to trust anyone other than Sidney. Kathleen had confirmed that Smith was in London at the time of Offerman's death, which meant he couldn't have been the mystery man who boarded the first-class compartment of the express with the victim and Miss Baverel. It also meant that he hadn't been the Smith who traveled to Holland

375

with her, and that made me suspicious that whoever that man was, they'd used the name Smith purposely to throw suspicion on the real Lieutenant Smith.

There was a small list of people who knew of their connection, and if Miss Baverel's traveling companion hadn't been another of Ardmore's men, that narrowed the field even further. One of those people in that narrow field happened to be Charlaix.

Neither Sidney nor I had yet had any great inspiration as to where in Baarle-Hertog we should look, but I had a small hunch, and like any respectable village, I knew the church was the place to start. We strolled into the stillness of the sanctuary and our eyes were drawn upward to the vaulted wooden roof supported by white pillars. Tall Gothic-arched windows allowed light to spill across the floor scuffed with age and wear. Such was the sense of light and space that we both paused involuntarily to soak it in.

A few moments later, the priest stumbled upon us still transfixed. 'Beautiful, isn't it?' he asked in Flemish, joining us in our contemplation.

'*Ja*,' I replied.

'We were fortunate in our location near the eastern Belgian border.' He sighed. 'Those in the west were not so lucky.'

I smiled tightly, not wishing to conjure the images of all the magnificent buildings destroyed by the shells and guns, chief among them being the churches with their soaring roofs and tall steeples which made them tempting targets.

Sidney turned to look at the grizzle-haired man politely, but I knew he hadn't understood what he said.

'Do you perhaps speak French or English?' I asked the priest.

'*Bien sûr*,' he replied. 'Would you like a tour?'

'We're actually looking for someone,' I demurred. 'And hoped you might be able to help us.'

'*Bien sûr*,' he repeated, clasping his hands behind his back. 'If I can.'

'Her name is Adele Baverel. And we believe she may have taken lodgings above a shop owned by the Huises or in a home they . . .' My voice trailed away as he began to nod vigorously.

'The Huises own a lodging house near the edge of town.'

My heart leaped into my throat at this confirmation my guess had proved correct. For *huis* was the Dutch or Flemish word for *house*, and Miss Baverel had said her proof was *safe as houses*. It seemed a small step to wonder if she'd been communicating that it was safe with the Houses.

'You simply follow this road south until it forks and go right; and then it forks a second time and go right again. It will be on your right. You can't miss it.'

I opened my mouth to thank him, but he wasn't finished speaking.

'I wish I'd realized this Mademoiselle Baverel

was lodging with the Huises.' His brow pleated fretfully. 'I'm afraid I told the other gentleman who asked after her that I didn't know where she might be.'

My stomach dipped in alarm. 'There was another gentleman here asking after Mademoiselle Baverel?'

'Oh, yes. Perhaps three days ago. He said he was her cousin and they'd lost track of each other during the war.'

Sidney and I shared a look of mutual skepticism. 'Did he give his name?' he asked the priest.

'No.' The older man's gaze darted between us, clearly sensing something was off. 'But he seemed perfectly in earnest.'

'It's just that we may know him,' I said with a smile, trying to reassure him. 'Could you describe him?'

'Above average in height, brown hair. Quite respectable looking.'

The description was vague and could indicate any number of men. In truth the only potential suspect it ruled out was Willoughby, whose hair was much too fair to ever be called brown. But I was leery of pressing the man for too many details, lest we draw too much attention to ourselves and our search. The last thing we needed was nosy locals poking their noses into the matter and complicating an already precarious situation.

So I feigned recognition and managed to extricate

ourselves with charm and a promise to return to the church for Maundy Thursday service the next evening if we were still in the area. I waved out the window of the Citroën as we drove away, water shushing beneath the tires. My smile dropped the moment we drew out of sight.

'That was some quick thinking,' Sidney remarked as we passed a newspaper office, a chocolatier, and a bicycle shop.

'The bit about the Huis name or distracting him from our questions?'

'Both. Though the insight about Huis-house is probably most important.'

'Yes.' I narrowed my eyes down the road. 'Now, the question is, did Miss Baverel's "cousin" think of it as well, or discover the connection by other means?'

Sidney shifted gears, gaining speed as the narrow street of shops widened to reveal more spacious lots filled with homes. 'Let's find out.'

We followed the priest's directions through the two forks, and soon enough came upon the small wooden sign advertising rooms for let just as the tidy lawns began to give way to open fields punctuated with the scraggily remnants of barley and straw from the previous autumn's harvest. We bumped down the short, rutted dirt lane strewn with puddles to the two-story brick house, and were met on the porch by a middle-aged woman drying her hands with a towel.

'Are you looking for a room?' she asked doubtfully

379

in somewhat halting French as she scrutinized our tailored attire.

I stepped up onto the porch, offering her my hand. 'Madame Huis, I presume?'

She accepted it hesitantly. 'Yes?'

'What a charming home,' I exclaimed, careful not to inject too much enthusiasm in my voice. 'It is no wonder Adele chose it. Mademoiselle Baverel,' I clarified.

Mrs Huis's eyes lit with recognition. 'You're Mademoiselle Baverel's friends. You're here for the cottage, then.'

'Yes,' I replied without missing a beat though my heart was now tapping a rapid rhythm in my chest.

'Let me fetch the key. I'll be just a moment.'

CHAPTER TWENTY-SIX

I nodded somewhat unnecessarily as Mrs Huis hastened into the house. I didn't dare look at Sidney until the door had closed behind her, lest my expression give us away. His was equally as surprised by this turn of events. I turned to stare out over the neatly laid paths of the front garden, restraining my rampaging thoughts. Most of the plants were dormant, but I imagined within a few weeks they would come alive with blooms.

'Here it is,' Mrs Huis declared, holding the key aloft. 'Just follow the lane on around past the barn,' she directed with a nod of her head. 'Leads straight to its door. You can't miss it.'

'Thank you,' I told her, accepting the key and then turning to go.

'Will you be wanting dinner this evening?'

I paused at the edge of the step, scrambling to decide what to do, and then turned to look back at her with a weary smile. 'Please excuse us. I'm very tired. I think I'd just like to rest this evening. We have a hamper of food with us in the car. If we get hungry, we can eat something from it.' The latter wasn't untrue. We had brought a hamper from the hotel with our lunch, uncertain what we would find in Baarle-Hertog. Even if the rest was a lie.

'Of course,' Mrs Huis replied uncertainly, and I hurried to the motorcar – though not too quickly – before she could question us further.

She stood watching us as we pulled past the house, and I gave a jaunty wave, hoping to set her at ease. We pulled through the yard and around the barn, as instructed. There, the lane became overgrown with tufts of winter grass sprouting between the ruts. On the right, the drive was lined with fig trees and ashleaf maples, which I suspected formed a border of some kind with the neighboring property. They led straight to a copse of taller trees some three hundred yards behind the barn.

Neither Sidney nor I spoke, too intent on the goal ahead of us and what we hoped to find there. He slowed the motorcar even further as we entered the trees, braking at the sight of the charming little cottage built of wood rather than brick nestled beneath the boughs.

Rain pattered softly against its shingle roof and in the dirt around us as we climbed from the Citroën to survey our surroundings. The cottage was certainly isolated, with naught but fields stretching in three directions. About two miles to the north as the crow flies, I could see the spire of St Remigius peeking through the trees.

'Shall we step inside?' Sidney suggested, and I handed him the key.

The lock opened without any fuss, and we entered the low-beamed room. For a moment, I thought Sidney was going to have to duck, but the lintel was just high enough for him to pass under it standing upright. The air smelled of dust, but I detected none of the must and mold that might have permeated the space. The ceiling was watertight, and Mrs Huis must clean and air it from time to time even if her tenant was not in residence.

How long had Miss Baverel rented this place? How far in advance had she paid for its lease? And what had compelled her to tell her landlady that she might have friends visiting? Mrs Huis had not seemed the least surprised by our appearance and had readily handed over the key as if she'd been forewarned of our eventual arrival. Or if not *our* arrival, then another friend's. But who, how, and why?

Miss Baverel might have sent a letter to Mrs Huis from jail, but that seemed too risky. Surely such an act would have been noted and led the gendarmes straight to Mrs Huis's door. No, it had to either be a standing order or someone else had forwarded such a message to Mrs Huis on Miss Baverel's behalf. Perhaps Miss Lemaire, her friend from Furnes. There was no way to know without asking Mrs Huis herself, and that could not be done without raising her suspicions, so for now the question would have to remain unanswered.

The cottage had no electric or gas lamps, but from the dim light filtering through the open door I could see that the contents appeared undisturbed. 'Open the shutters,' I instructed, moving to swing open the wooden louvers on the window closest to me. Though far from bright, the murky sunlight at least afforded us enough illumination to maneuver easily through the room. Its contents were sparse, leaving few places for a person to conceal a sheaf of documents unless Miss Baverel had pried up floorboards or fashioned a hiding spot among the eaves. However, the sight of the carvings on the wardrobe drew my steps immediately toward it.

I lifted my hand to trace the outline of a house engraved into the wood and then pulled open the doors. The scent of lavender washed over me as I eyed the three gowns hung there. Reaching inside, I trailed my hand over the wood at the bottom, the back, and along the sides. Then I began to shuffle through the dresses, searching for a bag or oilcloth or some sort of pouch that might have been suspended between them. I stilled after moving the gown on the left, wondering if it had felt a little stiff, a little heavy, even for a molded bodice of velvet. Turning the bodice toward me, I reached up to wrap my hands around it. It was definitely rigid. Then gathering the flounces of the skirt in one hand, I reached up inside the pool of indigo fabric.

My breath caught as my fingers met the familiar

rifled edges of paper. 'Help me,' I ordered Sidney. While he stepped forward to hoist the skirt even higher, I reached both hands into the bodice to find the mechanism by which the papers were suspended. Four gem paper clips were fastened around the documents at each edge, and then stitched to the bodice itself. Rather than waste time cutting the strings, I simply removed the papers from the clips and whisked them from the bodice.

Sidney allowed the fabric to slip from his hands, and the abrupt shift in weight pulled the gown from its hanger to pool at the bottom of the wardrobe. We paid it little interest, our attention being completely absorbed by the documents before us. I inhaled past the tightness in my chest, allowing my gaze to drift down the page over the list of dates and locations until one leaped out at me. The date of the bombing of Brigadier General Bishop's temporary HQ outside Bailleul. This must be the proof Miss Baverel had spoken of in Amiens. Or a form of it.

I glanced at my husband and then crossed toward the table. 'Light a candle.'

He did what I asked, igniting two with the cigarette lighter in his pocket while I set the documents in the center of the pool of illumination on the table and flipped the top page over to set it aside. The next one continued the list, but the third gave more details in a hasty scrawl. It was naught but her testimony – her observation of events and names – but if the specifics could be confirmed, it could prove damning enough on its own. At least for the people she mentioned being involved.

I noted Lieutenant Smith's name more than once, as well as Walter Ponsonby's and a few others who were familiar to us, but there was no mention of Ardmore. I looked. Not that that was surprising. He always did stick to the shadows, preferring to keep himself and his name far from any suspicious activity that might be linked back to him. But I well knew he was behind a number of these strokes.

What had been his game? He was involved with our Naval Intelligence in some unspecified role, and yet he'd promoted bombing a battalion's headquarters and fostered enemy collaborators. Why?

I remembered how my colleague Alec Xavier had told me he'd stumbled across Ardmore's name in a German Army report in Brussels a short time before Alec's identity was compromised and he'd been forced to flee Belgium. That Ardmore's inclusion in the report could mean one of only two things: he was being watched by the Germans, or he was providing information to them. When Alec was questioned upon his return to London about his decision to escape before he was apprehended by the Germans, as our intercepted reports indicated was about to happen, Ardmore had accused him of losing his nerve. The fact that Ardmore had attended Alec's hearing at all, let alone attempted to tarnish his record, made me highly suspicious that he'd known Alec had seen his name in that report. That Ardmore feared exactly what Alec knew about his involvement with the Germans.

Were all of Miss Baverel's notes more proof of his German sympathies, of his treason? Or was it all in aid of the sympathy we already suspected he held for the Irish rebels? With Britain's attention and manpower consumed by the war with Germany, it had less time and fewer resources to be directed at the unruly Irish.

I didn't have the answer to that, and any thought of uncovering one scattered with the wind clattering the branches against the walls outside when I flipped to the sixth page of the documents. It was Offerman's report.

Without a word, Sidney and I both yanked out the chairs on either side of the table and positioned them next to each other so that he could read over my shoulder. We discovered that several of the pages were written in code – one which seemed remarkably complex. But then at the end of the encrypted section was included a typed version of the deciphered text.

'I didn't know Miss Baverel was capable of advanced decryption,' I remarked in disbelief.

There was a note of consternation in his voice when he replied. 'I don't think she was.'

I turned my head to look at him. 'Then . . .'

I didn't know how to finish the thought.

Obviously, *someone* had possessed the capability of decoding the report. Had Miss Baverel shared it with that someone? My eyes dropped to the text. Or were these Offerman's originals? Had he either purposely or mistakenly included them with his enciphered text?

Shaking the question aside for the moment, we continued to read. It became apparent almost immediately that this report was not about the *Renate Leonhardt* or a gold wreck. Where and how that rumor had started, I didn't know, but with each page I read, the suspicion that it had begun with British Intelligence increased. All so they could draw scrutiny away from the truth should it begin to leak out.

For Landau had been right. Offerman *had* spoken with both former chancellor Bethmann Hollweg and Ambassador Bernstorff, as well as various other German officials – past and present. Offerman also possessed copies of memorandums and letters that I assumed they'd given to him.

On August 18, 1916, Bethmann had communicated to Bernstorff that he was to inform the American government that Germany was happy to accept mediation from President Wilson to end the war, and that they were setting no preconditions, but were prepared to restore Belgium as a sign of good faith and were open to important territorial adjustments with France, particularly in the Alsace-Lorraine region they'd annexed in 1871. With these statements, right out of the gate, the chancellor was addressing the key issues to the Americans and British, and to the French. What's more, Offerman had scrawled in the margin that the British Admiralty had decoded the German encryption buried in a Swedish cable to the United States relaying these peace overtures. How exactly he'd learned this, he didn't say, but he must have had a reliable informant inside British intelligence or the highest levels of government to know this and some of the other things contained in the report.

Wilson replied that he promised to make a peace move after he was reelected in early November, but Bethmann then pushed back, trying to convince him to take action sooner, while the Kaiser was still open to the gesture. Bethmann also made it clear that while Germany was anxious for peace, the Allies could not know that they had asked for it, so that they did not appear weak. Though, once again, Offerman noted that the British Admiralty was aware of all of this, presumably through intercepted and decoded messages.

Several memos followed, theorizing about the way to do this, and citing precedents like the Peace of Hubertusberg, which had ended the Seven Years' War between Prussia and Austria in 1763 and had resulted in essentially a prewar status quo, where both sides relinquished their conquests. There was discussion of possible terms, most of which were far better for the Allies than I would have ever anticipated Germany willingly ceding. But the chief hope appeared to be for Bethmann to find himself at the negotiating table with the then British prime minister Herbert Henry Asquith and Foreign Secretary Edward Grey. He seemed to strongly believe that if they could simply sit down together, they could negotiate a compromise. He just needed Wilson to get them to the table.

With each new page we read in the wavering light of the candles, I could feel Sidney's agitation growing. Many of these things were not a complete shock to me, even if seeing them laid out so starkly in black and while and understanding their implications was unsettling. But Sidney had still been mired down in the Somme while this was going on. His entire being had been focused on keeping himself and the too few men in his battalion who had survived the horrific battles of July and early August alive. He hadn't known the Germans – his enemy – were making a move to end all the bloodshed. A move the American president didn't seem to find pressing, and the British government seemed intent to ignore despite their knowledge of it.

Of course, I was also aware they hadn't completely ignored it. There had been a flurry of private discussions and meetings in August and September of 1916, but the government had been divided in what to do. And they couldn't risk letting the Germans know we'd broken their ciphers, or the Americans finding out we were secretly reading their cables.

'Isn't this about the time when Howard's article was published?' Sidney suddenly demanded to know as I flipped the page. His face was flushed with emotion, but his voice was carefully controlled. 'The one where he quoted Lloyd George.'

'Yes,' I replied softly.

Though I had not realized it at the time, I could now see the interview for what it was: a carefully orchestrated move by the newspaper magnate Alfred Harmsworth – Lord Northcliffe – to thwart an American peace move and establish his man Lloyd George as the politician who could lead Britain successfully through the war. At the time the article was published in late September 1916, Lloyd George was serving as the Minister of War, but everyone knew he was jockeying for prime minister and Asquith was in his way. His boast that Britain had only begun to fight, and that any step by the United States or any other neutral in the direction of peace would be construed as a pro-German move was a bluff. One meant to stir the weary British public's pluck.

Sidney nodded sharply, his gaze returning to the documents. I wanted to say something, to do something to blunt the pain of all we were learning, but I realized there was nothing I *could* say or do to make it better. I couldn't undo what had been done. And trying to lessen or brush aside its impact would be far crueler than acknowledging the brutal betrayal that it was.

Inhaling a shaky breath, I forced myself to continue reading.

In November 1916, with Wilson reelected the American president, the Germans continued to urge him to call for a peace conference. Chancellor Bethmann gave a speech to the Reichstag publicly welcoming a postwar league of nations to keep the peace. The Austrians indicated the Central Powers were willing to evacuate Belgium and northern France, restore Serbia, and take up other territorial questions. And Bethmann documented that he'd told the American diplomat Joseph Grew that if the Germans' press for peace continued to be ignored, the measures they would eventually be forced to take for their defense would not be their fault. That he could not stem the opposition of militant German right-wing newspapers and politicians and its battle-eager military commanders forever without results.

Offerman noted that in early November the Germans had delivered a new code to the United States via unarmed merchant vessel, and it had taken the British much of that month and December to break it, so their private dispatches had not been intercepted like many of the others. But that hadn't meant we weren't made aware of developments in other ways. Chiefly through intelligence officer Captain William Wiseman, who now had contact with Wilson's chief advisor – Edward House. Wiseman had communicated directly with C, so I was aware of some of the information

Offerman believed he had relayed, but not all. It seemed clear that Offerman hadn't actually had access to Wiseman's CX reports but must have been forced to rely on the word of House or a third party.

Or had he?

The name Wiseman prodded at me. Where had I heard it recently? Or had it merely entered my thoughts when I'd been thinking back over the war?

Then it struck me. Kick Schröder had used it. Or rather something similar. He'd told us that Offerman's letters had mentioned a Wijsman. That Offerman had read his reports and found them illuminating. I had suspected this Wijsman might have worked for Dutch Intelligence, but what if he was British instead? After all, the names Wijsman and Wiseman were remarkably similar. Could Captain Wiseman have been one of his sources? Could the wording of Offerman's report have been meant to obscure that fact?

I set aside the question for the moment to focus on the next section, in which Offerman paid particular attention to another significant event that occurred at the end of November 1916. The American Federal Reserve Board, with the encouragement of Wilson, had taken the drastic step of issuing a strong caution to its banks about the new, short-term, unsecured British and French Treasury bills being issued. The result of this move had been an almost instantaneous panic regarding *all* British and French securities. The British and French governments had been forced to act swiftly, rushing some of their dwindling gold reserves to New York in order to maintain the exchange rate and calm the markets.

Though I hadn't realized it until my friend George – a brilliant mathematician and code-breaker with the Admiralty – had pointed it out to me some months later, this moment had been indicative of just how disastrous the Allies' financial situation was. He had speculated that at that time we'd had, at most, four to five months' worth of reserves to fight the war, and then we would have been forced to make peace simply because we'd run out of money.

Offerman's report revealed he was aware of this as well. But he also raised questions that I echoed about why Wilson seemed to have finally apprehended the financial stranglehold he had over the Allies, and yet he hadn't used that leverage to the maximum effect: to force them to attend a peace conference. Offerman speculated on whether Wilson had simply been that bumbling and inept, or if he'd deliberately bungled the matter, wanting America to enter the war, despite all his protests to the contrary.

Sidney scoffed reading this remark. 'The trouble is, Wilson lives with his head in the clouds. He's filled with high ideals, but he doesn't know the first thing about how to implement them.'

My husband might have held more respect for

such a man when he was younger, but four years of war, when pie-in-the-sky thinking and the optimistic folly of generals had only gotten his men killed, had left him with little reverence for such mindsets.

He pressed a hand to his forehead, rocking himself slightly. 'Good God, we needed a man like Herbert Hoover, and we got Wilson.'

I pressed a hand to his upper back, though I wasn't certain he felt it, able to empathize with his thinking. The American financier Hoover had chaired the Commission for Relief in Belgium until America's entry into the conflict. It was largely due to his efforts and organization that the people of German-occupied Belgium and northern France had not starved. The position could not have been an easy one, and Hoover had continually needed to skillfully negotiate with both the Allies and Germans to make the program work. The world at large had needed that skillful negotiation in November 1916.

Instead, we had gotten Wilson's admittedly eloquent peace note in mid-December and his speech to the American Senate in January, but neither did anything practical to lay out the course to peace. He did not call for a peace conference, or demand the belligerents state their terms. He'd done nothing but spout more lofty principles.

In the void of Wilson's failure to act, Lloyd George's plans came to fruition in early December when, with Northcliffe's assistance, he forced

Asquith to resign and toppled the established government to take over as the new British prime minister, setting up a new cabinet.

However, the worst of Offerman's report was yet to come.

A flood of correspondence passed between hands in January 1917, with Bethmann and Bernstorff on one side seemingly trying to drag Wilson and House toward an understanding of how to proceed, and Captain Wiseman on the other side doing much the same thing. I recalled reading some of his reports to C, and the discussions he'd reported with House about a possible peace conference. Meanwhile, Wilson still seemed to be floundering. Perhaps he'd reached out to the British prime minister or foreign secretary in some meaningful clandestine manner, but if so, neither I nor Offerman, it seemed, knew how.

There were copies of a number of urgent coded telegrams sent from Bethmann in Germany to Ambassador Bernstorff in America. Telegrams that Offerman noted the British had surely obtained, as using such a method of transmission resulted in almost instantaneous interception by the Allies. This was an indication of just how desperate they were and how determined they were to make peace that they would willingly risk such a thing, particularly when the contents regarded Bernstorff's authority to deal with Wilson in laying out Germany's terms for the peace conference in black and white, and their instructions of what those terms should be. Particularly when the Allies had not yet stated anything remotely definitive about their own peace terms, instead spouting generalities.

By the end of January, Bernstorff had been fully armed with all of his chancellor's terms to make peace. But on February 1st the correspondence had all but stopped. The clock had run out. The German military had stubbornly gone through with their threat to reinstate unrestricted submarine warfare, and rather than continue to try to work the diplomatic option, Wilson and the United States had instead severed all diplomatic relations with the country.

I felt stunned and a little sick to discover that the German diplomats appeared to be doing all they could humanly do to stop the war, while the Americans fumbled and the British government merely sat back – even knowing all it did – and let more of the world slide into the abyss of the Great War. I knew it could never be stated in such black and white terms. There were always subtleties and nuances to every situation, especially when much of one's intelligence was being secretly gathered from both friends and enemies. But the last pages of Offerman's report left a rancid taste in my mouth, for I realized I'd read part of it before.

His words were pulled from a cable from James W. Gerard – the American ambassador in Berlin – to Secretary of State Robert Lansing and claimed to inform him of Germany's 'real' terms for peace – ones which were not so amenable. That anything else Bethmann might have sent Wilson was a sham. Captain Wiseman had reported that House had shown him this cable. However, we were almost certainly already in possession of the actual terms Bethmann had sent Wilson, the ones intercepted in their urgent telegrams.

Based on the cable House had shown Wiseman, the British government had brushed off all of the Central Powers' attempts to make peace – even their public announcement on December 12th – as being untenable because of their ridiculous demands. They claimed that the Entente Powers were being perfectly reasonable while Germany and her allies were not. Yet, all along we'd known the truth. We'd known Germany's terms for beginning the peace talks were more than fair. We'd simply ignored them, preferring instead to see the United States dragged into the war on our side. This meant prolonging the war, but what did another year or more matter when the Americans would be forced to take over the financing of the Allies in order to keep us afloat, and the ultimate result would be an all but guaranteed victory? After all, Germany would run out of soldiers eventually.

I lowered the last page to the table, my shoulders bowed from the weight of all these revelations, and my mouth twisted in anger and cynicism. I couldn't help but think of one statement from the memo Lord Lansdowne – a retired, but well-respected stateman – had circulated in November 1916 when all of this wrangling over peace was occurring. Lansdowne had summarized the moral conundrum our government had faced as this: 'The responsibility of those who needlessly prolong such a war is not less than that of those who needlessly provoke it.' If one believed that was true, then our government had *bitterly* betrayed us – in particular, its fighting men.

I turned my head to look at Sidney. Seeing the desolation written in his eyes tore at my heart. I lifted my hand to reach for him, but he abruptly pushed to his feet, nearly knocking over his chair. His arms rose and fell, as if he didn't know what to do with them, before he finally settled on raking his hands through his hair as he paced away several steps and then back. Then, suddenly he swerved toward the door, his panting breaths loud in the quiet of the room. He wrenched open the door and charged out into the rain.

CHAPTER TWENTY-SEVEN

'Sidney!' I called after him, pushing to my feet.

I didn't know what to do. Should I follow him? Should I give him space?

There were times when my husband was insistent I not approach him. Like when he woke from a nightmare and fled our bedchamber for the drawing room or even the dark streets of London, attempting to outpace the memories that haunted him. Or when he was unexpectedly confronted with a recollection he wasn't yet ready to discuss.

Over the ten months since his return, these episodes and events had occurred less and less, and I'd tentatively learned to navigate when to push him and when to hold back. But *this* . . . this was different. This was somehow worse than all those that had come before. Any sense of pain and betrayal I felt must be compounded tenfold for Sidney, particularly now knowing that he'd been part of the Battle of Passchendaele in the late summer and early autumn of 1917. A battle that wouldn't have occurred had peace been achieved.

Recognizing this, I realized I *had* to go to him. I had to try. Even if he screamed at me and told me go away, I had to try. I couldn't leave him alone to face this.

I scrutinized the papers, considered leaving them behind in my haste, but we'd already endured too much to abandon them now. Gathering them up, I hastily rolled the stack and stuffed it into the pocket inside my coat, ignoring the awkward bulge they made. Then I blew out the candles and pressed my hat firmly down over my curls before hurrying out into the rain after him.

I didn't have to search far. A swift look down the lane told me he hadn't ventured back toward Mrs Huis's house, so I turned to follow the narrow trail leading into the copse of trees. A copse which proved to be smaller than it first appeared, for about two hundred feet on it ended at a blunted hay field. At the edge of the trees stood Sidney, gazing out over the straggling, rain-drenched stalks.

The line of his back was rigid, and his hands clenched at his sides. I slowed my steps, approaching slowly and with no care to mask my progress through the detritus on the forest floor. The last thing I wanted to do was startle him, for I did not know what he was actually seeing – an empty field or a blood-soaked No Man's Land. Was his mind firmly in the present or mired in the past? I knew that one of the things Sidney most feared was that in a traumatized haze he would mistake me for a German intent on attacking him and that he would somehow harm me. Part of me didn't want to believe his mind could ever truly be so clouded that he would make that mistake, but today was not the day to test that theory.

He didn't move or speak, but there was some subtle shift in his muscles or perhaps the air between us that indicated he was aware of my presence. I hesitated slightly before taking the next step. 'Sidney,' I said, wanting to make it clear who I was, and that I wasn't sneaking up on him. Still, he didn't move, but I saw his shoulders raise and his torso expand as if he was inhaling deeply, and I stopped a few feet from him. 'Sidney,' I murmured again, hoping if anything it was my perfume filling his nostrils and not the gut-churning smells of the trenches from his memory.

He kept his face averted; his body tightly restrained. So tightly that he trembled slightly as the rain pattered down on his head and shoulders. He'd left his hat in the cottage, so his hair was now plastered to his head and the cold rain tracked down the sides of his face and neck in rivulets. But he made no move toward me, nor did he scream at me to go away. He merely stood there as I inched forward several more steps, close enough to see his profile. He quavered like a strong oak being battered by a windstorm, one mighty gust away from toppling.

I flexed my fingers inside my leather gloves, wanting to reach out to him, but knowing that would not be a good idea in his current state. So instead, I crossed my arms over my chest and huddled against the rain. Seeing him this way hollowed me out inside and caused an ache bone deep. Standing there beside him, knowing how terribly he was hurting, and yet being unable to do anything about it, was nearly unbearable. But I wouldn't abandon him. And I wouldn't force him to speak until he was ready. Averting my gaze, I turned my feet to stand side by side with him in solidarity like one of the men he'd served alongside in the trenches rather than continuing to scrutinize him like an outsider. I could only hope it was enough that I was there.

How long we stood that way, I don't exactly know, but without my mackintosh and his trench coat we would have been soaked completely through. As it was, his collar beneath his coat must have been sodden from the water running down his face seemingly unheeded. However long it was, I grew so accustomed to the silence that when he finally did speak it startled me.

'I'd accepted long ago that the war was utterly senseless.' His voice rasped as if being dragged from the depths of his lungs. 'That I was simply stuck. Just a little cog in a great monstrous machine that couldn't be stopped and would one day consume me as well.'

I blanched at the realization that this was what

he'd believed. This was what *any* of our men had thought.

'Not that I contemplated it all that much. It was best not to. Best to just get on with it. But if I had been forced to put it into words, that's what I would have said.' He inhaled a shaky breath. 'So to hear that there *had* been a way out, one that had been instigated by our *enemy*, and yet it was brushed aside by the very people who should have been looking out for us . . .' His words rang with a righteous fury that then abruptly drained away. 'That it wasn't taken . . .' His hand lifted to clutch his hair. 'My God, Verity! All those men who died after. All . . . those men . . . who were killed. Their deaths weren't just senseless, they were *thrown away* like so much wastage.' He began scrabbling at his head with both hands and turning in circles, sharp pants issuing from his mouth. 'They . . . they were *destroyed* . . . for nothing!'

'Sidney,' I gasped, reaching for him between hiccupping breaths. 'Sidney, stop,' I said, wrapping my arms around him as tears streamed down my face. His words had been like hammer strikes to my nerves, but only because they were true. That knowledge ate at my soul. It tore it to shreds. So much so that I felt I might be physically sick. But I had to keep it together for him. *He* deserved my comfort, not the other way around.

He resisted at first, continuing to try to spin, but eventually stilled, allowing me to embrace him, though his arms did not hold me back. After a few moments, when my own weeping was better under control, I relaxed my grip. Lifting my head, I looked up to find him staring bleakly across the field once again. I knew this time I couldn't let him disappear to wherever he went inside his head on his own. This was a wound that had to be lanced – now – no matter how painful.

'Sidney, what happened at Passchendaele?'

He flinched at the word and tried to pull away, but I held on tighter.

'I know that's what's haunting you. I see it in your eyes. Tell me.'

He jerked away harder, and finally I had to release him, lest he harm me or himself in his effort to break free.

'You're already reliving it over and over again in your mind. You need to let it out into the air.'

He shook his head. 'No.'

'Tell me, Sidney.'

He turned away.

'Tell me!'

'*No!!!*' he wheeled around to roar.

I shrank back a step, but then held my ground. His breaths heaved in and out of his chest as if he'd run ten miles and his eyes were stark with agony. But this was a battle I could not let him win, no matter what it cost me.

'Tell me,' I urged more quietly, but just as insistently.

He glared at me for several tense seconds, and then his head dropped forward, and his eyes squeezed shut. '*What* do you want me to tell you?' he challenged hoarsely. 'That it was hell on earth? That rather than postpone their battle plans for the weather, they sent us out into a muddy mire of sticky clay we could barely maneuver through, facing an enemy who held the Langemarck Ridge above us? That rather than call off the attack when the regiments of Gloucesters, and Oxfordshires, and Buckinghamshires were decimated, they urged us on and on and on again?'

His gaze drifted to the side as if returning to that hellscape in his mind, and I choked back the impulse to tell him to stop, swallowing the words even though they burned like acid going down, for I knew the worst was to come.

'All we could do during the day was cower in the craters and shell-holes and around the stranded and battered hulks of tanks, keeping our heads belowground. At night, we could hardly do much more but scamper between holes, trying to rally and coordinate our men as best we could, waiting for further orders or reinforcements. And the rain, the *bloody incessant rain.*' He clenched his teeth, looking up at the sky where even now rain fell on him. 'To charge up the hill was impossible. The mud was everywhere, dragging us down, breaking up our attacks. The only merciful thing about it was that it deadened the blasts of their shells, for they sank just as deeply in the quagmire, killing just the men directly in their path.

'We were relieved once – sent back to the

grounds of that demolished chateau. Our losses were horrific.' His tone was flat and numb now, rattling off the words almost as if he was reading statistics. This alteration in his demeanor was more alarming than the anguish and anger that had come before.

'I hoped that would be the end of it,' he said. 'But no, we were sent back out again. The rain had stopped for a few days. A nice drying wind,' he mocked as if reading a dispatch. 'And we were to be part of one wave of another tremendous push. But the ground was still impassable. It was nothing but a huge swamp of bodies and wire and broken ironwork, timber, and equipment littering the mud. Our opening barrage only made it worse.'

If I closed my eyes, I could imagine it. Or some semblance of it. After all, we'd driven through the landscape where this had occurred last July before I'd known any of this. It made Sidney's willingness to do so, and the courage it had taken to accomplish it, all the more moving. I'd known it had affected him greatly at the time, but not how much.

'The Jerries knew we were coming. There was no surprise.' Sidney scraped a hand down his face. 'We had to sling sandbags over our backs to have any hope of escaping their machine-gun fire. Those who were wounded could do little but drag themselves into the relative safety of the surrounding shell-holes. They cheered us on

407

as we crawled by. "Go on, boys! Give 'em hell!"' His voice cracked, but he kept going, and my nerves stretched ever tauter, not knowing what even greater horror lay at the end of this tale.

'We . . . we managed to capture a German pillbox. Sent back sixteen prisoners, but the Germans mowed them down with their machine guns. Maybe they thought they were Tommies. So we started putting the prisoners in shell-holes with our men because we couldn't spare anyone to take them back. By then the rain had begun again – pouring from the sky in buckets – and all we could do was sit and wait for reinforcements or further instructions.'

He fell quiet and I found myself holding my breath, my heart beating a rapid tattoo in my chest. My body trembled from the chill rain and my own dread as the silence stretched, but Sidney stood immobile. The desperate cast to his features was made all the more horrible by the empty hush that accompanied it. For he didn't yell or scream or rage, but faced his memories with a sort of desolate resolution.

'After nearly three years of war, you would think that I had become inured to everything. To the stench and the ghastly sights and the roar of the guns.' His voiced wavered. 'But it turns out there is a sound far worse than a shell exploding. It's . . . it's the moans and wails of men drowning.' His features scrunched and wavered under the weight of what he was trying to explain. 'We couldn't see them in the darkness, but we could hear them, on all sides. Our men who had crawled into the new shell-holes. They'd gone there for safety, but the water was now rising above them, and being too injured to move, they . . . they were slowly drowning.'

I pressed a hand to my mouth to stifle my gasp of horror, tears spilling down my cheeks.

Sidney looked down at me, his eyes two pools of anguish. 'I . . . I knew them. I knew those men lying out there wounded. I heard them sobbing and begging us for help. And yet there . . . there was nothing we could do,' he pleaded now. 'The Germans had their machine guns trained on us, and if we'd set one foot outside the pillbox . . .' His face finally crumpled, and his knees gave way. 'There was nothing we could do,' he wailed, adding his anguished moan to those of the men he'd lost.

I sank down on my knees beside him in the wet earth and wrapped my arms around his shuddering shoulders, pulling his face against my chest even as my own tears dripped into his hair.

It was no wonder Offerman's report had affected him so deeply. The pain of these men's losses, and his inability to help them, was terrible enough without the added realization that they might never have been on that battlefield in the first place had peace been achieved in late 1916 or early 1917. I'd known Sidney had long struggled with the disgust he felt for some of Britain's military commanders, and the unprecedented carnage caused by their continued insistence on pounding away at the Germans, hurling hundreds of thousands of men to their deaths in the fray. But our government's deliberate prolonging of the war in the face of having already achieved the aims they'd purportedly most wanted – the aims the public most wanted – with peace was an entire new level of betrayal all together.

I had never seen Sidney cry, let alone weep as if the entire world was breaking apart at the seams and him with it. It clawed at my heart and my very soul, and all I could think to do was hold him tighter, to pour every ounce of my love for him into my embrace.

This was something I could never fix. It was beyond us all. All I could do was love him.

Slowly, his racking sobs began to subside, and he pulled from my embrace. He lifted his hands to swipe at his streaming eyes and nose, before searching for his handkerchief in the pockets of his clothes. 'I'm sorry,' he began, his voice trembling. He turned away, ashamed. 'I . . . I shouldn't have . . .'

I shushed him. 'Yes, you should have,' I told him firmly.

But he still would not look at me.

My hands turned upward in supplication as I floundered for a way to reach him. 'Someone very wise told me once that everyone has their breaking points.'

His eyes lifted, recognizing I was quoting *him*,

repeating something he'd told me just a few short months ago.

'That it's not a weakness, just evidence of our humanity.' I reached out to touch his chin. 'Though frankly, the fact that you haven't fallen apart before now is astonishing.'

'Yes, well, what choice did I have?'

I didn't question that. For in the heat of the battle, he'd certainly had to hold it together for his men who were still living, and after, there was still a war on. By the time it had ended, stifling it all and swallowing it back had become second nature. Forcing himself to share this burden with me had been just as hard, if not harder than keeping it to himself.

'I'm sorry you had to endure that,' I told him, letting some of my own pain soften my voice. This time, when he started to turn away, I wouldn't let him, taking a firm grip of his chin. 'I'm sorry you had to endure any of it.' I could see the vulnerability glittering in his eyes, and I met it by pouring my heart into mine. Not so long ago, our situations had been reversed, and one of the things that had helped me to heal was the gift of his complete and absolute acceptance. Sidney needed to know that he was completely and absolutely accepted, too. That he was loved – self-perceived frailties and flaws and all. That the strength and intensity that so defined him didn't have to consume him.

I brushed his sodden hair back from the plaster

covering the cut above his right eyebrow. 'But you don't have to be invincible. Not for me, not for anyone. Just . . . *you.*' I pressed my hand to his heart. 'You simply have to be you. The man I love. Whether he's slaying dragons, or openly grieving the soldiers he cared for.'

He reached for me then, his eyes shimmering with need.

I cradled his damp face in my hands. 'Your care for others is not a weakness, but a strength.' My voice wobbled. 'And I love you all the more for it.'

His mouth pressed to mine, urgent and demanding. The heat of it sent a shiver of pleasure down my spine and raised gooseflesh along my rain-chilled skin, and I met his fervency with my own, trying to give him the love and reassurance he sought.

When he pulled away, we were both panting, and the shiver that had begun in delight was now turning to one in earnest. Sidney looked down at me and then blinked, turning to the left and then the right, as if only just realizing where we were – kneeling in the mud and rain, exposed. He scraped a hand back through his sodden hair awkwardly, and then began to help me to my feet. 'Let's get out of this rain.'

I nodded, eager to escape the dampness. Though I still had questions, and I knew if I didn't ask them now, I never would. 'What happened? How did you eventually escape that pillbox?'

Sidney's face was strained, but he answered softly. 'We waited all night and the next day, worried at any moment the Boche might make a counterattack. I'd sent back a runner to tell HQ where we were, but for all I knew, he'd been killed. We'd already lost seven of our eight signalers and runners in the early hours of our initial attack. But my message must have made it through, or we simply got lucky, for the following evening, we were relieved by another company.' He shook his head. 'The poor sods. I never did learn if they ever made it through alive.'

I pressed my hand to his arm, not wanting him to take on the burden of responsibility for those men as well. After all, he'd not given the orders for them to relieve him.

'We dragged the wounded men we passed who were still alive up onto the ridges so they wouldn't drown if it started to rain again, and promised to send the stretcher-bearers out for them. They cursed us for leaving them behind, but we couldn't take them with us. We could barely drag ourselves across the muddy morass, let alone another body. We were so filthy you could scarcely distinguish one person from another. I had to cut off my puttees with a knife.' He glanced at me. 'I'd been issued a private's uniform for the attack. Standard procedure.'

So the enemy couldn't tell who the officers were by sight and kill them first.

'How many of you survived?'

It took him a moment to answer, and when he did, his voice was bleak. 'Fifteen. Out of ninety.'

My hand squeezed his tightly where it gripped mine, icy fear seizing me even though he stood there with me now – proof that he'd survived. There was nothing I could say to ease the pain of such a truth. I could only hold fast to him and say a silent prayer for all the other lost souls and those they'd left behind, while thanking God he'd not been among them.

Sidney opened his mouth as if to say something more, but then hesitated, pulling me to a stop. I turned to him in alarm, which was only heightened by the staying hand he held up to stop me from speaking as he scanned the wooded path before us. Swallowing my retort, I slowly turned to do likewise, sensing what Sidney had perceived before I did.

Though the forest was silent except for the patter of rain, there was a trembling uneasiness in the air. The trees being devoid of leaves should have made it easier to see anything that moved among the dark trunks, but the copse was so dense, and dotted here and there with firs and pines, that there were still plenty of places to hide. The more optimistic side of my nature hoped we'd merely detected the presence of a fox, pine marten, or badger, but my war-hardened instincts agreed with Sidney's reticence.

How long had we stood at the edge of the trees, confronting his past and the pain Offerman's report had exposed? How oblivious had we become to our surroundings? Enough that we might not have noticed someone sneaking up on us?

I cursed my inattention. But honestly, how could I have remained vigilant when faced with the extremity of Sidney's despair? It had been all but impossible, but seeing Sidney's face now and the fury and frustration he was directing at himself for letting down his guard and allowing himself to be distracted, I cursed myself again for not managing it.

He released my hand and slid it inside the pocket of his trench coat where I knew he'd stowed his Luger pistol while I likewise reached for the Webley tucked in my own.

The click of a rifle cocking its hammer told us our movements had not gone unnoticed.

'I would stop right there if I were you.'

CHAPTER TWENTY-EIGHT

My heart kicked against my ribs as Lieutenant Smith stepped out from behind the branches of a Scotch pine, his rifle aimed directly at us.

'Withdraw your hand slowly, Kent, and leave the pistol behind.' When Sidney hesitated, Smith's voice sharpened. 'Unless you want to see your pretty wife bleeding all over the forest floor.'

The sour taste of fear flooded my mouth. I harbored no illusions after the tram explosion of what he was capable of. He would do it. And after being wounded by a bullet in December, I had no desire to repeat the experience, even if Smith didn't shoot to kill.

Sidney extracted his hand, holding it up for Smith to see that it was empty.

'You, too, Mrs Kent,' he ordered as his gaze snapped to me.

I gritted my teeth against the urge to hurl insults at him.

'What do you want, Smith?' Sidney growled, his face flushed red with anger and perhaps embarrassment over the prospect the other man might have observed his moment of weakness a short time ago.

The very thought of it made my skin prickle with outrage, knowing how hard it had been for my husband to share what he had without the threat of witnesses.

'Did you find Offerman's report?' Smith demanded to know, and I suddenly felt doubly glad I'd shoved it into my pocket before leaving the cottage. However, it also made a conspicuous bulge beneath my coat. One that was not as noticeable as before since I'd been pressed flush against Sidney, squashing it.

'We didn't kill Miss Baverel,' I retorted, hoping to distract him from his objective by dangling something more important before him. 'But we think we might know who did.'

From such a distance, I couldn't read his expression clearly, especially not with the rifle positioned before his eyes, but I could tell I'd captured his interest. It was written in the taut line of his shoulders and the intensity of his silent scrutiny.

'So do I,' was his unexpected response. Even more surprising was his act of lowering his weapon. 'And he's bound to appear shortly. So I certainly hope you removed the papers from that cottage.'

Sidney looked at me uncertainly, but I never removed my eyes from Smith as he began slowly making his way toward us over the fallen branches and brambles. I had no doubt he could still lift his rifle and fire in less than a second, but the very fact that he'd lowered the weapon in the first place seemed to be a complete contradiction to what I knew of the man. After all, my cheek still smarted from the blow he'd struck me. Was this some kind of trick?

'It's all he's after, you know,' Smith said. 'It's all Ardmore's after, too, for that matter.'

His outright mention of the man we all knew to be his employer and the mastermind behind most if not all of the nefarious things he'd done almost made my mouth drop open. His henchmen had always studiously avoided saying it, including Smith. Until now.

'And are *you* acting for Ardmore?' I queried, gathering my composure.

His eyes narrowed, but I could tell the fury glinting in them was not directed at me. 'No.'

I searched his features as he came to a stop several feet away, trying to figure out his game. 'Then what are you doing here? Don't tell me you're here to help us?'

It wasn't as laughable a question as it might seem. After all, a bullet from his rifle had saved me once before. But it still seemed improbable.

'I'm here to help myself,' he replied with relish.

Sidney shifted a step closer to me, perhaps fearing what exactly that meant.

'But not to the report, or either of you,' he clarified.

'You're after Miss Baverel's killer.' My husband's voice hardened. 'You mean to kill him.'

Smith didn't confirm this with words, but his determined stance and the mutinous glint in his eyes told us Sidney was right.

'But what if we're wrong?' I protested. 'What if he isn't the killer?'

'We're not wrong,' he stated with certainty. 'You just happen to be missing a few key pieces of information.'

Sidney's eyebrows arched. 'Then perhaps you'll enlighten us.'

He tilted his head, seeming to consider refusing. Rolling his shoulders in impatience, he peered down the path in the direction of the cottage before explaining in a low voice. 'Adele told me she was being coerced into helping some Belgian working for one of the French agencies. Apparently, he was aware of some of her . . . *activities* during the war, and so he was forcing her to accompany him to Amsterdam in order to retrieve a report from an old friend of his there. She didn't tell me the man's name, rightly suspecting I would have killed him for threatening her, but I reported Adele's difficulties to Ardmore anyway, thinking he would help.'

'Did he?' I asked.

Smith's face darkened. 'No. Instead he instructed Adele to go through with the plan, but to secure the report herself and bring it back to him.'

'But she didn't.' This much was easy to deduce.

'I don't know whether she realized what the report contained, or she simply saw it as her opportunity to escape, but she hid it and then proceeded to try to blackmail Ardmore into paying her passage to America in exchange for the report.' He shook his head. 'If I'd been there to counsel her, I would've told her not to do it. Ardmore always stacks the deck. He always wins. But she went through with it, and before Ardmore could make up his mind how to respond, the French authorities had arrested her.'

'With the man she double-crossed in on the scheme,' I deduced.

'Yes. I begged Ardmore to intervene, but he refused.' His jaw clenched. 'He told me she'd made her bed and now she had to lie in it, and he forbade me from intervening.'

'Which you ignored, traveling to Amiens anyway.'

'I had to try.'

I examined Smith's features for any sign of duplicity but found none. It seemed he truly had cared for Adele, and Ardmore's treatment of her had broken his hold over him.

'What makes you think Ardmore hadn't made up his mind how to respond?' Sidney asked pointedly. 'It seems just like him to let others clean up his messes and take care of his dirty work for him.'

Smith's eyebrows arched, clearly recognizing this was partly a dig at him, but then his brow furrowed, recognizing this was also an accurate assessment of Ardmore's modus operandi. It would be exactly like him not to lift a finger when he knew the French authorities would take care of his problem for him. Of course, there was the matter of the report Adele Baverel had hidden, but perhaps that was the real reason Willoughby had been in Furnes, and had followed us to Rotterdam. He'd been searching for it all along.

'Do you know what's in Offerman's report?' I questioned, curious just how much of the matter Smith was aware of.

His gaze riveted on me once again, sweeping over me from head to toe. 'I know what's supposed to be in it. Proof that the British government was aware of and ignored legitimate overtures from Germany to make peace with amicable terms.' His eyes darted toward Sidney and then back. 'And judging from your reactions upon reading it, I would say that's not just smoke.'

Sidney's posture turned rigid, and I had to stifle the urge to reach out to him in reassurance. I knew that was the last thing he would want me to do with Smith looking on. Part of me wondered if Smith was only baiting us anyway, for if he'd been watching us for that long, I hoped we would have realized it sooner, even in spite of our emotional distress.

'How do you know what's supposed to be in it?' I pressed, as this was far from common knowledge. No one had shared it with us until Landau. 'Who told you?'

'Ardmore.'

I frowned, wondering who he'd learned it from, and then it struck me. 'The intercepts!'

We knew Ardmore held some unspecified position with the Admiralty, just as we knew that many of the intercepted messages about the Germans' efforts to make peace had been decrypted by the Admiralty's codebreaking department – OB40. Why shouldn't Ardmore have read them?

Smith nodded. 'Apparently, he and Blinker Hall were great cohorts. He let him read the intercepts even when they weren't distributed.'

I pressed my hand to my mouth in realization. 'Of course. That's why Offerman wrote that the Admiralty *knew* things, not that they'd told anyone. Because he couldn't prove that.' I'd noted that wording while reading his report, but at the time it hadn't occurred to me why that distinction was important. My fingers twitched to remove the report from my pocket, curious how much of a difference that distinction made in telling us exactly what the prime minister and his cabinet had known and when. Perhaps they hadn't been aware of the particulars quite as early as it appeared on first reading.

'What does that matter?' Sidney demanded to know with a scowl. 'Wouldn't they have shared everything pertinent they knew?'

My lips twisted cynically. 'You would think. But the fact of the matter is that Blinker Hall liked to distribute the intelligence material they intercepted and decoded selectively.' I trusted Sidney to recognize that what I was repeating had come directly from George, who had worked under

Reginald 'Blinker' Hall, the former director of Naval Intelligence, in OB40. 'Hall was an extreme conservative and a hard-liner on the war, and so depending on the content of an intercept – and the impact it might have politically – he would either choose to distribute it or bury it in his files.'

Sidney's scowl deepened. 'So he wouldn't have taken kindly to the idea of Germany making peace before she'd been properly trounced.'

'Sadly, yes,' I replied with great distaste.

My husband looked as if he might haul off and punch a tree at any moment, and I couldn't blame him. Men like Hall had been playing god with other men's lives, and were clearly indifferent to the consequences.

'Though I deduce Ardmore wasn't aware of everything that might be contained in the report,' Smith chimed in to say. 'For he lost his connection in America sometime in late 1916.'

'He must be referring to Captain Gaunt.' Guy Gaunt had been a Royal Navy Intelligence Officer assigned to interact with President Wilson's advisor House on continental issues. As I recalled it, he'd been home on leave in late 1916. 'Captain Wiseman took his place in meeting with House, and House decided he preferred him to Gaunt. We certainly learned a great deal more from him through Wiseman.' But perhaps that had not been Gaunt's fault, but rather Blinker Hall censoring his dispatches. After all, Wiseman had been a

Secret Service Military Intelligence Officer, reporting to C, not Naval Intelligence.

I could only imagine how aggravated Ardmore must have been to suddenly find himself uninformed, and consequently that rather pleased me.

'Yes, I suspect that got under Ardmore's skin,' Smith remarked, following the same bent of my thoughts. He also seemed to relish this realization.

I was struck anew by the curiousness of this conversation. I had disliked Smith and his insolent, disrespectful, pucker-mouthed glares upon first sight some months back, and his subsequent actions and the revelation of his involvement with the bombing of General Bishop's temporary HQ had only proven my instincts about him correct. Even now, my hand twitched with the urge to slap the mocking grin from his face and deal back some of the pain he had caused me and Sidney, some of the pain he'd caused countless numbers of men and their families with his betrayals. But I couldn't deny the fact that he would make a significant ally in our quest to thwart and expose Ardmore. He knew the ins and outs of his organization, the extent of past operations, and likely some of the preparations for future ones.

The trouble was, he couldn't be trusted. Not unless our goals aligned. Even then, they could diverge just as swiftly. But how could we pass up the possibility to learn all he knew?

I altered my stance, crossing my arms over my

chest to conserve warmth. Here, in the denser part of the copse the skeletal canopy overhead absorbed more of the rainfall before it reached us, but I still shivered from the dampness that had worked its way inside my mackintosh. I could only imagine how chilled Sidney was without his hat.

'So you're here to confront Miss Baverel's killer. To kill him,' I stated bluntly, hoping a direct thrust at the dodgy fellow might reveal more than questioning him in a roundabout manner. 'Then what do you intend to do?'

He shrugged. 'Leave before the authorities arrive and I'm forced to shoot anyone else.'

My glower must have communicated how little I was impressed with this answer, for he suddenly flashed me a yellow-toothed grin.

'Then you're simply going to allow us to walk away with the report?' I clarified, not trusting he wouldn't turn on us.

'I told you, I'm not interested in it. That's Ardmore's affair.' His lips curled in a sneer. 'Which means Willoughby's probably lapping at your heels as well. But that's your problem, not mine.'

His comment alarmed me. 'Did you follow us here?'

He shook his head. 'No, I already knew about this place. But I didn't recognize its significance until I realized that Belgian bastard had been sniffing about the village.' His eyes narrowed in criticism. 'But Willoughby might have. That one's like a dashed bloodhound,' he groused, using much more offensive language.

I turned to Sidney, wondering what he thought of all of Smith's assertions, but there wasn't time or space to confer – and what choice did we have anyway? If we refused to work with Smith, then he would simply shoot us. Sidney might get one shot off before he fired at us both, but one of us would undoubtedly be killed. Our best, our *only* course of action was to cooperate and try to keep the upper hand.

There was always the hope Charlaix and Willoughby were nowhere near here, but proceeding based on that assumption would be foolhardy.

'All right,' I conceded as the first teasing scent of smoke reached my nose. 'But do you have to kill him? He should be taken into custody.' I ignored the smell, thinking it must have drifted here from someone's hearth. After all, it was a cold, rainy day, and a cozy, crackling fire sounded heavenly at the moment.

Smith's nostrils flared. 'The man *killed* Adele and tried to make it look like a suicide. And he deliberately used *my* name when he traveled to Holland to kill Offerman. So, no, I won't leave him alive.' He turned to stare through the forest in the direction of the cottage. The smoldering stench was growing stronger. 'Besides, which authority is going to take him into custody? The Dutch police don't know which way is up, and in

426

the meantime the French will swoop in and recover Charlaix with merely a slap on the wrist.'

By this point, we were all on alert. The smell of smoke was too strong to be coming from anywhere but very near. Sidney stood at attention, looking down the path through the clearest section of the wood. 'Bloody hell!' he exclaimed. 'He's set the cottage on fire!' He took several steps in that direction before stopping, coming to the realization Smith voiced.

'It's a trap. To draw us out.' He looked about him. 'He must know we're here.'

'Or at least that *we* are,' Sidney muttered. After all, the Citroën we'd borrowed was parked next to the cottage.

Smith seemed much struck by this thought. 'Then go confront him. I'll follow behind.'

I glowered at him. 'That's hardly a plan.'

'No.' He lifted his rifle. 'But it's what you're going to do.'

I glanced at Sidney. We were swiftly running out of options.

'Move!'

'Bloody hell,' Sidney muttered again through gritted teeth as we set off cautiously down the path.

I gripped his arm between mine, huddling close. 'We have to keep ourselves between Charlaix and Smith.'

'And how do you propose we do that when we don't even know from which direction Smith will be coming from?' he hissed. 'Not to mention the fact he's as likely to shoot through us as around us.'

He had a point. Smith was nothing if not ruthless, and unopposed to collateral damage.

'I don't know,' I snapped. 'But do you have any better suggestions?'

'Yes.' His deep blue eyes shimmered with intensity as they met mine. 'In this instance, we look out for ourselves. Charlaix caused this mess. I'm not risking my life or yours to save his sorry hide.' His hand pressed against mine where it rested against his bicep. 'I risked enough people's lives against my will for that godforsaken war. Now that it's my choice, I'm not risking any more. Especially not my wife's.'

A lump formed in my throat, making it impossible for me to form a response, but I nodded. He was right. There came a time when one's responsibility to others ended. Had Charlaix been innocent, matters might have been different. But considering the fact that his actions had set all of this in motion – his murder of at least two people, duplicity, and arson – our consciences should be clear in not sacrificing ourselves for him.

As we neared the cottage, the acrid stench of the smoke increased, but the flames I'd expected to see were not visible. Wherever Charlaix has set the fire, it had been on the inside. Smoke poured from the open door and the cracks around the windows, but it hadn't yet reached the exterior. Perhaps the rain had hampered its spread. I briefly thought of the wooden wardrobe with its lovely carvings, and then brushed it aside. We had far more pressing concerns. Like where was Charlaix?

Sidney and I hovered at the edge of the path, searching for any sign of the man, or anyone else for that matter, but the clearing was empty. There wasn't even a motorcar parked behind the Citroën, which meant that Charlaix, like Smith, must have parked at some distance so as not to rouse suspicion and walked across one of the fields.

I peered down the long lane toward Mrs Huis's house. She would undoubtedly see the smoke sooner or later and either come looking herself or send someone to investigate. Wouldn't it be better to warn her?

Sidney and I turned to each other. It seemed we'd had the same thought. As one, we broke free of the cover, dashing across the clearing toward the Citroën. Leave Smith and Charlaix to deal with one another. We had the report. As to what we would do it with, we still had to decide. But at least it wouldn't be in Charlaix's hands or on its way to Ardmore. All we needed to do was get out of there. Neither man would be able to follow us quickly.

We got as far as the front wings before the clap of a gunshot ripped through the air behind us. My shoulders shot up toward my hairline as I ducked, skidding to a stop in the dirt. I whirled about to see where the shot had come from and was shocked to find it wasn't Charlaix lying on the ground with Smith standing over him, but the other way around.

CHAPTER TWENTY-NINE

At the edge of the trees lay Smith, cursing a blue streak and clutching his shoulder as he scooted himself along the ground backward to put several more feet between himself and his shooter. Meanwhile, Charlaix kicked Smith's rifle away and aimed his pistol at his chest.

'I told you Smith was involved,' the French intelligence agent told us, looking up briefly in our direction. 'When I came to Rotterdam to check on you after the tram explosion I noticed him following you from the hotel. Decided I'd better tail you both.' His anger appeared genuine, his words truthful, but of course, he'd not yet outright lied. Smith *was* involved. And in a manner of speaking he *had* followed us. As for Charlaix checking on us, that was true, too, though not in the affable manner he implied.

My gaze slid sideways to meet Sidney's over the bonnet of the motorcar as the rain continued to fall, seeing in his eyes the same suspicion I held. Charlaix didn't yet know we were on to him, and we might be able to turn that to our advantage. As long as Smith didn't ruin this impression. But

431

other than his colorful curses, he remained quiet. Though the glare he aimed up at the Belgian promised brutal retribution.

'Thank goodness you did,' I finally managed to reply, pressing a hand to my chest as if to catch my breath, trying to cover the awkward lapse that had fallen between his words and mine. 'Then he must have set fire to the cottage.'

Charlaix nodded. 'When I saw the smoke, I feared I was too late.' The scrutiny he directed at me was more pointed than before. 'But you weren't inside.'

My eyes were beginning to water from the smoke in the clearing. I could only imagine how must worse it would be without the rain. However the dampness might also be obscuring its presence from the road, from anywhere in the distance others might see it and send assistance.

'No.' I coughed. 'We were investigating what was on the other side of the copse.'

'Anything of interest?'

'No, just trees,' I replied, perhaps inanely, but I needed to keep Charlaix's focus on me as Sidney withdrew his own pistol from his pocket. I tossed a glance over my shoulder in the direction of Mrs Huis's house. 'Shall we go fetch the authorities? You'll want to have Smith taken into custody.'

'Not just yet.' His words were rather chillingly indifferent to the man's pain in front of him, and I realized it was less an act and more the fact that he didn't intend for Smith to leave here alive. He

432

couldn't, considering everything the lieutenant knew. And of course, his real focus was on other matters. 'What of Miss Baverel's evidence? Did you find it?'

I couldn't outright lie, for Charlaix had undoubtedly seen the open wardrobe and the candles on the table, so I hedged around the truth. 'We found a book. Tolstoy, if you can believe it. It was hidden among the dresses in the wardrobe. We wondered if maybe there were notes written in invisible ink along the margins. As I'm sure you know, it was used often enough during the war, by both sides.' I looked anxiously toward the cottage where fire was now licking at the edge of the windows. I could feel the heat of it even from several dozen feet away. 'But I set the book on the side table when we went to explore the copse, intending to retrieve it when we returned. So unless Lieutenant Smith is carrying it with him, I'm afraid it's lost to us now.'

This pronouncement appeared to have startled Charlaix, who now stared at the cottage in dismay, clearly trying to recall whether he'd seen such a book on one of the tables and ignored it. Smith helped the falsehood along by sitting at his feet smirking.

'We'll go fetch the authorities now,' Sidney stated, moving toward the door of the motorcar. Perhaps remembering, as I had, that there had been no books inside the cottage, and sooner or later Charlaix was going to realize that. Best to leave while Smith had him riled by the idea he might have outwitted him.

But Charlaix's mind was quicker than we'd hoped.

'I wouldn't do that if I were you,' he cautioned, and we both turned to find his pistol aimed at us.

By his stance, and the way he'd opened the car door with his left hand, I knew that Sidney had, likewise, drawn his gun, though he still held it at his side, hidden by the folds of his trench coat.

'I'm not after you, only the report.' His tone of voice said he was being more than reasonable. 'But I *will* shoot you if I have to.' Gone was the friendly twinkle in his pale blue eyes. They were now deathly earnest when he shifted them to look at me. 'I presume your lovely wife has the documents.'

Repressed fury flooded my veins as I faced his threatening stare. This man who had purportedly been helping us, who was supposed to be seeking truth and justice, was the person we'd been searching for all along. He'd toyed with us, and killed in cold blood. If he was through with the pretense then so was I.

'*You* were the mystery man on the train with Offerman,' I charged. 'You knew him.'

A furrow formed between Charlaix's eyes, as if he didn't like being reminded. 'As boys. We grew up in neighboring villages near Mons.'

'Villages that were both overrun and ransacked by the Germans when they invaded,' I deduced.

434

His eyes were hard. 'Just so. When he contacted me, I hadn't heard from him in years.'

'Why *did* he contact you?'

His lips thinned as he formulated his response. 'He wanted my advice.' He turned away. 'He told me he'd worked for British Intelligence during the war. That they'd asked him to investigate one matter, but he'd uncovered something different. He wasn't sure he could remain quiet about what he'd found. So we agreed to meet on that train. It was supposed to appear like a robbery.'

I frowned. 'Then what happened? Why did he end up dead?'

'He . . .' Charlaix's feet shuffled in aggravation. 'He said he'd changed his mind. That he wasn't certain making everything he'd learned public would help anyone. That it would only hurt people who had been hurt enough. But how could we bury such a truth?' His face flushed with rage. 'How could we not let the world know what our so-called allies had done?'

'So you killed him?'

His mouth tightened at the bald truth of my statement.

'You killed your friend and stole his report,' I continued, unwilling to let him hide from what he'd done in his pursuit of revealing the report's contents. 'And Mademoiselle Baverel left the train with the report, as you'd planned all along, in case you were seized when Offerman raised the alarm about the feigned robbery. But rather than meet you at the Hook for the ferry bound for England, as planned, she double-crossed you. She disappeared with the report, presumably stashing it here, and then made her way back to Amiens.' I shook my head slowly. 'I can only imagine how angry that made you feel, especially after you'd *murdered* your friend to get your hands on it.'

His eyes narrowed, riveted on me as he relived that fury. Knowing that Sidney with his gun and Smith with his proximity to Charlaix had the best probability of thwarting him, I continued to hold that stare, hoping to continue to stoke that rage and keep him distracted from the others long enough for them to disarm him. However, it wasn't easy to stare him down, knowing he could turn his gun on me in any instant. My shoulder throbbed in remembrance of the last time that occurred.

'So you had her arrested, as you'd threatened to do. You interrogated her, and when she wouldn't crack and she asked for Mr Kent, you called him in, thinking you'd get your answers that way. But when she foiled you again, you snapped. You slipped into her cell and threatened her one more time, and when she *still* wouldn't cooperate, you broke her neck, and then tried to make it look like a suicide. Or tried to make it *look* like someone had tried to make it look like a suicide.' I arched a single eyebrow. 'I'm not sure how big of fools you took us for.'

Out of the corner of my eye, I could see Smith

toeing something with his foot and I did my best to ignore it, lest Charlaix notice my interest. Instead, I pressed on relentlessly. 'You followed us to Mademoiselle Baverel's flat, fed us your lies, and then sent us on to Achicourt to search for her "proof." It's our fault that we stupidly believed you were helping us, even keeping you apprised of our location. And so it was you who tried to hit us with that motorcar in the Hague.' I exhaled in disgust. 'The date of Smith's arrival in Holland was too late for it to be him. Besides, we should have realized the car was too poorly aimed to be the work of a former Royal Fusilier sniper.'

Charlaix's nostrils flared at the insult, and I half hoped he'd choke on the extra intake of smoke. It irritated my throat now, making it feel raw, but I pressed on lest he glance at Smith after he made his snort of amusement.

'But then you must have decided it would be more beneficial to let us continue investigating, all the while pretending to assist us.'

'What can I say? You were easy to mislead.' One corner of his lip peeled back in a sneer. 'It must be because you're a woman.'

Fiery outrage leapt in my veins, for I'd heard this similar infuriating refrain far too many times to count. But I tamped it back, recognizing he was playing the same game I was. I would *not* be the person whose attention fatally wavered first.

'I presume you sent those letters to prospective

bidders about the auction as well, in order to defraud them out of their money.'

'It wasn't a fraud,' he countered. 'I fully intend to have the report in hand by the end of the bidding tomorrow.' He narrowed his eyes. 'And I shall. So where is it?' His gaze slid up and down my figure. 'On your delightful person? Inside your coat, perhaps?'

That's exactly where it was, but I wasn't about to admit it.

He reached out his other hand. 'Bring it to me. Bring it to me *now*! The truth must be made known. The British and other Allies like to pretend they entered the war on the behalf of the Belgians, but they weren't thinking of us when they threw away our chance at peace in 1916. They weren't thinking of us at Versailles, where they treated Holland – a country who, if anything, helped Germany by remaining neutral – with more dignity than us. The pittance that Germany will actually pay us back in reparations will never cover a fraction of our losses.'

I hadn't closely followed the news coming out of Versailles where they had negotiated the terms of the peace treaty in the early months of 1919. At the time, I'd just been demobilized from the Secret Service and I'd still believed Sidney to be dead, and frankly I hadn't done much more than drink and dance and try to forget. But I'd heard rumblings about the Belgian delegations' dissatisfaction, as well as their attempts to redraw the border between them and the Netherlands. Their intent had been to create a more easily defensible position between themselves and any future incursion from Germany, or at least to gain control of at least one bank of the Scheldt estuary through which ships from Antwerp had to sail in order to reach the North Sea, but forcing such terms upon a neutral nation with whom all the belligerents still hoped to remain friendly was untenable.

However, having been in and out of Belgium during the latter years of the war and seen first-hand the destruction and devastation wrought upon them entirely through no fault of their own, the Belgians had all my sympathy. They were merely trying to find a way to move forward when their industries were in ruin – having been sabotaged and stripped of all capital by the invaders, when many of their cities and villages had been decimated, when great swathes of their land were either stark morasses littered with corpses and unexploded shells or inundated with seawater. Not only did they want to recover, they wanted to protect themselves from it ever happening again.

But that didn't mean the best way forward lay in publishing this report. Offerman was right – it would reopen wounds and create new ones. Worse, it might topple the already fragile state of affairs across Europe, harming even more people. Much as I believed in uncovering the truth and bringing it to light, I wasn't sure that doing so at this time was actually the best course. The time to do so would have been in early 1917, when something might still have been done. Not now, when all we could ask is, 'what if?' Conclusions might be jumped to without all the facts. While Offerman's report was thorough, we were already aware of a number of holes in it, a number of sources he'd not had access to. How many more were missing? Could we ever truly drill down to the core of the truth?

'Bring it to me!' Charlaix screamed when I remained immobile.

My heart jumped in my chest at the vehemence and desperation rung from his voice. If Smith or Sidney were going to act, it was now or never.

Smith kicked out with his foot, sending up a spray of muck and decomposing leaves from the forest floor at the same time Sidney ordered me to duck. I dove for the dirt, cowering behind the wheel of the Citroën in the mud. Three shots rang out in quick succession, and it was all I could do not to lift my head to see what was happening. *Please, not Sidney*, I begged over and over again in my head as I strained to hear the sound of his voice, of anyone's voice, but the rain dampened much of the noise, and the crackle of the cottage fire covered the rest.

So much so that when a figure approached me from behind, I didn't hear them coming. I startled as a hand touched my shoulder, and then exhaled in relief at the sight of Sidney crouching before me.

'Thank God!' I exclaimed, wrapping my arms around his solid form. But our embrace was by necessity brief. 'Are you injured?' I asked as I pulled back.

His expression was grave. 'No, but Charlaix's dead. And we have another problem.'

I allowed him to help me to my feet, turning to see that yet another individual had made his way onto the scene, even now squatting to search the Belgian's pockets.

'Good heavens,' I muttered. 'This is turning into a farce. Does anyone *not* know where this "secret" cottage is?'

'It's Willoughby,' Sidney informed me as he sheltered his pistol with his body, checking the cartridges. 'And while I appreciate his assistance in stopping Charlaix, I don't anticipate his remaining on our side for long.' He darted a glance toward the men as he slid the magazine back into place. 'Or Smith, for that matter.'

I wasn't sure I shared the same fear of their teaming up as he did, but I was well aware of the threat Willoughby posed. 'Do you think we could make a run for it? In the car?' I clarified.

Sidney shook his head, peering upward. 'Not reversing between these trees. Not without Willoughy getting off a few good shots.'

I nodded, readying myself to face Ardmore's man as he was rising to his feet, his watchful gaze on us. Sidney tugged at my sleeve, and I turned to find his face closer to mine than I'd expected.

'Our main objective is to stay alive.' His dark blue eyes bore into mine. 'None of the rest matters.'

I realized what he was saying. That the report didn't matter, not if it meant losing our lives. While the thought of handing such a damning document over to Ardmore made me recoil, I knew he was right. None of it mattered if we were dead.

'Do you understand?' he pressed urgently, as if worried I might object and do something foolish.

'Yes,' I replied as Willoughby bent to pick up Smith's rifle from where Charlaix had kicked it.

I tensed, waiting to see what he would do with it. Whether he would pass it back to Smith. Instead, he examined it idly before letting it fall to his side as he addressed the man reclining before him.

'You should have left it alone,' he told him with a sigh. 'She knew she was provoking him. And so did you.'

Smith called him something foul, and Willoughby shook his head, as if he was disappointed in him.

'Ardmore sends his regards.' Then before I could blink, Willoughby lifted his pistol and shot Smith in the chest.

It was so unexpected and so shocked me, even after all the rest, that I actually gasped out loud.

Willoughby turned to me with a weary look of resignation, and I knew then that he was merely carrying out his orders, at all costs. That there would be no talking him down from his goal – an item that was burning a hole in my pocket.

'Just give it to me,' he directed impassively,

turning the gun on us. 'And you can go on your way. Otherwise . . .' He tipped his head toward the gun.

'You'll shoot me?' I was incredulous. 'After you just killed Smith for hurting me?'

His eyes dipped to the man in question before he retorted callously. 'He's not dead yet. But you're right. Ardmore does want you alive.' His weapon swung marginally to my right. 'Him, he doesn't care so much about.'

Sidney raised his own pistol in response, stepping in front of me.

The corner of Willoughby's mouth lifted fractionally. 'You may get a shot off, Kent, but so will I. And I never miss.'

'Neither do I,' my husband replied.

'Stop, just stop,' I told the men, reaching into the interior pocket of my coat to extract the tightly rolled report with a trembling hand. It was a bit damp and crushed from the rain and Sidney's earlier embrace, but still whole. 'Here, see?' I held it aloft. 'I've got it.' My eyes shifted to meet Sidney's as I added under my breath, 'Stay alive, remember?'

'There, now. Cooperation is much better,' Willoughby cooed, almost making me wish I had let Sidney shoot him. 'Bring it here.'

What I wanted to do was hurl the thing at his head, but then the papers would just scatter in the mud, and he'd make *me* gather them up. My thoughts drifted to the fire, which was burning

443

even brighter, its heat warming the right side of my body. If the papers were incinerated, if they were consumed, then we would no longer possess them, but neither would Ardmore.

It was not an easy thing to contemplate. For not only would we be destroying Offerman's report, but also Miss Baverel's proof. Proof we had searched so long and so hard for. Proof that might finally bring down Ardmore. The very thought of it made me ill, but I knew what had to be done.

Pretending to stumble over the uneven ground, I staggered as close to the cottage as I dared. Then with one mighty throw I hurled the roll of paper into the doorway. It sailed through the air and disappeared inside the billowing roils of smoke just as a single sheet separated and fluttered to the ground.

We all seemed to stand transfixed for a moment, perhaps equally surprised by what I'd done. When I finally turned away from the blaze, I was half afraid Willoughby would shoot us anyway, for in my impetuousness I'd not fully considered the matter. Instead, his weapon lowered as his wide stare shifted to meet mine, bright with a curious mixture of bemusement and perhaps a touch of reluctant pride.

'Well done,' he asserted quietly, perhaps wishing he could do something similar. He took a firmer grasp of the rifle, still holding it at his side. His expression turned shrewd. 'But then, the damage is already done, isn't it?'

With this parting comment, he turned his back on us, seemingly unconcerned by Sidney's pistol still aimed at him. I watched as he disappeared behind the burning cottage, a sickening feeling filling me. For he was right. The damage *was* done. I had read the report, and my possibly naïve faith in C and the agency had now been shattered.

Not that I believed that had been Ardmore's sole intention. I was certain he would have loved to get his hands on those documents. But aided by Ardmore or not, that report had driven a splinter between me and my blind trust in British Intelligence, one that would never fully make its way out again. Not knowing everything I did.

I turned to Sidney, suddenly uncertain what to do. His compassionate expression told me he'd also understood what Willoughby had meant, and how unsettled that would make me. Ardmore had been trying to worm his way under my skin for more than six months, to make me doubt myself and those around me, to make me question my objectives. And he'd finally done it.

I waited for Sidney to speak, but a wet cough from the opposite side of the clearing made my head whip around. Somehow, Smith was still alive. We ran to him, kneeling down beside his form. Blood ran from the corners of his mouth only to be washed away by the rain. He didn't have much time left.

'Take this,' he gasped painfully, gesturing toward his right side.

Sidney gingerly reached inside his coat pocket and wiggled free a leatherbound book.

I looked to him in shocked inquiry.

'If . . . you're . . . as clever . . . as Ardmore thinks, you'll . . . figure it out,' he stammered between gurgling breaths. His body shook with a great racking cough, and more blood flowed from his mouth.

I sat stunned that it was Smith who might be giving us the evidence we needed, the evidence we'd sought for so long to incriminate Ardmore. The evidence we'd thought we'd just thrown away. If we'd believed Miss Baverel knew much, how much more did Smith know?

Smith scrabbled for my hand, and I gave it to him. 'The gas,' he gasped. 'The . . .' He broke off, fighting to draw breath as more fluid filled his lungs.

Tears welled up behind my eyes watching him struggle, and I pressed his hands between my own, letting him know I understood what he meant. There could only be one gas. The phosgene cylinders we'd been searching for since our discovery more than five months ago that Ardmore had contrived to have them stolen and smuggled out of England during the midst of the war.

'It's . . . in . . . Dublin.' Smith's final word was barely distinguishable as he choked on his last breath and then fell silent.

I stared down through a blur of tears at his cold, sightless eyes staring toward the heavens, rain glistening off their lashes. I despised Smith. He had been a merciless opportunist, a heartless assassin. And yet, I couldn't help but be moved by his death. Especially since he'd chosen to do the right thing in the end and shared what he knew.

Sidney reached out to close his eyes and then rounded his body, tugging me to my feet. Blindly, I allowed him to pull me back toward the Citroën, slowly at first, and then with more urgency as I comprehended the same thing my husband clearly had.

Smith and Charlaix were both dead. There was nothing we could do for them. It was left to us now to look out for ourselves, and if we were found next to a smoldering cottage with two dead bodies it would cause more than a simple scandal. It would be an international incident. It would be bad enough when the bodies of an SCR agent and a former British soldier were found shot to death in the Belgian countryside, but if war-hero Sidney Kent and his intrepid bride were discovered with them there would be far too many questions we couldn't answer.

We tumbled into the motorcar, dripping mud and water all over the seats, and Sidney reversed to a spot where he could turn the vehicle around. Then we tore off down the lane, slowing only as we passed Mrs Huis's house so as not to draw attention. I felt a pulse of dismay for the destruction of the woman's property, even though we

447

hadn't been the ones to set the fire. But once again, there was little we could do. The cottage was not salvageable.

Sidney turned the motorcar southwest before swinging back to the north to avoid Baarle-Hertog, flooring the gas pedal to put miles between us and the destruction behind us. Neither of us spoke until we neared the village of Chaam. Then about a mile from the cluster of buildings which had appeared on the horizon, he pulled into a narrow lane and stopped.

He sat staring out the windscreen in front of him, his hands still on the driving wheel, evidently struggling to come to terms with what had just happened, the same as I was. When he suddenly got out of the motorcar, I made a move to follow him, but my hands were shaking too much, and I fumbled with the door latch. Hearing him rustling around in the boot of the car, I elected to stay put, and was rewarded when he returned with a pair of blankets.

'I'm not sure how clean they are, but they're dry,' he told me as he passed me one.

'Bless you,' I replied, wrapping it around my shoulders and swaddling myself.

Sidney scrubbed his damp hair with the blanket and swiped at his neck and collar before draping it over his seat and climbing back behind the wheel. However, he made no move to turn the starter, but simply sat with his head bowed. His dark hair was a rumpled mop of curls, the pomade he used to restrain it having rubbed off. 'Do you think they recognized us?' he finally turned to ask.

I tilted my head to consider the question, knowing who he meant. We hadn't given either Mrs Huis or the priest our names, but he was right. Our photographs in the papers had made us familiar figures to many. But perhaps not to those in a rural village like Baarle-Hertog.

'No. But if we were, and the authorities dare to believe it, we'll simply have to brazen our way through. Though it would certainly be easier if we were back in London when they tried to contact us.'

He nodded in agreement. 'When we return to Rotterdam, I'll make arrangements for us to sail this evening.'

He reached into the pocket of his coat and extracted the brown leatherbound volume Smith had given him. I leaned closer to see the book as he brushed away the droplets of rain still speckling its cover and opened it to leaf through the pages. The contents were written in some sort of code, though I'd expected nothing less given what Smith had said about my being clever enough to figure it out.

'I suspect it won't be an easy cipher,' I remarked, studying the letters and numbers inscribed in neat rows. 'Maybe I can enlist George to help me.'

'And resist Smith's dig at your intelligence?'

'Yes, well, intelligence isn't merely about the

449

amount of knowledge and skills one possesses, but also knowing when it's best to utilize someone *else's* knowledge and skill set.'

The hard line of his mouth softened fractionally, but there was still a deep well of pain behind his eyes. 'If only others could be that wise,' he answered softly, and I knew he was thinking of the military leaders and politicians who far too often had refused to listen to the advice of those who were better informed. Had they heeded that guidance, countless numbers of lives might have been saved.

I pressed my hand to his wrist, letting him know he wasn't alone in his grief.

He closed the book and passed it to me, his features grim. 'Perhaps it will tell us what Ardmore intends to do with that phosgene in Dublin.'

I forced a breath past the tightness in my chest. 'I'm just afraid I already know.'

Sidney's gaze met mine, rife with the same foreboding. For the Irish rebels were most active in Dublin, along with the British forces combating them. If Ardmore contrived to have the phosgene fired into a crowd there, the casualties would be horrific, and the consequences more far-reaching than we could anticipate.

CHAPTER THIRTY

Upon our return to London, life settled back into its old routines as if we'd never left. The bureau in the entry hall where we kept our mail was overflowing with invitations to spring parties, including the Duchess of Albany's Ball at resplendent old Devonshire House, the last grand event to ever be held beneath its roof before its scheduled demolition. We might have kept ourselves busy day and night, whirling from one society event to the next and then on to a nightclub, had we wished. And yet, we felt no desire to take part in any of it.

The trouble was, neither Sidney nor I knew what to do with everything we'd learned – from our most recent investigation and Offerman's report. We rarely spoke of it, and yet I knew he turned it over in his thoughts as often as I did. In truth, I didn't know that there was anything *to* do with it, but it had changed us irrevocably all the same, and forced us to confront some things in ourselves and others that were not pleasant.

We didn't inform T, or consequently C, that we'd read the report, simply that it had been destroyed.

Part of me wanted to confront C with what we'd learned. After all, he had been a servant of the government as much as any of us, passing along the information he received for the political leaders to make the decisions on which course of action to take. But the other part of me dreaded what I might learn, for clearly he'd not wanted me to discover what Offerman was looking into. Not when he'd lied about the contents of the report to begin with and then ordered me not to read it.

I also feared the possibility that C might sever our clandestine relationship, and we needed the information he could provide to help us track down the phosgene cylinders we had now confirmed Ardmore had sent to Dublin. Upon learning of their location, Sidney and I had discussed traveling to Ireland ourselves to search for them, but then we'd realized how foolish it would be to stumble onto the scene blindly. It would be better to utilize our contacts already in place and find out what they could uncover before making any hasty decisions. I wished I could send a message to Alec Xavier, but he was deep undercover and the last thing I wanted to do was put him in greater danger by trying to contact him.

As for Smith's coded notebook, after making a few rudimentary attempts to decipher it myself, I'd elected to hand it off to my codebreaker friend George, who now served as a mathematics professor at Oxford. I reasoned that Ardmore must not yet know of its existence. Otherwise,

Willoughby would never have left it on Smith's body for us to find. So George would be reasonably safe holding it in his possession, as long as Ardmore didn't find out. George was certain to decode it faster than I could, and speed was rather of the essence. Even so, the key to the cipher continued to elude him for longer than any of us anticipated.

Therefore, in both instances, Sidney and I were simply forced to wait. Which led to thinking. And thinking led to brooding on what might have been, particularly in Sidney's instance. Since Baarle-Hertog, he no longer tried to hide his struggle from me, and I didn't try to cajole or reason him out of it. From everything I'd learned, I knew the only way past these dark feelings was to go through them. I trusted the same would prove true for Sidney, and I would be beside him all the while until he emerged on the other side.

Without the proof contained in Offerman's report, without verifying its facts and filling in the holes that had remained, we couldn't state definitively how close we'd come to peace or who was at fault. And we certainly couldn't leak the matter to the press, if any of the newspapers – so many of which were controlled by Prime Minister Lloyd George's backer, Northcliffe – would carry the story anyway and not squash it. Not that we would attempt to share it even if we could. Our loyalty to king and country, and the necessity for discretion which had been hammered into us by our upbringing and four years of war, not to mention the Official Secrets Act we'd signed, were difficult to circumvent. Particularly when we weren't certain whether the revelation of such facts would be more damaging and hurtful at such a fragile time than keeping it quiet.

Ultimately, the heartbreak at the crux of the matter was that we wished our government had tried as hard to make peace as it had war. That it had poured as many of our resources into saving our men and those of other nations when the glimmer of an amicable peace presented itself as it had in trouncing our enemy. Whether or not the rest of the world would ever know about the knife's edge of peace and continued war we'd stood on in late 1916 and early 1917, we didn't know. But we both feared that the utter destruction the last two years of war had wrought and the resulting fragile and uneven peace hammered out at Versailles would come back to haunt us.

So we carried on the best we could until one day I received a summons via telegram from Kathleen, C's secretary. I wasn't completely surprised, as I'd been waiting for an update on the exact location and intentions for the phosgene in Dublin. However, I'd expected a coded briefing, not to be asked to meet her. She must have important news, indeed, to request such an assignation.

We met at our usual place in St Paul's Churchyard in Covent Garden. Arriving a quarter of an hour early, my footsteps nearly faltered at the sight of

Kathleen already perched on one of the benches beneath the towering lime trees. My first thought was that I must have gotten the time wrong, for normally I arrived first to wait for her. But when she looked up, I could read the apprehension she was struggling to hide.

My heart rate accelerated as I sat beside her and briefly scanned the churchyard, which was all but empty on this breezy morning. Save for an older man seated on the opposite end of the lane lined with benches reading a newspaper, we were alone.

'Blustery morning, isn't it?' I opened with, much as she always did.

'Yes, a trifle too cold for my taste,' she managed to reply in kind after a slight pause.

I turned to look at her directly then, noting the worry lines etched across her forehead, and decided there was no point in beating around the bush. 'What's happened?'

'What makes you think anything is wrong?' she replied with a false laugh, which only heightened my alarm.

'Don't play games,' I pleaded quietly. 'I worked at the desk beside yours for two years. I can tell.'

She nodded, dropping all pretense. 'Matters in Ireland have grown increasingly tense.'

'The phosgene?' I whispered aghast.

She shook her head. 'We've not located it yet. Nor has it been used.'

I exhaled in relief. 'Then what's this to do with me?'

Her lips flattened as she hesitated once again to say what she'd called me here to tell me.

I held my breath, somehow knowing whatever it was would alter the course of events drastically.

'Captain Xavier has gone missing.'

My stomach dipped.

'He hasn't reported to his handler or made a drop at his letterbox in over a month. There's been no report of his death, or . . . or discovery of his body, and the IRA' – the Irish Republican Army – 'doesn't usually hide their victims, wanting them to serve as examples for others of what could happen if you cross them. So we believe he may still be alive.'

'Could he have simply been sent to another part of Ireland, perhaps on a special mission?' I asked, anxious to explain his sudden disappearance.

'Possibly.' But from the sound of her voice, I knew she thought this doubtful.

'What's being done to locate him?'

She reached up to clutch her dark woolen coat closed around her throat as a gust of wind swept through the churchyard, sending a scattering of last autumn's dried leaves clattering over the walkway. I felt too chilled inside to notice it without.

'His handler is making discreet inquiries.' She leaned closer. 'But you understand he can only risk so much.'

I nodded. After all, Alec's handler wouldn't be responsible just for him, but several agents. If he was found out, he might compromise them all.

'Then what are you asking me to do?' The fact that she was telling me at all must mean that she – or rather C – wanted something from me.

Before she even spoke, I could already decipher in her wary expression what they wanted.

'We need someone on the outside, someone who knows him . . .'

'Someone who's already risked her life extracting him once before,' I finished for her, masking my fear with exasperation.

'Yes.'

I turned away, fighting the surge of emotion rising inside me. Dread for Alec. Trepidation at the idea of traveling to Ireland with all its unrest. Distress at what we might encounter there. And uneasiness at the thought of explaining all of this to Sidney, at the possibility of making the wrong choice.

But mingled in with that confusing muddle was also a pulse of eagerness and excitement at the prospect of testing my mettle in the field again, at getting our hands dirty in not only locating Alec, but also those phosgene cylinders and whatever Ardmore intended them for. Of being useful instead of sitting idly about or flitting from soiree to soiree.

'I'll need to speak with Sidney,' I told Kathleen. 'I won't make this decision without him.'

'We understand,' she replied, telling me she and C had already discussed the matter.

What Sidney would say, I suspected I already

knew, but I would not take that choice from him. Not when it could alter our lives so drastically.

True to expectation, he didn't even bat an eyelash when I relayed all of this to him, listening with an unruffled demeanor. But then perhaps he sensed I was ruffled enough for the both of us.

Having paced before the sofa where he sat while I finished explaining C's request, I crossed to one of the tall Georgian windows and stared down at the square below, allowing him time to consider the matter. Motorcars sped along the roads, but the garden at its center sat empty, the wind and sporadic rain driving everyone inside.

A few moments later, I heard Sidney rise and come to join me. Resting his hands on my shoulders, he turned me to face him, his deep blue eyes bright with concern.

'Ver, do you *want* to go to Dublin?'

'How can I *not* go?' I replied, agitation stretching my voice. 'If Alec is in trouble . . .' I broke off, struggling to put my thoughts into words. 'What would *you* do if it were one of your men or fellow officers in danger and you could do something that might help?'

His lips curled into a humorless smile, for we both already knew the answer to that. After all, he feigned his death to catch a traitor for them.

'There's no chance Xavier severed communication for a reason?'

'Of course he could have,' I retorted, gesturing

with my hands. 'Maybe he knew either the handler or the letterbox, or both, had been compromised. But there's no way to know that until we make contact with him. Just the possibility that he's fallen out of contact because he's in trouble . . .' My throat closed around the thought.

Sidney's hands tightened around my upper arms. 'Don't leap to that conclusion. Don't borrow trouble. Not yet.'

I nodded, inhaling deeply to try to still my racing thoughts.

'We'll find him.'

I looked up into his beloved face as he tried to reassure me, overwhelmed by his willingness to not only help me, but the man who had slept with his wife when I'd believed him to be dead. His willingness to venture into danger to do so. Tears pricked the back of my eyes.

'We will, Ver,' he repeated, misunderstanding the reason for my emotion.

I cradled his face between my hands. 'You're a good man, Sidney Kent,' I murmured hoarsely. 'Perhaps a better man than I deserve.'

His arms tightened around my waist, pulling me close. 'No, just one trying to be worthy of you.'

I pressed my lips to his in both an offering and an oath.

'To Ireland, then,' he whispered when our kiss ended, the softness of his voice befitting the solemnity of the pronouncement.

I took a bracing breath to reply. 'To Ireland.'